The
Summer
Seekers

Center Point
Large Print

Also by Sarah Morgan and available from
Center Point Large Print:

Family for Beginners

The Summer Seekers

SARAH MORGAN

CENTER POINT LARGE PRINT
THORNDIKE, MAINE

This Center Point Large Print edition
is published in the year 2021 by arrangement with
Harlequin Books S.A.

The text of this Large Print edition is unabridged.
In other aspects, this book may vary
from the original edition.
Printed in the United States of America
on permanent paper.
Set in 16-point Times New Roman type.

ISBN: 978-1-64358-976-3

The Library of Congress has cataloged this record under
Library of Congress Control Number: 2021935050

For Susan Ginsburg,
the best of the best,
with thanks for the support,
guidance and friendship

it's never too late for adventure.

I

KATHLEEN

It was the cup of milk that saved her. That and the salty bacon she'd fried for her supper many hours earlier, which had left her mouth dry.

If she hadn't been thirsty—if she'd still been upstairs, sleeping on the ridiculously expensive mattress that had been her eightieth birthday gift to herself—she wouldn't have been alerted to danger.

As it was, she'd been standing in front of the fridge, the milk carton in one hand and the cup in the other, when she'd heard a loud thump. The noise was out of place here in the leafy darkness of the English countryside, where the only sounds should have been the hoot of an owl and the occasional bleat of a sheep.

She put the glass down and turned her head, trying to locate the sound. The back door. Had she forgotten to lock it again?

The moon sent a ghostly gleam across the kitchen and she was grateful she hadn't felt the need to turn the light on. That gave her some advantage, surely?

She put the milk back and closed the fridge

door quietly, sure now that she was not alone in the house.

Moments earlier she'd been asleep. Not deeply asleep—that rarely happened these days—but drifting along on a tide of dreams. If someone had told her younger self that she'd still be dreaming and enjoying her adventures when she was eighty she would have been less afraid of aging. And it was impossible to forget that she *was* aging.

People said she was wonderful for her age, but most of the time she didn't feel wonderful. The answers to her beloved crosswords floated just out of range. Names and faces refused to align at the right moment. She struggled to remember what she'd done the day before, although if she took herself back twenty years or more her mind was clear. And then there were the physical changes—her eyesight and hearing were still good, thankfully, but her joints hurt and her bones ached. Bending to feed the cat was a challenge. Climbing the stairs required more effort than she would have liked and was always undertaken with one hand on the rail *just in case.*

She'd never been the sort to live in a *just in case* sort of way.

Her daughter, Liza, wanted her to wear an alarm. One of those medical alert systems, with a button you could press in an emergency, but Kathleen refused. In her youth she'd traveled the world, before it was remotely fashionable to do so. She'd sacrificed safety for adventure without a second thought. Most days now she felt like a different person.

Losing friends didn't help. One by one they fell by the wayside, taking with them shared memories of the past. A small part of her vanished with each loss. It had taken decades for her to understand that loneliness wasn't a lack of people in your life, but a lack of people who knew and understood you.

She fought fiercely to retain some version of her old self—which was why she'd resisted Liza's pleas that she remove the rug from the living room floor, stop using a step ladder to retrieve books from the highest shelves and leave a light on at night. Each compromise was another layer shaved from her independence, and losing her independence was her biggest fear.

Kathleen had always been the rebel in the family, and she was still the rebel—although she wasn't sure that rebels were supposed to have shaking hands and a pounding heart.

She heard the sound of heavy footsteps. Some-one was searching the house. For what, exactly? What treasures did they hope to find? And why weren't they trying to at least disguise their presence?

Having resolutely ignored all suggestions that she might be vulnerable, she was now forced to acknowledge the possibility. Perhaps she shouldn't have been so stubborn. How long would it have taken from pressing the alert button to the cavalry arriving?

In reality, the cavalry was Finn Cool, who lived three fields away. Finn was a musician, and he'd bought the property precisely because there were no immediate neighbors. His antics caused mutterings in the village. He had rowdy parties late into the night, attended by glamorous people from London who terrorized the locals by driving their flashy sports cars too fast down the narrow lanes. Someone had started a petition in the post office to ban the parties. There had been talk of drugs, and half-naked women, and it had all sounded like so much fun that Kathleen had been tempted to invite herself over. Rather that than a dull women's group, where you were expected to bake and knit and swap recipes for banana bread.

Finn would be of no use to her in this moment of crisis. In all probability he'd either be in his studio, wearing headphones, or he'd be drunk. Either way, he wasn't going to hear a cry for help.

Calling the police would mean walking through the kitchen and across the hall to the living room, where the phone was kept and she didn't want to reveal her presence. Her family had bought her a mobile phone, but it was still in its box, unused. Her adventurous spirit didn't extend to technology. She didn't like the idea of a nameless faceless person tracking her every move.

There was another thump, louder this time, and Kathleen pressed her hand to her chest. She could feel the rapid pounding of her heart. At least it was still working. She should probably be grateful for that.

When she'd complained about wanting a little more adventure, this wasn't what she'd had in mind. What could she do? She had no button to press, no phone with which to call for help, so she was going to have to handle this herself.

She could already hear Liza's voice in her head: *Mum, I warned you!*

If she survived, she'd never hear the last of it.

Fear was replaced by anger. Because of this intruder she'd be branded Old and Vulnerable and forced to spend the rest of her days in a single room with minders who would cut up her food, speak in overly loud voices and help her to the bathroom. Life as she knew it would be over.

That was *not* going to happen.

She'd rather die at the hands of an intruder. At least her obituary would be interesting.

Better still, she would stay alive and prove herself capable of independent living.

She glanced quickly around the kitchen for a suitable weapon and spied the heavy black skillet she'd used to fry the bacon earlier.

She lifted it silently, gripping the handle tightly

as she walked to the door that led from the kitchen to the hall. The tiles were cool under her feet—which, fortunately, were bare. No sound. Nothing to give her away. She had the advantage.

She could *do* this. Hadn't she once fought off a mugger in the backstreets of Paris? True, she'd been a great deal younger then, but this time she had the advantage of surprise.

How many of them were there?

More than one would give her trouble.

Was it a professional job? Surely no professional would be this loud and clumsy. If it was kids hoping to steal her TV, they were in for a disappointment. Her grandchildren had been trying to persuade her to buy a "smart" TV, but why would she need such a thing? She was perfectly happy with the IQ of her current machine, thank you very much. Technology already made her feel foolish most of the time. She didn't need it to be any smarter than it already was.

Perhaps they wouldn't come into the kitchen. She could stay hidden away until they'd taken what they wanted and left.

They'd never know she was here.

They'd—

A floorboard squeaked close by. There wasn't a crack or a creak in this house that she didn't know. Someone was right outside the door.

Her knees turned liquid.

Oh Kathleen, Kathleen.

She closed both hands tightly round the handle of the skillet.

Why hadn't she gone to self-defense classes instead of senior yoga? What use was the downward dog when what you needed was a guard dog?

A shadow moved into the room, and without allowing herself to think about what she was about to do she lifted the skillet and brought it down hard, the force of the blow driven by the weight of the object as much as her own strength. There was a thud and a vibration as it connected with his head.

"I'm so sorry—I mean—" Why was she apologizing? Ridiculous!

The man threw up an arm as he fell, a reflex action, and the movement sent the skillet back into Kathleen's own head. Pain almost blinded her and she prepared herself to end her days right here, thus giving her daughter the opportunity to be right, when there was a loud thump and the man crumpled to the floor. There was a crack as his head hit the tiles.

Kathleen froze. Was that it, or was he suddenly going to spring to his feet and murder her?

No. Against all odds, she was still standing while her prowler lay inert at her feet. The smell of alcohol rose, and Kathleen wrinkled her nose.

Drunk.

Her heart was racing so fast she was worried

that any moment now it might trip over itself and give up.

She held tightly to the skillet.

Did he have an accomplice?

She held her breath, braced for someone else to come racing through the door to investigate the noise, but there was only silence.

Gingerly she stepped toward the door and poked her head into the hall. It was empty.

It seemed the man had been alone.

Finally she risked a look at him.

He was lying still at her feet, big, bulky and dressed all in black. The mud on the edges of his trousers suggested he'd come across the fields at the back of the house. She couldn't make out his features because he'd landed face-first, but blood oozed from a wound on his head and darkened her kitchen floor.

Feeling a little dizzy, Kathleen pressed her hand to her throbbing head.

What now? Was one supposed to administer first aid when one was the cause of the injury? Was that helpful or hypocritical? Or was he past first aid and every other type of aid?

She nudged his body with her bare foot, but there was no movement.

Had she killed him?

The enormity of it shook her.

If he was dead, then she was a murderer.

When Liza had expressed a desire to see her

mother safely housed somewhere she could easily visit, presumably she hadn't been thinking of prison.

Who was he? Did he have family? What had been his intention when he'd forcibly entered her home?

Kathleen put the skillet down and forced her shaky limbs to carry her to the living room. Something tickled her cheek. Blood. Hers.

She picked up the phone and for the first time in her life dialed the emergency services.

Underneath the panic and the shock there was something that felt a lot like pride. It was a relief to discover she wasn't as weak and defenseless as everyone seemed to think.

When a woman answered, Kathleen spoke clearly and without hesitation.

"There's a body in my kitchen," she said. "I assume you'll want to come and remove it."

2

LIZA

"I told you! Didn't I tell you? I *knew* this was going to happen."

Liza slung her bag into the back of the car and slid into the driver's seat. Her stomach churned. She'd missed lunch, too busy to eat. The school where she taught was approaching summer exam season and she'd been halfway through helping two students complete their art coursework when a nurse had called her from the hospital.

It was the call she'd dreaded.

She'd found someone to cover the rest of her classes and driven the short distance home with a racing heart and clammy hands. Her mother had been attacked in the early hours of the morning, and she was only hearing about it *now?* She was part frantic, part furious.

Her mother was so cavalier. According to the police she'd left the back door open. It wouldn't have surprised Liza to learn she'd invited the man in and made him tea.

Knock me over the head, why don't you?

Sean leaned in through the window. He'd come straight from a meeting and was wearing a blue shirt the same color as his eyes. "Is there time for me to change?"

"I packed a bag for you."

"Thanks." He undid another button. "Why don't you let me drive?"

"I've got this." Tension rose up inside her and mingled with the worry about her mother. "I'm anxious, that's all. And frustrated. I've lost count of the number of times I've told her the house is too big, too isolated, that she should move into some sort of sheltered accommodation or residential care. But did she listen?"

Sean threw his jacket onto the back seat. "She's independent. That's a good thing, Liza."

Was it? When did independence morph into irresponsibility?

"She left the back door open."

"For the cat?"

"Who knows. I should have tried harder to persuade her to move."

The truth was, she hadn't really wanted her mother to move. Oakwood Cottage had played a central part in her life. The house was gorgeous, surrounded by acres of fields and farmland that stretched down to the sea. In the spring you could hear the bleating of new lambs, and in the summer the air was filled with blossom, birdsong and the faint sounds of the ocean.

It was hard to imagine her mother living anywhere else, even though the house was too large

17

for one person and thoroughly impractical—particularly for someone who tended to believe that a leaking roof was a delightful feature of owning an older property and not something that needed fixing.

"You are not responsible for everything that happens to people, Liza."

"I love her, Sean!"

"I know." Sean settled himself in the passenger seat as if he had all the time in the world. Liza, who raced through life as if she was being chased by the police for a serious crime, found his relaxed demeanor and unshakeable calm occasionally maddening.

She thought about the magazine article folded into the bottom of her bag. "Eight Signs That Your Marriage Might Be in Trouble."

She'd been flicking through the magazine in the dentist's waiting room the week before and that feature had jumped out at her. She'd started to read it, searching for reassurance.

It wasn't as if she and Sean argued. There was nothing specifically wrong. Just a vague discomfort inside her that reminded her constantly that the settled life she valued so much might not be as settled as she thought. That just as a million tiny things could pull a couple together, so a million tiny things could nudge them apart.

She'd read through the article, feeling sicker and sicker. By the time she'd reached the sixth sign she'd been so freaked out that she'd torn the pages from the magazine, coughing violently to cover the sound. It wasn't done to steal magazines from waiting rooms.

And now those torn pages lay in her bag, a constant reminder that she was ignoring something deep and important. She knew it needed to be addressed, but she was afraid to touch the fabric of her marriage in case the whole thing fell apart—like her mother's house.

Sean fastened his seat belt. "You shouldn't blame yourself."

She felt a moment of panic, and then realized he was talking about her mother. What sort of person was she that she could forget her injured mother so easily?

A person who was worried about her marriage.

"I should have tried harder to make her see sense," she said.

They would have to sell the house—there was no doubt about that. Liza hoped it could wait until later in the summer. It was only a few weeks until school ended, and then the girls had various commitments until they all went on their annual family holiday to the South of France.

France.

A wave of calm flowed over her.

France would give her the time to take a closer look at her marriage. They'd both be relaxed, and away from the endless demands of daily life. She and Sean would be able to spend some time together that didn't involve handling issues and problems. Until then, she was going to give herself permission to forget about the whole thing and focus on the immediate problem.

Her mother.

Oakwood Cottage.

Sadness ripped through her. Ridiculous though it was, the place still felt like home. She'd clung to that last remaining piece of her childhood, unable to imagine a time when she would no longer sit in the garden or stroll across the fields to the sea.

"Dad made me promise not to put her in a home," she said.

"Which was unfair. No one can make promises about a future they can't foresee. And you're not 'putting' her anywhere." Sean was ever reasonable. "She's a human being—not a garden gnome. Also, there are plenty of good residential homes."

"I know. I have a folder bulging with glossy brochures in the back seat of the car. They make them look so good I want to check in myself. Unfortunately, I doubt my mother will feel the same way."

Sean was scrolling through emails on his phone. "In the end it's her choice. It has nothing to do with us."

"It has a lot to do with us. It's not practical to

go there every weekend, and even if they weren't in the middle of exams the twins wouldn't come with us without complaining. *It's in the middle of nowhere, Mum.*"

"Which is why we're leaving them this week-end."

"And that terrifies me too. What if they have a party or something?"

"Why must you always imagine the worst? Treat them like responsible humans and they'll behave like responsible humans."

Was it really that simple? Or was Sean's confidence based on misplaced optimism?

"I don't like the friends Caitlin is mixing with right now. They're not interested in studying and they spend their weekends hanging out in the shopping mall."

He didn't look up. "Isn't that normal for teenage girls?"

"She's changed since she met Jane. She answers back and she used to be so good-natured."

"Hormones. She'll grow out of it."

Sean's parenting style was "hands off." He thought of it as being relaxed. Liza considered it abdication.

When the twins were little they'd played with each other. Then they'd started school and invited friends round to play. Liza had found them delightful. That had all changed when they'd moved to senior school and Alice and Caitlin had made friends with a different group of girls. They were a year older. Most of them were already driving and also, Liza was sure, drinking.

The fact that she might not like her daughters' friends was a problem that hadn't occurred to her until the past year.

She forced her attention back to the problem of her mother. "If you could fix the roof in the garden room this weekend, that would be great. We should have spent more time maintaining the place. I feel guilty that I haven't done enough."

Sean finally looked up. "What you feel guilty about," he said, "is that you and your mother aren't close. But that isn't your fault, you know that."

She did know that, but it was still uncomfortable hearing the truth spoken aloud. It was something she didn't like to acknowledge. Not being close to her mother felt like a flaw. A grubby secret. Something she should apologize for.

She'd tried so *hard,* but her mother wasn't an easy woman to get close to. Intensely private, Kathleen revealed little of her inner thoughts. She'd always been the same. Even when Liza's father had died, Kathleen had focused on the practical. Any attempt to engage her mother in a conversation about feelings or emotions was rebuffed. There were days when Liza felt that she didn't even truly know her mother. She knew what Kathleen did and how she spent her time, but she didn't know how she *felt* about things. And that included her feelings for her daughter.

She couldn't remember her mother ever telling her that she loved her.

Was her mother proud of her? Maybe, but she wasn't sure about that either.

"I love her very much, but it's true that I do wish she'd share more." She clamped her teeth together, knowing that there were things she wasn't sharing either. Was she turning into her mother? She should probably be admitting to Sean that she felt overloaded—as if the entire smooth running of their lives was *her* responsibility. And in a way it was. Sean had a busy architectural practice in London. When he wasn't working he was using the gym, running in the park or playing golf with clients. Liza's time outside work was spent sorting out the house and the twins.

Was this what marriage was? Once those early couple-focused years had passed, did it turn into this?

Eight signs that your marriage might be in trouble.

It was just a stupid article. She'd met Sean when she was a teenager and many happy years had followed. True, life felt as if it was nothing but jobs and responsibility right now, but that was part of being an adult, wasn't it?

"I know you love your mother. That's why

we're in the car on a Friday afternoon," Sean said. "And we'll make it through this current crisis the way we've made it through the others. One step at a time."

But why does life always have to be a crisis?

She almost asked, but Sean had already moved on and was answering a call from a colleague.

Liza only half listened as he dealt with a string of problems. Since the practice had taken off it wasn't unusual for Sean to be glued to his phone.

"Mmm . . ." he said. "But it's about creating a simple crafted space . . . No, that won't work . . . Yes, I'll call them."

When he eventually ended the call, she glanced at him. "What if the twins invite Jane over?"

"You can't stop them seeing their friends."

"It's not their friends in general that worry me—only Jane. Did you know she smokes? I'm worried about drugs. Sean, are you listening? Stop doing your emails."

"Sorry. But I wasn't expecting to take this afternoon off and I have a lot going on right now." Sean pressed Send and looked up. "What were you saying? Ah, smoking and drugs . . . Even if Jane does all that, it doesn't mean Caitlin will."

"She's easily influenced. She badly wants to fit in."

"And that's common at her age. Plenty of other kids are the same. It will do the twins good to fend for themselves for a weekend."

They wouldn't exactly be fending for themselves. Liza had already filled the fridge with food. She'd removed all the alcohol from the kitchen cupboard, locked it in the garage and removed the key. But she knew that wouldn't stop them buying more if they wanted to.

Her mind flew to all the possibilities. "What if they have a wild party?"

"It would make them normal. All teenagers have wild parties."

"I didn't."

"I know. You were unusually well-behaved and innocent." He put his phone away. "Until I met you and changed all that. Remember that day on the beach when you went for a walk? You were sixteen. I was with a crowd."

"I remember." They'd been the cool crowd, and she'd almost turned around when she saw them, but in the end she'd joined them.

"I put my hand up your dress." He adjusted his seat to give himself more legroom. "I admit it— my technique needed work."

Her first kiss.

She remembered it clearly. The excited fumbling. The forbidden nature of the encounter. Music in the background. The delicious thrill of anticipation.

She'd fallen crazily in love with Sean that summer. She'd known she was out of step with her peers, who'd been dancing their way through different relationships like butterflies seeking nectar. Liza had never wanted that. She'd never felt the need for romantic adventure. That meant uncertainty, and she'd already had more than enough of that in her life. All she'd wanted was Sean, with his wide shoulders, his easy smile and his calm nature.

She missed the simplicity of that time.

"Are you happy, Sean?" The words escaped before she could stop them.

"What sort of a question is that?" Finally she had his full attention. "The business is going brilliantly. The girls are doing well in school. Of course I'm happy. Aren't you?"

The business. The girls.

Eight signs that your marriage might be in trouble.

"I feel—a little overwhelmed sometimes, that's all."

She tiptoed cautiously into territory she'd never entered before.

"That's because you take everything so seriously. You worry about every small detail. About the twins. About your mother. You need to chill."

His words slid under her skin like a blade. She'd used to love the fact that he was so calm, but now it felt like a criticism of her coping skills. Not only was she doing everything, but she was taking it all too seriously.

"You're suggesting I need to 'chill' about

the fact my eighty-year-old mother has been assaulted in her own home?"

"It sounded more like an accident than an assault, but I was talking generally. You worry about things that haven't happened and you try and control every little thing. Most things turn out fine if you leave them alone."

"They turn out fine because I anticipate problems before they happen."

And anticipating things was exhausting—like trying to stay afloat when someone had tied weights to her legs.

For a wild moment she wondered what it would be like to be single. To have no one to worry about but herself.

No responsibility. Free time.

She yanked herself back from that thought.

Sean leaned his head back against the seat. "Let's leave this discussion until we're back home. Here we are, spending the weekend together by the sea. Let's enjoy it. Everything is going to be fine."

His ability to focus on the moment was a strength, but also a flaw that sometimes grated on her. He could live in the moment because *she* took care of all the other stuff.

He reached across to squeeze her leg and she thought about a time twenty years ago, when they'd had sex in the car, parking in a quiet country lane and steaming up the windows until

27

neither of them had been able to see through the glass.

What had happened to that part of their lives? What had happened to spontaneity? To joy?

It seemed so long ago she could barely remember it.

These days her life was driven by worry and duty. She was being slowly crushed by the ever-increasing weight of responsibility.

"When did we last go away together?" she asked.

"We're going away now."

"This isn't a minibreak, Sean. My mother needed stitches in her head. She has a mild concussion."

She crawled through the heavy London traffic, her head throbbing at the thought of the drive ahead. Friday afternoon was the worst possible time to leave, but they'd had no choice.

When the twins were young they'd traveled at night. They'd arrive at Oakwood Cottage in the early hours of the morning and Sean would carry both children inside and deposit them into the twin beds in the attic room, tucking them under the quilts her mother had brought back from one of her many foreign trips.

"I really don't want to do it, but I think it's time to sell Oakwood Cottage. If she's going into residential care, we can't afford to keep it."

Someone else would play hide-and-seek in the

overgrown gardens, scramble into the dusty attic and fill the endless bookshelves. Someone else would sleep in her old bedroom, and enjoy the breathtaking views across fields to the sea.

Something tore inside her.

The fact that she couldn't even remember the last time she'd had a relaxing weekend in Cornwall didn't lessen the feeling of loss. If anything it intensified the emotion, because now she wished she'd taken greater advantage of the cottage. She'd assumed it would always be there . . .

Ever since her father had died, visits home had been associated with chores. Clearing the garden. Filling the freezer. Checking that her mother was coping with a house that was far too big for one person, especially when that person was advanced in years and had no interest in home maintenance.

She'd thought that the death of her father might bring her closer to her mother, but that hadn't happened.

Grief sliced through her, making her catch her breath. It had been five years, and she still missed her dad every day.

"I can't see your mother selling it," Sean said, "and I think it's important not to overreact. This accident wasn't of her own making. She was managing perfectly well before this."

"Was she, though? Apart from the fact she

did leave the door open, I don't think she eats properly. Supper is a bowl of cereal. Or bacon. She eats too much bacon."

"*Is* there such a thing as too much bacon?" Sean caught her eye and gave a sheepish smile. "I'm kidding. You're right. Bacon is bad. Although at your mother's age one has to wonder if it really matters."

"If she gives up bacon maybe she'll live to be ninety."

"But would she enjoy those miserable, bacon-free extra years?"

"Can you be serious?"

"I *am* serious. It's about quality of life, not just quantity. You try and keep every bad thing at bay but doing that also keeps out the good stuff. Maybe she could stay in the house and we could find someone local to look in on her."

"She's terrible at taking help from anyone. You know how independent she is." Liza hit the brakes as the car in front of her stopped, the seat belt locking hard against her body. Her eyes pricked with tiredness and her head pounded. She hadn't slept well the night before, worrying about Caitlin and her friendship issues. "Do you think I should have locked our bedroom?"

"Why? If someone breaks into our house they'll simply kick the doors down if they're locked. Makes more mess."

"I wasn't thinking of burglars. I was thinking about the twins."

"Why would the twins go into our bedroom? They have perfectly good rooms of their own."

What did it say about her that she didn't entirely trust her own children? They'd been suitably horrified when they'd discovered that their elderly grandmother had been assaulted, but had flat-out resisted her attempts to persuade them to come too.

"There's nothing to do at Granny's," Alice had said, exchanging looks with her sister.

"Besides, we have work to do." Caitlin had gestured to a stack of textbooks. "History exam on Monday. I'll be studying. Probably won't even have time to order in pizza."

It had been a reasonable response. So why did Liza feel nervous?

She'd do a video call later so that she could see what was going on in the background.

The traffic finally cleared, and they headed west to Cornwall.

By the time they turned into the country lane that led to her mother's house it was late afternoon, and the sun sent a rosy glow over the fields and hedges.

She was allowing herself a rare moment of appreciating the scenery when a bright red sports car sped round the bend, causing her almost to swerve into a ditch.

"For—" She leaned on her horn and caught a brief glimpse of a pair of laughing blue eyes as the car roared past. "Did you see that?"

"Yes. Stunning car. V-8 engine." Sean turned his head, almost drooling, but the car was long gone.

"He almost killed us!"

"Well, he didn't. So that's good."

"It was that wretched rock star who moved here last year."

"Ah yes. I read an article in one of the Sunday papers about his six sports cars."

"I was about to say I don't understand why one man would need six cars, but if he drives like that then I suppose that's the explanation right there. He probably gets through one a day."

Liza turned the wheel and Sean winced as branches scraped the paintwork.

"You're a bit close on my side, Liza."

"It was the hedge or a head-on collision." She was shaken by what had been a close shave, her emotions heightened by her brief glimpse of Finn Cool. "He laughed—did you see that? He actually smiled as he passed us. Would he have been laughing if he'd had to haul my mangled body out of the twisted wreckage of this car?"

"He seemed like a pretty skilled driver."

"It wasn't his skill that saved us. It was me driving into the hedge. It isn't safe to drive like that down these roads."

Liza breathed out slowly and drove cautiously down the lane, half expecting another irresponsible rock star to come zooming around the corner. She reached her mother's house without further mishap, her pulse rate slowing as she pulled into the drive.

Aubretia clung to the low wall that bordered the property, and lobelia and geraniums in bright shades of purple and pink tumbled from baskets hung next to the front door. Although her mother neglected the house, she loved the garden and spent hours in the sunshine, tending her plants.

"This place is a gem. She'd make a fortune if she ever did decide to sell it, leaking roof or not. Do you think she will have made her chocolate cake?" Sean was ever hopeful.

"You mean before or after she tackled an intruder?"

Liza parked in front of the house. She probably should have baked a cake, but she'd decided that getting on the road as soon as possible was the priority.

"Can you call the kids?"

"Why?" Sean uncoiled himself from the front of the car and stretched. "We only left them four hours ago."

"I want to check on them."

He unloaded their luggage. "Take a breath, will you? I haven't seen you like this before. You're amazing, Liza. A real coper. I know you're shaken up by what's happened, but we'll get through this."

She felt like a piece of elastic stretched to its limits. She was coping because if she didn't what would happen to them? She knew, even if her family didn't, that they wouldn't be able to manage without her. The twins would die of malnutrition or lie buried under their own mess because they were incapable of putting away a single thing they owned or cooking anything other than pizza. The laundry would stay unwashed, the cupboards would be bare. Caitlin would yell, *Has anyone seen my blue strap top?* and no one would answer because no one would know.

The front door opened and all thought of the twins left her mind because there was her mother, her palm pressed hard against the door frame for support. There was a bandage wrapped around the top of her head, and Liza felt her stomach drop to her feet. She'd always considered her mother to be invincible, and here she was looking frail, tired and all too human. For all their differences—and there were many—she loved her mother dearly.

"Mum!" She left Sean to handle the luggage and sprinted across the drive. "I've been worried! How are you feeling? I can't believe this happened. I'm so sorry."

"Why? You're not the one who broke into my house."

As always, her mother was brisk and matter-of-fact, treating weakness like an annoying fly to be batted away. If she'd been frightened—and she must have been, surely?—then there was no way she would share that fact with Liza.

Still, it was a relief to see her in one piece and looking surprisingly good in the circumstances.

If there was one word that would accurately describe her mother it would be *vivid*. She reminded Liza of a hummingbird; delicate, brightly colored, always busy. Today she was wearing a long flowing dress in shades of blue and turquoise, with a darker blue wrap around her shoulders. Multiple bangles jangled on her wrists. Her mother's unconventional, eclectic dress style had caused Liza many embarrassing moments as a child, and even now the cheerful colors of Kathleen's outfit seemed to jar with the gravity of the situation. She looked ready to step onto a beach in Corfu.

Despite the lack of encouragement, Liza hugged her mother gently, horrified by how fragile she seemed. "You should have had an alarm, or a mobile phone in your pocket."

Instinctively she checked her mother's head, but there was nothing to be seen except the bandage and the beginnings of a bruise around her eye socket. Even though she'd tried to enliven her appearance with blusher, her skin was waxy and pale. Her hair was white and cropped short, which seemed to add to her air of fragility.

"Don't fuss." Kathleen eased away from her. "It wouldn't have made a difference. By the time help arrived it would have been over. My old-fashioned landline proved perfectly effective."

"But what if he'd knocked you unconscious? You wouldn't have been able to call for help."

"If I'd been unconscious I wouldn't have been able to press a button either. The police happened to have a car in the area and arrived in minutes, which was comforting because the man recovered quickly and at that point I wasn't sure what his intentions were. Charming policewoman, although she didn't seem much older than the twins. Then an ambulance arrived, and the police took a statement from me. I half expected to be locked up for the night, but nothing so dramatic. Still, it was all rather exciting."

"Exciting?" The remark was typical of her mother. "You could have been killed. He hit you."

"No, I hit *him*—with the skillet I'd used for frying bacon earlier." There was an equal mix of pride and satisfaction in her mother's voice. "His arm flew up as he fell—reflex, I suppose— and he knocked it back into my head. That part was unfortunate, but it's funny when you think that bacon may have saved my life. So no more nagging me about my blood pressure and cholesterol."

"Mum—"

"If I'd cooked myself pasta I would have been using a different pan . . . nowhere near heavy enough. If I'd made a ham sandwich I would have had nothing to tackle him with except a crust of bread. I'll be filling the fridge with bacon from now on."

"Bacon can be a lifesaver—I've always said so." Sean leaned in and kissed his mother-in-law gently on the cheek. "You're a formidable adversary, Kathleen. Good to see you on your feet."

Liza felt like the sole adult in the group. Was she the only one seeing the seriousness of this situation? It was like dealing with the twins.

"How can you joke about it?"

"I'm deadly serious. It's good to know that I can now eat bacon with a clear conscience." Kathleen gave her son-in-law an affectionate smile. "You really didn't have to come charging down here on a Friday. I'm perfectly fine. You didn't bring the girls?"

"Exams. Teenage stress and drama. You know how it is." Sean hauled their luggage into the house. "Is the kettle on, Kathleen? I could murder a cup of tea."

Did he really have to use the word *murder?* Liza kept picturing a different outcome. One where her mother was the one lying inert on the kitchen floor. She felt a little dizzy—and she wasn't the one who had been hit over the head.

Of course she knew that people had their homes broken into. It was a fact. But knowing it was different from experiencing it.

She glanced uneasily toward the back door. "You left it open?"

"Apparently. And it was raining so hard he took shelter, poor man."

"Poor man?"

"He'd had one too many and was most apologetic, both to me and the police. Admitted it was all his fault."

Apologetic.

"You look pale." Kathleen patted Liza on the shoulder. "You stress about small things. Come in, dear. That drive is murderous . . . you must be exhausted."

Murderous. Murder.

"Could everyone stop using that word?"

Her mother raised her eyebrows. "It's a figure of speech, nothing more."

"Well, if we could find a different one I'd appreciate it." Liza followed her into the hallway. "How are you feeling, Mum? Honestly? An intruder isn't a small thing."

"True. He was actually large. And the noise his head made when it hit the kitchen floor—awful. I never should have asked your father to lay those expensive Italian tiles. I've broken so many cups and plates on that damned surface. And now a man's head. It took me forever to clean up the blood. It's fortunate for all of us that he wasn't badly hurt."

Even now her mother wouldn't share her true feelings. Her talk was all of bacon, broken plates and floor tiles. She seemed more concerned for the intruder than herself.

Liza felt exhausted. "You should have left the cleaning for me."

"Nonsense. I've never been much of a house-keeper, but I can mop up blood. And I prefer not to eat my lunch in the middle of a crime scene, thank you."

Her mother headed straight for the kitchen. Liza didn't know whether to be relieved or exasperated that she was behaving as if nothing out of the ordinary had happened. If anything, she seemed energized, and perhaps a touch trium-phant, as if she'd achieved something of note.

"Where is the man now? What did the police say?"

"The man—his name is Lawrence, I believe—is doing very well, although I don't envy the head-ache he'll have after all that drink. I remember one night when I was in Paris celebrating—"

"Mum!"

"What? Oh—the police. They came back this morning and took a statement. A very pleasant man but not a tea lover, which always makes me a little suspicious."

Liza wasn't interested in his choice of beverage. "Are they charging him? Breaking and entering?"

"He didn't break anything. He leaned against the door and it opened. And he apologized profusely, and made a full admission of guilt. He had impeccable manners."

Liza fought the urge to put her head in her hands. "So will you have to go and give evidence or something?"

"I truly hope so. It would be exciting to have a day in court, but it seems unlikely I'll be needed as he admitted everything and was so remorseful and apologetic. I thought my life would be considerably enlivened by an appearance in my own courtroom drama, but it seems I will have to content myself with the fictional variety."

Her mother fussed around the stove, pouring boiling water into the large teapot she'd been using since Liza was a child. The tea would be Earl Grey. Her mother never drank anything else. It was as familiar as the house.

The kitchen, with its range cooker and large pine table, had always been her favorite room. Every evening after school Liza had done her homework at this same table, wanting to be close to her mother when she was at home.

Her mother had been one of the pioneers of the TV travel show, her spirited adventures around the world opening people's eyes to the appeal of foreign holidays from the Italian Riviera to the Far East. *The Summer Seekers* had run for almost twenty years, it's longevity due in no small part to her mother's popularity. Every few weeks Kathleen would pack a suitcase and disappear on a trip to another faraway destination. Liza's school friends had found it all impossibly glamorous. Liza had found it crushingly lonely. Her earliest memory was of being four years old and holding tight to her mother's scarf to prevent her from leaving, almost throttling her in the process.

To ease the distress of Kathleen's constant departures, her father had glued a large map of the world to Liza's bedroom wall. Each time her mother had left on another trip, Liza and her father would put a pin in the map and research the place. They'd cut pictures from brochures and make scrapbooks. It had made her feel closer to her mother. And Liza's room would be filled with various eclectic objects. A hand-carved giraffe from Africa. A rug from India.

And then Kathleen would return, her clothes wrinkled and covered in travel dust. She'd bring with her an energy that had made her seem like a stranger. Those first moments when she and Liza were reunited had always been uncomfortable and forced, but then the work clothes would be replaced by casual clothes, and Kathleen the traveler and TV star would become Kathleen the mother once again. Until the next time, when the map would be consulted and the planning would start.

Liza had once asked her father why her mother always had to go away, and he'd said, *Your mother needs this.*

Even at a young age Liza had wondered why her mother's needs took precedence over everyone else's, and she'd wondered what it was exactly that her mother *did* need, but she hadn't felt able to ask. She'd noticed that her father drank more and smoked more when Kathleen was away. As a father, he had been practical, but economical in his parenting. He'd make sure that she was safe, but spent long days in his study or in the school where he was head of the English department.

She'd never understood her parents' relationship and had never delved for answers. They seemed happy together and that was all that mattered.

Liza had thought about her mother exploring the desert in Tunisia on the back of a camel and wondered why she needed her world to be so large, and why it needed to exclude her family.

Was it those constant absences that had turned Liza into such a home lover? She'd chosen teaching as a career because the hours and holidays fitted with having a family. When her own children were young she'd stayed home, taking a break from her career. When they'd started school she'd matched her hours to theirs, taking pleasure and pride in the fact that she took them to school and met them at the end of the day. She'd been determined that her children wouldn't have to endure the endless goodbyes that she'd had as a child. She'd prided herself on connecting with them, and encouraging conversations about feelings, although these days those conversations were less successful. *You can't possibly understand, Mum,* as if Liza hadn't once been young herself.

Still, no one could accuse her of not being attentive, another reason she was feeling uneasy right now.

Sean was chatting to her mother, the pair of them making tea together as if this was a regular visit.

Liza glanced around her, dealing with the dawning realization that clearing out this house would be a monumental task. Over the years her mother had filled it with memorabilia and souvenirs from her travels, from seashells to tribal masks. There were maps everywhere—on the walls and piled high in all the rooms. Her mother's diaries and other writing filled two dozen large boxes in the small room she'd used as an office, and her photograph albums were crushed onto shelves in the living room.

When her father had died, five years before, Liza had suggested clearing a few of his things but her mother had refused. *I want everything to stay as it is. A home should be an adventure. You never know what forgotten treasure you might stumble over.*

Stumble over and break an ankle, Liza had thought in despair. It was an interesting way of reframing "mess."

Before her mother could sell this place it would need to be cleared, and no doubt Liza would be the one to do it.

When was the right time to broach the subject? Not yet. They'd only just walked through the door. She needed to keep the conversation neutral.

"The garden is looking pretty."

The French doors in the kitchen opened onto the patio, where the borders were filled with tumbling flowers. Pots filled with herbs crowded around the back door. Scented spikes of rosemary nestled alongside the variegated sage which her mother sprinkled over roast pork every Sunday— the only dish she ever produced with enthusiasm. The flagstone path was dappled by sunlight and led to the well-stocked vegetable patch, and then to a pond guarded by bulrushes. Beyond the garden were fields, and then the sea.

It was so tranquil and peaceful that for a moment Liza longed for a different life—one that didn't involve rushing around, ticking off items from her endless to-do list. She just wanted to *sit*.

Her quiet fantasy of one day living near the sea had all but died. There had been a time early in their relationship when she and Sean had discussed it regularly, but then real life had squeezed out those youthful dreams. Living on the coast wasn't practical. Sean's work was based in London. So was hers. Although teaching was more flexible, of course.

Sean brought the food in from the car and Liza unpacked it into the fridge.

"I had a casserole in the freezer, so I brought that," she said. "And some veg."

"I'm capable of making food," said her mother.

"Your idea of food is bacon and cereal. You're not eating properly." She filled a bowl with fresh fruit. "I assumed you weren't set up for an invasion of people."

"Can two people be an invasion?" Her mother's tone was light, but she gripped the edge of the kitchen table and carefully lowered herself into a chair.

Liza was by her side in a moment. "Maybe I should take a look at your head."

"No one else is touching my head, thank you. It already hurts quite enough. The young doctor who stitched me up warned me that it would leave a scar. As if I'm bothered by things like that at my age."

Age.

Was this the moment to mention that it was time to consider a change?

Across the kitchen, Sean was pouring the tea.

Liza paused, nervous about disturbing the atmosphere.

She tried again to encourage a deeper conversation. "You must have been frightened."

"I was more worried about Popeye. You know how he dislikes strangers. He must have escaped through the open door and I haven't seen him since."

Liza gave up. If her mother wanted to talk about the cat, then they'd talk about the cat. "He's always been a bit of a wanderer."

"That's probably why we get on so well. We understand each other."

Was it crazy to be jealous of a cat?

Her mother looked wistful and Liza resolved to do what she could to find Popeye. "If he's not back by the morning we'll search for him. And now I think you should have a lie-down."

"At four in the afternoon? I'm not an invalid, Liza." Kathleen put sugar in her tea—another unhealthy habit she refused to abandon. "I don't want a fuss."

"We're not fussing. We're here to look after you, and to—" *To make you think about the future.* Liza stopped.

"And to what? Persuade me to wear an emergency buzzer? I'm not doing it, Liza."

"Mum—" She caught Sean's warning glance but ignored it. Maybe the subject *was* best raised right now, so that they had the whole weekend to discuss details. "This has been a shock for all of us, and it's time to face some difficult truths. Things need to change."

Sean turned away with a shake of his head, but her mother was nodding.

"Things *do* have to change. Being hit over the head has brought me to my senses."

Liza felt a rush of relief. Her mother was going to be reasonable. Turned out she wasn't the only sensible person in the room.

"I'm pleased you feel that way," she said. "I have brochures in the car, so all we have to do now is plan. And we have all weekend for that."

"Brochures? You mean travel brochures?"

"For residential homes. We can—"

"Why would you bring those?"

"Because you can't stay here any longer, Mum. You admitted things have to change."

"They do. And I'm in the process of formulating a plan I will share with you when I'm sure of the details. But I won't be going into a residential home. That isn't what I want."

Was her mother saying she wanted to come and live with them in London?

Liza swallowed and forced herself to ask the question. "What is it that you want?"

"Adventure." Kathleen slapped her hand on the table, setting cups rattling. "I want another adventure. I was the original Summer Seeker and I miss those days terribly. Who knows how many summers I have left? I intend to make the most of this one."

"But Mum—" *Oh this was ridiculous.* "You're going to be eighty-one at the end of this year."

Her mother sat up a little straighter and her eyes gleamed. "All the more reason not to waste another moment."

3

KATHLEEN

Kathleen woke with a pounding headache. For a moment as she drifted between sleep and wakefulness she thought she was back in Africa suffering from malaria. It had been a miserable experience, and not one she was in a hurry to relive.

Struggling awake she sat up, felt the bandage on her head and remembered everything.

The drunk man dressed in black.

The police.

Popeye missing.

Her head.

The headache wasn't malaria, but a result of her self-inflicted injury. Which, thinking about it, was a great deal more exciting.

Since Brian died, it had felt as if someone had pressed Pause on her life. She'd been living here in her safe little world, moored in a harbor instead of heading boldly out to sea.

Liza didn't want her in the harbor, she wanted her in dry dock. She wanted her safely shut away in a place where no harm could come to her.

Her daughter's intentions were good, but

the thought of selling the home she loved had brought Kathleen to the edge of panic. She'd been so horrified by the idea that she'd blurted out that wild statement about wanting adventure.

Liza's expression of shock wasn't something any of them were likely to forget in a hurry.

She'd obviously thought that the bang on the head had affected her mother's thinking.

Mum? Are you sure you're feeling all right? Are you dizzy? Do you know what day it is?

Yes, she knew what day it was. It was the day to make a few decisions.

She eased herself out of bed, ignoring the aches in her limbs, and took painkillers for her headache. From her bedroom window she could see the ocean in the distance and had a sudden yearning to be skimming the waves in a catamaran with salt air stinging her face. She'd once spent a month sailing the Mediterranean as part of a flotilla. She'd spent most of the time barefoot, her skin burnt from the hot sun, and her hair stiff from seawater. Most of all she remembered feeling alive and free.

She wanted to feel that way again. It wasn't age dependent, surely?

Was Liza right? Was she being stubborn? Unrealistic? What did she expect at eighty years old? Did she really think she was going to dance barefoot across the sand and haul in a sail? Drink tequila in Mexico?

Those days were behind her, although she still had the memories and the evidence of the life she'd once lived.

The house was silent and she walked into the room that had been her study for all the years she'd lived here. The walls were lined with maps. Africa. Australia. The Middle East. America. The whole world was right there in front of her, tempting her.

How she missed exploring. She missed the bustle of the airport, the scents and sounds of a new country, the excitement of discovery. She missed sharing it with people. Go here, see this, do this. *The Summer Seekers* had been her baby. Her show.

What use was her experience to anyone now? She'd thought she might write a book about her travels, but it turned out that writing about it had been nowhere near as exciting as doing it. She'd scribbled a couple of chapters and then abandoned them, bored with sitting and drowning in a sea of nostalgia. She didn't want to write, she wanted to *do*.

It had been eight years since she'd last traveled out of the country, a sedate trip to Vienna to celebrate their wedding anniversary. They'd eaten Sachertorte, richly chocolatey and unquestionably indulgent. Flavors had been one of the pleasures of exploring new countries. Flavors were memories for Kathleen. When she smelled spices, she was transported to the palm-fringed beaches of Goa. The soft sizzle of garlic in olive oil made her think of long, slow summers in Tuscany.

She'd always had a passion for adventure. For travel. She hadn't paused long enough to let life settle on her.

She stood in front of the map of North America, marked with the historic Route 66.

That particular road trip had long been on her wish list. She would have taken the trip many years back were it not for the fact that it ended in California. California was a big place, of course, but still it was too uncomfortable.

Thinking about California made her think of the letters. She reached out to open the drawer in her desk, but then snatched her hand back.

It was far too late now. You couldn't change history. All she could do was look at the maps and the photographs and dream.

She looked at the box files, bulging with maps and notes.

Selling this place wouldn't just mean selling her home, it would mean leaving her past. Her house wasn't stuffed full of meaningless objects, it was full of pieces of her life. Everything came with meaning and memory attached.

She locked the door of the study, and returned to the bedroom where she hid the key in a drawer.

That man breaking into her house had made her evaluate her life.

Yes, she was vulnerable, but so was every human being. Most didn't realize it, of course. Most people believed they were in control of everything that happened to them and perhaps it took age and long experience to know that life could deliver blows you never could have deflected, not even with a skillet.

She'd never let fear stop her living. Instead she'd made the most of every moment, dealing with trouble as it came her way. If anything she'd been reckless.

She was no longer reckless, but nor was she ready to live out her days in a room with a call button.

A restless feeling stirred inside her. Excitement. Anticipation. A thirst for adventure. Lately it had been absent and it was reassuring to know she was still capable of feeling it. It gave her an energy and a drive that was much needed.

She walked to the bathroom and removed the bandage from her head. Enough of that.

She scrubbed at the dried blood and cleaned herself up as best she could, deciding that washing her hair probably wouldn't be the wisest move right now. She tried not to look directly at her reflection. In her mind she was youthful, but the mirror mocked her attempts at self-deception.

Turning away, she dressed as quickly as her body would allow and walked down to the kitchen. She was disappointed to find no signs of Popeye. She was ridiculously fond of the cat, and not entirely because he expected very little of her.

She'd always been an early riser and she began the day with strong coffee. The sun was shining, so she carried her cup to the small marble-topped table she'd had shipped from Italy. The moment she stepped outside, her mood lifted.

It promised to be a perfect day, the air filled with the scent of flowers and a sweet chorus of birdsong.

This moment with her coffee was a brief respite before what she knew would be a difficult weekend. She excelled at some things, but parenting wasn't one of them. She'd been forty when she'd married, and Liza had been born nine months later. Of all the adventures Kathleen had faced, nothing had frightened her more than the thought of being a mother and having someone emotionally dependent on her.

She didn't fit the template that many used to measure parental performance. She'd missed almost every sports day, had never attended a ballet class and had treated parent teacher conferences as optional. She *had* read to her daughter, although she'd always favored travel books over fiction. She'd wanted her to understand how big the world was, and she took some credit for the fact that Liza had achieved top grades in geography. But it was also true that the first time Liza had put two words together it had been to say "Mummy gone."

Kathleen had always struggled to balance her own needs with society's expectations.

And now she found herself in that position again. Someone of her advanced years wasn't supposed to have a sense of adventure.

What was she supposed to do? Sell her home and move into residential accommodation to please her daughter? Protect herself and not move from her chair until her heart gave up?

In the sixties she'd smoked marijuana and danced to rock and roll.

When had she become so careful?

She finished her coffee and bent down to tug up a weed growing between the paving slabs. The garden was her pride and joy, but keeping it tidy was an endless task. She could pay someone, but she didn't like having strangers in her home. She wanted to be able to drink her morning coffee in her nightdress.

The sun was already hot and she lifted her face and soaked up its warmth. Sunshine always made her want to travel.

"Mum?" Liza's voice came from the kitchen door. "You're awake early. You couldn't sleep?"

"I slept perfectly." Kathleen decided not to mention the headache. "You?"

"Yes."

Kathleen could see that was a lie. There were dark shadows under her daughter's eyes and she looked exhausted. Poor Liza. She'd always been so serious, weighed down by her sense of responsibility and devoted to keeping everyone's lives on what she considered to be a safe track.

Kathleen had occasionally lamented the fact that her daughter seemed not to have inherited even a sliver of her own adventurous spirit. When Liza was six years old, Kathleen had wondered if it was healthy for a child to be so biddable. She'd half hoped to see at least a tiny hint of rebellion in the teenage years, but Liza had remained steady and reliable, an adult before her time, vaguely reproachful of her mother's slightly unconventional antics. She hadn't died her hair pink, drunk herself into a stupor or, to the best of Kathleen's knowledge, kissed an unsuitable boy. It seemed to her mother that Liza lived a life regrettably lacking in daring.

But there was no doubt that she was caring and selfless. More selfless than Kathleen had been.

Kathleen had told herself that by pursuing her own passions she was setting an example to her child but if anything her experiences had caused her daughter to become more careful not less.

And here she was causing her anxiety yet again.

Liza put her coffee down on the table. "You removed the bandage."

"It was annoying me. And the wound will heal better exposed to the air." Kathleen pressed her fingertips to her head. "They had to shave some of my hair. I look like something from a horror movie."

Liza shook her head. "You look good. You always do."

Kathleen felt guilty for wishing she could have had a few more moments alone with her coffee and the birds.

Her daughter had dropped everything to drive here through hideous Friday traffic. No mother could have a more attentive daughter.

"How are the girls doing?"

"I don't know. It's too early to call them. They never emerge until midmorning. It's not the easiest age. I assume they're alive, or I would have heard something." Liza sat down opposite her mother and lifted her face to the sun. She was wearing navy linen trousers with a tailored white shirt, an outfit that would have taken her from the classroom to a parent-teacher conference. Her shoes had a small heel and her hair hung smooth and sleek to her shoulders. Everything about Liza was safe and controlled from her attitude to her dress to the way she lived her life.

"You worry too much about them. Things have a way of turning out fine if you leave them."

"I prefer to take a more hands-on approach than you." Liza colored. "Sorry. I shouldn't have said that."

It was so unlike her careful daughter to be unguarded in her remarks that Kathleen took heart. There was spirit there, even if it was rarely permitted to see the light. If only she could encourage more of it.

"Never apologize for saying what's on your mind. It's true that I wasn't a hands-on parent. I did leave you, frequently, although you were with your father. You were never unsafe. I could say that it was my job—and that would be true—but it's also true that I needed to travel."

"Why? What was missing at home?"

Kathleen wished her daughter had overslept. Of the conversational topics she avoided, emotions were right up there with religion and politics. She didn't talk about her feelings, and she didn't talk about the past. Liza *knew* that. There were some things better kept private. Kathleen had learned to protect herself and was far too old to change. "It was complicated. But it had everything to do with me, not you."

Liza put her coffee down. "I shouldn't have asked."

"You think I was selfish. You think I'm selfish now by not agreeing to go into a residential home."

"I'm worried, that's all. I love you, Mum."

Kathleen squirmed. Why did Liza say th
like that?

"I know you do." She saw something flicker in
her daughter's eyes. Disappointment? Resigna-
tion?

"I understand that it isn't easy to leave somewhere you love, but I want you to be safe."

"What if that isn't what I want for myself?"

"You don't want to be safe?" Liza gently
brushed away a bee that was hovering around the
table. "That's the strangest thing I ever heard."

"I'm saying that there are other things more
important than safety."

"Like what?"

How could she explain? "Happiness. Adventure. Excitement."

"Surely tackling an intruder is more than
enough adventure and excitement for a while?"

"That wasn't an adventure, it was a wake-up
call."

"Exactly. It was a painful reminder that living
in this house by yourself is impractical, but of
course we'll support whatever you want to do."
Liza sounded tired and Kathleen could see her
mentally adding to her already-bulging to-do list.
Keep an eye on mother.

There would be regular phone calls and twice-
monthly visits and another worry to add to the
many that already kept her daughter awake at
night.

Kathleen wondered how to free her daughter of the crushing sense of responsibility she felt for those around her.

"I'm not your responsibility, Liza."

"Mum—"

"I'm willing to live with the consequences of the decisions I make. I've always valued independence—you know that. I'm sure many people considered me selfish traveling the world when I had a young child at home, and maybe I was, but it was my job and I loved it. *The Summer Seekers* was part of me. Is it selfish to sometimes put your own needs first? I don't think so. I was a mother, but not only a mother. A wife, but not only a wife. And of course, if I'd been a man, no one would have questioned it. The rules were always different for men, although I hope that's changing now. Progress."

"I don't look at it the way you do. I'm part of a family."

"Family can be your priority without you waiting on them hand and foot." She expected her daughter to argue with her and defend the way she lived her life, but instead Liza slumped a little.

"I know. And I don't know how it got to be this way. I think it's because it's simpler to do things myself because then they get done."

"And if things don't get done, what's the worst that can happen?"

"I end up unraveling the mess, which is usually more work than if I'd done it in the first place." Liza finished her coffee. "Let's not have this conversation."

Given that the conversation was starting to veer toward the personal, something Kathleen made a point of avoiding, she readily agreed. There was an awkward silence. "I hear Sean in the kitchen."

"I'll make breakfast." They spoke at the same time and Liza stood up quickly, knocking the table and sending the remains of Kathleen's coffee sloshing onto the table. She paused, seemed about to say something and then turned and walked back into the kitchen.

Kathleen stared after her for a moment feeling frustration and regret.

She'd thought that her travels would make her daughter more independent and in a way that had been the case. Liza had learned to cook and care for the home. She'd provided the cozy warmth that Kathleen hadn't. What was lacking was emotional independence. Liza had become insecure and clingy when Kathleen had returned from her trips.

Was that why her daughter had married so young? Had she been seeking security?

Kathleen had taken the opposite approach. She hadn't married until she was forty and even then it was on the third time of asking. She felt a strange pressure in her chest and realized it was grief. It had been five years since Brian had died, but still she missed him terribly.

She stood up, her bones aching. People who said that eighty was the new sixty had never been eighty. At her age only one thing was certain, and that was that nothing was going to get easier.

She waited for the stiffness to pass, and then joined them in the kitchen.

"Morning, Kathleen." Sean pulled a face when he saw the ugly wound and the traces of blood in her hair. "That's quite a wound. But I'm sure the other guy is worse. You're an example to us all."

"Sean!" Liza was exasperated. "Are you hungry? I'll make breakfast."

She opened the fridge and removed eggs, while Sean sat down and chatted about golf, fishing and the outrageous cost of property in London.

Liza moved quietly round the kitchen, laying the table and cooking.

Kathleen watched her daughter as she whisked eggs and expertly produced fluffy omelets which she sprinkled with fresh chives cut from Kathleen's herb pots. Caring for people came naturally to her, but at some point she'd forgotten to include herself.

Sean picked up his fork. "My favorite comfort food."

Liza made a fresh pot of coffee and put it in the center of the table, along with bowls of fresh berries and yogurt. "I brought you fresh oranges, Mum."

"Delicious," Kathleen said. "Let's have fresh juice right now. Such a treat."

Liza shook her head. "You should keep them."

"Why? What use is an orange in a bowl? The bowl is decorative, but the orange isn't." Kathleen studied her daughter. "You need to squeeze every last drop of juice from it and enjoy it while you can. When it's gone, it's gone."

"Is that supposed to be a metaphor? Life giving you lemons and all that?" But Liza squeezed juice and put the jug and glasses on the table.

"What's the plan for the day?" Sean cleared his plate. "Shall we take a walk to the beach later?"

"This isn't a minibreak." Liza put two slices of toast in front of him. "We need to help Mum with the house."

"I know, but in between helping, we can have some fun." Sean spread butter on his toast. "Might see if the surfboard is still in the garage."

Kathleen glanced up. "It is."

Liza poked at her eggs, as if she was too tired to lift the fork to her mouth.

After breakfast, they all moved into the living room.

Sean looked a little lost. "Do you need me to mow the lawn or something? Call an estate agent? Give me orders."

Kathleen breathed in sharply. "You will not

be calling an estate agent. I'm not selling this place so please don't waste your time trying to convince me." Was this what it was going to be like from now on? Was every conversation with her family going to be them trying to persuade her to move, and her refusing? How dull and frustrating that would be for all of them. What was it going to take to get them to understand that she had no intention of selling? Didn't they understand how she felt about this house?

She ignored the little voice inside her telling her that they couldn't possibly know how she felt about the house because she'd never shared her feelings on the subject.

"Right." Sean glanced at Liza who was dusting surfaces. "One option would be for you to stay here and we could arrange some help."

"What help do I need? A bodyguard?"

Liza shook her head. "That man probably knew you were alone and vulnerable, Mum."

"He was too drunk to know anything."

Sean laughed. "I was going to suggest buying you a scary dog with an extra row of teeth, but nothing could be scarier than the sight of you brandishing a skillet in a nightdress. If the press got hold of the story, you'd be the headline."

Liza clutched the cloth she was holding so tightly that the blood fled from her fingers. "She could have been killed, Sean."

"But I wasn't." Kathleen was calm. "And if

that had been the end of me—well, so be it. I will not sell this place. If you really want to do something useful, you can look for Popeye. He's missing."

"I'll do that." Sean stood, apparently grateful for something that gave him an excuse to leave the house.

"I'm going to spend the morning going through this room," Liza said. "Clearing the bookshelves. They haven't been touched in decades."

Kathleen bristled. "I'd rather wrestle another intruder than throw out books."

"But there has to be stuff here you'll never read again."

"Possibly. But if we throw it out we remove the option. And there is no reason to clear them. I've already told you—"

"You're not selling the house. I know. But that doesn't mean it's not a good idea to occasionally have a clear out. We don't have to rush any decisions." Liza clearly wasn't going to give up and Kathleen decided that the simplest solution was to allow her daughter to load a few things into boxes. It would give her a feeling of control, and Kathleen could always unload them again after she'd gone.

"In that case you can start on those shelves in the corner."

The morning passed, bathed in tension rather than a companionable silence.

Occasionally Liza would hold up a book. "This one?"

"Keep it," Kathleen would say, or "put it in the box."

Sean returned, but with the news that Popeye was nowhere to be found. "He's probably off exploring."

Kathleen had never thought she'd find reason to envy her cat.

On the other hand if a one-eyed, three-legged cat could go exploring, why couldn't she? There were no rules that demanded a person be in perfect condition in order to travel beyond one's own walls.

Liza was sorting through photo albums, flicking through the pages. "There's a lovely one here of you with Dad." She put it to one side and picked up the next book. "This must be one of your earliest albums." She turned a page and smiled. "Here's your graduation photo. Look at your hair! Why haven't I seen these before?"

"Because I tend to focus more on the present than the past." It was Brian who had put the photos into albums. Brian who had turned their house into a home and their little trio into a family. Kathleen had taken thousands of photographs of her travels, but they were stored in boxes in her study.

"Who are these two?" Liza pointed and

Kathleen walked across the room and looked over her shoulder.

Emotion lodged in her throat.

She should have destroyed the photo.

"Mum?"

"Mmm?"

"The two other people in the photo. Who are they?"

"Friends. We were all on the same course at college. The three of us were inseparable. That was taken in Oxford."

"The guy is very good-looking. What was his name?"

"Adam." Did her voice sound normal? "His name was Adam."

"And the girl?"

"Ruth." Her voice most definitely didn't sound normal. "She was my roommate." *My closest friend.*

"You've never mentioned her. What happened?" Liza turned the page. "Did you lose touch?"

"We—yes." Kathleen's legs suddenly turned wobbly and she sat down hard on the nearest chair. She thought about the letters, tied together and safely hidden in the back of one of her drawers. Unopened. "Not all friendships last."

"And Adam? Did you stay in touch with him?"

"No."

"But here you are again—the three of you. Do you know where Ruth is now?"

"Last time I heard she was living in California." Kathleen felt a sudden pang.

She took the book from Liza. There was Ruth smiling at the camera, her hair falling long and loose over one shoulder. And there was Adam with those blue eyes and movie star looks.

She remembered the nights she and Ruth had lain on the banks of the river in Oxford and talked until dawn. Kathleen had been an only child and for a while, with Ruth, she'd tasted what life might have been like if she'd had a sister. There had been nothing she didn't know about Ruth, and nothing Ruth didn't know about her. She'd truly believed that nothing would ever get in the way of their friendship.

She placed her finger on the photograph, touching Ruth's smile and remembering the sound of her laugh.

Brian had encouraged her to make a trip to California, but she'd refused.

She'd been cowardly.

Kathleen felt something stir inside her.

She looked up and there was Popeye, standing in the doorway of the living room, the angle of his head suggesting he was less than impressed by the number of people currently crowding his territory. He stalked across to Kathleen with a swish of his tail.

Kathleen put the album down and scooped up her cat who tolerated a few moments of affection before easing himself away from her grasp and heading into the kitchen.

Dear Popeye. If he could have an adventure, why couldn't she? Instead of sitting here reliving things that had happened in the past, she should be living in the present.

Liza picked up the abandoned photo album. "I'm sorry if looking at these upset you."

"They didn't upset me. They made me think." Kathleen felt stronger. "They made me realize it's time to do something I should have done a long time ago."

"You mean clear out the albums?"

"No." Was courage one of those things that dwindled with age, along with memory and muscle tone? "Sit down, Liza."

Liza joined her on the sofa without question, her brows meeting in an anxious frown. "Mum?"

"I'm lucky to have a daughter who cares about my welfare. Look at you, driving up here on the weekend to be with me when you have such a busy life of your own. I am grateful to you for all the research you've done on residential homes—" she looked at Liza "—but I won't be needing the information yet." *Never,* she thought, but she didn't say that because she suspected she needed to give her daughter the idea that she might see sense at some point.

"Mum—"

"I know you're acting out of love, but I'm in

sound mind and capable of making my own decision on what's best for me."

Liza's expression was one of pure frustration.

Stubborn. So like her father. Kathleen hadn't been interested in marriage after everything that had happened. Fortunately for her, Brian had refused to accept that. If he hadn't been so persistent and proposed three times, she would have missed out on the happy life she'd had. She never would have had Liza, who was now staring at her nervously, worried about her next move.

"You can't stay here, Mum."

"I don't intend to, but nor do I intend to move into a home and wait patiently for death."

"Not death, but—"

"I'm going to take a trip to California." It was a big place. There was no likelihood that she would bump into someone she didn't want to see.

"Cali—" Liza choked. "Are you kidding? That's a twelve-hour flight."

"I won't be flying all the way. I'm taking a road trip across America. Route 66." The moment she said the words she felt her insides lurch with a mixture of excitement and trepidation. Was this bold or foolish?

It didn't matter. She'd waited long enough. Too long. She wasn't going to let the past stop her from doing something she'd always wanted to do.

But even without the emotional pressure, it

was an ambitious trip. There were days when her bones ached so badly she could barely drag herself from her bed, and here she was blithely talking about driving two thousand four hundred miles—she hated thinking in kilometers—as if it was nothing more than a trip to the village.

Sean was the first to speak. "Exciting. How can we help?"

Dear boy.

Liza opened her mouth but Kathleen spoke first. "I'd appreciate a lift to the airport when I've made all the plans." She almost asked for help booking her flight, but she knew she'd have to find the confidence to do that herself. Ridiculous that the thought of a flight booking scared her more than a road trip. She found it impossible to believe that pressing a button and inserting a credit card number was enough to ensure her a seat on a plane.

Liza finally found her voice. "Route 66? You can't possibly be serious."

"I've never been more serious about anything in my life. I've already done the research." Kathleen thought about the box file under the desk in her study, bulging with maps and guidebooks.

"But why California? If you want sunshine, then come to the South of France with us. Or is it because you want to see Ruth after all these years?"

"I don't know if Ruth is still there. She might

have moved, or—" She might be dead. At their age, it was a distinct possibility. But this trip wasn't about Ruth. Kathleen had no wish to see her, and she was sure Ruth would feel the same way.

The past could never be undone.

"I don't want sunshine. I want adventure. And I've wanted to do Route 66 for a long time."

"So why didn't you do it?"

"It never seemed to be the right time." Kathleen kept her reply purposefully vague. "But now it does."

Liza appeared to be struggling for words. "You're ignoring one very big problem."

There were a million problems. It made her dizzy to think of them all, but she was determined to handle each and every one.

She'd beaned an intruder with a skillet. She was confident she could handle anything that came her way, even an uncomfortable set of memories.

"I have a passport, if that's what you're worried about. It's right here in my bag." She closed her fingers around the handle and pulled it a little closer.

Liza glanced from her mother to the bag. "You carry your passport with you?"

"Yes."

"To the village shop? To the post office?"

"I have it on my person at all times." Not that she'd traveled anywhere for years, but carrying her passport around made her think she might.

Liza looked aghast. "What if someone snatches your bag?"

"What will they do? Clone my identity? Frankly they're welcome to it, providing I can have theirs and they don't suffer from creaking bones."

Her daughter shook her head. "You don't just need a passport, Mum. You need a driving license. A road trip across America requires you to have a car and drive it. You don't drive anymore."

Kathleen sat up a little straighter. "Then I'll need to find someone who does."

4

MARTHA

"Will you at least listen to me?"

"No." Martha stalked up the path to the house, her bag of library books knocking against her legs. She couldn't wait to lose herself in a fictional world, which was currently her only escape from the real world. Anxiety swarmed through her. "There is nothing you have to say that I want to hear."

"I know it's mostly my fault, but everyone makes mistakes, right?" Steven stumbled as he tried to keep up with her. "And you've got to admit you've let yourself go a bit. Although your bum does look good in those jeans."

"I don't want to see you again." Martha elongated her body in order to look slimmer and hated herself for doing it. Her jeans *were* too tight. She should have bought new ones, but if there was one thing that was tighter than her jeans, it was money.

How had her life turned out like this? And how was she going to get out of this mess?

She was starting to dread leaving the house, and it wasn't as if home was a sanctuary. Things were almost as bad inside as they were outside.

She wanted to run away, but you needed money to run away.

Steven stuffed his hands in his pockets. "Do you want to know your problem, Martha?"

"No." She didn't need help identifying her problems. She could list them easily, thanks to the people around her who never let her forget her shortcomings.

"You expect too much. People are human. We're not all bloody perfect."

She fumbled in her bag for her keys.

"Martha, are you even listening?"

"I've done all the listening I intend to do. Bye, Steven. Don't call me." Proud of her restraint, she slammed the front door and heard her mother call from the kitchen.

"Was that Steven? Invite him in. He could take a look at the pipe in the kitchen. We have a leak."

Only her mother could put the state of the plumbing above her daughter's happiness.

"Ask Dad to do it."

There were many downsides of living with her parents at the age of twenty-four, but being trapped with people who didn't understand you was the biggest one. Lack of privacy came a close second. There was no space to lick your wounds, or mope with your head under a pillow. No chance of seeking emotional comfort from the TV and a box of chocolates because someone would change the channel and eat half of whatever you were about to put in your mouth.

And there was no way of avoiding an inquisition.

"Your dad is out." Her mother emerged from the kitchen, a cleaning cloth in her hand and a frown on her face. "And Steven is a plumber. He knows his way around a pipe."

But very little else.

The last thing she wanted was a conversation with her mother, but their house was small and what she wanted didn't figure much in anyone's plans. "He's gone."

Her mother flicked her cloth over the mirror. "You've been very unforgiving. You should at least talk to him."

"I've said all there is to say."

"Oh Martha." Her mother gave her a look of weary despair.

"What?" She did *not* need this. "What now?"

"He's nice enough and handy around the house. You shouldn't be so quick to dismiss someone in a steady job."

"Settling for someone because they know how to fix a toilet is a pretty low bar. I'm hoping for more than that."

"You are too fussy—that's your problem. Real life isn't like it is in those books you read, you know. I will never understand you, Martha."

That went both ways.

When she was ten she'd actually asked her parents if she was adopted because she saw nothing of herself in either of them. She'd secretly dreamed of a lovely woman knocking on the door one day to claim her. But it had never happened.

Each time her mother criticized her it chipped another piece from Martha until she felt less and less like herself.

"It's over."

Her mother tensed. "All men have frailties. And urges. Sometimes it's best to turn a blind eye. If you'd—"

"I don't want to talk about that."

"All I'm saying is that blame is never all on one side."

"It is in this case."

"Is it? You've put on a lot of weight since you lost your job. Too much sitting around moping. You might think that's harsh, but I'm your mother and it's my job to speak the truth." Her mother scrubbed at a stubborn mark on the mirror. "At your age I could fit into the same clothes I wore when I was sixteen. Never put on an ounce of weight."

Chip, chip, chip.

How did famous sculptors know exactly when to stop chiseling? At what point did they turn a masterpiece into a ruin?

"It's kilograms now, Mum."

"In your case, maybe. You're beyond being measured in ounces, that's for sure. You're eating because you're bored and unhappy, and that's your own fault for giving everything up so easily. First college, and now Steven. You should have stuck it out and graduated like your sister instead of throwing it all away. At least then you'd stand a chance of finding a job. You're paying the price for your bad decisions."

Her mother, whose own life had been a disappointment, had hoped for more from her two daughters. She'd wanted to live vicariously through their business lunches, international travel or endless promotions. Martha's older sister, Pippa, had gained favor by qualifying as a physiotherapist and securing a very glamorous job at a swanky private gym where a few famous names trained, thus giving her mother plenty to boast about over the garden fence.

Martha, unfortunately, had provided her with nothing but embarrassment.

"I didn't graduate because I wanted to take care of Nanna." And she missed her grandmother as much now as she had in the beginning. There was a corner of her heart that felt numb and lonely. "After she had her stroke I didn't want to miss a single moment of being with her. I couldn't concentrate on lectures or essays thinking of her all on her own. It didn't seem important."

"But now you're realizing it *was* important."

"Nothing is more important than the people you love." She didn't say family. Her family drove her to distraction. Whatever she did, she seemed unable to gain their approval. Her opinion seemed worth nothing. Her wishes even less. She wasn't sure she would have given up her degree to care for any of them. But her grandmother—"I will never regret the time I spent with her."

She'd always had a special relationship with her grandmother. When Martha was eight years old and bullied in school, she'd run away to her grandmother's house. Her grandmother had held her and listened, something her mother never did. Her mother's advice had been to "ignore them," but that wasn't so easy when they'd wrapped the strap of your school bag around your neck and were trying to hang you from a fence.

Martha had started going to her grandmother's for tea every day after school. There had been comfort in the routine. The cheerful teapot covered in red cherries. The delicate cups that had belonged to her great-grandmother. But the biggest comfort came from being with someone who was interested in her. It was a routine that had continued until she'd left for college to study English literature.

She'd been starting her third and final year when her mother had called to tell her about her grandmother's stroke. Martha had packed her things and returned home to care for her.

How could she concentrate on Tolstoy or Hardy when her Nanna was sick? Her mother had been appalled, but Martha had ignored her disapproval and slept on the sofa in the living room. Her grandmother had made a surprisingly good recovery. She and Martha had played cards, discussed books and giggled over racy TV shows. They'd even managed to take short strolls in the garden. It had been precious time that Martha would never forget.

And then one night her grandmother had suffered another stroke and that had been it.

Numb with grief, Martha had ignored her mother's advice that she should return to college and instead taken a job in a coffee shop a short walk from the house.

There was something comforting about making a good cappuccino, creating patterns in the foam. She could cope with it even when she was ambushed by sadness. She liked the fact that she often saw the same people every day. There was the woman with the laptop who made one coffee last all day while she wrote her novel, and the elderly man whose wife had died who could no longer stand being in the house on his own all day.

She'd enjoyed chatting to people and liked the fact that when she left the café she didn't have to take her work with her.

But then the coffee shop had closed, along with

many others, and suddenly what little work there was to be had was being chased by what seemed like thousands of people. She'd worked in the local animal shelter for six months before they'd run low on funds and had to stop paying her.

Her mother never missed an opportunity to remind her that she had no one to blame but herself. Her father, who liked a quiet life, chose to agree with her mother on every topic.

"If you hadn't thrown everything in, you wouldn't be in this situation now."

"Being a graduate isn't everything, you know. There are thousands of graduates who can't get jobs."

"Exactly. So why would an employer pick someone like you? You have to give yourself an edge, Martha, and you just don't have that much going for you."

She had no edges.

That sounded uncannily like the insult Steven had just thrown at her.

"I liked the job I had."

"You can't spend the rest of your life working in coffee shops or animal shelters. You should have studied for a profession like your sister, although you're far too old now, even if you did go back to finish your degree."

"I don't want to go back to college. And I'm only twenty-four."

"Ellen's daughter is twenty-four and she has

qualified as a doctor. She's saving lives! And what are you doing with your day?"

"I've put in a hundred applications in the last four months, but there are thousands of people applying for every job. Most of the time people don't even reply. It's soul destroying."

"All the more reason why you should have done a proper training like your sister, but you've missed that boat now."

Martha had a mental image of a flotilla of boats floating into the distance. She badly wanted to be on one of them. Preferably sunbathing while someone poured her an iced drink.

"Thanks for making me feel better."

"Well, if your own mother can't tell you the truth, who can? But there's no point in sitting around and moping about the bad decisions you made. You should go running with your sister."

Running with her sister would be another bad decision. Not only would it mean leaving the house, which meant bumping into Steven, but Martha would lag behind, which was pretty much the story of her life. She'd always been ten steps behind her sister, and there was no chance of her forgetting that.

Martha knew she wasn't as pretty as her sister. She wasn't as thin as her sister. She didn't make great choices like her sister.

She knew all the things she wasn't but wasn't sure what she was, apart from sturdy.

She made a great cappuccino and was good at talking, but that was more of a flaw than a skill. *Martha would talk the hind leg off a donkey* her mother would say, a statement accompanied by an exaggerated eye roll. *If there was an award for who talked the most, Martha would win it.*

She might not be as smart as her sister, but she knew enough to understand that living with people who made you feel worse about yourself wasn't good for the soul. She needed a job and a little place of her own, but there was no chance of either in London.

After everything that had happened, she'd had no choice but to move back with her parents. She hoped they didn't reach the point where they killed each other.

"Hi, Martha!" Pippa bounced down the stairs, hair swinging in a sleek ponytail. "How is Steven? Still behaving like a shit?"

She couldn't even lose at love without her sister knowing.

Martha looked gloomily at the shiny ponytail. Pippa even won at hair.

"Pippa! Don't you look a picture." Their mother beamed. "Are you off to work? Treating anyone famous today?"

"Day off. I have a yoga class in thirty minutes. I need something to eat before I leave." Pippa headed for the kitchen and Martha followed her.

She'd made cupcakes the day before using her

grandmother's favorite recipe, and there were still a couple left. She offered one to her sister who shook her head.

"No thanks. I'm making myself a green smoothie."

Winning at the healthy diet too, Martha thought, watching as her sister dropped apple, spinach, cucumber and various other healthy ingredients into the blender and proceeded to whiz it together into an unappetizing-looking pale green liquid. If Martha had found a blob of it on the kitchen surface she would have covered it in antibacterial spray.

Her mother reappeared. "Don't forget to clean the kitchen floor, Martha."

Her life was so exciting she could hardly bear it.

She finished the cupcake and unlocked the back door. Across the fence she saw their elderly neighbor, Abigail Hartley, struggling to hang her sheets on the line. The edges were hanging perilously close to the ground.

"I'll do that for you, Mrs. Hartley." Martha sprinted round the side of the house and into the adjoining garden. "You shouldn't be doing that with your arthritis."

"You're a kind girl, Martha."

"It's no trouble." At least Abigail thanked her for helping with laundry. In her own house everyone took it for granted.

"I struggle to lift my arms above my head."

"I know. It must be so hard for you." Martha pegged the sheets securely. "I'll come back later and bring them in so don't worry about that."

"You're very flexible and strong."

Flexible. Strong.

No one hung sheets like she did. She was winning at laundry.

Mrs. Hartley tried to push money into her hand and Martha was appalled that for a moment she was tempted to take it. Right now she couldn't even afford to buy a new hair clip and every little bit helped.

No way. The rest of her family might not like her very much, but if she started taking money for helping friends and neighbors then she wouldn't like herself either.

"I don't need payment." She almost said that it was a pleasure to do something for someone who appreciated the effort, but that would have felt disloyal. Family were family, even when they drove you to screaming pitch. "Happy to help."

"Was that Steven I saw just now?"

"Yes. I can't get him to leave me alone." Martha checked that the sheets weren't going to blow away.

"You're upset." Mrs. Hartley patted her arm. "Don't worry. Plenty more fish in the sea."

Martha had no interest in fishing.

Why did people commit to each other? She

had no idea. She'd had years of experience of watching her parents together and frankly there was nothing about their relationship that inspired her. Her mum was always yelling at her dad, who had selective hearing. There wasn't a lot of affection on display.

But what did she know about relationships?

Nothing it seemed.

"Mum wants me to be a high-flying career woman, but for that I'd need a career and right now that's not looking good. There are more people than jobs."

"But someone has to get the job. And that someone could be you. A girl like you can do anything she wants to do."

Her grandmother would have said the same thing, and although it sounded great it did nothing to lift Martha's spirits. "That's kind of you, Mrs. Hartley, but not quite accurate."

"You can't wait around for a job to fall into your lap. You need to put yourself out there." Mrs. Hartley stuck her chin forward. "What's your dream?"

Her dream was to be happy and look forward to each day, but that was never going to happen while she was living with her parents. She needed to be independent. She needed to not feel like a failure. She needed to get Steven out of her life.

And all that needed one thing—

"My dream is to find a job." She picked up the laundry basket. "Any job."

"Nonsense!" Mrs. Hartley waggled her finger. "You need to find something you're going to love."

"What did you do?"

"I worked at Bletchley Park during the war with all the codebreakers. I can't tell you more than that or I'd have to kill you and dispose of your body." Mrs. Hartley gave an exaggerated wink. "It was all very secretive and in those days we didn't gossip the way everyone does now."

Martha tried to imagine her mother in Bletchley Park. There wouldn't have been a secret the enemy didn't know. "I bet you were a force to be reckoned with."

"My husband used to say the same thing."

"How long were you married, Mrs. Hartley?"

"Sixty years. And I would have chosen him again at any point during that time. Not that I didn't want to occasionally kill him, but that's normal of course."

Martha hugged the empty basket. "You were lucky."

"You've had a rough time, but everything will work itself out." Mrs. Hartley patted her arm. "You're a good listener and very cheerful."

Not around her family. The cheer was sucked out of her.

"I'd better go. My dream job isn't going to present itself unless I look for it."

Martha walked back into the kitchen of her parents' house and found her mother scowling into the fridge.

"There's nothing much to eat. I'll go to the shops, but you need to clean the kitchen floor."

"Later. I'm busy."

"Doing what?"

"Job hunting. Trying to find a boat I haven't missed." Hatching an escape plan. She'd reached the point where she'd do anything.

"I forgot—" Her mother pulled an envelope out of her pocket. "This came for you. I hid it from your father because I knew how upset he'd be if he saw it on the mat."

Martha took the letter, hoping her mother didn't notice her shaking hand. "Thanks."

That was it then. All done. Finished.

No turning back now.

Sliding the letter into her pocket, Martha washed her hands, made herself a mug of tea and disappeared up to her bedroom.

She had the smallest room in the house, which meant she had room for a bed and not much else. There was a small recess where she hung her clothes, and a desk that folded away when she wasn't using it.

The wall opposite her bed was covered in a map of the world. Sometimes she lay in bed at night, dreaming about all the places she was never going to visit.

She pulled the letter out of her pocket and stared at it for a moment. Then she ripped it open, feeling sick even though she already knew what it would say.

She read it and felt her eyes fill with tears.

Her mother was right. She made bad decisions. What had she achieved in her life?

She folded the letter carefully and stuffed it into her bag.

She was keeping it as a reminder to make better decisions in the future.

Next to her on the bed her phone buzzed. Steven.

She rejected the call.

The summer stretched ahead like a long, gloomy road. She checked her social media and saw that one of her friends was now in Ibiza posting the most enviable beach selfies, while another was spending a week on a canal boat with her family and kept posting photos of rippling water, sunsets and glasses of wine balanced on the deck. Martha threw her phone on the bed. It wasn't that she cared massively about social media, but it said a lot about your life when you had nothing at all to post.

She stared out the window. The nearest thing she'd had to excitement in the last few weeks was when a fox had climbed into Mrs. Hartley's garden and dug up her flower beds. Martha had spent the morning clearing up fox poo so that Mrs. Hartley's little dog wouldn't roll in it.

Kicking off her shoes, she balanced her tea on the shelf above the bed and opened her ancient, temperamental laptop. Her hands hovered over the keys. She didn't even know what job to search for anymore.

Great with laundry, good at cleaning up fox poo weren't exactly assets.

What she needed was a job that came with accommodation so that she could get away from her family home.

She scrolled through the website.

Someone was looking for a live-in companion, to include full nursing care. What exactly did that entail? Martha, who was horribly squeamish, decided she didn't want to find out.

A professional couple were offering free accommodation in return for cat sitting, but there was no additional payment. How was she supposed to feed herself? She imagined herself coming home to visit her parents and being so svelte and slim they didn't recognize her.

She was about to give up when another job caught her eye.

Do you love driving?

Martha closed the laptop and reached for her tea. No, she didn't love driving. In fact it was no exaggeration to say she loathed driving, and driving loathed her. She'd failed her test five times and eventually passed only because the examiner had been worried about his pregnant wife who had texted in the middle of Martha's lesson to say that she was having contractions. He'd been so distracted he hadn't noticed that Martha was in the wrong lane approaching a roundabout, and he hadn't reacted at all when she'd failed to demonstrate even a hint of skill at reversing. She was used to inducing raw fear in her passengers, including her regular driving instructor, so it had been a relief and a surprise when the examiner had simply nodded as he'd discreetly checked his phone. When he told her that she'd passed she'd had to stop herself from saying, *Are you sure?*

Still, she'd been delighted and vowed to live up to his faith in her, only every time she slid behind the wheel she broke into a sweat. She felt like a fraud and an imposter. She expected the police to pull her over and tell her that they had CCTV footage that proved she hadn't really passed her test at all.

Driving scared Martha. It might have been all right if she'd been the only person on the road, but everyone seemed to either be stuck to her bumper, or overtaking her like a racing driver competing for a trophy. She knew that what she needed was more practice, but ever since she'd driven his car into a ditch during a practice session, her father had refused to let her behind the wheel. It didn't matter that he was an appalling teacher.

Wait until you can afford your own car.

As if that was ever going to happen.

She finished her tea and gazed out the window. From the bed she had a perfect view into the gardens of the houses opposite. Mrs. Pettifer, who was eighty-five and recovering well after receiving a new hip, was watering her plants.

What stories would she have to tell when she was eighty-five? Unless something dramatic changed, nothing that was likely to interest anyone.

She heard her mother clattering in the kitchen below.

"Martha!" her mother called up the stairs. "Kitchen floor!"

"I'm job hunting!" Martha opened her laptop again. She was ready to do anything. Better to do the wrong thing than nothing.

The driving job was still on the screen.

Are you ready for the adventure of a lifetime?

Yes, she was definitely ready for that.

Curious, she read on.

Enthusiastic and competent driver needed for a road trip across America, driving from Chicago to Santa Monica. Generous salary, all expenses paid. Must be good-humored, flexible and friendly. Clean driving license.

Martha stared at it.

She definitely wasn't an enthusiastic driver, and not by any stretch of the imagination could she be described as competent, but she was friendly, and she was also flexible, always assuming that they were talking about attitude to life rather than the ability to touch her toes without pulling a muscle because that was more her sister's province.

She scanned the details again.

A road trip across America.

Why did it have to be a road trip? But hadn't she read somewhere that America didn't have many roundabouts? If it was all straight roads and no roundabouts then she'd probably be fine. Providing she didn't have to reverse.

Her driving license was definitely clean, even if that was because no one in uniform had so far witnessed one of her misdemeanors. Also it had gone through the washing machine three times before she'd realized it was in her pocket.

How far was it from Chicago to Santa Monica?

She typed the question into a search engine and stared at the answer.

Two thousand four hundred miles.

She couldn't begin to imagine a distance like that.

It was two miles from her house to the nearest supermarket.

Two thousand four hundred . . . basically one

thousand two hundred trips to the supermarket.

She gulped and studied the map, and then looked at the map on her wall. Route 66. The road wound its way through multiple states and ended on the Pacific Coast. She'd studied Steinbeck at school, and *The Grapes of Wrath* hadn't made the Mother Road sound appealing.

On the other hand it was one of the most iconic roads in the world.

She searched for images of Santa Monica, and found herself staring at sandy beaches, palm trees, a girl cycling with the wind in her hair and a smile on her face. A couple gazing at each other in a restaurant. She could almost hear the crash of the waves in the background.

The place looked so *alive.*

She glanced out the window again and saw Mrs. Pettifer deadheading geraniums.

California.

It looked like another world, and right now that was exactly what she wanted. Any world other than the one she was currently inhabiting. Best of all, it was thousands of miles away from her crappy life here.

She read the words again, trying to find a way to make herself fit the job. She was definitely good-humored. She'd kept smiling all the way through the fox poo incident, and not only because her sister had trodden in it on her way to work. If the person she was supposed to be driving was good-humored too, then they might just about get by.

Why weren't they driving themselves?

Presumably they either couldn't drive, or didn't want to. Both options worked in her favor. If they couldn't drive then they wouldn't know when she was making mistakes, and if they didn't want to then they'd be sympathetic to the fact that she generally didn't want to either.

They wanted a competent driver. How exactly did they define competent? It was hard to be competent when you couldn't afford a car and no one would lend you theirs.

If she could fake it at the beginning, then by the time she'd driven two thousand four hundred miles there was a strong chance she might actually *be* competent. As long as she could make it out of Chicago without crashing into something, she'd be fine. She'd be ecstatic! She'd never achieved anything in her life, as her mother was always pointing out, but driving across America—that would be an achievement. And it would get her away from her family for the summer. Best of all it would get her away from Steven. She wouldn't have to look over her shoulder every time she left the house.

And a road trip would give her the chance to think about what she wanted to do with her life.

Maybe it would even lead to another job.

Martha Jackson, long-haul truck driver.

She imagined herself checking into a motel with a glowing neon sign. Maybe walking into a traditional diner and ordering a juicy burger.

America.

It sounded unbelievably glamorous compared to her little part of outer London.

"Martha! *Kitchen floor!*"

Martha was dragged from her fantasy of feeding coins into an old-fashioned jukebox and dancing round a bar to country music.

She felt like one of the ugly sisters. She was expected to scrub the floor while her sister was paid to prance around in leopard print yoga pants.

A new determination spread through her as she reached for her phone and dialed.

She had no idea who exactly wanted to be driven across America, but they couldn't be more annoying than her own family. Somehow she had to sound like a perfect candidate.

Martha Jackson, personal chauffeur. Calm (except when there's a roundabout), confident and reliable.

She waited until she heard a voice on the other end of the phone and then she smiled, trying to inject an appropriate level of friendly and flexible into her voice.

"My name is Martha and I'm calling about the job . . ."

Flexible, friendly and possibly the worst driver on the planet.

5

LIZA

"Who is this girl? We don't know anything about her." Liza paced across her mother's kitchen. It was her third trip to Cornwall in a month and each visit was more frustrating than the last, and not just because the traffic was starting to heat up along with the weather. It was as if dealing with an intruder had made her mother give up all thought of personal safety. Or maybe it had given her rather too much confidence in her own ability to survive the worst.

Whatever the psychology, nothing Liza said could make her see sense. "If you're determined to do this trip then book a tour. Go with a group. And a guide."

"I don't want to be part of a group. I'm too old to tolerate people whose company I haven't chosen and will no doubt find annoying. I shall go where I wish and stay as long as it pleases me to stay. It's not as if I have anywhere in particular to be at my age."

"Mum—"

"You didn't want me to stay alone in the house, and this way I won't be alone in the house."

There were days when Liza felt as if she was banging her head against a wall. "What if something happens?"

"I hope something *does* happen. It would be a crushing disappointment to travel two thousand four hundred miles and not encounter a single adventurous moment."

"You don't think you should start with a less ambitious trip?" Liza cleared the breakfast things into the dishwasher and set it to run. "You haven't been anywhere since Dad died."

"That was a mistake." Kathleen set a box of maps on the kitchen table. "Confidence and bravery can be lost if they're not used. I've spent far too long at home."

"You can't travel across America with a stranger."

"Why not?" Kathleen pulled out a map and spread it across the table. Then she found a large notepad.

"It isn't safe." Why was she the only person who thought this was a bad idea? Sean had refused to get involved. *It's her life, Liza. Her choice.*

Her mother peered at her over the top of her reading glasses. "Could you pass me the guidebook please."

Everyone in her life seemed determined to make foolish choices. Before she'd walked out the door to drive to Cornwall Caitlin had informed her that she was going to a party with Jane and if Liza tried to stop her she'd run away. Liza had been too nervous to leave her in the house, but Sean had intervened, persuaded Caitlin to have a few friends over instead, and everything had calmed down. Until next time. What had happened to her adorable daughter, who had loved dressing up and playing "school"? What had happened to the hugs and affection? These days Liza was greeted by rolled eyes and attitude.

Liza intended to spend the summer holidays rebuilding her relationship with her daughters. And with Sean too, because so much of the time it seemed their relationship revolved around the people they were caring for.

Eight signs that your marriage might be in trouble.

The article was still squashed in the bottom of her bag. Buried, but not forgotten.

She watched as her mother squinted over the map.

It was a mammoth trip for anyone, let alone someone who would be eighty-one on their next birthday.

Liza's strong sense of duty nudged at her.

She'd already started dreaming about their two weeks in the South of France. Her holiday reading was stashed away in the suitcase along with her sun hat.

But now here was her mother needing someone to drive her on her ridiculous road trip.

And then a thought occurred to her. Wouldn't this be the perfect opportunity for her and her mother to grow closer? Cocooned in a car, her mother would have to open up a bit, surely?

She felt something close to excitement. "I'll drive you. I'd really like to."

It was difficult to tell who was most shocked by that announcement, her mother or her husband.

"Er—Liza?" Sean scratched his head. "France?"

"You could go without me this year." The more she thought about it, the more excited she was. As a child she'd longed to be taken along on her mother's travels. This was the perfect time. They'd bond over the adventures. Emerge with a new closeness.

"It wouldn't be the same without you." Sean's appalled expression made her feel better about life.

She'd started to feel that people saw her only as a killjoy. Someone to put the brakes on their more impulsive decisions.

But Sean wanted her there.

Perhaps all that was wrong with their marriage was that they'd stopped creating time for themselves as a couple.

"You'd miss me?"

"Of course." Sean, who had obviously decided that nothing but coffee was going to get him through the weekend, was pouring a third cup. "How would we manage without you? I don't even know where we get the keys for the place. You always deal with the scary Madame Laroux. You're the best French speaker. And then there's the food. We'd probably starve if you weren't there."

The excitement oozed out of Liza.

He wanted her there because she made his life easy? That was it?

Did he even love her? Not her organizational abilities, but *her,* Liza, the woman he'd married?

"I'm sure you're capable of booking a restaurant." And now she was even more determined to go with her mother. It would bring them closer and also give Sean and the girls the opportunity to see how much she did for them.

"Don't panic, Sean," her mother said. "I appreciate the offer, but I don't want Liza to drive me. She would be the wrong person for this kind of trip."

The rejection tore open an old scar. She'd been eight years old and clinging as her mother had walked out the door. *Take me with you!* On one occasion she'd even sneaked her own packing into her mother's case and then howled when it was gently removed.

"Why would I be the wrong person?"

"Apart from the fact you love your annual trip to France and you'd resent not being there, you like everything to be in your control, and on a trip like this nothing is going to be in your control. You would worry about your family constantly and spend half your time phoning home. And you'd nag me to eat the right things and be careful. It would be stressful for both of us." Kathleen smoothed the map flat on the table. "This is one trip I'm doing alone."

She'd done every trip alone, Liza thought, absorbing the pain while outwardly keeping herself composed. She should be used to rejection by now, so why did it hurt so much?

She had to accept that they'd never be close, no matter how much she wanted it to happen. She needed to stop hoping for that.

She'd go to France, even though that felt tainted now.

She was processing the fact that Sean saw her as a tour operator when she heard the sound of a car engine through the open window.

Kathleen straightened, one hand on the map. "That's her. Martha. My driver. Why don't you and Sean go and breathe in the sea air?"

Her mother didn't want her around.

Only her sense of responsibility forced her to stay put and meet the girl. "Have you checked her credentials? How do you know she's a safe driver?"

"The roads that lead to this house are narrow and twisty. If she managed it without having an accident, then she's a good driver. I'll meet her," Kathleen said. "I don't want you scaring her off or sending her away." She left the kitchen and Liza stood there feeling unappreciated, alone and misunderstood.

Sean gave her shoulder a squeeze. "Narrow escape there, Liza. She might have said yes and then where would we have been?"

She would have been driving across America spending quality time with her mother.

But Kathleen didn't want that. She'd rather spend weeks with a stranger than her own daughter. Liza wasn't adventurous enough.

"Is that all I am to you? Someone to organize your holiday?"

"No." Sean finished his coffee. "Although you *are* good at that. Thanks to you, life runs smoothly."

The holiday, which she'd been looking forward to for so long, no longer seemed as shiny. She wanted to tell him how she felt, but she couldn't do that with a stranger about to join them in the kitchen.

Grabbing Sean's mug, she refilled it.

She needed to stop overthinking everything, particularly her marriage. Sean had made an insensitive comment. So what? People said the wrong thing all the time. She said the wrong thing. It was important not to overreact. She was going to throw that stupid article away.

She heard laughter from the hallway and then her mother came back into the room, accompanied by a girl who looked barely older than Caitlin.

Her curls bounced around her shoulders and her jeans and her top clung to her curves. She had a dusting of freckles on her nose and a friendly smile that made you want to smile back.

Sean stepped forward. "Nice to meet you. Martha, is it? Good journey?"

"Great, thanks. Straight through from London."

Liza looked at her stupidly. "You came by train?"

"Train, and I splurged on a taxi from the station. He moaned all the way." Martha seemed sympathetic rather than annoyed. "Something about the roads being too narrow and the hedges too high."

She made Liza feel old. "I assumed you'd drive."

"I don't have a car, and anyway I like the train. It's a good time to read and I always find the rhythm soothing."

"I am the same," Kathleen said. "I once traveled from Moscow to Vladivostok on the Trans-Siberian Railway."

Liza remembered that trip. She'd had meningitis and been so ill she'd had to spend weeks in the hospital. People had talked in hushed voices around her. Her father, white-faced and tense, had never left her bedside. For a short time she'd been the focus of attention, and then her mother had arrived home with postcards and souvenirs from her trip and the focus in the house had shifted.

Did her mother even remember she'd been ill?

"Come and sit down, Martha." Kathleen rummaged in her file and brought out some pictures. "What do you know about Route 66?"

"I studied *The Grapes of Wrath* at school, so I know about the people escaping the Dust Bowl in the 1930s, traveling from the Midwest to the California coast. Route 66. The Mother Road. Hated the book as a child, but I've reread it five times since then and it's one of my favorites. Weird how school can put you off something, instead of inspiring you. Apart from that," Martha pondered, "I know the road was decommissioned and replaced by the interstate, but presumably you want to stick to the historic Route 66 wherever we can?"

"I do." Kathleen looked delighted. "My dream is to rent a classic Ford Mustang and travel in style, but then I thought maybe I'm too old for that."

Finally, Liza thought. *Some common sense on display.*

Kathleen continued. "Instead I've decided that we'll rent the fanciest, most up-to-date Mustang convertible available. With air-conditioning of course, because when we reach Needles, on the state line between Arizona and California, the temperatures will be hot enough to roast a hog."

A Mustang convertible?

Martha leaned over the pictures, her curls tumbling forward. "We'd look cool, but we'd be boiling to death?"

"Exactly." Kathleen was charmed. "It's a subtropical desert climate, with huge thunderstorms during the hot summer."

Liza couldn't believe what she was hearing. "I assumed you'd rent a safe, modern SUV."

"Where's the fun in that?" Kathleen was studying the map. "I read an article that said as long as you drive early in the morning, you can avoid the heat of the day. Can you travel light, Martha? There's not a lot of room for luggage."

"Wait—" Liza interrupted. "You're basically hiring a sports car?"

"It will be fun for Martha."

Liza thought she saw a flash terror in Martha's eyes, but decided she was probably seeing a reflection of her own emotions.

"What if you break down?"

"What if we don't? And anyway, the company said there was a number we could call. With luck they might send a hot guy for Martha." Kathleen winked at Martha, who laughed.

"If we break down in the desert, we'll all be hot."

"This sounds like such fun I'm tempted to hide away in the back seat," Sean said and Liza wondered why it was left to her to ask the important questions.

"But you *can* drive, Martha? The minimum age to rent a car in the US is twenty-five."

"I was twenty five last month."

She looked younger. Liza resisted the temptation to ask if she could check her birth certificate. "And you don't mind being away for half the summer?"

"Thank you, Liza." Her mother gestured to the map. "Come and take a look, Martha. Exciting, isn't it?"

"Very." Martha leaned closer. "I've been studying the route. I can't wait to see the Grand Canyon."

"Me too." Kathleen urged Martha to sit down. "I will take care of all expenses of course. You won't have to pay for a thing."

What if the girl had extravagant tastes and wanted to order a massive steak in every restaurant or diner?

"Mum—"

"Are you able to be flexible? Because although we will book a few places along the way, I'd like to give ourselves time to be spontaneous. Stay longer if we feel like it. Move on if we don't."

"Sounds good. Let's go where no one can find us." Martha blushed. "I mean, it sounds exciting, that's all. And I can sleep anywhere."

Liza frowned. Why would she want to go where no one could find her?

"I'm planning on taking two weeks to do the

trip, perhaps more, and then spending a few weeks in California. I'll be away for a month at least." Kathleen folded the map. "What date do you have to be home?"

"I don't have to be home at all. I can stay forever if that's what works for you."

Forever? What sort of person could stay away forever?

Did she have nothing going on in her life at all?

Liza's frustration turned to suspicion. Something about this didn't feel right.

And what about the practicalities? *Visas? Immigration?*

"Do you have family, Martha?"

"Yes." Martha took a mug of tea from Sean with a smile of thanks. "I live with my parents and my sister because I'm in between jobs right now."

"What was your last job?" Liza ignored her mother's exaggerated sigh.

"I worked in an animal shelter. I've been looking at millions of things, but there aren't any jobs right now."

"If we could have the details of your last employer, that would be good. We need references."

Kathleen put the map away. "References won't be necessary." She stood up. "Tell me what you love most about driving, Martha."

"The best part is when I reach my destination

and I'm still alive. That's always a cause for celebration. Not an alcoholic celebration though, obviously." Martha gave a burst of laughter, and Sean and Kathleen joined in.

Liza breathed deeply. "What about accidents?"

Martha took a sip of tea. "Just the one. No casualties, although I took a chunk out of my dad's affection for me."

"I had three accidents in my first year of driving," Kathleen said. "Accidents teach one to drive more carefully."

Unless they killed you.

Liza forced a smile. "I expect you want to ask about qualifications?"

"Ah yes. Qualifications." Kathleen looked Martha in the eye. "Can you make a good cup of tea? I'm partial to Earl Grey."

"I make the best tea," Martha said. "Before the animal shelter, I worked in a café."

"Then you're perfectly qualified for the job," Kathleen said. "I can tell we're going to get along famously. The job is yours, if you're happy to spend your summer with a badly behaved octogenarian who has an annoying tendency never to do as she's told." Kathleen glanced at Liza with a twinkle in her eye and Martha smiled.

"I never do as I'm told either. My mother says I'll be the death of her."

Perfect, Liza thought. *Two irresponsible people together. What could possibly go wrong?*

Martha must have recognized that Liza was the one who needed to be won over because she leaned forward. "I promise to take good care of your mother."

"Thank you." Liza could hardly argue with her enthusiasm or intention, even if the reality promised to be somewhat different. "What will your parents think of you flying to America for the summer?"

"They'll be thrilled I've got a job."

That response did nothing to reassure Liza, but Kathleen stood up.

"That's settled then. Do you have a passport?"

"Yes." Martha nodded. "I went on a school trip to Italy in my final year of school and it's still valid."

Liza was scrolling through the facts in her head.

How many twenty-five year olds would choose to drop everything to drive across America with an eighty-year-old? Why wasn't Martha spending the summer with her friends, or a boyfriend?

Something wasn't adding up, but it was too late because her mother was already rummaging in a drawer for the envelope where she kept her cash.

"I'm going to give you some money now so that you can equip yourself ready for the trip." Kathleen opened a drawer. "I hope you don't mind not having a bank transfer. I don't like the idea of my money moving around in space. All you have to do is type one number incorrectly and suddenly you've handed over your life savings."

"Whatever works for you, Mrs. Harrison. But what do you need me to buy? If you make me a list, then I can go and buy whatever you need. Tea?"

"You can leave the tea to me. This is for your personal items. You'll need comfortable clothes for driving. A soft bag that will squash into a small space. Sunglasses so that we both look cool when we're driving our cool car. A scarf to stop your lovely curls blowing across your face as we're speeding along the highway? A couple of dresses?"

Martha tugged at her T-shirt. "I'm more of a jeans girl, but thank you. That's generous. Are you sure?"

"If I'm expecting you to drive two thousand four hundred miles then the least I can do is make sure you're comfortable doing it." Kathleen handed over a thick wad of cash. "Ignore Liza's frown. My daughter is careful about everything."

What was wrong with being careful? Since when was it a sin to be reliable?

Where was the virtue in throwing off responsibility giving no thought to others?

Liza felt a hot stinging behind her eyes.

Never mind that she'd spent every other weekend in Cornwall since her mother's "incident."

Never mind that she'd had little time with her own crumbling family.

None of her efforts had brought her closer to her mother and they never would.

Hurt, she gave a brief smile and walked to the door. "I'm going for a walk. Nice to meet you, Martha. Enjoy the trip." She almost felt sorry for Martha, who was so smiley and optimistic. Whatever her reasons for agreeing to this, Liza was confident she had no idea what she was letting herself in for. And as for the promise to keep Kathleen safe—well, good luck with that.

Suddenly she badly wanted to go home. Maybe they'd leave after breakfast tomorrow, instead of waiting until lunchtime as planned. She'd make a nice supper for the girls. They'd eat as a family.

As she and Sean walked across the fields to the beach, Liza breathed slowly and deeply. It was beautiful, but she couldn't ever properly relax here. Part of relaxing was being able to leave all the jobs behind, and here in Oakwood Cottage there were far too many jobs glaring at her. Future complications loomed. Her mother falling. The house crumbling.

Sean stooped to pick up a shell from the sand. "Martha seems great."

"Mmm." She watched the waves break onto the shore. She'd always felt a sense of responsibility. Even as a child, she'd felt it. She'd cooked for her father and tried to make up for her mother's many absences.

Sean looped his arm round her shoulders and tried to kiss her, but she eased away and strolled forward along the beach. She was still upset, and she couldn't so easily flip the switch from irritation and hurt to affection. His thoughtless words had created a barrier between them and she didn't know how to reach across it. For her, sex was closely tied to emotion. She'd never been the type to use sex as a way of making up after a fight. She had to feel loved and nurtured, and right now she felt neither.

Sean caught up with her. "I know you're upset. But that's your mother being your mother."

It wasn't only her mother who had upset her, but this wasn't the time to have such an important conversation. She was tired and hurt and didn't trust her own feelings.

They walked together in awkward silence and by the time they returned to the house, Martha was gone.

While Sean called the girls, Liza threw together a selection of summer salads, tearing fresh basil leaves over mozzarella, adding toasted almonds to green beans as she half listened to the conversation.

"Everything quiet there, Caitlin?" Sean reached past Liza and stole an olive. "House still standing? No calls to the emergency services . . .

What? . . . Yes, of course I'm joking." He gave Liza a look that said, *You see? I'm checking on them.* "Make sure you lock up properly before you go to bed. And check you haven't left the freezer door open."

Liza sprinkled chopped garlic over baby tomatoes, red onion and peppers and put them in the oven to roast.

"That smells good." Sean hung up. "The twins sound fine. They're having a quiet night in and all is well."

"What about the party?"

"You told them they couldn't go."

"Since when did anyone listen to me?" Liza sliced a sourdough loaf and pulled butter out of the fridge.

"They obviously *are* listening to you."

She felt guilty for not being as trusting as he was. "Did you talk to Alice?"

"No. Why?"

Because she wasn't as good a liar as her sister.

Caitlin was very much the dominant one.

"Nothing. Ignore me."

Why didn't she feel reassured? It was that look Caitlin had given her before she'd left the house. The *yes Mum,* that didn't mean yes at all.

These were her children. She loved them more than anything. She should trust them too. She was never going to heal the relationship unless there was trust involved. She was going to be more like Sean, and always assume the best and not the worst.

"Thank you for checking. I appreciate it." She kissed Sean on the cheek and took the glass of wine he offered.

The first sip was bliss, like tasting sunshine in a glass. Some of the tension left her.

They ate dinner outside, watching the sun dip over the fields and the ocean in the distance.

Popeye appeared, as he so often did when there was food to be had.

They talked about the trip, and Liza talked about the summer plans for France, and carefully resisted all temptation to urge her mother to be careful.

She closed her eyes, savoring the wine and the sunshine until the air grew chilly. When the sky darkened, she cleared the plates into the kitchen and Kathleen headed for bed.

Liza had the feeling she would have been as happy to be alone.

It was clear that her mother was frustrated by her attempts to be caring, and Liza didn't know how not to care.

"We should have an early night too," she said to Sean. "All that sea air has made me tired."

Feeling isolated and unappreciated, she took ages in the bathroom and was relieved to find Sean already asleep when she eventually slid into bed next to him.

It took a long time for her to fall asleep but eventually she did and she was dreaming of the South of France when Sean's phone rang.

He groped for it in the dark and Liza switched on the light, heart pounding.

"Is it the girls?"

He focused on the screen. "No, it's Margaret and Peter from next door. Why on earth would they be calling in the middle of the night?" He sat up and answered the phone. "Margaret? Yes—don't worry about that—" He listened and rubbed his hand over his face. "You're kidding—oh no—"

"What?" Liza mouthed the question but he shook his head and held up his hand.

"All I can do is apologize . . . Yes, absolutely. We'll leave now, but it will take four hours to get home. Of course you called the police—I understand."

"Police?" Liza, who didn't understand at all, was frantic. "What is going on?"

"Yes, Liza and I will be dealing with them I can assure you." Sean finally hung up and swore under his breath. "We need to leave."

"Is it the twins? Did they have an accident?"

"No, they had a party." Sean's expression was grim as he threw their clothes into the overnight bag. "They've wrecked our house and, it seems, broken our neighbors' dining room window and destroyed their precious herbaceous borders. We have to go home."

6

KATHLEEN

Two weeks later Kathleen sat clutching her bag on her lap as Liza drove her to the airport.

She felt old, but that was what two nights with teenagers could do for you.

Was it wrong to feel relieved that part of her trip was over? She was starting to understand why Liza looked drained the whole time.

Liza gave her a wan smile. "Sorry. It wasn't the most relaxing stay."

"It was a treat to see the girls." Kathleen forced herself to lie, a challenge for someone who believed in speaking the truth. It seemed the polite thing to do, even though they both knew that the twins had been a nightmare. They'd behaved delightfully to her of course—*Granny! It's great to see you*—and appallingly to their mother—*We could all go out for a nice family dinner but Mum's taken away all the fun in our lives.*

Given the level of hostility, Kathleen admired her daughter for sticking to the sanctions she'd imposed. In the same situation she doubted she would have been so resolute. But

Liza had always been an easy child, so discipline of any sort had been unnecessary.

What a horrid, conflict-ridden, joyless world her daughter was inhabiting.

"No internet, no TV, no phone, for a *month*." Caitlin had stomped around the kitchen. "It's an infringement of my human rights."

Alice, a conflict avoider, had covered her ears and left the room.

Liza had stayed calm. "It was an infringement of our neighbors' rights when you kept them awake, broke a window and destroyed half the plants on their border."

"That wasn't my fault." Caitlin was mutinous. "I'm not responsible for other people's actions."

"You are when they are guests in your home."

"They weren't guests! I didn't even know them. And taking everything away is—is—it's medieval. Granny, tell her it's medieval."

"Nothing about your life is medieval." Kathleen had tried to stay impartial. "In medieval times you probably wouldn't have survived to teenage years. Infant mortality was alarmingly high."

"Are you saying you never had a party when you were our age?"

Oh dear. "Yes, I suppose—"

"You see?" Caitlin turned to Liza, triumphant. "Granny said she had a massive party when she was our age."

"I didn't say massive," Kathleen said, but no one was listening to her.

Liza was working so hard to stay calm her body was vibrating.

"Firstly, this is about you, not Granny. Secondly, social media hadn't been invented when Granny was a teenager and even if she *did* have a party, I'm willing to bet she knew everyone there. Thirdly, her guests didn't destroy the house and also the neighbors' house."

"*We* didn't destroy the house," Caitlin mumbled, but she had the grace to look a little sheepish. "We didn't invite those people."

"But someone did, and you need to find out who and make them accountable."

"No way. That is not cool."

Kathleen waited for Liza to say *While you're living under my roof, you will live by my rules,* but she didn't.

Instead she sat down at the kitchen island, shoulders slumped as if the weight of life was too much to carry. "Caitlin, if a stranger who you hadn't invited into your room, went in and destroyed the things you love, would you be upset?"

Caitlin had paused. "That's different."

"It's not different. The insurance company sent someone round to assess the damage yesterday, and it's going to cost thousands of pounds to put right."

"That's crazy. It's a scam."

"It's reality. Your 'friends' left the tap running in the downstairs bathroom, and the water flowed into the hallway, causing irreparable damage to the wooden floor. There are cigarette burns on the sofa in the living room, and wine stains on the carpet. The glass in the patio doors is cracked. And none of this is counting the damage done to our relationship with Mr. and Mrs. Brooks next door. I feel so embarrassed I can hardly face them. Apparently one of your so-called 'friends' used their front garden to relieve himself."

Caitlin looked less sure of herself. "I don't know anything about that."

"You were responsible for caring for this property."

"I didn't know they were going to invite a ton of people I didn't know!" There was a note of panic in her voice.

"That happens when you share details of a party on social media."

Caitlin was a little paler. "I didn't do that."

"Someone did, and you need to find out who. And you need to ask yourself some serious questions about your friendship with that person."

"Oh why don't you just say it?" Guilt made Caitlin more fractious than usual. "You think it's Jane. I bet you're hoping it is Jane because then you'll have an excuse to keep her out of my life. You've hated Jane from the beginning. Just because she's a year older and really cool. But I'm old enough to make my own choices about my friends."

"You're not making your own choices," Liza said. "You're following her choices. That's what worries me. You're going along with everything she does and says, even though it goes against your own values. If you are old enough to make choices, you're also old enough to take responsibility."

Sean had walked into the room at that point and immediately left again.

Kathleen had caught Liza's look of frustration as she opened her mouth to call him back and then thought better of it.

Strange, Kathleen had thought, that they hadn't handled it together. A united front.

And then she remembered all the times she'd been absent, traveling somewhere exotic, leaving Brian to handle all those small family crises himself.

Caitlin was still in full flow. "You want me to have a boring life, like you. But I'm more like Granny. Adventurous and fearless. It's in my DNA. I was born this way."

In different circumstances Kathleen might have admired the clever, if manipulative, way Caitlin had shifted attention from herself.

DNA. Apparently this episode was now somehow her fault.

Kathleen had made a tactful exit at that point and escaped to her room to study her guidebook. Traveling was the perfect way to step out of one's life, and right now she was ready to do that. She wished her daughter could do the same because her life didn't seem a particularly pleasant place to be.

For the first time ever she was questioning that part of her that had wished Liza had been a little more rebellious. If Caitlin was an example of what rebellion looked like, she was glad she hadn't had to handle it.

And now they were in the car and Kathleen couldn't help but be aware that she was escaping, but Liza was returning to that toxic atmosphere.

Her daughter looked pale and tired, but resolute and determined as if she was in the midst of fighting an exhausting battle.

Whatever had happened to fun? Relaxation?

Kathleen sat a little straighter, her brain working hard. She hadn't been the best mother in the world, but it was never too late to do better.

But how? How could she persuade her daughter to take time for herself? She hated it when people told her how to live her life, so she was hardly going to deliver a lecture or even offer advice. And they'd be at the airport soon, surrounded by strangers and noise and life at its most frenetic. Hardly the moment for a heart-to-heart, particularly for someone as averse to emotional conversations as her.

Sitting in stationary traffic, Liza drummed the wheel with her fingers and glanced at her. "Are you having second thoughts about this trip? Because you know that if something happens, you can call me and I'll help."

Kathleen felt an ache in her chest. Her daughter thought what she was doing was a bad idea, but she was still willing to help if something went wrong. Never mind that she was handling a crisis at home. It was so typical of Liza to put everyone's needs in front of her own.

But people made sacrifices for those they loved. No one knew that better than her.

She pushed aside thoughts of herself, and not only because dwelling on the past was her least favorite thing. This wasn't about her.

"I was thinking about you." *Go on, Kathleen. Say something deep and helpful. Acknowledge feelings.*

"It's been a pretty stressful time." Liza turned her attention back to the road. "Hopefully the holidays will calm everything down and I'll be able to relax. I can't wait."

"You can't live your life waiting for two weeks a year when you enjoy yourself, Liza. What about the other fifty weeks?"

"I don't only enjoy myself two weeks a year." Liza frowned. "It's true that day-to-day it feels

123

a bit exhausting, but this is life, isn't it? And it's the same for everyone. Everyone has something."

But not everyone handled their "something" with the same diligence as her daughter.

"You need to find that summer feeling for the rest of the year, not only for two weeks in August." Kathleen licked her lips. "I'm worried about you."

"*You're* worried about *me?*" Liza laughed. "You're the one driving across America with someone you don't know."

But that suited her. She had no desire to know Martha. Superficial relationships had always been her preference.

"I'm worried that you never put up boundaries."

Liza adjusted her grip on the wheel. "We're different that way, you know we are."

"Yes, but you allow people to feed on your good nature until all that's left is—is dust. Have you painted lately?"

"Caitlin's bedroom."

"You know that wasn't what I meant."

"No, I haven't painted." Liza sounded tired. "No time."

"You should make time."

"I haven't felt like it. There's no pleasure in trying to create something in a snatched moment when everyone is trying to take a piece of you. It becomes another chore. And I'd feel guilty taking that time for myself when there is so much to be done."

This wasn't good. This wasn't good at all.

Kathleen trod cautiously, like an explorer venturing into a new land. "You're the glue that holds the family together, but do you know what happens to glue over time? It dries out. And then everything falls apart."

"You think I'm drying out?" Liza's response was light, but her hands tightened on the wheel. "I need to change my moisturizer."

"Do you use moisturizer?"

"When I remember." Liza drew breath. "You think I'm weak. You think I let people walk all over me."

"No. I think you're a giver. You're the kindest person I know, and generous, but for some reason you forget to extend that kindness to yourself. Which part of your life is for you and no one else? *Liza!*" She squeaked a warning as her daughter almost drove into the car in front.

Liza slammed on the brakes. "Sorry. I— Did you say you think I'm kind and generous?"

"Yes." Why would a few words of praise elicit such a dramatic response? And were those tears in Liza's eyes? No, no!

Her daughter blinked rapidly. "You think I'm boring. And careful."

"Not boring. Careful, maybe. Caring, definitely." Maybe this conversation had been a mistake. She wasn't in a position to help or influence even if she wanted to, and generally she was of the opinion that a person had the complete right to mess up their own lives free of interference. But this was her daughter. "You care deeply about those close to you and you always put their happiness first. You were the same as a child."

"Is that a bad thing?"

"It can be bad if it means people take advantage of you. If something needs doing, they know you'll do it." And suddenly it came to her. The answer. It wasn't interference if you gently nudged someone in a particular direction. They still had choice. "And because I know you'll do what people need you to do, I'm going to ask one more thing of you." She didn't need to extend this uncomfortable conversation, she simply needed to manipulate the situation to achieve the outcome she wanted.

"You told me I should start saying no," Liza said, "and now you're asking me to do something else?"

"Yes," Kathleen said. "Selfish of me, I know, but I need someone to help me out with this. I should have asked you sooner." If she'd thought of it, she would have. She'd been tackling this the wrong way. "Would you check on Popeye a couple of times when I'm away?"

"I thought you said someone was feeding him?"

"They are, but you know Popeye. He's an independent soul, and I've never left him for this long. I'd be happier if I knew someone I trust is keeping an eye on him. Maybe giving him a cuddle." She sent a silent apology to Popeye who, generally speaking, wasn't big on cuddles. Any guilt she felt at exploiting Liza's good nature and sense of responsibility, was diluted by the fact that her request was in a good cause.

"I'll try, but the girls are busy and there is no way we're leaving them after what happened last time—"

"Why not go alone? Leave Sean to keep an eye on the girls. You might enjoy it. There is nothing like an early morning walk on the beach when you're the only one there. Sometimes I take my coffee down there and sit on the sand."

"You do?" Liza glanced at her. "I didn't know that."

"Now you're going to tell me it sounds like a risky undertaking."

"I think it sounds blissful. I'd give a lot to have a peaceful half hour on the beach with no one around."

"Then do it. Spend the weekend at the cottage. Have some time to yourself. Why not?"

"Well, because—" Liza frowned. "I never go anywhere by myself. We do everything together."

And that, Kathleen thought, *was the problem.*

She worked hard at looking pathetic. "I

wouldn't ask, but I'm worried about Popeye, the dear soul."

"I know he means a lot to you." The traffic started moving and Liza eased the car forward. "I promise I'll keep an eye on Popeye. Although I won't be responsible if he runs off."

"He never runs off. He goes exploring, but then he always comes home."

Liza smiled. "I never realized before how alike the two of you are."

"Indeed. All I need is the freedom to roam." It wasn't so far from the truth. "If you go to the cottage for the weekend, don't bother shopping and cooking. There's a wonderful deli in the village that opened recently. Tell them you're my daughter. And if you walk a mile down the beach, the Tide Shack makes a wonderful burger. The salty fries are spectacular."

"Your diet is shocking, Mother." But this time Liza was laughing, not lecturing. The traffic had finally eased and they were now only minutes from the airport. "Please try and eat the occasional vegetable or piece of fruit when you're in the US."

"I promise to eat nothing but broccoli." Kathleen reached for her bag and checked her passport again. She felt a little nervous, but there was no way she was going to admit that to her daughter. She could just about handle a conversation about emotions providing they weren't her own. "It's been so long since I traveled properly, I've forgotten my routine. I keep having to check my passport and credit card are there, even though I've already checked twice."

"You're going to be fine." Liza took the turnoff to the airport. "You have a phone. Martha has my number. If you need anything at all, or get into any sort of trouble, call me."

"I hope I do get into trouble." Kathleen patted her daughter's leg. "That's why I'm going."

Liza pulled in at Departures. "You're incorrigible."

"I know. Please do check Popeye for me."

"I'll check Popeye." Liza opened the car door and walked around to help Kathleen with her bags. "I should have parked. Then I could have come in with you."

"I hate prolonged goodbyes." They exchanged a look, both of them remembering all the stressful partings when Liza was a child. Emotions had tentacles, Kathleen thought. They wrapped themselves around you and pulled you down. They dug themselves into your heart and caused pain. She gave Liza's shoulder an awkward pat. "Thank you. Enjoy France."

A strange pressure built in her chest.

She should walk away right now, but for some reason her legs wouldn't move.

Liza stepped forward and hugged her. "Have fun. I love you."

The pressure grew until it felt as if someone had inflated a balloon in her chest.

She licked her lips and tried to speak but the words wouldn't come. How was it possible to feel so much and yet say so little? And yet that was her world. She kept feelings inside that balloon and hoped that one day it wouldn't burst.

Liza stepped back, gave an awkward smile and turned back to the car.

Kathleen gave a wave, unsettled by the sense of loss she felt.

She stood still as Liza eased into the never-ending flow of traffic, and it didn't just feel like goodbye. It felt like a moment gone forever. An opportunity lost.

I love you too. You do know that, don't you?

She turned, battling that feeling of disappointment that comes when you've failed an exam, or missed a goal. That feeling that came when you knew you should have done better.

The moment she entered the terminal building, the bustle and the echoing noise closed around her and her mood lifted. The present could always drown out the past if you made your present loud enough.

The feeling lasted until a young man almost knocked her flying with a *Look where you're going, Grandma.*

Up on the departures board were all the destinations, reminding her of how big the world was, and how small she'd allowed hers to become.

She spotted Martha standing by the automatic check-in, looking lost.

Kathleen waved and trailed her suitcase along the gleaming floor, weaving her way through the passengers as Martha approached with the excitement and enthusiasm of a Labrador.

"Kathleen!" Martha enveloped her in a big hug. "Our flight is on time, I checked. Chicago, here we come." Some of her vibrant energy flowed into Kathleen, and the pressure in her chest eased. Those uncomfortable emotions slid back deep inside her where they belonged.

For the next month she had no need to think about them.

What a perfect pair she and Martha would make. Her wisdom and experience, combined with Martha's youth and energy.

Her new companion would compensate for all those parts of her that no longer seemed to work properly.

Three time zones, eight states, one incredible adventure.

It was going to be perfect.

7

MARTHA

Forty-eight hours later, Martha stared at the sleek high-performance car in front of her and gave a silent apology for what she was about to do to it. Why, oh why, hadn't she been honest about the fact she hated driving?

Her mother was right. She always made bad decisions.

It was all very well faking confidence—*Yes, I love driving*—but sooner or later you had to face your own lies and she was facing hers now. The thought of climbing behind the wheel of that sports car made her feel nauseated. It was like riding a racehorse when you'd only ever been on a fairground horse.

Oh Martha, Martha.

This was not going to end well. By the time she'd driven to the end of the street they'd either be dead or she'd be fired. It would be the shortest employment in history, which was a shame because she was starting to love Kathleen and so far this trip had been more exciting than she could possibly have imagined. She'd never had the chance to travel and she had to stop herself from pointing at everything and saying, *Look at that!*

She was trying to appear like a sophisticated woman of the world, which wasn't easy.

And now they'd reached the moment of reckoning.

"Ford Mustang, right?" The tall, lanky guy with bad skin who had introduced himself as Cade handed her the keys. "You're lucky. They're in demand and we don't always have one. You're sure this is what you want? You could have had a Corvette or a Camaro. Or an SUV. You'd have more room."

What I want, Martha thought, *is something older and slower.*

But Kathleen shook her head. "One of the advantages of being challenged in the height department, is that we don't need legroom. I want the Mustang."

Two days in Kathleen's company had taught Martha that what Kathleen wanted Kathleen got.

She thought back over the whirlwind of the past forty-eight hours.

After they'd landed in Chicago, they'd checked in to a smart hotel, where Kathleen had reserved a suite with two bedrooms. Martha's bathroom had been bigger than her bedroom back home.

Kathleen had flung open the doors to the balcony and breathed deeply, as if she was inhaling oxygen for the first time in years. She'd stood there, gazing at the view of Chicago and then said *yes,* in a voice that suggested she was more than satisfied.

The whole trip was getting a big *yes* from Martha too.

Apart from the driving part, she was living the dream. Luxury! A room big enough to dance in without the risk of smacking your limbs on the walls. No family pointing out all her faults. Best of all, no chance of Steven turning up on the doorstep.

The suite was incredible, but how on earth could Kathleen afford it? Had she robbed a bank in her youth? The wicked twinkle in her eye made Martha think that anything was possible.

And what exactly were the rules of this trip? Was she supposed to stay out of the way or join Kathleen?

This job hadn't come with any instructions, apart from the fact that she was expected to drive. She was looking forward to spending a quiet evening with a large burger, and her tattered copy of *The Grapes of Wrath* to get herself in the mood, although she hoped there would be considerably less drama and hardship in her version of the journey across America.

Overwhelmed by gratitude for her new life, Martha had joined Kathleen on the balcony.

"Shall I order something to eat from room service, Kathleen? You'd probably like an early night." Her grandmother had always had a nap in the afternoon. She knew Mrs. Hartley did too because she yelled at anyone who knocked on her door between three and four.

Kathleen, however, was buzzing. "Early night? It's five in the afternoon."

Her skin was pale and her eyes looked tired but they gleamed with an excitement that spiked Martha's excitement too.

It wasn't her job to argue with her new employer. She was a driver and companion, not a minder. And if you didn't know what you wanted by the time you were eighty, then what hope was there?

Liza's concerned frown slid into her mind. Martha had enough experience of disapproval to know that Kathleen's daughter had disapproved of her. She was a little daunted by Liza, and not only because she envied anyone with well-behaved hair. Liza's was as smooth and pale as buttermilk. And then there was her air of competence. Martha hadn't needed to be told she was a teacher. She doubted there had ever been an issue Liza couldn't solve, or a class she couldn't control.

But she wasn't employed by the daughter, was she? She was employed by the mother.

Still, there was no harm in checking. "It's ten o'clock back home. No, wait—it's a six-hour difference. So it's eleven at home." Her mother

135

would be cleaning her teeth and yelling at her dad to check that he'd locked the doors. Martha was grateful she wasn't there.

"You're on Chicago time now. We have a couple of hours to shower and freshen up, and then we're going for dinner and cocktails."

"Cocktails?" Her grandmother had always drunk hot cocoa before bed. Martha had made it for her, using exactly the right amount of milk and sugar. Sometimes she'd eaten a nice digestive biscuit.

Kathleen gazed out over the skyline. "Last time I was here, I drank cocktails. I want to do it again."

"You've been here before? When?"

"I was thirty. It was my first trip to Chicago."

"I can't wait to hear all your stories. You can tell me over drinks." It sounded so adult and sophisticated. She, Martha, was going to drink cocktails and talk about exotic travel. Her conversation was normally restricted to the mundane, but tonight she was going to travel through Kathleen's experiences. Or maybe she was being too presumptuous. "I don't have to join you of course. If you'd rather be by yourself—"

"Why would I want to be by myself? You're part of this adventure." Kathleen beamed. "You're a jet-setter now, Martha."

Martha didn't feel like a jet-setter and she was pretty sure she didn't look like one either, but she was willing to do whatever it took to embrace that lifestyle.

"What should I wear?"

"Casual chic."

What exactly was that?

In the end she wore the only dress she owned. She grabbed her denim jacket in case she was chilly and slid her feet into a pair of white running shoes.

Kathleen was wearing her customary floaty layers in jewel colors, with a narrow gold watch on one wrist and multiple bangles on the other. With her cropped white hair and her effortless elegance, she looked impossibly glamorous.

When you looked at her you saw bone structure and poise rather than age, Martha thought.

"You look beautiful, Mrs. Harrison."

"Call me Kathleen." Kathleen picked up her purse. "We're heading up to the roof terrace, where we will drink Manhattans and eat lobster risotto."

Was that going to be delicious or disgusting? Martha pictured herself in the local pub at home on her return. *I'll have a Manhattan and lobster risotto.* The response would probably be, *What, love?* accompanied by a blank look, a plate of fish fingers and half a pint of beer.

The roof terrace turned out to have views over downtown Chicago, and the lake beyond that.

"This is very cool." Martha settled herself at the nearest available table but Kathleen gestured to the waiter.

She said something that Martha couldn't hear, and the next moment they were being ushered to a table by the balcony, with the best views of the skyline.

Martha sneaked a look at the people around her, relieved to see a variety of clothing. Some were casual, some dressier in their approach, but they all had one thing in common—confidence. They all looked as if they belonged.

Martha sat up a little straighter and tried to look as if this glamorous bar was her normal habitat even though she was sure she wasn't fooling anyone. She probably stood out like a zebra on a sandy beach.

And then the cocktails appeared, delivered with a flourish.

"To adventure." Kathleen raised her glass and Martha, half dizzy with jet lag, tiredness and an overdose of excitement, lifted hers too.

"To adventure." And a new life, far away from her old one.

Martha, explorer and drinker of exotic cocktails.

Take that, Slimy Steven.

She took a mouthful of the cocktail and almost choked. Her alcohol intake was restricted by her lack of funds, and when she drank she usually drank the beer her dad kept in the fridge. She probably had the most unsophisticated palate on the planet.

It took three sips for her to discover that the cocktail was the best thing she'd ever tasted and four to decide she'd be quite happy never to drink anything else. By the time she'd emptied her glass she realized that Kathleen was nothing like her own grandmother.

There was a strange spinning feeling in her head. Jet lag? Cocktail? Having had no experience of either before this moment, it was impossible to tell.

Kathleen ordered another and Martha was about to point out that drinking so much on an empty stomach might not be such a good idea when the lobster risotto arrived.

Chicago was spread before them, glittering and bright.

"What did you say that persuaded them to give us this view?"

"I told them the truth." Kathleen picked up her fork. "That I'm of somewhat advanced years and one never knows if this could be my last supper."

Martha wasn't used to people acknowledging their own mortality so openly. What should she say? *Don't be silly, you're going to be fine.* But what if she wasn't fine? What if Kathleen died on this trip?

She took another slug of her drink. She'd never seen a dead body.

Was it selfish to hope that Kathleen at least didn't die until the end of the trip? She didn't want this adventure to end yet. Nor did she want to be blamed by scary Liza for leading her mother to her doom.

Maybe it was in her interests to be at least a little protective.

"Are you generally well? Anything I should know about?" She probably should have asked Kathleen to have a medical check, or produce a certificate of health, but given that Kathleen hadn't asked her for proof of her driving experience that wouldn't have been fair.

"I'm eighty. You could say I'm like a classic car. I need maintenance. My engine stutters and I have scratches on my paintwork, but still I endure." Kathleen raised her glass. "To living in the moment."

Martha raised her glass too. "Living in the moment." Which was fine, as long as her moment didn't include having to deal with Kathleen's dead body. They were going to be driving through Death Valley, weren't they? It didn't sound auspicious. Maybe they should take a different route. Also the car analogy didn't thrill her because she didn't have a good track record with cars. She didn't want to be responsible for putting another dent in Kathleen's paintwork. "Shall I order you a juice? Water?"

"I'll have one more cocktail to celebrate our first night. You?"

One more cocktail would ensure she woke with a headache, so Martha shook her head. She had a feeling she would have enough reasons for headaches on this trip without adding an excess of alcohol to the mix.

"Sparkling water, please."

Kathleen beamed at the waiter and gestured to her glass. "That man is very dishy. You probably don't even know what that word means, do you? Your generation would say cute, or so my granddaughters tell me."

"Cute works."

"Fifty years ago I would have invited him back to my room. He has wonderful eyes and a cheeky smile." Kathleen looked at Martha thoughtfully. "Maybe you—"

"No. Thank you. I'm not interested." Adventure, yes. Road trip, yes. Cocktails, definitely. Men? No way. What did it say about her life that an eighty-year-old was trying to fix her up with someone?

Kathleen leaned in. "You're gay?"

"No, not gay. A bit off relationships right now." She thought about Steven and thinking about Steven made her wish she'd ordered another cocktail instead of water. "I should take a photo of you to send to Liza. I promised her I would. Should you put the drink down? Will she be concerned?"

"She would probably be more concerned if I wasn't drinking." Kathleen posed against the skyline as Martha took photos on her phone.

As she put her phone away she noticed that she had two missed calls from Steven. Some of the magic oozed out of the moment. Even this far from home, he could still ruin her evening.

She was tempted to send a photo of herself sipping cocktails together with a message, *Can't talk now, I'm busy.*

Kathleen was watching her. "Everything all right?"

"Fine." She zipped up her bag and tried to forget about it. "Tell me more about you, Kathleen. Did you always travel a lot?"

"Yes. And this place is as exciting as I remembered. Doesn't it raise your pulse looking at it?"

"Your pulse is raised?" Martha sat up straighter. "Any pains in your chest or anything?" She should have done a first aid course before coming on this trip.

Kathleen seemed untroubled. "At my age there are always aches and pains. It's best not to dwell on them."

Martha had a few pains of her own, mostly around her heart. Her feelings and her confidence were bruised and battered. She was all for trying not to dwell on it.

"Did you come here as a tourist?" She realized that the only thing she knew about her employer was that she lived in a nice house in the middle of nowhere, seemed to have enough money to pay for expensive hotels and was determined to live out the rest of her years in a manner unbecoming for her age.

"I was working." Kathleen put her fork down. "I presented a travel show. Decades before you were born, of course. I traveled the world. I was a household name for a while."

"What was the show called?"

"*The Summer Seekers*. You're far too young to remember it, but your mother might."

Martha had no intention of communicating with her mother. She was enjoying the break, and she had no doubt that the feeling was mutual. "You were a journalist?"

"I started working at a television company when I finished college. I did a number of jobs, but then it turned out I was rather good at presenting. I worked on a few different shows, including one for children. And then came *The Summer Seekers*. Have you ever done a job in your life that felt absolutely right?"

"No." Martha saw no reason not to be honest. "I suppose you could say I'm still—finding my way. Trial and error, you know?" There had been more errors than she cared to remember.

"Well, *The Summer Seekers* was right for me. Right from the beginning, I loved it. What I tried to do in my reports was to give people a taste of the place. I wanted people to make up their minds if they wanted to visit, and armchair travelers— and there were plenty of those—to feel as if they'd visited even though they hadn't left the comfort of their own homes. Once we arrived in a place it was up to me to decide what to highlight. I'd look at the culture, the food, but I'd always cover a few places that were off the beaten track. If I was lucky I'd find a local willing to join me for a day and take me to all their favorite haunts. That insider perspective gave viewers a feel for the real place."

Martha was fascinated. "Are any of your old shows on the internet?"

"I have no idea. I don't use the internet. I do have them on DVD, but they're at home."

"If you don't use the internet, how did you book the flight tickets, the hotels and the car?"

Kathleen paused. "If I tell you, you need to promise not to tell Liza. She would disapprove."

It seemed funny to Martha that Kathleen was keeping secrets from her own daughter. Maybe she wasn't the only one who found Liza a little scary.

"I promise."

"My neighbor did it for me."

Martha ate her risotto slowly, savoring each mouthful. "Why is that a problem?"

"Because he is considered to be a little on the disreputable side."

"Disreputable. I love the way you talk." Martha grinned. "What does he do?"

"He enjoys life," Kathleen said calmly, "a trait that tends to induce a state of envy in those observing his more extreme antics. Envy masquerading as disapproval. He's a rock star. Highly successful, so I'm told by people who know more about these things than I do. Successful enough to have bought all the land around me and several fast cars. His house is spectacular. Glorious sea views."

"What's his name?"

"Finn Cool."

Martha dropped her fork. "You're kidding. *The* Finn Cool? I love his music. I mean, he's quite old obviously—" Too late she realized that Finn must be half Kathleen's age. "But I still think he's great. He booked your tickets?"

"Not personally. He consulted me on my preferences and contacted his manager who arranged everything. He was most accommodating, and I was grateful because I couldn't bring myself to ask Liza to do it. It doesn't look good to say I want adventure, and then to be afraid of the internet."

Martha thought it was adorable. "How did you

meet Finn Cool? I thought most celebrities were pathologically private."

"It was rather amusing." Kathleen picked up her glass and the bangles on her wrist jangled. "The entrance to his house is difficult to locate. I assume that's why he chose the property. I'm forever having people knocking on my door asking where he lives."

"That must be annoying."

"Not at all. It's entertaining. I once sent a grubby-looking news hack with a camera across two fields in the wrong direction." Kathleen leaned forward. "I never trust a man flaunting a large camera lens, do you? One wonders what they're trying to prove."

Martha choked on her drink. "I don't know anyone who owns a camera. Everyone uses their phones."

"Well, he was one of those men one dislikes on sight, so I sent him on his way. But he somehow missed the notice about there being a bull in the field and had to be rescued by the farmer."

It was the funniest story she'd heard in a while. "Did Finn Cool know?"

"Not at first. But then I rerouted a car full of young hopeful women to the next village, believing I was helping. Turned out they were guests who had been invited to one of his outrageous parties."

"How did you find out?"

They called him for directions, and no doubt mentioned the unhelpful old lady who lived down the road. The next day he appeared at my door with a large bunch of flowers and a bottle of excellent gin to thank me for being the dragon at his gates. We drank some of the gin together in the garden and when I told him about the photographer he roared with laughter. After that we agreed that anyone who was a welcome and expected visitor would be issued with a code word that would be changed monthly. That way if someone knocked on my door and didn't use the right word, I would send them on a long and interesting diversion."

Martha decided she loved Kathleen. "What's this month's code word?"

"I'm sworn to secrecy. But he and I have an understanding. He's not at all the way people say he is, although it's true he does have the most enviable parties. There was one occasion when a few of his guests went for a midnight wander and ended up in my garden. Delightful women, although very economical with their clothing."

"You mean cheap?"

"I was referring to the volume rather than the value." Kathleen sipped her drink. "One was wearing the bottom half of a very brief bikini, and nothing else. Finn might consider it presumptuous of me to say so, but I consider us to have a friendship of sorts."

"That's a great story." Was that why they'd been upgraded at the hotel? Maybe management thought Kathleen was related to Finn Cool. Hilarious. With luck they'd have rock star treatment all the way. "So you've been to Chicago before. How about California?"

Kathleen put her glass down. "Never."

"This is a dream trip for you?" She could see from Kathleen's expression that she'd asked the wrong question, and quickly moved on. "I've never been to America before. I've been to Italy. On a school trip. That's it."

Kathleen was staring across the skyline with a faraway look in her eyes.

"Kathleen?" Martha was tempted to snap her fingers to check that she was conscious. "Would you like another drink?"

Kathleen blinked. "I'd better not." She picked up her empty glass. "I'm not supposed to drink with my blood pressure tablets."

Martha thought about the three cocktails. "What happens if you do?"

"I don't know. We might be about to find out."

Hopefully not. "The risotto was delicious. So was the cocktail. Thank you."

"Have another." Kathleen waved at the cute waiter. "If you don't misbehave when you're twenty-five, you don't have anything to look back on when you're eighty. If the time comes when I'm too decrepit to travel and maintain my independence I shall spend my days traveling through my memories, and when that happens I should very much like them to be interesting. I'm sure you will feel the same."

Martha couldn't imagine being eighty, but she'd allowed herself to be persuaded, and she'd allowed herself to be persuaded the night after too, which was why she was now standing in front of a sports car with the aftereffects of the three cocktails still hammering away at her brain. The hot sun beat down on the shiny red sports car, making the paintwork gleam and dazzle.

She'd had two blissful evenings and had spent the whole of the day before exploring Chicago on her own because Kathleen had decided to have a quiet day before their journey began. It had been more exciting than Martha could have imagined. For a brief time her anxiety about the driving had vanished, but now it was back with a vengeance as was the sickening realization that she was about to be responsible for two lives— hers and Kathleen's. Also the lives of anyone else who happened to be on the road in front of her.

Cade was still waiting for a response from her and she tried to focus. "What did you say again?"

"I was checking that this is really the car you want." Cade looked between the two of them, as if he'd never seen such an unlikely pairing.

Martha didn't blame him. She opened her

mouth to say, *Of course this isn't what we want,* but Kathleen was talking.

"This is perfect." She stroked her slender wrinkled hand over the shiny surface. Her rings looked too big for her fingers. "Is it fast?"

"Fast?" The guy transferred his gum from his right cheek to his left. "Lady, this baby has a 5.0 liter V-8 engine and it'll go from zero to sixty in under four seconds. That about fast enough for you?"

Kathleen tilted her head. "It sounds sufficient for our needs."

The guy grinned and shook his head. "You're really something." He obviously thought Kathleen should be renting a wheelchair, not a high-performance car.

Martha felt out of her depth. Age was supposed to make you careful, wasn't it? Mrs. Hartley next door never went anywhere without her walking stick. She didn't answer the front door without checking the spy hole first.

It was clear now why Liza had looked anxious and asked so many questions.

But this was Kathleen's trip. Surely she had a right to live life the way she wanted to? Although she didn't have all the facts, of course. Lacking full disclosure from Martha on the quality of her driving, Kathleen had probably underestimated the risk.

"This model has redesigned cylinder heads

and a new crankshaft—" Cade droned on and Martha's mind glazed over. What exactly was a quad tip dual exhaust and why did she need to know about it?

Cade opened the door and gestured. "You've got your sport setting, your track setting—"

Martha looked inside, relieved to see automatic transmission. *P* for Park and *D* for Drive. That was all she needed to remember. She had no intention of reversing. This journey was going to be forward all the way. In fact that could be a metaphor for her life. No going backward.

Cade straightened. "You want to take her for a ride?"

And give him visible evidence of her lack of skill? He'd probably refuse to rent it to them.

"Not right now. Let's finish up the paperwork. We need fully comprehensive insurance." She caught his eye. "Not that we're going to need it, but probably best to be safe. In case someone reckless drives into us." Like a tree. Or a post. That had been known to happen.

"Sure. That's it? Then we're done here." Cade shrugged. "Any questions?"

"I have a question." Kathleen removed her sunglasses and the wicked gleam in her eyes made Martha almost as nervous as the prospect of driving the car.

"Kathleen—"

"What's the speed limit?"

Oh for . . .

"Why? Are you on the run, lady?" Cade laughed and scratched at his skin under the T-shirt. "You robbed a bank? Police chasing you?"

"No, although I did recently have dealings with the police when they came to remove a body from my kitchen."

Cade stopped laughing. "Body?"

Body? It occurred to Martha that she really didn't know that much about Kathleen at all. She'd talked a lot about her work, and her travels, but hadn't revealed anything personal. She knew about Liza only because she'd met her.

She could be traveling across America with an eighty-year-old serial killer. "Kathleen? You didn't—er—mention—"

"It slipped my mind, dear. Or perhaps subconsciously I've been trying to forget it. The mind has a way of blocking out trauma, doesn't it?"

Hopefully that was true, because right now it seemed that this trip might be unforgettable for all the wrong reasons. "Tell us about the body, Kathleen."

"It wasn't a random body. It belonged to an intruder who entered my home in the middle of the night."

"Oh that's terrible." Martha put her hand on Kathleen's arm. "How very frightening."

"He didn't seem frightened. In fact, he was rather bold."

"I meant frightening for *you.*"

"I know. I was teasing you." Kathleen patted her hand. "It was the most excitement I'd had in a long time, although I admit I was lucky he was alone and inebriated. A word of advice—" she leaned closer to Cade "—if you intend to break into a house, stay sober and always take an accomplice. It's much harder to fight off two people."

Cade took a step back, eyes wide and staring. "Right. So—you killed him?"

"No. He is very much alive." Kathleen frowned. "Probably because I used the eight-inch pan, and not the twelve-inch. I only use the twelve-inch if I'm frying eggs and mushrooms with my bacon."

"Good to know." Cade's gaze skittered to Martha and she saw pity there. "Speed limits and general information on driving here in the US is right here in our book—" He thrust it at her. "In the trunk you've got your flashlight, a blanket, jumper cables, flares and a first aid kit. We advise you to always carry water, particularly when you reach the desert, and keep your phone charged although you might not have a signal of course. Everything you need is right there. And if you get into trouble—" the look on his face suggested he thought that to be highly likely "—you can call the number on the back."

"Thank you." Kathleen took the book and beamed. "It's all most exciting."

Martha wasn't finding it exciting. Flares? Why would they need flares?

Cade cleared his throat. "So—any more questions or are we done here?"

I have a question, Martha thought.

Why, oh why, did I take this job?

8

LIZA

Liza glanced at the picture of her mother raising a glass with the spectacular Chicago skyline shimmering behind her. Martha had added a quick caption: *Living the dream.*

It had been a thoughtful gesture on Martha's part to send the photo, but it was making Liza take a long, hard look at her life.

Envy stabbed her in the chest and she sat down at the kitchen counter she'd been cleaning moments before.

Her world seemed gray and mundane by comparison. Her mother was surrounded by flickering candles and cocktails. Liza was confronting an empty cereal bowl.

Today was her wedding anniversary. Not that she had high expectations, but a small celebration would have been nice. It wasn't as if they didn't have an excuse.

Her mother didn't need an excuse. She celebrated every moment.

How had Liza ever thought that was irresponsible? It was a good way to live life.

What had she done the night before while her

mother had been drinking, laughing and watching the sun go down over Lake Michigan? She'd been catching up on ironing and doing some last-minute planning for France.

Her mother stayed in hotels. She wouldn't even have to make her own bed. If she was engrossed in a book, she could pick up a menu and order room service. All she had to do was decide when she wanted to eat, and someone else would do all the work.

Liza stood up and threw the cleaning equipment back in the cupboard.

Enough feeling sorry for herself.

She had to find a way to be more enthused about the moment she was in, rather than always hoping that things would improve in the future. There were days when her entire life felt like a postponement. She'd waited for the twins to grow out of colic, for the nights when they started sleeping, for the day the tantrums stopped. Now she was waiting for them to move past this "difficult" teenage phase. Was there ever going to come a point where she was happy with life in the present?

Sean walked in. He was wearing a suit and was reading the news on his phone. Without lifting his head, he put his breakfast bowl on top of the counter.

That one small bowl, abandoned, seemed to symbolize her whole life.

Happy Anniversary, darling.

"The bowl doesn't load itself into the dishwasher, you know."

He glanced up from his phone. "It's one bowl."

"Someone has to put it into the dishwasher. That someone is always me."

The article in her bag would have advised that she broached any issues calmly, expressing her concerns in a constructive way. No snappy, snide remarks. But his response made her snappy and she was tired of trying to be perfect.

Sean opened the dishwasher, put the bowl inside and closed it with a decisive click.

"Happy now?"

No, she wasn't happy. Today was their anniversary and he'd forgotten.

He could have put a bottle of something fizzy in the fridge for later. He could have told her he was whisking her off to dinner.

"I shouldn't have to ask, Sean."

"Yeah, right. Sorry." The ends of his hair were still damp from the shower. "What's wrong?"

My mother is drinking cocktails on a roof terrace while I'm cleaning up other people's mess.

Her mother was squeezing every last moment of joy from life. Perhaps that made her reckless or selfish, or perhaps it made her sensible.

"I spend too much time clearing up after other people, that's all."

157

"We'll all try and help a bit more." He flashed her a smile and dropped his phone into his pocket.

"When you say you'll *help,* that still puts the responsibility squarely on me. It implies that the job is mine, but you'll assist me. I don't want 'help.' I want other people to take responsibility."

The book she'd bought had suggested she started with "I feel" and she'd messed that up again.

I feel, I feel, I feel.

"I feel taken advantage of, Sean."

"What? Oh—that's not good. And we're going to talk about this. Properly." He walked back to her and gave her a brief kiss on the cheek. She smelled the faint smell of shaving gel and felt something uncurl deep in her stomach.

It was their wedding anniversary. She should be feeling romantic, not mad.

They needed to pay more attention to each other. Perhaps that was *all* that was needed.

She lifted her hand on her chest. "I'm glad you said that. I think we do need to talk."

"And we will." He glanced at his watch. "But I have a nine o'clock meeting in the office with the pickiest client it has ever been my misfortune to work with, and I need to leave now if I'm to stand a chance of making it."

She let her hand drop.

Is your marriage in trouble?

Yes, it definitely was.

Was she being unfair? She couldn't expect him to blow off a meeting because she wanted to talk. He had responsibilities to his partners and clients. And any conversation they had now would be tainted by the fact that he was stressed about being late for work.

"Let's go out for dinner tonight." If he wasn't going to suggest it, then she would.

"Tonight?" He looked panicked. "I have drinks after work with the partners. Didn't I mention it?"

"No."

"How about tomorrow? We should celebrate."

A warmth spread through her. He hadn't forgotten. "Celebrate?"

"Beginning of the holidays, for you and the girls at least—" He flashed her a smile. "We could go to that Italian place. The twins would love that. And tomorrow works for me because it's Saturday and I won't be breathing garlic over everyone at work."

"I wasn't planning on inviting the girls."

"Oh—you mean a romantic night. Great." He grabbed a protein bar from the cupboard. "Any night except tonight."

Any night except tonight.

Their anniversary.

The warm feelings withered and died.

She watched as Sean grabbed his gym bag from

the laundry room and stuffed the nut bar into a pocket on the side.

"Sean—"

"You book somewhere. Anywhere you like. Looking forward to it." He was out through the door, leaving before she could say, *I feel it would be more romantic and special if you chose somewhere.*

The front door slammed behind him and she flinched as if he'd trapped her finger in it.

Happy Anniversary, Liza.

She topped up her coffee. Was she wrong to expect romance? Did every relationship feel this way after two decades and two children? For their first anniversary they'd had a weekend in Paris. They'd done it on a shoestring, staying in a seedy hotel on the Left Bank and loving every minute. For their second they'd taken a picnic to the river and spread everything out on a blanket in the shade of a weeping willow.

It had been years since they'd done something special.

Eight signs that your marriage might be in trouble.

Why was it bothering her so much? And why eight signs? Why not seven or nine? Someone had probably sat at their desk throwing out ideas and eight sounded like a good number.

Caitlin came thundering down the stairs. "Have you seen my jeans?"

"It's a school day. No jeans."

"Last day. We can wear what we like, remember?"

No, she hadn't remembered. "Your jeans are in the wash. You'll have to wear something else."

"What?" Caitlin's shriek brought her sister running to the top of the stairs.

"What's wrong?"

"Mum washed my jeans! Can you believe that?"

"Thank you for washing my jeans, Mum," Liza said, and Caitlin flushed.

"I needed them today, that's all."

"If you needed them, why were they in the laundry?"

"Because they needed a wash—but I thought you'd have done it by now. I put them there on Monday."

"I've had a busy week too. I'm sure you can find something else to wear."

"I wanted my jeans. I'm going to look awful in all the photos, and that will be your fault. You're still punishing me because of the stupid party. I hate my life!" She thundered back upstairs and reappeared ten minutes later wearing a pair of thigh-length boots with bare legs and a miniskirt.

Still blindsided by the fact that her daughter thought she hadn't washed the jeans out of spite, Liza blinked. "Where did you get those boots?"

"Jane lent them to me."

"Well, you can give them back." *Stay calm.*

Do not escalate the tension. "You're not wearing that outfit to school, last day or not. It's inappropriate."

Caitlin's eyes sparked. "I know you like to control absolutely *everything* about our lives, but you're not controlling what I wear. I decide. I do have a brain, you know."

"And it would be good to see you using it." This was exhausting and thankless. "Go and change."

"No time." Caitlin swung her bag over her shoulder and headed for the car.

Alice was right behind her. "Don't start a fight," she begged. "I can't be late today. I'm reciting a poem, remember? Doing that is enough of a horror without being late."

Why was she always the one who had to deal with these moments?

She'd give anything to swap places with Sean. She'd take a picky adult over a teenager in a tantrum any day.

"Can we go?" Alice tugged her sleeve. "People wear anything on their last day. No one cares."

"Do people wear barely anything? Because that seems to be the look your sister is going for." Liza looked at her daughter's sleek bare thighs as she folded herself into the car.

She really ought to stand firm on this one, but Alice was right. If she stood her ground and argued they would all be late, her included. It wasn't fair to expect her colleagues to cover her classes because her daughter was determined to make life as difficult as possible.

Shame washed over her.

She was allowing herself to be manipulated, and she'd almost given up caring. She was too tired to resist.

Defeated, she locked the front door and drove to school.

Caitlin scowled from under her fringe for the short journey and the moment Liza stopped the car she sprang out and headed through the gates, all sweet smiles and waves when she saw her friends.

"Bye, Mum." Alice slammed the car door behind her and followed her sister.

Liza sat in the silence of the car and then glanced back at the twins. Caitlin was now convulsed with laughter, arms round her friends. Less than fifteen minutes earlier she'd behaved as if her life was over. Now she looked as if she didn't have a care in the world.

Hurt slid into her.

Breathe, Liza, breathe.

They'd come through this phase, as they had all the others. One day she'd laugh at it. *Would she?*

She wanted so badly to be close to them. She'd never wanted them to think *I wish I was closer to my mother,* as she so often did. But they didn't seem interested.

What was she to them? She was a chauffeur, a housekeeper, a chef.

And whose fault was that?

Liza swallowed. What had her mother said? *Which part of your life is for you and no one else?*

The answer was none of it.

She forced herself to take a hard, brutal look at the truth. Gradually, over time, they'd learned to expect her to do things for them. They didn't see it as an act of love. They took advantage. *Where are my jeans? Have we run out of milk?*

The girls didn't appreciate her affection or her interest. *Stop the inquisition, Mum.*

All she had to show for the last sixteen years of homemaking was two young women who expected her to cook their meals, do their laundry and be at their beck and call.

Right on cue, her phone rang.

Caitlin.

Liza reached out to take the call and then changed her mind. No. If she wasn't always available, maybe the girls would start thinking for themselves.

She let the call go to voice mail and immediately felt anxious. What if it was an emergency? Or what if Caitlin wanted to apologize for her rude, selfish behavior?

Hating herself for not being stronger, she checked the message.

"Mum!" Caitlin's voice barked down the phone. "I've forgotten to bring the school drama cup from home and it's the last day. I'll lose house points if I don't, and everyone will hate me. I need you to drop it into reception at lunchtime." There were giggles in the background and then the phone went dead.

Please, Mum. Thank you, Mum.

I love you, Mum.

Liza stuffed her phone into her bag.

It was time to make changes. And no doubt she'd pay a high price for that and life would be stressful for a while, but no matter how much unpleasantness her actions caused she wasn't going to budge.

Fueled by anger and hurt, she drove to the school where she taught and arrived in the staff room just before the bell.

"One more day." Her colleague Andrew was pouring hot water onto instant coffee. "The summer cannot come soon enough. You look stressed—everything okay?"

Everything was not okay, but she wasn't going to say anything. She was upset, but that didn't mean she was ready to discuss her teenagers in the staff room. Also, the conversation wouldn't reflect well on her and she was already feeling like a bad mother without needing reinforcement from others.

"End of the school year. You know how it is."

He probably had no idea how it was, but this was a staff room not a psychiatrist's waiting room. Confessions weren't appropriate.

He stirred sugar into his coffee. "You doing anything exciting this summer, Liza?"

Washing. Cleaning. Cooking. Organizing. Loading the dishwasher.

"Liza?"

She gave a start. "Sean is working on a big job right now, and then we're going to France. You?"

"Jen and I are having two weeks touring the Greek Islands. First trip without the kids. Can't wait."

"You're not taking the kids?" Liza decided she didn't have time to wait for her coffee to cool, so she drank a glass of water instead.

"Phoebe has tennis camp, and Rory got a place on a youth orchestra so they're both going to be away for the same two weeks. Jenny and I thought we'd make the most of it. Enjoy some couple time, you know?"

No, she didn't know. But she'd dearly love to find out. But would that solve her problem? Maybe not. The truth was, she felt lonely. She didn't feel close to her mother, she wasn't close to the girls, and right now she didn't feel close to her husband.

Andrew blew on his coffee. "Your girls doing anything this summer?"

"Two weeks of theater workshops but living at home."

Hardly a holiday by any stretch of the imagination.

Andrew ate a chocolate chip cookie, even though it was technically still breakfast time. "You and Sean going away by yourselves?"

"No." Even if she'd wanted to, how could they trust the girls after what had happened the last time? As it was, she was going to be doing favors for her neighbors for the rest of her life to compensate.

And she no longer had any confidence that the twins were capable of looking after themselves.

She was planning to go to Oakwood Cottage at some point in order to check on Popeye as she'd promised her mother, but she had no idea how she was going to make that work. They would all have to go, which would stress Sean who couldn't afford to take the time off right now.

"See you later, Andrew."

She taught her morning classes, allowing the students latitude because they were excited about it being the last day.

At lunchtime she joined her colleagues in the staff room for a final lunch.

She had three missed calls from Caitlin, all of which she ignored. If she'd had an accident the school would have called.

This was her last opportunity for adult conversation for a while, and on balance she'd rather hear about Wendy's new herb garden than chase through lunchtime traffic to pick up the trophy Caitlin should have remembered herself.

It was time to get tough. Not by grounding them, or removing privileges as she'd done up until now, but by forcing them to take responsibility. She should have done it before now.

"I can't believe you didn't bring the trophy." It was the first thing Caitlin said when she walked through the door. "I called and called. Why didn't you pick up the phone?"

"I was teaching."

"But you always answer the phone, in case it's an emergency."

"It never is an emergency." Would Sean be home early? She could use some moral support.

And then she remembered. Drinks. Which meant that she was here alone with the girls.

Happy Anniversary, Liza.

Caitlin was still giving a performance worthy of the drama award. "I could have been bleeding to death."

"But you weren't." Liza opened the fridge. "You're the one who forgot it, Caitlin. You need to be more organized."

"But I asked you to bring it! That's being organized."

Teenage logic.

"I was working."

"But you could have driven home at lunch-time."

No one asked her how her day had been, or how she was feeling. No one cared.

Her insides felt hollow. She missed her mother. How ridiculous was that? She wasn't any closer to her mother than she was to her children but right now she felt closer. It was that conversation in the car. That strange, surprising conversation where her mother had been kind, and praised her. Liza had thought about it a lot. She'd come close to breaking down and telling her mother everything. Not because she was close to her mother, but because there was no one else she felt able to talk to.

She missed intimacy. She missed feeling as if she was special to someone.

Liza closed the fridge slowly. Why had she opened it? She couldn't remember.

Her head was full of her own mistakes.

She'd been determined to create a warm, comfortable home and to be the attentive loving mother she'd dreamed of having herself, but what she'd done was create the equivalent of a five-star hotel with room service.

She was a one-woman concierge. A fixer.

And the worst part was, they didn't even notice. They were so used to having everything done for them it never even entered their heads to do it themselves. They complained about the service.

If this had been a paid position, Caitlin probably would have fired her.

She felt a moment of something close to panic. She'd been so sure—*smug*—that she was a much better parent than her own mother. But she'd left home able to look after herself, because she'd been doing it since she was young. It never would have crossed her mind to demand that her mother drive to fetch something she'd forgotten. She either wouldn't have forgotten it, or she would have figured out a way to get it herself.

She'd failed her children. A parent was supposed to raise a child to be independent. Respectful of another person's time. And what had she done? She'd raised them to yell for their mother when there was no pizza in the freezer or when a strap top had gone missing from the laundry.

How were they going to cope when they left home?

And how was she going to cope right now?

She felt as if her head was exploding. There was a crushing weight on her chest and breathing felt difficult.

The long-awaited summer stretched ahead, but it was going to be more of the same.

She would soothe and smooth until all the lives of the various members of her family were wrinkle-free. It was what she did.

"Can we order pizza tonight?" Alice pushed

her sports bag into the laundry room. "As a cele-bration?"

"How about ordering from that amazing Thai restaurant?" Caitlin ate a yogurt from the fridge and left the empty container on the countertop. "Or maybe Indian."

What would you like, Mum? Let's let Mum choose.

Enough!

Ignoring the empty yogurt container, Liza walked out of the kitchen and was halfway up the stairs by the time Caitlin caught up with her.

"Mum? We've decided on pizza. What toppings do you want?"

Liza headed for the bedroom. "No takeaway. You and Alice can make something from the fridge."

"What? Why?" Alarmed, Caitlin followed her into the bedroom, watching as Liza pulled out an overnight bag and started throwing in some clothes. "What are you doing? Where are you going?"

"Away." Liza swept her toiletries out of the bathroom and into the bag without bothering to filter them.

Alice appeared in the doorway. "What's going on?"

"Mum's going away."

"Right now? You never said anything. Is Dad going too?"

"No." Liza stuffed a pair of shoes into her bag. "Dad is at a work event. And someone has to stay with you."

"But where are you going? You never go away without Dad."

Another thing that had to change.

Liza grabbed her keys and money. "I'm driving to Oakwood tonight."

"Why?" Alice frowned. "Granny isn't even there."

"I know. Granny is probably drinking cocktails on a rooftop bar in Chicago, because she's sensible and knows how to enjoy life." *I'm a novice at that,* Liza thought, *but I'm going to learn.* "I'm going to check on Popeye and have some time for myself."

She could see the girls looking at each other, trying to figure out how serious this was. For once their mother seemed to be following her own agenda, and that was so alien to them they had no idea how to handle it.

"Does Dad know you're going?"

"I'm going to write him a note right now." She snatched a pen from her bag and found a scrap of paper.

Sean, I've decided to go to Oakwood. I want to check on the house, the cat, and spend some time there. She almost scribbled, *keep an eye on the girls,* but then remembered she was going to stop organizing other people's lives. Let him decide whether he needed to keep an eye on them, or not. Should she wish him Happy Anniversary? No, that would be petty, and he might think this was all about the fact he'd forgotten when it went so much deeper than that. Instead she signed off *Love Liza x.*

She left the note on the pillow, proud that she hadn't given way to her inner toddler who was ready to yell, *You forgot our anniversary.*

Caitlin looked alarmed. "But what are we supposed to do?"

"Do about what?" Liza transferred her purse, phone and car keys to a bag that didn't remind her of work. Did she have everything she needed? Probably not, but the most important thing was to leave before she changed her mind. Her sense of responsibility was already tapping on the edges of her conscience. *Hello, remember me?*

Liza ignored the tapping. Just because someone knocked on the door, didn't mean you had to open it.

"We have lots going on this week," Caitlin said. "Summer activities. You always drive us. What about lunches?"

"Figure it out. Think of it as another summer activity, only instead of learning tennis, or drama, you'll be learning self-sufficiency." Liza grabbed the books she'd been saving for France and tucked them into her bag.

"But the difference is that tennis and drama are, like, *fun*."

"Life can't always be fun. There's a lesson right there. A good life is a balance between doing what you have to do and what you want to do. I'm sure you're both going to rise to the challenge." And so was she. She was going to take a close look at the balance in her own life.

"But if you're not cooking and we can't order pizza, what do we eat tonight?"

"That's up to you." For the first time she was giving them neither the menu, nor the ingredients. "Be creative."

"We'll probably die of malnutrition." Caitlin, the drama queen.

"I doubt that." Liza carried her bag to the door. Was this too extreme? Was she overreacting? By leaving them to cope alone would she simply increase her workload when she returned?

"But when will you be back?" Alice added her voice to her sister's. "There's always so much to do before our holiday."

Liza paused in the doorway. "And I'm the one who does all of it. Right now, I'm not sure I have the energy."

Ignoring Alice's shocked expression, she headed down the stairs and opened the front door. The car sat in the drive like a friend, waiting to whisk her away. On impulse she opened the garage, pulled out a large box and loaded it into the car.

Alice and Caitlin hovered on the doorstep.

"You said you didn't trust us after what happened last time."

They didn't want her to leave, but Liza knew that right now that had less to do with affection and more to do with the fact that she was inconveniencing them.

"You think I'm controlling, and you want me to leave you alone so that's what I'm doing. Consider this to be an advanced course in Looking After Yourself. I expect you to graduate with top marks."

"But—" Alice looked alarmed. "You'll be back for France, right?"

Would she?

Liza slung her bag into the car and slid into the driver's seat, feeling liberated. For the first time in as long as she could remember, she had only herself to think about.

She turned off her phone.

"Wait!" Caitlin hammered on her window. "You didn't answer the question about France."

Because she didn't have the answer. All she knew for sure was that she needed to get away. She needed to do something for herself. And so far that felt *good*.

Liza opened the window a crack. "Behave yourselves."

With a quick wave to the girls, she reversed out of the drive.

Next stop Oakwood Cottage.

Her mother wasn't the only one going on a road trip. Hers might not be considered glamorous by comparison, but right now it felt like the biggest adventure of her life.

Happy Anniversary, Liza.

9

KATHLEEN

CHICAGO~PONTIAC

At the same time Liza was leaving on her road trip, Kathleen and Martha were leaving on theirs.

Kathleen was unsure whether to attribute the throbbing in her head to her rather reckless ingestion of alcohol or the six-hour time difference. Either way she was secretly relieved to be leaving Chicago behind after two nights. It was all so large and loud and contributed to an excess of stimulation which did nothing to ease her headache.

Martha had spent the free day sightseeing while Kathleen had stayed in the hotel and enjoyed the city from the relative peace of her balcony, her comfort enhanced by the delightful young man who brought her room service order.

Peace had been shattered when Martha had burst back into the room (on the fourth attempt because she seemed not to have a natural affinity to key cards), bubbling with stories and excitement. *She'd seen this, been there, tasted this, met this person, did Kathleen know that . . .*

She'd talked nonstop, while devouring the remains of Kathleen's afternoon tea. Kathleen had found her breathless enthusiasm surprisingly invigorating. How could one feel flat and old around Martha, who seemed to exude not only youth but a certain naive innocence? It was as if she was seeing the world for the first time.

Listening to her, Kathleen wasn't sure that she'd ever felt quite the same level of enthusiasm for tall glass skyscrapers that Martha seemed to feel, but she gave what she hoped were suitably encouraging responses. Yes, it was an unbelievable amount of glass. No, it probably didn't mean that everyone in the city liked looking at their own reflection. Yes, it really was true that the lake froze in winter—Kathleen had witnessed it. Yes, it most certainly was called the Windy City for a reason.

Martha's enthusiasm had continued unabated throughout their predinner cocktails and then through their meal. She ordered the lobster risotto for a second time because, as she informed Kathleen in a serious tone, she was *never likely to get a chance to eat it again and anyway you could never have too much of a good thing*.

Was that true?

Kathleen, who had turned down a third cocktail under the suspicion that she may indeed have had too much of a good thing, wasn't so sure.

Like a long-life battery, Martha had eventually

run out of energy and taken her flagging self to bed where no doubt she had slept the enviably deep sleep of the young.

Kathleen, to whom sleep never came easily, had turned and wriggled, plumped the unfamiliar pillow and eventually dozed, floating on a dream of past memories.

Today was the first day of her longed-for road trip and she felt as if she was dragging every one of her eighty years along with her. Maybe it had been a mistake to indulge in cocktails. On the other hand it had been a memorable experience and she'd always believed in living in the present. When she'd been filming *The Summer Seekers* she and the crew had started each trip with a celebration.

She felt a pang of nostalgia for those days.

Traveling for the show had meant stepping into an alternate reality. There had been a sense of life suspended, their enjoyment intensified because they all knew it wasn't going to last. Eventually they'd had to emerge from the bubble and return to real life and the collision between their carefully constructed temporary world and the real world had been jarring. It had always taken Kathleen a while to adjust. Liza would demand time and attention from the moment she stepped through the door, while part of her had still been inhabiting the other half of her life. She'd felt disconnected and disorientated as she'd made the change from one life to another, and frequently she'd missed a step.

She was uncomfortably aware that she hadn't been the best mother. She'd married late in life, and pregnancy had come as a surprise. Her first reaction when the midwife had put Liza into her arms had been one of terror. A baby was more than a baby. It was responsibility, a lifetime of worry and a love so huge it threatened to burst out of you at inconvenient moments.

And there was no going back. It didn't matter that she didn't feel qualified, or that she knew she lacked the essential skills. Reliability, constancy and the ability to be present—that wasn't who she was. If things had gone differently for her earlier in her twenties when she was still romantic and idealistic then maybe she would have slid more comfortably into the role, but life had shaped her differently. She'd navigated life alone successfully for almost four decades, so marriage had seemed like a big step which was why Brian had gone down on one knee three times before she'd said yes.

And then Liza arrived.

She'd felt as if her life, who she really was, had been permanently hijacked.

Confident and in control in her working life, in the role of parent she'd felt like an imposter. She wasn't good at sharing herself emotionally. Brian had understood that. He'd understood all of it and given her the space she needed. But with her daughter she'd kept a large part of herself locked away.

Was that why Liza allowed her life to be consumed by the demands of her family? Was she compensating for Kathleen's deficiencies?

The thought added further discomfort to her already-throbbing head.

She couldn't forget that moment at the airport. Liza had hugged her so tightly she'd thought her ribs might crack. *I love you.*

Kathleen had patted her, unable to shake the feeling that she was failing her daughter again.

What was Liza doing now? She almost wished she hadn't stayed with them before her trip because now her daughter was constantly on her mind. Liza was the one who put in the hard work maintaining a relationship with Kathleen too. Any deficiencies were not her fault.

Kathleen reached into her bag for her sunglasses. It was a scorching day, the sun blazing through the glass into the cool car.

Those cocktails were making her maudlin.

Presumably Martha was suffering a similar attack of regret because yesterday's chatter and enthusiasm had been replaced by tense silence.

Her gaze was fixed intently on the road in front as if it were an enemy to be defeated. Her lips moved slightly, as she conducted a silent conversation with herself.

Kathleen realized the girl hadn't said a word aloud since they'd climbed into the car.

Martha had checked Kathleen's seat belt three times and would have checked it a fourth had Kathleen not pointed out calmly that they were going for a drive, not space travel, and that the heavy crush of traffic seemed to preclude any racing tendencies that might be built into their rather flashy vehicle.

"Are you all right, dear?" Kathleen had welcomed Martha's endless, bubbly chatter. It made her feel young again and gave her something to focus on other than her aching bones and unsettling thoughts. And it wasn't as if their verbal exchanges were deep or probing. Apart from that one innocent query about whether Kathleen had visited California, there were no uncomfortable questions to deflect. It was Kathleen's idea of perfect conversation. But from the moment Martha had helped Kathleen into the car, she'd stopped chattering and now her eyes—slightly wild, Kathleen thought—were fixed on the road as if she was braced for catastrophe.

"I'm concentrating. It's—busy."

It was a city, so of course it was busy. But Kathleen didn't believe in stating the obvious, so she stayed silent and drank in the experience. Cars thronged bumper to bumper, crawling forward to a soundtrack of shouts and blaring horns. Drivers made sudden turns without giving any prior indication of their intentions. On top of that, navigating the route had proved challenging—a fact Kathleen considered to add an extra frisson of excitement, but which had caused Martha to breathe deeply several times and had no doubt added to her stress and punctured ebullience.

And now they were creeping along the edge of Lake Michigan with the Chicago skyline towering above them.

Kathleen felt she should say something reassuring. "I'm sure it will calm down once we leave Chicago."

"I hope so or I estimate it's going to take us at least a year and a half to complete this road trip. Not that I'm in a hurry. Or that I don't love driving in traffic! It's great practice." Martha snatched a breath. "I'm not saying I need practice. I don't want you to be nervous. Are you nervous?"

Someone in this car was nervous, Kathleen thought. And it wasn't her.

"Why would I be nervous? You're an excellent driver." She had no idea if Martha was indifferent or excellent, but after that encounter with Liza in the car on the way to the airport she'd learned that a little encouragement went a long way.

"You think so?" Martha's hands were locked around the wheel so tightly that if it had been a living thing it would have been long dead. "If you need me to slow down, tell me."

If they drove any slower they'd be stationary. "Drive at any pace you wish. I hope you're finding this car enjoyable to drive?"

"Oh it's—" Martha licked her lips. "It feels as if it would like to go fast."

As if the car had a mind and life of its own. "You're the one in charge."

Martha sat up a little straighter. "Yes, I am."

Finally they left Lake Michigan and the buzz and bustle of Chicago behind them and headed southwest out of the city. Martha's hands gradually relaxed on the wheel. Her mouth still moved occasionally, and Kathleen managed to work out by a determined effort at lip reading that she was saying, *Drive on the right.*

Kathleen was reassured. A reminder was vastly preferable to a head-on collision.

They drove through the towns of Joliet, Elwood and Wilmington before crossing over the Kankakee River and continuing the journey south toward St. Louis. Each town was studded with nostalgia and quirky attractions. They passed neon signs advertising hot dogs and hamburgers, vintage diners, historic buildings and restored gas stations where they stopped to take photos in front of the shiny red gas pumps.

"I compiled a playlist," Martha said. "But I'm thinking maybe I'll get used to the car before adding music. Unless you'd like music. Some people hate silence."

"Silence is underrated." *Particularly after three cocktails.* "But it was thoughtful of you to put together appropriate music."

"I've picked tracks for each place we're visiting." Martha's focus on the road would have made a meerkat proud. Nothing escaped her attention. "Maybe later."

Kathleen had the guidebook open on her lap, and also a notebook where she scribbled thoughts and observations. Even now, after so many years, it was instinctive to plan how she would present a place to the public. Part of her skill had been to get straight to the heart of the locality, showing what made it unique and special, knowing what would appeal and draw people in.

In her head she recorded a piece to camera.

When you hear the words road trip *what do you imagine? Established in 1926, Route 66 has become one of the most famous roads in North America. There's a reason it's on the bucket list of so many people around the world. Over the next couple of weeks we'll be traveling the 2,448 miles from Chicago to Santa Monica, crossing eight states and three time zones. We'll be tasting food in historic diners, admiring murals, taking a side trip to the Grand Canyon and driving through flat planes, deserts and mountains before finally ending up on the shores of the Pacific Ocean. So join us as we take you on a journey not just through a varied landscape, but through American history.*

At that point she'd smile at the camera, Dirk would yell "cut," and they'd all celebrate with drinks in the nearest bar.

She'd prided herself on rarely needing more than one take. It helped that she always wrote the words herself.

"Are you feeling okay, Kathleen?" Martha glanced at her, the first time her eyes had left the road. "You're quiet."

"I was imagining how I would introduce this place if I were recording the show."

"I'd love to see some of your shows. I'm going to see if I can find them on the internet." Martha's eyes were back on the road. "Do you need me to stop? Do you want a coffee?"

Kathleen checked the guidebook. "There are a few recommended stops ahead, one of which includes a particularly interesting historic diner. I presume it's the building itself that's historic, and not the contents of their fridge."

The towns fell away, the road became quieter as drivers chose the faster route and each side of them were fields and farmland.

They stopped for a delicious lunch of fried chicken and Martha ate while she studied the guidebook, tracing the route with her finger.

"When we reach this point we have to decide which road to take."

"Route 66." Kathleen smiled her thanks as the waitress topped up their drinks.

"It's more complicated than that because the route deviates from the original road. According to this book, there have been improvements and realignments. And there are faster routes if we want them."

"We don't." Kathleen was determined to stick as closely as possible to the original historic Route 66. She wanted to savor every moment.

"It says here that there are two choices. We can drive on the road as it was in 1926 or pick the route from 1930." Martha abandoned the book and returned to her chicken. "This is delicious. I've decided this trip might be all about the food. I ate this amazing slice of pizza yesterday, by the lake."

"You mentioned it." *Five times.*

"We should take the route that has the best restaurants." Martha turned her attention back to the guidebook.

"That plan works for me. I'm enjoying myself tremendously."

Martha looked up. "You're enjoying yourself?" A tentative smile formed. "You're sure?"

"It's all thrilling." Kathleen finished her chicken and wiped her fingers. "You have no idea how I've longed for this. I'm living the dream."

"As long as my driving hasn't turned it into a nightmare." Martha handed her the book. "You might need to give me instructions. It says here that SatNav tries to take you on the interstate, not the old route."

They headed back to the car and Martha eased her way cautiously from the parking lot to the road. Her lip was caught between her teeth and her knuckles were white on the wheel.

Kathleen wondered what she could do to help the girl relax.

"Tell me a little about yourself."

"Oh—" If anything the question seemed to add to Martha's tension. "I'm pretty boring. Nothing to tell."

"You live with your parents?"

"Yes."

"And is that a harmonious arrangement?"

"Harmonious? Oh, you mean do we get on? Yes." She slowed as they reached an intersection. "Actually no, not really."

Having discovered that Martha didn't need much encouragement to talk, Kathleen shame-lessly encouraged her. "It can't be easy. A girl like you needs independence."

"Needing independence and being able to afford independence are unfortunately not the same thing. Do I go right up ahead?"

Kathleen checked the map. "Yes." She waited until Martha made the turn. "Are you close to your mother?"

"No. Are you close to Liza?"

Kathleen wished she hadn't asked the question. "We have a satisfactory relationship." That was true on her part. Probably not true for Liza, but she had no intention of discussing such an intimate topic with anyone. "Have you never been close to your mother?"

"No. She prefers my older sister."

That humble confession startled Kathleen. She'd undoubtedly failed in many areas of parenting, but she was confident that if she'd had more than one child, she would have failed them equally. She wouldn't have had a favorite.

"Are you sure?"

"Yes. If I had money for every time she says *Why can't you be more like your sister,* I would have been able to afford a more interesting life."

"What exactly does your sister do that makes her so worthy of your mother's approval?"

"She makes good choices."

"Choices, surely, are subjective and only the person who makes those choices can comment on the quality of those decisions, and usually with the benefit of hindsight?"

"Not in my house." The road opened up and Martha drove a little faster. "Commenting on choices is a free-for-all, providing it's my choices we're talking about and doing it in real time is considered normal. And she's probably not wrong. I was doing English at college until Nanna got ill."

Became ill, Kathleen thought, but managed not to interrupt the conversation with the correction. It was the curse of being a presenter, and of being married to an English teacher.

"What happened?"

"I came home to look after her. My mother thought I'd lost it of course, but Nanna was like a mother to me. I adored her, and not only because she made the most spectacular chocolate cake and always encouraged me to be myself. She was kind. Not enough people are kind. She never once made me feel bad about myself and I miss her horribly, even after all this time." There was a crack in her voice and Kathleen felt a flicker of alarm.

She was interested in hearing more about Martha, but not if the revelations came with tears. She'd wanted to unlock facts, not emotions.

She reached across and patted Martha's leg awkwardly. "Your grandmother was lucky to have someone like you."

"Maybe. I don't know." Now that the roads were quieter, Martha seemed more relaxed. "I suppose in a way my mother isn't wrong. I have struggled to get a job, although I don't know for sure that finishing college would have helped. I probably would have ended up with even more debt and no salary to pay it off. It's tough out there, whether you're a graduate or not."

Kathleen was relieved to see that Martha was back in control. "What would you like to do if you had a choice?"

"I loved working in the coffee shop, but it wasn't the coffee part as much as the people. I liked chatting. I suppose if there was a job for a professional chatter I'd apply for that." She grinned at Kathleen. "Vice President of Chatting. Does that exist? Hey—" she pointed "—that's a pretty gas station by that Route 66 sign. We should stop and take your photo and send it to Liza." She pulled over and Kathleen dutifully posed for a photograph.

Martha, she thought, needed to get a job that paid enough for her to be able to afford her own place.

"Where shall I stand?"

"Right there is good. So if you were presenting a program from here, what would you say? I'll video you—" Martha hit a couple of buttons on her phone and held it up. "Whenever you're ready."

"Ready for what?"

"Ready for whatever it is you do. Take one. Action. Rolling, rolling, rolling."

"But what will you do with it?"

"I don't know. Send it to Liza. Keep it as a souvenir. We can talk about that later. Ready when you are. Go!"

Since the girl didn't seem about to take no for

an answer, Kathleen dutifully struck her best presenting pose.

"Look beyond the neon signs and restored gas stations, and what you find is history. In the 1920s—" She talked for about three minutes, repeating what she'd read in the guidebook and when she finished Martha gave her a strange look. "What? I had lipstick on my teeth?"

"You were incredible. Such a pro." Martha pressed something on her phone and held it out to Kathleen. "Watch."

Kathleen took the phone and removed her sunglasses. Was that really her? And did she really look that old?

But underneath the self-consciousness was a certain pride. She might be slower and have an excess of wrinkles, but she hadn't lost her abilities.

"You filmed that with your phone?"

"Yes. It was a gift from my grandmother and it has a great camera. I'm going to edit this later and we'll post it online. It's too good not to use it. I bet we'll get a ton of views." Martha pocketed it. "Better get going. Still have a way to go before we get to tonight's stop."

They'd been driving for half an hour when Kathleen noticed Martha's phone light up. "Someone called Steven is calling you. Would you like me to answer it?"

"No!" Martha grabbed the phone and turned it over. "Leave it."

Interesting, Kathleen thought, that Steven was the only thing that had tempted Martha to release her grip on the wheel.

The phone stopped ringing and then immediately started again.

"He's persistent."

"One of his many annoying traits." Martha pushed her hair away from her face with a shaky hand. "Sorry."

"I have no objection to personal calls. If you want to pull over and call him back—"

"I don't." But Martha swerved to the side of the road and stopped the car. Breathing deeply, she grabbed her phone and switched it off. "There. No more calls. At least he can't turn up at the motel where we're staying so I suppose I should be grateful for small things."

It had been a long time since Kathleen had witnessed the fallout of a bad romance, but that didn't mean she'd forgotten how it looked. "Was he a scoundrel?"

"A sc—" Martha gave a choked laugh. "Yes. He was a real scoundrel, Kathleen. A megascoundrel. A *superscoundrel.*"

"Scoundrel is an adequate descriptor. Hyperbole is unnecessary. I gather he broke your heart."

"Along with a few other things, including a

teapot my grandma gave me which is something I'll never forgive him for."

As a tea lover, Kathleen could understand the outrage. "Describe the teapot."

"It was white and covered in red cherries. It made me think of summer and smiling." Martha sucked in another breath and steered the car back onto the road. "I refuse to let him intrude on my life, or this special trip."

"Was it serious?"

"For me? Yes. For him—it turned out the answer was no. My mother took it as yet more evidence of my inability to make good choices."

"She clearly didn't understand scoundrels. They're charming and convincing and they seem like a good choice at the time." *She should know.* "Is he the reason you took this job?"

"What?" Martha braked sharply and Kathleen lurched forward, her seat belt locking.

She should have waited until they'd arrived at the motel before asking the question.

"I assumed you were running away from something. Or someone."

"You—what made you think that?"

"That day you came to visit, you seemed a little—desperate. Keep your eyes on the road, dear."

Martha was gripping the wheel. "You noticed? And you gave me the job anyway?"

"You were exactly what I needed. Someone

young with enough energy to compensate for my occasional lack of it, and someone who had absolutely no reason to change their minds and go home in the middle of our trip."

"Kathleen—"

"It was only a suspicion at first, but I'm sure now that nothing less than desperation would have persuaded you to take a job that involved driving when you clearly hate driving."

Martha wiped sweat off her forehead and mouthed an apology to the car behind who was now leaning on his horn. Fortunately, the sign for the motel flashed up ahead and she pulled in with visible relief and parked.

"How do you know I hate driving?" She turned to Kathleen, stricken. "Am I scaring you? Am I doing something wrong?"

Kathleen was beginning to wish she hadn't said anything. Liza had wanted her to check Martha's license, but what she really should have done was utilize some kind of psychological test that would have revealed that her prospective driver was a seething mass of emotions. "You're not doing anything wrong, but you don't seem comfortable. Every time a car approaches your jaw is clenched, you lean forward in your seat and you grip the wheel until you almost cut off the blood supply to your fingers. And I don't understand why because you are an excellent driver."

Martha stared at her. "Excellent? You really think I'm excellent?"

"Yes. Why would you think otherwise?"

"I'm—not confident."

"I would describe you as careful. And given that you're driving on the wrong side of the road and sitting on the wrong side of the car in a country unfamiliar to you, I have reason to be grateful for that. The last thing I would want is some cavalier individual who harbors a secret desire to become a racing driver. Do you want to tell me why you took a job driving, when you hate driving?"

"I never said I hated driving."

"Martha—" Kathleen was gentle "—we are spending the next few weeks in extraordinarily close quarters. It would be exhausting to keep up an act. It's important that I understand you."

She didn't need, or want, Martha to understand her.

Martha tipped her head back against the seat. "You're right. I hate driving. I find it terrifying. And I failed my test five times although in my defense I have to tell you that the last time was *not* my fault. And if you'd asked me outright I would have told you—I'm not a liar—but you didn't ask so I decided not to tell you. Because I *needed* the job. And you seemed like a nice person. And also, you're right—I was desperate." The words tumbled out and left her slumped and miserable. "Are you going to fire me?"

"Why would I fire you? How would I then continue on Route 66? I can no longer drive, and my physical condition won't allow me to push the car."

"You could find someone else."

"I want a driver exactly like you."

Martha's eyes were brimming with tears. "Rubbish, you mean?"

"There is no problem with your driving, my dear, only your confidence levels."

Martha rummaged in her bag for a tissue. "Confidence comes from achieving something, and I've never achieved much. I'm a bit of a disaster."

That emotional confession made Kathleen's skin prickle.

If her hips weren't so painful she might have run from the car. She'd never been one of those people who knew exactly what to say when someone was upset, so she took the bracing approach. "Nonsense. Confidence comes from knowing your own worth. From liking who you are. You're kind, funny, smart, warm and obviously loyal. On top of that you clearly had the sense to remove yourself from the path of a scoundrel, which also makes you a woman of good judgment."

Martha blew her nose hard. "I should have shown that judgment a lot sooner."

"Had you known him long?"

"The scoundrel? Yes, we met at school. Dated on and off. I should have paid more attention to the off parts instead of marrying him." She mangled the tissue. "How could I have been so *stupid?*"

"You were hopeful. Optimistic. Both admirable traits." She could have been describing herself. "It's your husband who keeps calling?"

"Ex-husband." Martha nibbled the side of her nail. "Shocking, right? I'm twenty-five and I have no college degree, no place to live of my own and no job but I do have an ex-husband. My mother says the only thing I'm good at is giving up."

Kathleen's opinion of her own parental performance was improving by the minute. "You *do* have a job. You have this job. For the foreseeable future you also have somewhere to live." She might not be the best at emotional support, but she was excellent at delivering practical help. "I fail to see how a college degree or similar would aid you in your current situation. How long were you married?"

Martha reached into the back of the car for her bag, tugging it between the seats so violently that she almost removed the strap. "Not long."

The girl was clearly raw and angry and Kathleen felt a rush of sympathy.

"Are we talking months or years?"

"I left him after four days, after I found him

in bed with someone. I'm a terrible cliché."

The pain was unexpected. It tore through her, ripping at wounds that had taken decades to heal, opening up a part of her life she'd tried to forget.

She had to remind herself that this was about poor Martha, not her.

Martha glanced at her. "The divorce came through a few weeks ago."

Say something, Kathleen. Say something.

"That must feel painful."

"I felt terrible when it happened, but it was months ago and now I'm mostly just steaming mad, which I actually prefer. It's easier to be mad than sad." Martha opened her bag and dropped her phone inside. "I'm mad with him. And with myself."

Kathleen's mouth was dry. "Why with yourself?"

Martha shrugged. "My mother has always said I'm not a good judge of character. I guess she was right about that."

"Why would you blame yourself for something that was patently not your fault?" *Yes why, Kathleen? Why?*

"I should have been less trusting. And honestly I don't get why he's calling me. I mean he slept with someone else, so why would he want me back?" Martha's voice rose and Kathleen could tell that although she might be mad, she was also deeply wounded.

And no one understood that better than her.

"I'm no psychologist but it's probably some-thing to do with the unobtainable." Kathleen felt a little dizzy. Her mind had been swamped by a dark cloud and she could no longer see the sun.

"Kathleen? Are you okay? Have I shocked you?"

Kathleen made a supreme effort to pull herself together. This wasn't about her. This wasn't her story. "One of the few advantages of being eighty, is that not much shocks you. Apart from one's reflection in the mirror of course. That's always startling, particularly first thing in the morning." A joke. Well done, Kathleen. "Shall we go inside? I think I'm ready for a lie down and a nap before we sample the local delicacies, whatever they may be."

"Corn dogs," Martha said absently.

"You should delete his number of course." She'd close her eyes for half an hour and try and pull herself together. Kathleen gathered up the guidebook, her glasses and her bag. "Sooner rather than later."

"I haven't been able to do that, but I probably should. You're a good listener. I was worried that if you knew the truth, you wouldn't want me to drive you."

"I can't imagine why you would have thought that. We women must stick together."

Martha slid her water bottle into her bag. "You

probably think I'm a coward running away. I mean, you're so bold. Fearless. You hit an intruder with a skillet when most people would have stood there frozen. And look at you now— eighty years old and crossing America. You're not even daunted." Martha gave a watery grin. "You're incredibly brave, Kathleen."

"You're doing it again, Martha. Hyperbole."

"Truth. You're the bravest person I've ever met. I don't expect you to understand how it feels to want to run away."

Kathleen clutched her bag and stared through the window. She was a fraud. A damn fraud.

Martha frowned. "Kathleen?"

She could make some vague remark and change the subject. That was what she did. She never talked about that time. Even Brian had known it was off-limits.

So why, for once, did she feel like telling the truth? What was it about this young girl that made her want to pass on the lessons learned by her experience?

"I've spent my life running away." The words emerged without her permission. "It's fair to say I'm something of an expert. You're not the only one with a scoundrel in your past, you know."

Oh Kathleen. You foolish, foolish woman.

Now there would be follow-up questions, none of which she intended to answer.

"You?" Martha sounded incredulous. "But you

have everything sorted. You're incredible. No man would dare treat you badly."

Martha wasn't a relative. There was no obligation on her to offer advice, or the benefit of her experience.

She could leave the girl to her illusions.

She glanced at her companion, intending to do exactly that and saw Martha's swimming eyes.

Kathleen felt something tug at her. She remembered feeling that same pain, and handling it all alone.

"No one has everything 'sorted,' Martha, whatever that means. I'm a coward." There, she'd said it. "After my encounter with a scoundrel I made sure I protected myself from pain. It's a human response of course."

Maybe age didn't give you wisdom, but it gave you the benefit of hindsight.

She couldn't change how her life had played out. She couldn't undo the decisions she'd made. But she could do her best to make sure Martha didn't go down the same road.

"I may not have been afraid of living, but I was afraid of loving." Given that she'd never spoken the words before, they were remarkably easy to say. "I'd hate to see you make the same mistake."

10

LIZA

Liza woke to the sound of birdsong and the smell of fresh linen. Cool air drifted through the open window, bringing with it the scent of sea salt and honeysuckle. Her head was nestled deep in the softest pillow and for a few blissful seconds she basked in extreme comfort, and then life intruded.

She was in Oakwood Cottage.

She'd driven the whole way without stopping, with the music of her choice blaring through her speakers. She'd arrived in the dark and collapsed on top of the bed fully clothed, too drained by the whole emotional experience to do more than remove her shoes.

Despite everything, she'd fallen asleep easily and slept deeply, which at least meant she was rested for the moment of reckoning.

She sat up, braced to experience a pounding of difficult emotions.

What had she done?

She'd left her family. No, not *left* them. That sounded permanent, and this wasn't permanent. But whichever way she framed it, family was everything to her and right now she should be feeling terrible. It came as a shock to discover that she wasn't.

Last night's feeling of panic had faded, but the hurt and loneliness was still there.

She wasn't even sure why she'd walked out the way she had. It had been a culmination of emotional pressure that had built over the day until she'd thought she might burst. From Sean forgetting their anniversary to Caitlin demanding that she bring the cup to school in her lunch break, the whole day had been a stark reminder of all the things that were making her unhappy in her life.

She hadn't left to make a point. She'd left because it had been necessary for her sanity.

She needed space and thinking time. Her brain wasn't given sufficient respite from stress to figure out what she really wanted.

Still, it felt unnatural being here on her own.

She'd chosen to sleep in the bedroom she'd used as a child rather than the bigger guest room that she and Sean occupied on their visits. Why had she done that? Perhaps because it was a way of winding back time to the life she'd been living before this one. The person she'd been before the woman she was now.

The oversize map of the world was still stuck to the wall, complete with the markings she'd made with her father. Gathering dust on the shelves were all her old books, favorites that she'd never part with. Usually they were held in place by the art award she'd won at school, but that seemed to be missing.

Her mother must have stowed it away some-where.

Feeling ridiculously disappointed that her untidy mother would choose to tidy up that particular item, she walked to the window and gazed out over the fields to the sea. This had been her view every day when she was growing up.

The sun blazed and she could feel the heat pumping into the room even though it was still early. It was going to be a scorcher.

She undressed, put her clothes in the laundry hamper and took a long shower.

Wrapped in a towel, she unzipped the bag she'd packed. She'd randomly pushed various things into the space without giving real thought to what she was going to wear.

Why on earth had she packed that shirt? She hated it.

Every item she pulled out of the bag reminded her of home and the life she wasn't sure she liked that much. And there was nothing suitable for relaxed outdoor living during a heat wave.

In the end she picked out a fitted white shirt with shell buttons, a pair of cropped linen trousers, and stuffed everything else back in the bag. She zipped it up and stowed it under the bed.

It wasn't only her life that needed an over-haul—her wardrobe did too.

Maybe she'd pay a visit to the boutique in the village later.

Only when she'd dried her hair did she finally switch on her phone.

She had several missed calls from Sean, and before she could decide what she was going to do about that, he called again.

She picked up, not sure what to expect from the conversation. "Hi."

"Liza? Thank goodness. I've been worried sick about you." The tone of his voice and the faint crackle told her he was calling her from the car.

"Why would you be worried about me?"

"Because you took off with no warning! I had no idea you were intending to go to Cornwall this weekend. And I feel—" The phone went dead.

"Hello?" She checked the screen to see if they were still connected. "Sean?"

"Yes. Are you there?"

"Yes. I missed what you said." How did he feel? Had he realized he'd missed their anniversary?

She waited, determined to be relaxed and for-giving. He was busy. They both were. It was one of the many things that needed addressing.

"I feel frustrated that you did that without talking to me, without checking that the plan would work for me."

She forced herself to breathe. She could discuss

206

it, right here and now, but she knew what would happen. For all his faults, Sean was a good man. If she confessed how she was feeling, he'd turn the car round and head straight down to Cornwall to see her and she didn't want that. She wanted time on her own, and for once in her life she was going to do what she wanted.

"I promised my mother I'd keep an eye on Popeye."

"Well, the timing is bad. I am buried under work. I had to leave the house this morning before the girls were awake, and I'll be home late so the last thing I need is to be clearing up the mess they make in the kitchen."

Were they even capable of having a conversation that didn't involve managing tasks and the girls? At the beginning of their relationship they'd played a game, *Big Dreams, Little Dreams*, sharing everything they'd hoped for, but those dreams were like an old threadbare rug. Trodden on and mostly forgotten.

"If they make a mess, they can clear it up themselves. If they need to be somewhere they can take public transport. They're old enough to figure it out."

"Who are you and what have you done with Liza?"

She licked her lips. "You're always telling me we need to trust them."

"That was before they wrecked the house. The

builders are coming in this week, by the way. Can you be in on Tuesday?"

"No. Leave them a key."

"You never leave builders in the house without supervision."

"If you trust them then so do I?" She didn't care about the builders.

There was a silence. "Are you sure you're all right?"

No, but she wasn't ready to talk about it. "I'm tired after the drive. You know how it is at the end of the school year." She heard him curse under his breath. "Are you all right?"

"Traffic is bad. I'm going to be late."

"Where are you going?"

"On-site meeting."

"It's Saturday."

"This project is a nightmare. I don't see how I can join you with things the way they are right now."

The feeling of relief was swiftly swamped by guilt. What did it say about her that she was pleased that her husband couldn't join her?

"Don't worry."

"Will you keep your phone on? They can call you if they have a problem."

They'd call her for every little thing. "I can't guarantee I'll pick up. There's a lot to do here and you know the signal is patchy."

"Liza—" He sounded exasperated. "I can't

208

take calls at work right now. You couldn't have chosen a worse time to do this."

To do what? Take time for herself? "I don't expect you to take calls."

"I don't understand. You worry about these kids every second of the day. You check they've cleaned their teeth, and taken vitamins. And now you're refusing to be there in an emergency?"

"What I'm doing," she said slowly, "is teaching them to problem solve and also take responsibility. Something I should have done a long time ago. If they turn to me for everything, they'll never learn. Hope your meeting goes well."

She ended the call and gazed across the fields to the sea, her mind battling between her needs and their needs.

With no to-do list and no people to make demands, the day stretched ahead, empty of everything except possibilities. Free time was so alien to her that she had no idea how she wanted to spend it.

Walk? Maybe she'd sit on the patio on her mother's comfortable swing chair and read one of the books she'd been saving for her summer trip. Just because she couldn't sip cocktails on the roof terrace of a swanky hotel in Chicago, didn't mean she couldn't spoil herself in other ways.

She picked up her book, made herself a coffee in the sunny kitchen and took it into the garden. The place felt strangely empty without her mother. Liza was used to seeing her bent over by the flower beds, weeding and deadheading.

Popeye wandered in front of her and she reached down to stroke him, but he whisked away from her, rejecting her attempts at affection before walking in the direction of the kitchen and his food bowl.

Was there anyone who wasn't interested in only what she could do for them?

She fed the cat, then opened her book but found it difficult to concentrate.

She felt restless and on edge. Her instinct was to clean cupboards and dust shelves. Polish the sea spray from a few windows.

No.

She tightened her grip on her book.

She never did this. At home her reading was restricted to a few snatched pages before she fell asleep. Sitting in the sun with a book felt decadent and indulgent. It made her feel guilty. She needed to retrain herself to relax.

She struggled through a few pages and then stood up and pulled at her shirt which was already sticking to her skin. It was so *hot*.

The clothes she'd brought with her were scratchy and uncomfortable. She felt ready to teach a class, not sit in the sun.

Maybe there was at least something cooler in her bag, or something of her mother's she could borrow. She went upstairs and rummaged through her mother's dresses and was immediately trans-ported back to childhood. Whenever Kathleen had vanished on another of her trips, Liza had sought sanctuary inside the racks of her mother's clothes, allowing the scent to fill all the little gaps created by her absence. And here she was, doing it again even though she was past the age where she should be missing her mother.

She had her face buried in a vintage silk shirt when she heard the sound of footsteps in the kitchen.

She froze. Had she locked the back door when she'd come upstairs? Yes! She remembered turning the key. But despite that someone was in the house.

What was she going to do?

Hide? Here in the clothes? Under the bed? No, that would be the first place an intruder would look and then she'd be trapped.

She could jump out her mother's bedroom window which faced over the fields, but then she'd probably break a leg.

Fear trapped the breath in her lungs. Her heart tried to hammer its way to freedom.

Could it be the same man who had broken in a few weeks ago? No. He'd been drunk and seeking shelter.

She stood up slowly. Her legs were shaking so badly she wasn't sure she was capable of running anywhere even if the opportunity arose.

She heard the sound of a kitchen cupboard opening and closing.

Whoever it was didn't seem to be making any effort to disguise his presence. Perhaps they hadn't yet realized the house wasn't empty.

She eased her phone out of her pocket and called the emergency services, then tiptoed into the bathroom and locked the door.

"Hello?" she whispered, terrified that any moment now the door would be smashed down. "There's an intruder in the house. Help me."

11

MARTHA

ST. LOUIS~DEVIL'S ELBOW~SPRINGFIELD

"Are you sure you feel up to traveling today? You're quiet." Martha loaded their bags into the trunk of the car. She'd learned that they had to be loaded in the exact same order or they didn't fit. For someone whose underwear drawer was usually a tangled mess, she was proud of her achievement. The neatly packed trunk seemed to represent something, although she wasn't sure what. Order?

"I can confirm my wish to travel." Kathleen clutched the small bag that she kept with her in the car at all times. "We're on a road trip and after those delicious pancakes for breakfast I'm full of energy."

"You mentioned that you didn't sleep well. Probably all that talk of scoundrels." Martha still couldn't believe that something similar had happened to Kathleen when she was young. Kathleen's experience had been worse, in some ways. Hearing about it had made Martha feel a little less bad about herself. If it could happen to someone like Kathleen, it could happen to anyone.

Not that she knew many of the details. All Kathleen had told her was that she'd been engaged to a man who had then had an affair with her friend. Having revealed that, she'd then cleverly deflected all follow-up questions and instead encouraged Martha to talk about herself.

She'd done so willingly. There was plenty Martha didn't know, as her mother was always quick to point out, but she knew when someone didn't want to talk about something.

Kathleen handed her the last of the bags. "It's true that I didn't sleep well, but that's a common occurrence and nothing that should alarm you."

Martha squashed the bag into the remaining space, closed the trunk and glanced at Kathleen. There were no outward signs that her companion was flagging. She was wearing her usual floaty, elegant layers and had taken the time to apply lipstick.

Martha felt a rush of admiration and an even bigger rush of affection. She'd known Kathleen for only a few days, but she hadn't felt this comfortable with someone since she'd lost her grandmother. Kathleen was so easy to talk to. Warm, hilarious and delightfully frank. But she was also supportive and greeted all Martha's tentative suggestions with so much enthusiasm that Martha found herself becoming less tentative. It made her realize she'd been living her life in defense mode, constantly on edge and ready to defend herself against her mother, her sister and Steven. Not beginning each day braced for combat was a good feeling. The knot in her stomach had eased.

And if a small part of her warned that she should have been more cautious about being so open with a stranger, she ignored it.

Was that why Kathleen had suddenly backed off?

"Are you wishing you'd never told me that personal stuff?" Martha held the car door open for Kathleen. "Because you don't need to worry. I'm chatty, but I'm not a gossip. There's a difference."

"I'm aware of the distinction. And I have no regrets."

"I know you only did it because you were trying to make me feel better. And it did." Martha closed the door, sprinted round the car and slid into the driver's seat.

"I'm nowhere near as kindly and unselfish as you seem to believe." Kathleen secured her seat belt. Her hands were still elegant, even though the skin was wrinkled and darkened in places from overexposure to the sun. "I don't fully understand why I shared my own experience. It was an impulse."

Martha adjusted her mirror. "That's what you said when you ordered the bacon."

"Generally I find food impulses to have fewer immediate consequences than those of an emotional type. I do hope you'll heed my advice and not let your lamentable experience with Scoundrel Steven influence the choices you make for the rest of your life."

Martha hesitated. "Like you did?"

"We have done enough talking about me." Kathleen slid her sunglasses onto her nose. "Shall we drive? That way we might stand a chance of arriving in California before I reach my hundredth decade."

Martha snorted with laughter. "You're so funny."

"Your entertainment is high on my priority list, so I count that as excellent news. Drive, Martha!"

Martha discovered that the driver's seat felt a more comfortable place than previously. She no longer felt as if it might eject her as an imposter at any moment. She was in charge, not the car. "You don't like talking about yourself, do you?"

"I've already given an extensive account of my travels."

"That, yes." Martha checked the traffic and pulled onto the road. "But I mean emotional stuff. You don't like talking about emotional stuff. I can tell. It's hard for you."

"You are perceptive."

"I'm good at reading people. And everyone is different, aren't they? And that's okay. Nanna used to say that a person had to be allowed to be the way they wanted to be. Some people are chatty, some people are quiet. You can't change that. Take me for example—" she increased her speed as they headed out of town, shifting the focus of the conversation to herself to give Kathleen some space "—my school reports were all *Martha needs to concentrate more and talk less,* but what no one gets is that it's really hard for me to talk less."

"As I am discovering."

Martha laughed. "People never tell a quiet person to be noisier—have you ever noticed that? They never say *talk more.* Or *why can't you be more chatty.* But for some reason people have always felt the right to tell me how I could improve myself. It's annoying, actually."

"I can imagine the frustration."

"The weird thing is, I don't chat that much at home. It's mostly arguing about who is doing what chores." She thought about her mother and sister. "I have a lot to say, and no one to say it to. All I get is *shut up, Martha.* That's another reason I need to move out. I'm not allowed to be me."

"You not being you would indeed be a loss to the world."

Martha felt herself blush and glanced at her companion. "Do you mean that?"

"I may, on occasion, withhold information, but I'm not in the habit of saying things I don't mean. The point of speech is to communicate clearly."

Martha focused on the road. "Well, I know I communicate more frequently than the average person, so if you want me to be quiet, say so. Say, *Martha, enough!* I won't be offended."

"Your good nature is a remarkable quality, and it is my good fortune to be traveling with you."

An expert on identifying sarcasm thanks to long experience with her family, Martha decided that Kathleen meant what she said. A feeling of contentment settled around her. She was used to spending her time around people who constantly tore her down and this was a refreshing change. "Well, I feel lucky to be traveling with you. Go me, I say! Most of my friends are busy this summer—holidays, jobs and stuff—so I was bracing myself for a lonely, miserable summer until I saw your ad for this job." And her friends had been impressed when she'd told them about it. Less so her family, who seemed incapable of being impressed by anything she did.

"I cannot imagine you being miserable, Martha. And I'm sure someone like you has more friends than there are hours in the day to connect with them."

Was that true? "Well, I know a lot of people—

but friendship is a weird thing, isn't it? There are friends who would drop everything to help you in a crisis—they're like gold dust. And then friends who you meet in the pub and you chat about your week but they don't really have a clue what's going on in your head, or in your life. I'm not saying that's not friendship, but it's a different type of friendship, isn't it? A good friend can feel like family." In her case, better than family, but admittedly it was a pretty low bar.

"Yes. A true friend can indeed be like family." The wistful note in Kathleen's voice made Martha wonder.

She had a feeling that for all her reticence, Kathleen *did* want to talk about it. Just because you didn't find talking easy, didn't mean you didn't want to do it. Like everything, it took practice.

She tried a little encouragement, promising herself she'd back off at the first sign of retreat on Kathleen's part. "After the affair—you and Ruth lost touch?"

Kathleen shifted in her seat. "She wrote to me, but I never opened her letters."

"I get that. You wanted to keep it in the past. Move on. Not look back. I mean, that's human. I wish Steven was in the past." Martha frowned. "But Ruth was your friend, so that had to be tough."

"It was indeed a trial." Kathleen's voice was faint.

"I bet you missed her. But at the same time wanted to kill her. It's hard when emotions get all mixed up like that. You don't know what you're supposed to feel. It's all wrong, like—like—someone pouring chocolate sauce onto spaghetti Bolognaise. I mean, what even is that? Or like when Nanna dropped her knitting—hard to unravel the mess."

"I prefer the knitting analogy. I don't love having my food tampered with."

"And you were brokenhearted, so that made it even tougher."

"Indeed. I loved him deeply."

Martha's chest ached and she reached out and squeezed Kathleen's arm. "But you moved on. I can't tell you how much that inspires me. I was feeling all flimsy and pathetic when I came to your house that day, like a silk shirt that's been through a hot cycle in the laundry instead of being hand washed—"

"Your analogies are continually intriguing."

"—but hearing your story makes me feel a lot more confident. And I don't blame you for wanting to leave it all in the past. I was the same. That was one of the reasons I called you when I saw the ad." And she was relieved she had. If she hadn't been desperate, there was no way she would have considered a job that involved driving, and yet here she was having the time of her life.

Kathleen clutched the bag on her lap. "I am the fortunate beneficiary of that decision."

"I know our situation isn't the same, though. If I'm honest, I don't feel that brokenhearted about Steven. I was at the beginning, but mostly I felt stupid. Stupid for thinking he was the right one. Stupid for making the decision to marry him. I don't think I would have done that if Nanna hadn't died, but I'd known him forever and I was clinging to something familiar."

"You have remarkable self-insight."

"Never before the event, sadly. Only after and then it's too late."

"How well I understand that."

Martha glanced at her. "You were the same? So did you burn Ruth's letters? Cut them into pieces? If you'd rather not talk about it, that's fine."

"The letters currently reside in a drawer at home, along with the ring."

Maybe she hadn't opened the letters, Martha thought, but nor had she thrown them away. If she really didn't want any contact ever, wouldn't she have thrown them away?

"And you don't know if she's still in California? Or if they're together?"

"I doubt they're together. He wasn't capable of commitment. But the letters were always postmarked California, so it seems reasonable to assume that Ruth still resides there."

"And that's why you looked a bit funny on that first night when I mentioned California. Going there makes you feel a bit weird. Big place though. You won't bump into her unless you want to." But maybe she wanted to. Was that why Kathleen had chosen this particular trip? Had she consciously, or subconsciously, been keeping her options open? Martha stifled the million questions bubbling in her brain and asked just one. "Were you very good friends?"

It took Kathleen a long time to respond and when she finally did, her voice was faint. "Yes," she said. "The very best. We were like sisters."

How terrible must that have been? To lose the man you were engaged to was bad enough, but to lose your best friend too?

She was starting to think her situation wasn't so bad after all. Okay, so she was twenty-five and already divorced, which didn't look good from the outside to people who didn't know the whole story, but what other people thought shouldn't matter, should it? Kathleen hadn't made her choices based on what other people thought.

Martha lifted her chin. *Be more Kathleen.* That was her new motto.

Maybe she should see divorce as a life experience instead of a failure. Things happened in life, to everyone. She needed to focus more on the *now,* and less on the *then.* She was young, healthy and didn't have kids to worry about. She didn't have to stay in touch with Steven. She was in a position to move on, as Kathleen had.

Except Kathleen had also lost her closest friend. That was a double blow.

Martha had a sudden urge to help. Kathleen had already helped her, so the least Martha could do was repay the favor.

"If you wanted to look her up then we could."

"I don't want that."

The flat-out rejection of that suggestion made Martha wonder at the pain hidden behind those words.

What exactly had happened?

Martha decided it was time for distraction. "How about some music?"

"We tried that yesterday. My ears are still in a state of recovery."

Martha grinned. "That's my fault for singing along. I can't help it. I burst if I don't sing. Forget music. How about I put the top down?" It was a hot day. The sun beamed its approval of that suggestion.

"The top of what, dear?"

"The car. We have this fancy, sexy sports car. We might as well use some of its features. It will probably blow your hair around."

"That sounds marvelous. Do it."

Marvelous. When had she last heard anyone use that word?

Grinning, Martha pulled over next to a field. She hit the button, fascinated by the way the roof opened. "It's very cool."

"I doubt it will be cool when we hit Arizona."

Martha started the engine and saw a man gazing at them from a house across the road. She was beginning to understand that far from being everyone's worst nightmare, this car was considered a dream. It wasn't quite *her* dream, but they might get there yet.

Kathleen wound her scarf around her hair and Martha grabbed her phone and snapped a few pictures.

"You look like a glamorous movie star. And if you're not too old for an epic road trip, I don't see why you'd be too old to contact an old friend." Maybe she shouldn't have pushed, but if it was the wrong thing to do then Kathleen would tell her. If not with words, then with one of her looks.

Kathleen adjusted her sunglasses. "She's probably dead."

"That's not very optimistic. She might be very much alive, and hoping to hear from you." Martha pulled onto the road. The sun was on her face and a light breeze played with her hair.

"She probably wouldn't even remember me."

Martha raised an eyebrow. "When did the last letter arrive?"

"Last year."

"So she was obviously still thinking of you then." Martha settled herself more comfortably in the seat. The car was starting to feel familiar. She no longer had to stare at the pictures on the key for five minutes while she tried to work out how to lock and unlock the doors. True, there were still lots of buttons she hadn't touched, but overall, she was proud of herself. "I understand why you were so reluctant to be involved with anyone else after that. But it's funny how life works out, isn't it?" She slowed down as they approached an intersection. "If my relationship hadn't ended, I probably wouldn't be here with you now having the time of my life."

Kathleen turned her head. "Are you having the time of your life?"

"Are you kidding? This whole trip is brilliant. It's hard even to pick out a highlight so far. I mean—Chicago was incredible. And yesterday, crossing the Mississippi River and seeing The Chain of Rocks Bridge. I loved driving through the little hamlets and passing all those corn and soybean fields. Not that I would have known what was growing if that woman hadn't told us. Everyone is so friendly and welcoming. Oh and that hamburger! And talking to that French couple. I never realized that this route had such international appeal. I want to stay longer in each place, but at the same time I can't wait to move on and see what's next. I feel excited the whole time. It's made the world seem bigger. It's made my whole life seem bigger. It's as if—" she struggled to explain "—my experience with Steven filled my very small world, and now my world is so much larger and filled with possibilities that he no longer dominates. He's become a small part of my big life, instead of a big part of my small life. This has shown me how important it is to reach outside your normal world. To embrace new experiences. Does that make any sense?"

"It does. I'm glad you're finding it all so enriching."

Martha loved the way Kathleen talked. "It's all thanks to you. I think you might have saved me, although you've also probably cost me a fortune. Now I've got the travel bug and I don't have the money to subsidize my new passion, but I'll figure something out. Maybe you'll need a driver for your next exciting road trip." She'd already started thinking. There was no way she was returning to her deeply unsatisfying life back home. Maybe she could work for a tour company. Or maybe she'd backpack around the world for a couple of years with nothing but a rucksack and her wits. She could work in bars or cafés. There were no rules that said you had to have a big corporate-type career or a professional qualification to enjoy life. And if her parents didn't approve—well, tough. This was her life, not theirs. Their judgment was not going to affect her choices. That part of her life was in the past, along with Scoundrel Steven, as she now thought of him. "All I'm saying is that it's funny how life turns out, isn't it? Good can come from bad. If your relationship hadn't ended you probably wouldn't have had the career you did. Traveling the world. Making all those TV shows. You were a superstar." She'd managed to find some clips of *The Summer Seekers* on the internet and she and Kathleen had watched them together the night before. "I'm talking too much."

"I enjoy your conversation. Do continue."

Kathleen enjoyed her conversation.

"I mean let's say you'd married him—" Martha followed the Route 66 sign and made a right turn. "He might have cheated on you *after* you were married and already had two kids. That wouldn't have been fun."

"No fun at all."

"It would have been harder to move on, and your options would have been limited. Instead of which you had this wonderful, exciting life and then fell in love and had kids later. That sounds good to me. Like the best of both worlds. Did Brian really have to propose three times?"

"Yes." Kathleen's voice was faint, as if she couldn't quite believe she'd told Martha that.

"You probably protected yourself. Like one of

those ancient castles they built in Roman times. An emotional fortress." She glanced at Kathleen. "I'm not saying you're crumbly or anything."

Kathleen adjusted her glasses. "Many would consider me to be something of a ruin."

"I think you're great. And I understand. I'm not interested in another relationship, that's for sure."

"That needs to be remedied with some urgency."

"How can you say that, when you've just confessed you avoided relationships?"

"We might have to entertain the possibility that I'm a hypocrite." Kathleen reached for the little mirror she kept in her purse and checked her lipstick. "Or it could be that I don't want you to make the mistakes I did."

"But you had a full and happy life."

Kathleen stared out the window. "Until I met Brian, it was lacking in intimacy. I kept myself apart from people, male and female." The waver in her voice made Martha suspect that was a significant admission from Kathleen.

Had she ever said these things to anyone else?

"Self-protection." Martha nodded. "That's natural. You put your heart on ice. Like the fish counter in the supermarket where they keep it all cool. Shrimp on ice."

"You're comparing me to a fish?"

"Not *you*. Your heart. Heart and sole. Get it? Sole. Never mind. Maybe champagne on ice would have been more appropriate." Particularly for Kathleen who seemed to drink only Earl Grey tea or bubbles. "Whatever. It was frozen."

"It was fear. And fear narrows your choices and your life experience. I don't want that for you. We need you to have a nice rebound relationship as soon as possible to get your confidence back."

Martha hit the brakes, relieved there were no cars in front or behind. "A rebound relationship?" Changing the subject was one thing, but this went beyond her comfort zone. Maybe she did have a few boundaries after all.

"Yes. How would you put it? Get back on the horse."

"Get back on—Kathleen! I can't believe you said that."

"We've already established that I say what I think, although maybe it is presumptuous of me to make such a personal observation given the length of our acquaintance."

Martha smiled. "It's probably because we've bonded so quickly."

"Bonded?"

"I like you. I think you like me a little too, although I get that you probably won't say so because you don't like to talk about your emotions. And that's fine. Probably a generation thing. But it's not always about words, is it? Sometimes it's how a person behaves. You want me to be happy. And that's nice."

Kathleen cleared her throat. "It's true that I

may have developed a certain fondness for you, Martha."

Martha felt a pressure in her throat. "I've developed a fondness for you too. Weird, isn't it? After only a few days?"

"I've never believed that the quality of a relationship is dependent on its length."

Was she thinking about her friend?

"I'm the same. I've known my mother all my life and I don't feel as close to her as I do to you."

"Concentrate on the road, Martha, or the next person we meet might well be pulling us out of the ditch. We're going to find you someone. I've always been very good at spotting a partner for other people. Not so good with myself."

"That's not true. You said yes to Brian. And honestly Kathleen, I'm very touched that you're thinking of me, but the last thing I need now is a man. I'm still getting over the last one."

"Let's use an analogy. I know you like those." Kathleen tapped her fingers on her bag. "If you eat a meal you don't like, do you stop eating? No. You select something different from the menu. If you visit a place you don't like, do you stop traveling? No. You choose a different destination."

"That's all logical but doesn't make me inclined to throw myself back into the dating pool."

"Not all men are like Steven."

"But how do you find out what they're like? I don't trust my judgment."

"You keep things casual until you know them better."

"It's easy for you to say."

"No, it isn't. The *road,* Martha! You're driving in the middle."

"Fox!" Martha turned the wheel and adjusted her position. "Sorry."

"You saw a fox?"

"No, fox is an exclamation. The *F* word."

Kathleen blinked. "I may be approaching fossilization, but even I know the *F* word doesn't refer to an animal."

"It does when I say it." Martha grinned. "When I was nine I asked Nanna what the *F* word was. She couldn't bear bad language, so she told me it stood for *fox.* I've been saying it ever since. It's a habit."

"I suppose no harm will come of it providing you're not transporting a carload of chickens with a nervous disposition."

"It was your fault for distracting me with all that talk about casual relationships. I hope you're not about to grab some unsuspecting, innocent man from the next diner."

"You don't need someone innocent. You need someone experienced who can show you a good time."

Martha managed not to swerve into the oncoming car. "I can't believe you just said that."

"I will remain alert to a suitable candidate. As

you say, one never knows what opportunities life will place before you."

Should she laugh or protest? "Well, right now I don't need life to place a man before me, but thank you for the thought." They were surrounded by fields, the light playing across the grass and crops. "Did Liza think you should try getting in touch with Ruth?" When Kathleen didn't answer, Martha glanced at her. "Kathleen?"

"She doesn't know the whole story. Only that Ruth and I were friends in college."

"She doesn't know that you were engaged? Or that you have letters?" Martha broke off, shocked. "None of it?"

"Liza and I don't talk about personal things. The responsibility for that is mine."

"Don't feel bad about it. It's who you are. You don't find it easy to talk about emotional stuff. I'm sure Liza gets that."

"I'm not sure she does. Liza has always wanted more than I felt able to give her. That's a matter of regret for me."

"If you can talk to me, you can talk to her."

"Perhaps, although your delightfully unguarded nature does rather remove all barriers."

"It's probably different when it's mother and daughter. I don't talk to my mother either. Not even about neutral subjects like books. We don't read the same thing. I like novels, and she reads magazines full of articles on how to avoid wrinkles, even though we all know that the only way to avoid wrinkles is to die before you're thirty."

"A sobering observation indeed."

"My mother is nothing like you. I'm sure you could find a way to get closer to Liza. It's never too late to do any of these things." The traffic was lighter than it had been the day before. They drove past farms, the land stretching into the distance. "We're stopping for lunch in a place called Devil's Elbow. I'm going to take photographs of you and record another video so you might want to start doing your research. I think we should start a social media account for you. I've been wondering what to call it. It's a shame you're not eighty-six."

"Why would I want to wish my life away when I have so little of it left?"

"You don't know how much of it you have left. I mean, none of us do, do we? I could be dead tomorrow."

"If you kept your eyes on the road the chances of living beyond that might be vastly improved for both of us."

Martha laughed. "That was one of the things I loved about watching *The Summer Seekers*. You were hilarious. Anyway, as I was saying, you could live to be 106, in which case you're only three quarters through. The best might be yet to come."

"I doubt that, although I admit my zest for living is considerably enhanced by the prospect of pairing you up with a suitable candidate for your affections."

"That's not fair." The sun was bright and Martha pulled her baseball cap farther down over her eyes. "I'm supposed to tolerate your matchmaking in order to brighten your days?"

"That would be a kind gesture."

"I hate to disappoint you, but my affections aren't up for grabs at the moment. As I was saying, if you were eighty-six, I could call our social media account '86 on 66' or something." Martha pondered. "Or maybe '86 meets 66. Or how about Old But Bold? No, that sounds rude."

"We could call it 'Martha finds a new man.' "

"We are not calling it that."

"Martha's Rebound Road Trip?"

"Maybe we'll call it *The Summer Seekers*. That's what we are. We're seeking summer. Seeking adventure. Pick up that guidebook and start studying." Martha felt more relaxed than she had in a long time. Kathleen's confidence in her had boosted her self-confidence. "Don't die of shock, but I'm starting to enjoy driving. I'm feeling happy."

"I can tell. Your increase in speed appears to directly correlate with your elevated mood. Let me know when you hit a moment of ecstasy so that I can take the appropriate safety precautions."

And now they were heading across Missouri on their way to Kansas with the sun on their faces and the breeze blowing their hair.

"Have you been looking at the guidebook? Is there anything in particular you'd like to see?"

Kathleen adjusted her scarf. "Yes. I'd like to see you with a man."

"I meant sightseeing."

"Well, that's a sight I'd like to see."

"Kathleen, are you going to embarrass me when we stop?"

"I aim to try. That was a pretty drive, by the way."

Unable to shift the conversation, Martha pulled up at Devil's Elbow and parked. "We're going for a stroll to see the bridge and the Big Piney River and then we'll get something to eat. We're right in the middle of the Ozarks. Loggers used to float the logs down the river here and they had to negotiate this horrid bend, which is why it's called Devil's Elbow. I read that they didn't have a barrier on the road originally. I think we both know where I would have ended up. Floating down the Big Piney River along with the logs."

Kathleen was staring along the dusty road. "We appear to have struck lucky. And so soon! Over there—" She pointed. "That man is handsome, although no doubt you would use a different word. What would you call him? Cute?"

"I'd call him a stranger." Was Kathleen really

going to do this? Martha had assumed she was joking. "Could you at least not point?"

"How else will you know who I've identified? It would be terrible if you picked the wrong man."

"Yeah, well I'm good at that." Martha locked the car and glanced over at the man. He was leaning against a wall, deep in conversation with another man. His jeans rode snugly around strong legs and his shoulders were broad and solid. He held himself with a certain relaxed confidence that was undeniably attractive. *Hot,* she thought. She'd call him hot, but there was no way she was admitting that. Kathleen was already out of control. And also watching Martha closely.

"What do you think? His hair could do with a cut, and he needs a shave but he's probably been traveling like us, so we'll forgive him that."

Martha slipped the car keys into her bag. "He's too far away for me to see his face."

"We'll move closer."

"No way. I'm buying us food and we're going to walk to the river and eat there. Any preferences? Are you coming in with me?"

"I'll stay with the car."

When Martha came back loaded with food and drink Kathleen was deep in conversation with the man she'd identified as "cute."

"Martha!" Kathleen waved. "Over here."

"I'm going to kill her." Martha tried to find a reason not to join her, but failed to find one that didn't sound rude so she gave in to pressure and joined Kathleen and her new friend.

"Josh here was telling me that we absolutely have to stay an extra day in Arizona and see the Grand Canyon. He's doing Route 66 too, can you believe that?"

Martha didn't point out that since they were, in fact, on the old section of Route 66 that point was pretty obvious. Nor that they already had a visit to the Grand Canyon planned. "What a coincidence."

His eyes crinkled at the corners and he extended a hand. "Josh Ryder. Kathleen here has been telling me all about your trip so far. Traveling with her must be an eye-opener."

"In more ways than you can possibly imagine."

Kathleen winked at her.

Subtlety, Martha thought, wasn't one of her skills. "I bought us both a pulled pork sandwich. I thought we could eat it near the river. Goodbye, Josh. Safe travels."

"Josh is hitchhiking," Kathleen said. "Isn't that intrepid?"

"Very." Martha waved the bag and Josh smiled. "Smells good."

Okay so he *was* very sexy, Kathleen wasn't wrong about that.

"I need to visit the restroom. You two young things get to know each other in my absence." Kathleen headed away from them and Martha stared after her with exasperation, which mounted when she turned and found Josh laughing.

"It's been a while since I was described as a 'young thing.' She's quite a character."

No kidding.

"She really is." Martha spoke through her teeth. "One of a kind."

"She's eighty? That's quite something. She was telling me about your adventure."

As long as that was all she'd told him. If she'd mentioned that Martha needed a rebound relationship Kathleen's next adventure on Route 66 would be a dip in the Big Piney River. Forget Devil's Elbow, it would be courtesy of Martha's Elbow. In her ribs.

"Yes, it's been a dream of hers to do Route 66. I applied for the job of driving her, so here we are. How about you?" She needed to fill the time until Kathleen came back, and she'd rather they talked about him than her.

"I—needed a change of scenery." He drained a can of soda and tossed it into the bin, his aim perfect. "This seemed as good a way of getting it as any."

Why had he needed a change of scenery? *None of your business, Martha.* She wasn't interested, she really wasn't. "You've come from Chicago?"

"Vermont. I was staying with friends."

"You hitchhiked all that way? Isn't that dangerous?"

He shrugged. "Not so far. Everyone has been friendly and helpful."

"I suppose having muscles helps," she said and then saw amusement in his eyes and her face grew hot. "I just meant that you probably don't have to worry too much about— Oh never mind."

Her mind was going in directions she didn't want it to.

She was definitely going to kill Kathleen.

"How about you?" He leaned against the wall, as comfortable as she was uncomfortable. "How are you finding the driving?"

"It's been great," she lied. "A bit hair-raising in Chicago, but getting easier."

"You have a nice set of wheels there, that's for sure." Josh nodded to the car and she was relieved that Kathleen had insisted on hiring a small, sporty car rather than a big SUV. There was no room for an additional passenger.

Finally Kathleen emerged and Martha decided this was her cue to end this exchange before something embarrassing happened.

"Safe travels, Josh."

He held her gaze for a moment. "Perhaps we'll meet again farther down the road."

Her heart was beating a little too fast. The heat in her cheeks had nothing to do with the sun. "Yeah, maybe. Take care." She gave an awkward smile and slid her arm into Kathleen's, propelling her along so that she didn't linger. "We're walking to the river. It's so pretty here and I want to feast my eyes on Ozark scenery."

Kathleen didn't protest but she did glance over her shoulder at Josh. "One wonders what a man like that is doing alone? It seems like an opportunity."

"It seems like a warning. Maybe he's a serial killer and he doesn't like accomplices." Martha handed over a bag. "Sandwich. Eat. Food will help your brain function and hopefully stop you plotting."

"I'm enjoying plotting. And it's beautiful here. A perfect place to stop, you clever girl." Kathleen stared down at the sun shimmering across the surface of the river. Trees stretched into the distance and overhung the water, creating shadows and shade. "The Ozarks, you say."

"Mmm." Martha had a mouth full of delicious pulled pork but that didn't stop her from enjoying the view.

They stood in companionable silence, both of them eating.

Finally Kathleen spoke. "Josh seems delightful. It's hard to believe we struck lucky so quickly, don't you think?"

Martha managed to swallow before she choked. "We did not strike lucky. We greeted a fellow traveler. That's it."

"It doesn't look as if anyone has stopped for the poor man. We should offer him a ride."

"Kathleen, he is not a poor man, and we are not picking up a hitchhiker."

"Have you ever picked up a hitchhiker before?"

"Never."

"Didn't you say that you were ready to embrace new experiences?"

"Not that kind of new experience." Martha wiped her fingers and scrunched up the bag. "Are you done?"

"The more I think about it, the more I'm convinced this is a wonderful idea."

"The more I think about it, the more I'm convinced it's the worst idea in the world."

"But it would cheer me up. Would you really deny a frail old lady some happiness in what might be her final days?"

Martha rolled her eyes. "I do not respond to emotional blackmail. And if you carry on trying to pair me up with every man we pass, these will be your final days."

"This convinces me that we need to be spontaneous. I hate to see you so suspicious." Kathleen patted her on the arm. "We never really know anyone, dear. You and I both have experience that supports that."

"Mmm." Martha took some photographs with her phone.

"All we can do is take a chance."

"Kathleen, this is ridiculous." She lowered her phone. "All we know about him is that he 'needed a change of scenery.' Maybe he murdered someone. He could be on the run."

"But have you seen him close up? Those eyes." Kathleen finished eating and scrunched up the bag. "What a way to go. And anyway, you're lucky enough to be traveling with a woman who beaned an intruder with a skillet, so you should feel very safe."

"I think that experience might have given you a slightly overinflated opinion of your own self-defense skills."

"This is my trip—it's up to me who I invite."

"I'm the driver. I could go on strike." And then Martha realized she was using all the wrong arguments. "Anyway, there is no room in the car. He tops six foot. Long legs. Not that I've been looking—"

"I've seen you looking."

Martha sighed. "There is no way he is fitting in the back."

"He doesn't have to. I will fit in the back perfectly and he can sit in the front with you."

"I'd be trapped with him."

"Exactly! You never know—the two of you could be a perfect match."

"That would be a miracle."

"A good relationship doesn't require a miracle. It requires the right person at the right time." Kathleen slid her sunglasses onto her nose. "Onward."

12

KATHLEEN

ST. LOUIS~DEVIL'S ELBOW~SPRINGFIELD

Kathleen closed her eyes and pretended to sleep.

She hadn't been exactly honest with Martha when she'd said she was fine. She didn't feel fine at all. Her insides were all churned up, and it had nothing to do with the pulled pork sandwich. Thoughts and feelings that she'd managed to outrun for so many years had all finally caught up with her. They seeped past all the barriers and buried themselves in her brain where she couldn't shake them off.

It was that conversation with Martha that had started it all. Why hadn't she shut it down?

It was Martha, of course. Her warmth and kindness had a way of melting all Kathleen's usual reserve. *Shrimp on ice.* No matter how serious the topic, Martha still managed to make Kathleen laugh.

And now she couldn't stop thinking about Ruth.

Should she have opened those letters?

"Are you all right back there, Kathleen?"

Martha glanced at her in the mirror, a dangerous glint visible in her eyes before she covered them with sunglasses. "Not too squashed?"

"Never better." Her discomfort was caused by something less easy to fix than a lack of legroom in the rear seat.

She knew Martha was frustrated that she'd offered Josh a ride, but she was willing to weather her new friend's disapproval if it meant coaxing Martha out of the little protective bubble she'd formed around herself. Kathleen recognized fear when she saw it. She didn't think for one moment that Josh was a serial killer, or a threat of any kind. And the last thing Martha needed for the next month was to be closeted with an eighty-year-old, however much they enjoyed each other's company. The girl needed youth and excitement.

But so far Martha had shown no inclination to engage their new passenger in conversation, so if this was going to happen then it was all up to Kathleen.

Fortunately she'd always been a skilled interviewer. There was no reason why she couldn't use those skills to discover more about Josh.

"Vermont, you say. I've never been to Vermont, although I am partial to maple syrup. Is it home for you, Josh?"

"Home is California. I was visiting friends in Vermont."

"And Route 66 has always been a dream of yours?"

It took him a long time to answer. "It's something I've thought about doing for a while, but it's taken me until now to do it."

Kathleen sensed there was something he wasn't saying.

Interesting.

Relieved to have something to focus on rather than her own problems, she waited for Martha to follow the obvious lead and ask why it had taken him until now, but Martha was silent, her eyes fixed on the road.

A silent Martha was concerning.

Kathleen could almost hear her saying, *You invited him to join us, so you can make the conversation.*

She sighed. It seemed she was going to have to do all the work.

"What made you suddenly decide to make this dream a reality?"

"A number of things, but it culminated in a friend pointing out that I hadn't taken a vacation in three years."

"Three *years?* Why?"

"I was busy working. I put my career first."

So he was a man able to show commitment, Kathleen thought. That wasn't a bad quality to have, providing he was able to apply it to other situations across his life and not only work.

"Your boss didn't encourage you to take time off?"

There was a pause. "He didn't see the point of vacations. He was—focused."

"What job do you do?"

"I work in tech. I'm a computer engineer."

Kathleen had only a vague notion of what that involved. She certainly knew too little to feel confident engaging him in conversation on the specifics. "No doubt he was one of those driven types who set up a business from his bedroom at college."

Josh laughed. "That's exactly what he did."

"And no doubt upset his parents by not graduating."

"No, he did graduate. He had too much respect for his parents and the sacrifices they'd made to throw that away."

"He can't be all bad then." Kathleen was smug that she was managing to converse despite her lamentable lack of knowledge. "But I'm sure someone like that would make a difficult boss. Probably expected everyone around him to have the same drive and commitment to growing the company."

"He had a degree of tunnel vision, that's for sure."

"Ambitious?"

"Definitely."

Kathleen made a clucking sound. "He sounds

rather formidable. No doubt he ran a cold, macho-like culture and treated people like machines. Balance is so important in life." Not that she'd had much balance when she was young. She'd worked too. She'd put her work above every-thing, including intimacy. But that was different. She'd had a bad experience. Work had been her safe place. "But here you are taking a vacation, so what happened? Did his company eventually go bust? Was he part of the tech bubble?"

"The company was successful. Beyond his wildest dreams."

Kathleen studied his profile thoughtfully. Then she tried to see Martha's face but being in the back put her at a disadvantage. "But he still didn't feel his staff should embrace work-life balance? Well, I respect your decision to leave. That can't have been easy. Perhaps that will make him think, although people like that don't tend to care too much about staff. And now you're taking some time out to decide what you're going to do, and this road trip will give you the thinking time."

"Something like that."

Kathleen reached out and gave him a reassuring pat on the shoulder. "I'm sure you won't have trouble finding another job when you're ready. My granddaughters tell me that tech is the place to be these days."

He smiled. "Tell me about your grand-daughters."

The road from Devil's Elbow passed through rolling hills, the landscape thick with trees.

"My daughter has twin girls. Alice and Caitlin. They're teenagers and at a difficult age, which doesn't make things easy." Poor Liza. What was she doing at the moment? Probably cooking a meal for someone or ferrying them across town to some commitment or other. "They spend their lives glued to their phones, messaging friends. In my day we saw friends in person, but I accept that I'm from a different age. A few more years and they'll put me in a museum."

"You're traveling Route 66 at the age of eighty. I don't think you're ready for a museum yet. Do you see a lot of your granddaughters?"

"Not as much as I used to. When they were very young they loved visiting. My home is near the sea, so they'd come with their buckets and spades and make castles and eat ice cream. As they grew older they were more reluctant to leave friends behind. These days it tends to be my daughter and her husband who visit." And her concern about that had simmered in the back of her mind since that journey to the airport.

She felt a flutter of anxiety. "Martha, when we reach our next destination perhaps you would be kind enough to send another photo and message to my daughter. Perhaps even an email."

Martha glanced in the mirror. "Of course. I've

been sending her loads of photos. We've got a relationship going."

It was the first thing she'd said since they'd left Devil's Elbow. Kathleen was relieved to know she was at least alive, and not only because she was the one driving.

"I expect you know a great deal about social media, Josh? Martha here has started a social media account for us, cataloguing our adventures. It's beyond me, of course, but it's all rather fun. We're photographing and videoing our trip across America. In my youth I presented a rather popular travel show called *The Summer Seekers.*"

"You did?" Josh turned, intrigued. "Tell me about it."

And so she did, and it turned out that Josh was a remarkably good listener, something she'd always considered to be an important quality in a man. Hopefully Martha could see that.

Was she going to talk at all?

Josh was obviously wondering the same because he glanced at her. "How about you, Martha? Are you taking the summer off?"

"I am."

With the exception of the early part where she was becoming accustomed to the car, Martha had talked nonstop since they'd started this trip but now, when Kathleen needed her to engage Josh in conversation, she was silent. "Martha is also taking some thinking time," she said, "so the two of you have that in common. Josh, you seem like a well-connected young man. Perhaps you have some career tips for Martha. She's looking for a change of direction."

Martha kept her gaze fixed on the road. "Don't need anyone's help, thank you." She slammed her foot on the brake as a car pulled out. "Fox!"

Josh looked confused, and Kathleen gave a weary sigh.

"Don't ask."

Josh obviously realized that Martha wasn't going to engage, because he turned back to Kathleen.

"And how about you, Kathleen? This is an ambitious trip for—" He broke off and Kathleen waved a hand.

"For someone of my age? No need to be tactful. It is ambitious in some ways, but I have dear Martha who is a wonderful driver and has kept me entertained with her chatter—" She emphasized the word slightly, in case Martha had forgotten how to speak.

"What happens when you reach California?"

Kathleen's insides gave another lurch. Ruth. For a moment she'd forgotten, but now all those thoughts, doubts, questions and regrets were back.

What if . . .

Were there two more torturous words in the English language?

She'd never been a person to dwell on "what-if" but for some reason she felt as if she was unraveling. It was all Martha's fault. Being with her had encouraged an openness that was new to Kathleen, and now she didn't know how to close herself down again.

Josh was waiting for an answer, and she truly had no idea what answer to give.

"Kathleen hasn't decided what to do yet." Martha finally spoke, filling the silence. "She may spend a little time soaking up the Californian sunshine. Part of the joy of this trip is having a flexible schedule."

Kathleen felt a rush of gratitude and affection. Dear girl. She knew exactly what Kathleen was thinking.

Josh seemed satisfied with the answer. "California is my home state, so if you need any suggestions of places to visit while you're there, don't hesitate to ask."

"Most kind of you." Kathleen secured her scarf. "Do you have particular places you're planning to see on this trip?"

"The Grand Canyon. I'm embarrassed to admit I've never seen it."

"You shouldn't be embarrassed. You've obviously spent too much time working, thanks to your unfeeling boss." She glanced at Martha, but the girl had returned to a state of silence. "I'm pleased you're finally able to explore the world a little. Don't rush to get back to work. I was lucky of course, because travel was my work, so I did both."

They drove through another small hamlet where the smell of barbecue filled the air, and gradually they left the hills and forest behind them.

By the time they arrived at their stop for the night Kathleen was tired and her mind was floating off in directions that normally she didn't permit. Should she contact Ruth? No, that would be most unwise. Particularly as she hadn't even opened the letters.

She should have read them. Or at least brought them with her. But the knowledge that they were in her bag would have weighed her down. This trip had been about making the most of the time she had, not about confronting the past.

Was Ruth even in California? Martha had said she would look her up, but really there was no way Kathleen would encourage that.

But what if she arrived home, read the letters, and then wished she'd reached out to Ruth?

She felt a rush of panic that she'd done the wrong thing.

Martha parked. "Are you all right, Kathleen?"

"Never better." For the first time she wished she hadn't invited Josh to join them. She might have had a short nap in the car as they were driving. As it was she was exhausted with keeping up

252

jolly conversation, and the past kept nagging at her, ending all hope of relaxation.

To her mortification she needed Martha's help to get out of the back of the car.

"It's the angle," Martha said gently, supporting Kathleen so that she could lever herself from the back seat.

"It's the age." Kathleen straightened and felt the world spin. She clung to Martha.

"Kathleen?" Holding her tightly, Martha aimed the key at the trunk and opened it. "Josh? Could you bring our luggage so that I can help Kathleen inside?"

Kathleen tried to steady herself. "I've been sitting too long, that's all. My body has seized up. I need a moment, and then I'll be fine."

"You prebooked?" Josh unloaded their luggage. "Why don't you let me go and sort out your rooms. I'll bring your key back. Save you an extra walk to the reception desk."

Was she really going to let a spell of dizziness stop her enjoying her trip? No, she wasn't.

"Thank you, but we can manage. Are you staying here too, Josh?"

"That was my plan." He picked up their cases. "And I'm grateful for the ride this far. Can I buy you dinner as a thank-you?"

All Kathleen wanted to do was lie down, but she knew that if she suggested they went without her Martha would accuse her of matchmaking.

But Martha was looking at her with concern. "I think what we need right now is to settle into our rooms and have a nice cup of Earl Grey tea before we decide about the evening. How does that sound, Kathleen?"

It sounded idyllic.

Swamped by gratitude, Kathleen slid her arm through Martha's as they walked to reception.

Martha stroked her hand. "We've overdone it. Don't you worry. You'll feel good as new once you've had a nice sit down and a cuppa."

It was remarkable how comfortable she felt with Martha.

Why were things not this easy with her own daughter? Perhaps it was because being with Liza reminded her of her own failings. Whether it was refusing to quietly relocate to a home, giving up bacon or having an emotional conversation, she felt as if she couldn't be what Liza wanted her to be.

Martha was swift and efficient, the staff at the motel were equally efficient and in less than ten minutes Kathleen was in her room, sitting on the edge of the bed while Martha filled the kettle Kathleen had insisted on bringing from home. You couldn't have a proper cup of tea without boiling water, and Kathleen had never trusted the machines in hotel rooms.

It was a pretty room, with views across the fields that stretched behind them. Wherever possible they'd tried to avoid staying in busy towns.

Kathleen relaxed a little. She'd be fine after a rest.

"There." Martha put a cup of Earl Grey on the table near the bed, along with a shortbread biscuit. "I'm right next door, so I'll go and settle in and then check on you in an hour."

There was a tap on the open door. Josh stood there.

"How are you feeling? Is there anything you need?"

"I'm feeling good." To prove it, Kathleen stood up and walked over to him, intending to thank him for his kindness. Halfway across the room she realized she'd made a mistake.

Her surroundings started to spin and she reached out to steady herself only to realize that there was nothing nearby that she could grab.

"Martha!" she cried out and was braced to hit the floor when strong arms caught her and broke her fall.

"You're all right." Josh's voice was calm and rock steady, confirming Kathleen's original suspicion that he was the perfect choice for Martha. She'd always considered a crisis to be a good test of a man's character. A woman's too, come to that.

"Put her on the bed! Kathleen?" Martha was the one who sounded panicked. "Do you have pain anywhere? I'm going to call the doctor."

"You are not going to call the doctor. We're going to wait for this to pass." Kathleen lay back and closed her eyes, but the room swirled alarmingly so she opened them again.

Her tea would grow cold, and she couldn't bear cold tea.

Was this it?

If she died here she'd never make it to California, and she'd never know what was in those letters.

Ruth.

Her old friend was the last thing on her mind before the world went black.

13

LIZA

Liza paused at the entrance of the lane. The beach house was set back from the road, almost impossible to find if you didn't know where the turning was.

The house itself was protected from prying eyes and unwanted camera lenses by large iron gates, equipped with state-of-the-art security. It was the ideal property for someone high profile who didn't want to be found.

The sun burned the back of her neck, and her feet felt hot and uncomfortable in the flat pumps she'd brought from home. The bag she was carrying smacked against her legs.

What was she doing here?

She should forget the whole thing and nurse her embarrassment in private.

She was about to walk away when a voice came through the intercom.

Liza froze.

She pictured herself being watched by a team of guards in a control room.

She'd spent the whole of Sunday feeling ridiculous and fighting the temptation to drive home. But then she decided to do what she was encouraging her children to do—take responsibility.

"Hi. I'm Liza." She stepped closer to the camera and the intercom. "My mother owns the house down the lane—I'm staying there. I'm here to see Finn Cool, although he probably won't—" There was a buzz and the gates opened.

"Oh. Right."

Left with no choice, Liza walked through the gates and they closed smoothly behind her, sealing her inside.

She walked along a winding drive shaded by huge bushes of rhododendrons and azaleas, and finally the house came into view.

It was spectacular, of course, which was nothing less than she would have expected. The front seemed to be constructed almost entirely of glass, with views across sloping gardens which dropped away sharply above a small beach accessible only from this property.

How the other half lived.

She drank in the view for a few moments and then the front door opened.

She'd expected a burly bodyguard or a scary housekeeper. What she hadn't expected was to see Finn Cool himself, lounging against the door frame.

With his lean, handsome face and sleepy eyes he looked as dissolute and dangerous as he had when she'd first seen him in her kitchen, although at the time she'd been too stressed to admire him. He was wearing board shorts and a black T-shirt. His feet were bare and his jaw shadowed. She couldn't work out if he'd just woken up, or hadn't bothered shaving.

"Did you come alone, or are the police following you? If so, I need to open the gate again."

The heat in her cheeks had nothing to do with the sun. "I came to apologize for calling the police. *Obviously* I had no idea—I mean, my mother never mentioned you." There wasn't much she could say to redeem herself so she flourished the bag she'd carried all the way from the cottage. "I brought you a peace offering." She'd spent hours wondering what to give the man who had everything, and in the end settled on something homemade. Probably another mistake, but what was one more amidst so many?

He straightened. "You beat me to it. I was planning on coming over this afternoon to apologize to you."

"You were going to apologize to *me? Why?*"

"For frightening you half to death. Luckily for me you have a gentler disposition than your mother or I'd currently be lying unconscious in hospital with a dent in my skull." He flashed her a smile. "Sorry. I should have rung the doorbell instead of walking into the kitchen, but I didn't know anyone would be there, so I used my key."

He stood back and pushed open the door. "Come in."

"Oh there's no need to—I mean, I wanted to give you—" Distracted by that smile, her words tripped over each other and she walked up the steps to the door and thrust out the bag. "It's a lemon meringue pie, and a batch of my chocolate chip cookies. Two of my specialties. I wasn't sure what to bring." The fact that Finn Cool had a key to her mother's house still hadn't quite sunk in. Why hadn't her mother mentioned it?

"You have more than two specialties? In that case you need to call the police on me more often so I can eat my way through your repertoire. Thank you, Liza. That was thoughtful. I'd say you shouldn't have bothered, but I never turn down food. Come into the kitchen." He took the bag and walked into the house.

Was he being polite? Surely the last thing he wanted was a strange woman in his home.

She waited a moment and then followed him, closing the door behind her.

She had to admit she was curious about the house, and it didn't disappoint. Light flowed through a glass atrium high above them, bouncing off acres of white floor tiles. *Italian,* she thought, and almost drooled with envy. The designer had played with space and color, keeping the scheme mostly white but introducing flashes of blue that gave a Mediterranean feel. Liza had more than a passing interest in interior design. She'd even explored the idea of joining Sean in his practice, but in the end they'd decided that two people working in the same business wasn't a good idea. And teaching had meant she was able to spend more time with the girls.

But still she occasionally hankered after it. She was incapable of walking into a property and not immediately imagining how she would change the interior.

But she'd change nothing about this house.

It was a modern architectural masterpiece. Sean would have appreciated the simplicity.

Thinking of Sean created a pang. The state of her marriage was never far from her mind, gnawing at her like toothache.

All she'd had from him this morning since that one conversation was a quick text. Have you seen my blue shirt?

It had made her question whether she'd been right to delay the conversation about the way she was feeling. At some point she needed to be honest with her family, and also tell them that things needed to change. They weren't mind readers. If they were, then they wouldn't still be texting her expecting her to sort out all their trivial problems. But the moment she did that any chance of having breathing space would be over and she badly wanted some time to herself. She deserved this!

So she'd ignored Sean's message, and the two from Caitlin asking about laundry.

Not one of them had asked how she was.

What would she have said?

I'm worried I might be on the verge of a breakdown, and by the way I had to call the police because there was an intruder in my kitchen but don't worry about any of it. I'll handle it myself because that's what I always do.

Pushing thoughts of her family out of her head, she followed Finn Cool through to a large airy kitchen.

"This is perfect." Although if she tried to cook here she'd burn everything because she'd be looking at the ocean views. "I feel terrible about what happened. I never should have called the police."

"You were right to call them. Particularly after what happened with your mother." He put the bag on the countertop. "No harm done. I had to sign a few autographs and smile for a few selfies, that's all. I've dealt with worse."

"I had no idea you knew my mother."

"She's a very discreet woman is Kathleen. Also a total badass." He pulled a couple of plates out of one of the cupboards. "We've been friends for a while. If I was a few years older I'd marry her and believe me that's a compliment because I'm not the marrying type."

She wasn't one to read gossipy newspapers or

magazines, but even she knew he had an active and interesting social life. Which made it all the more bizarre that he was friends with her eighty-year-old mother.

"I can't believe she asked you to feed her cat." Only her mother would ask a celebrity to walk round to her house and open cat food.

"Popeye and I are best friends. He often visits."

"You know Popeye?"

He grinned. "There aren't many one-eyed, three-legged cats around here. I consider him an example of resilience at its finest. Nothing stops him exploring, not even my dogs. Popeye is boss of the world." As he said the words there was a cacophony of barking, a blur of tan and black and three large German shepherd dogs streaked up from the bottom of the garden to the house.

Liza eyed them nervously as they slithered across the tiles. "Are they going to take revenge on me for calling the police?"

"More likely to lick you to death or slide into you. They hate these tiles." He snapped his fingers and the dogs skidded to a halt, tongues lolling as they looked at him stupidly. "Sit."

They sat, one with more reluctance than the others.

Liza looked at the rows of sharp teeth. "I'm starting to understand why you don't need body-guards."

"These boys are a deterrent, that's for sure."

263

He crouched down and made a fuss of the dogs and she did the same, although a little more cautiously.

One of them rolled over, exposing his tummy, and she rubbed it gently. "They're gorgeous. What are they called? Not that I'm going to be able to tell them apart."

"One, Two and Three. Seemed a simple way of naming them at the time. Don't be fooled by the size of them. They're terrified of Popeye." He rose to his feet and so did she.

"We're all a little terrified of Popeye. He's the most judgmental cat I've ever met. And very emotionally distant." *Like her mother.* "And talking of meeting, how did you get to know my mother?"

"Long story. We need food for that." He washed his hands, then opened the bag she'd handed him and explored the contents. "I haven't had a lemon meringue pie since I was a kid. I'll cut us both a slice and we can take it onto the terrace."

"I made it for you."

"I believe in indulgence at all times, but even I can't eat an entire pie myself."

"You're on your own here? I assumed you'd have lots of staff."

"I'm the only permanent resident, although I am subject to a regular invasion from London. My long-suffering housekeeper occasionally visits and rescues me from the depths of my own mess. Her husband does the gardens and the pool. They live in the cottage five-minutes walk from here. They're around, but not around if that makes sense. They treat me like a son, which is lucky for me." He cut large slices. "This looks incredible." His accent was somewhere between an American drawl and a soft Irish lilt. She decided she could listen to him talk all day.

"The eggs are organic. They're from the Anderson farm." Why on earth had she told him that? He probably couldn't be less interested.

"I never eat eggs from anywhere else." The laughter in his eyes made her flustered.

"You're teasing me."

"I'm not. My freezer is also full of their organic, grass-fed beef. I virtually subsidize that place, but still he takes pleasure in driving his tractor at a snail's pace and making me late for everything. He's determined to slow the pace of my life from turbo to tractor. He has the biggest scowl in the West Country."

She'd expected Finn Cool to be aloof, and to try and get rid of her as quickly as possible. She hadn't expected him to be warm and approachable. She'd smiled more since she'd walked into his house than she had in the past week. *Month?*

His phone rang but he ignored it. "Drink?"

"Oh—it's far too early for me but thank you."

"I was thinking tea or coffee." He pulled two

mugs from a cupboard. "Despite the scurrilous rumors you might hear in the village, I do try and spend at least part of the day sober."

"I didn't mean—" She backed away, embarrassed again. "I need to leave. This is too awkward."

"You don't need to leave. You need to relax. Come into the garden. It's impossible to frown while listening to the sounds of the ocean and indulging in lemon meringue pie. Cappuccino? My machine makes the best cup you'll ever drink."

She accepted his offer and a few minutes later was sitting on a large terrace with the sun on her face and the sea breeze gently lifting the edges of her hair. Below them was the swimming pool, and beyond that the sea.

Palm trees shaded one side of the terrace and the dogs sped off across the lawn, rolling over each other as they played.

"It always amazes me that palm trees grow here in Cornwall. My mother has the same in the corner of her garden."

"I know. She's given me a lot of advice on this garden. Even a few cuttings."

Her mother had given cuttings to a rock star.

It felt unreal. She, Liza Lewis, was sitting in what was probably the most expensive house in the west of England, with Finn Cool.

The twins would have been impressed. Except

266

they wouldn't have taken the time to ask her what she was doing.

It felt good to have this tiny slice of herself that no one else knew about.

"This place is incredible. Has my mother ever been here?"

"Many times." He sliced off a piece of lemon meringue.

"I had no idea. And what I don't understand," Liza said, "is why she'd make such a point of insisting I come down here to keep an eye on the cat, when she knew you were keeping an eye on the cat. Why didn't she tell me?"

"That, I can't answer." He devoured the lemon meringue pie as if he hadn't seen food for a month. "Could she have had another reason for wanting you to be here?" Dark glasses made it impossible to see his expression, but she had a feeling he was watching her closely.

She thought about the tense few nights her mother had spent with them before she'd driven her to the airport. She tried to remember exactly when her mother had asked her to keep an eye on the cat.

It had been at the last minute, after a conversation about how Liza put everyone else first.

Could her mother have been intervening? No, she wouldn't do that.

Would she?

The idea settled in her mind. "It's possible that

she wanted to encourage me to take a break. And if she'd told me you were keeping an eye on Popeye, I wouldn't have come. Popeye was the excuse. I haven't told her I'm here yet. I need to call her."

Her mother had noticed that something was wrong. She'd cared enough to try and help, even if her methods were a little clumsy.

She was surprised by how good it felt.

A bird skimmed the swimming pool and fluttered away again. Bees hummed in the bushes and a bright blue butterfly fluttered around the terracotta pots that surrounded the terrace.

She felt the sun burning her face and felt more peaceful and relaxed than she had in a long time.

Finn scraped the last of the crumbs from his plate. "You need an excuse to take a break?"

"I'm not good at it." She picked up her fork and took a small mouthful of her own pie, savoring the sharp, lemony flavor.

"What is it you do? No, wait—" he lifted a finger "—let me guess. You're in charge of a major corporation and without you to keep it afloat thousands of people would lose their jobs."

This time he was definitely teasing her.

"I'm an art teacher."

He pushed his plate away. "I'm surprised. You have a corporate look about you. I see you working in a glass skyscraper in the city, not a studio. I wouldn't have guessed artist in a million years."

"I'm not really an artist. Not anymore." Laying claim to that title would have made her feel like a fraud. "I haven't painted anything in a long time. I teach others to paint." She taught them about space and form, about tone and texture, about color.

"But presumably there was a time when you painted yourself?"

"Yes. I loved it."

"Then why don't you consider yourself to be an artist?"

Liza considered. "An artist is someone who creates art, and I'm not doing that."

"Why not?"

The question created a layer of intimacy that was at odds with their brief and casual acquaintance.

"It was squeezed out by other things. And you'll probably say that we can always make time for something we want to do, but—"

"No, I understand. Creativity requires space and time, and those two things are in short supply in the world we live in. Your brain is crushed under the weight of mundane demands." He steered a wasp away from the table. "Being overwhelmed can zap every last drop of creativity from your cells."

How could this man who didn't know her,

understand so perfectly? "You sound as if you know."

"Why do you think I'm living here? Although I also have the advantage of being intrinsically selfish, which helps." He gave a half smile and stood up. "Come with me. I want to show you something."

She followed him across the terrace, down steps to the tranquil pool area and then across the lawns to the sea. A small sandy path led steeply down to the small beach protected on both sides by cliffs. Here the Atlantic Ocean crashed onto the shore, surging forward and then retreating. The rhythm was mesmerizing, the wildness a contrast to the sheltered stretch of beach on the estuary near Oakwood Cottage with its sun-drenched sand dunes.

"I didn't even know this existed."

"It was the reason I bought the house." He headed down the path and she followed.

Halfway down they passed a life preserver, secured to a post.

He gestured to it. "In case someone goes for a midnight dip during one of the many wild, drunken parties I'm rumored to throw between these walls."

She trod carefully, trying not to slip. "I've seen the way you drive your car, so at least some of the rumors are true."

He flashed her a grin. "Cars are my vice."

"The roads around here are frustratingly twisty and narrow for a fast car."

"The problem isn't the roads. It's the other drivers."

The dogs bounded past her and would have knocked her off balance if he hadn't shot out a hand to steady her.

"Sorry. They have no concept of civilized behavior. They forget we don't all balance on four legs." He kept hold of her hand as they headed down the path and she was conscious of his fingers, wrapped tightly around hers. She felt as if she should tug her hand away, but left it there until they reached the bottom of the path.

Liza slid off her shoes and felt instant relief as her bare feet touched the soft sand. The beach was secluded and private. It was like stepping into another world.

"Do people ever climb over the cliffs?"

"No. Too steep. They try coming across the fields but fortunately the farmer keeps his bull two fields across in that direction—" he waved an arm "—so that's a kind of built-in security. They can come by road, but I have Kathleen to protect me from that."

Liza closed her eyes briefly and breathed in salt air and sunshine. Her usual daily view was buildings and streets choked with traffic and people. Her soundtrack was engines, car horns, airplanes overhead. Now there was nothing but sea, sky and seabirds.

She opened her eyes. "How does my mother protect you?"

"She has numerous interesting strategies. She misdirects people. Sends them across country, or to the next village. Occasionally she pretends to be deaf and lets them shout louder and louder until they give up." He took off his glasses. His hair was tangled and tousled from the breeze, his eyes were bright with laughter. "She's never told you?"

"Would it damage your ego to tell you that she barely mentions you?"

His smile deepened. "It would confirm my suspicion that she's probably the best neighbor on the planet."

Liza rolled up the bottom of her trousers. The pale skin around her feet and ankles was evidence that she hadn't stayed still long enough for her skin to see the sun. She needed to do something about that, and she definitely needed to do something about her wardrobe which was entirely unsuited to relaxation or beach life.

"How often do you see her?"

"Most weeks when I'm here." He stooped to pick up a shell. "We drink coffee in her garden, or she comes up here to swim in the pool and we have a glass of something cold afterward."

"Every week?" Liza couldn't believe what

she was hearing. "She swims in your pool?"

"She used to swim twice a day in the sea, but after she had that dizzy spell I persuaded her that the pool was safer."

Dizzy spell?

If she asked him for details he'd think she was a terrible daughter. And there was no point in asking herself why her mother hadn't mentioned it. She would have been afraid Liza would have lectured her on safety. And no doubt she would have done exactly that.

Maybe she *was* a terrible daughter. She'd been trying to help and protect, but in doing so had cut herself off from a large part of her mother's life. Her constant urging to stay safe didn't have any impact on her mother, who always did exactly as she pleased. All it did was encourage her to keep things from Liza, to avoid any fuss. But it seemed she didn't keep things from Finn.

"She took your advice and stopped swimming in the sea?"

"Not at first, but I told her that if her body were to wash up on the shore one evening she might ruin one of my beach parties. She laughed and agreed to use the pool instead." He glanced at her. "Glenys, my housekeeper, is always around when she uses the pool so she's safe enough."

Liza tried to think of a time she and her mother had shared a conversation that made them both laugh.

"You're fond of her."

He shrugged. "I don't have parents or grand-parents alive. I guess I see Kathleen as someone older and wiser."

"Really?" That wasn't how she saw her mother at all. "I tend to think of her as reckless. She gives me constant anxiety attacks."

"I guess it's different when it's your mother." He walked to the water. "Has she always been the way she is?"

"Stubborn?"

"I was going to say adventurous. Bold."

"I suppose so, yes."

"Must have made for an interesting childhood."

It had made for a lonely childhood. But that wasn't something she intended to discuss with Finn Cool.

"I always got good grades in geography. I'm the person you want on your team in a pub quiz."

"I watched a few of her old shows on the internet. Incredible. She had such presence."

She hadn't watched *The Summer Seekers* since she was a child. They reminded her of absences. "She has them all on DVD."

"You're kidding." The breeze had blown strands of hair across his face. "But they would have been shot on 16mm film, surely?"

"I don't know. All I know is that they gave them to her on DVD as a gift on her sixtieth birthday."

He raised an eyebrow. "That's quite a gift. On

274

the other hand she was something of a legend. I bet they all adored her. She must have been fun to work with. Are those DVDs in the house?"

Was he expecting her to invite him over? And how would she feel watching them? She'd always felt mildly resentful of *The Summer Seekers*. As a child she'd felt it was competition for her mother's time and affection. "I don't know where she keeps them, but I can ask."

"You should keep them under lock and key. They're probably collector's items." He turned to look at the sea, his gaze fixed on the horizon. "She knows how to live life. And she never conforms to society's expectations. She was presenting long after other people would have been pushed aside, presumably because she was irreplaceable at the time. And look at her now—most people would expect her to be living in some sort of residential accommodation, and she's traveling across America." His shoulders shook with silent laughter. "She's amazing. She knows how to hunt down every last delicious crumb of happiness and devour it. Most people tread those crumbs into the carpet. You must be pleased that she's still so active and engaged in life."

She felt guilty that she'd ever considered trying to persuade her mother to move out of the house. "Her lifestyle causes me anxiety." And she'd been thinking about herself, not Kathleen. In her own way she'd been as selfish as the twins.

"She's lucky to have a caring daughter like you."

Was she? She had a feeling Kathleen would have chosen an adventure-seeking, globe-trotting daughter.

There had been a reason she hadn't wanted Liza to drive her on her special trip.

She changed the subject. "Martha sent me a photo of her sipping cocktails on a roof terrace in Chicago." She showed him the photo on her phone and he took it from her, shaded the screen with his hand.

"Brilliant. Are there more?"

She leaned across and swiped. "Martha took a photograph of the car."

His smile widened. "Well, dammit—she went ahead and rented the Ford Mustang."

"You knew she was planning to rent a sports car?"

"She asked me about cars. Wanted to know what I'd rent if I was doing that trip. Easy enough to answer, because I've done that trip—in that car." He handed the phone back to her. "She'll have the best time. So who is Martha?"

"Martha is a stranger who she hired without even checking references. Typical of my mother." But in fact Martha had proved to be thoughtful. She was sending photos every day, along with amusing updates and videos. It seemed her mother had chosen her companion well. "You seem to know a lot about her trip."

He hesitated. "She didn't talk to you about the planning?"

"No. I kept waiting for her to ask for help because she hates the internet, but she never did." She paused. "What are you not telling me?"

"She's discreet. I feel I should be too." He rubbed his hand over his jaw. "My team helped her with the arrangements. As you say, she's not that comfortable with the internet."

"You booked it? Why didn't she ask me? I would have done it."

"I offered. I would have been offended if she'd refused."

"I suppose that explains why she stayed in the Presidential Suite in Chicago."

"They gave her that? I hoped they would, but it always depends who else is staying of course."

"It was thoughtful of you." She tried not to be hurt that her mother hadn't turned to her for help. "I misjudged you. I thought you were a complete rogue."

"Rogue? I've never actually heard someone use that word outside a costume drama." He leaned closer, a wicked gleam in his eyes. "I am a rogue, Liza. I'm selfish, and if I've done something that helped someone it probably benefited me too."

She couldn't imagine how helping her mother could have helped him.

They walked across the sand until they reached the water's edge.

"Tide is coming in. I could sit here and watch it all day. Sometimes I do just that." He stooped and picked up another shell. "I hadn't written anything in a year when I found this place."

"You mean music?" Liza was embarrassed that she knew more about his reputation than his music.

"Music and lyrics." He turned the shell over and rubbed at the sandy interior. "It's a funny thing. You can sit forever and try and force yourself to produce something. Hard work always plays a part, but in the end it's about a magical something that's as delicate as the new shoots of a plant. And you can't force that. You're an artist. You understand."

Oh yes, she understood. "I've told you, I'm a teacher. I don't think of myself as an artist."

"Presumably you thought of yourself that way once?"

She remembered the days when she'd slept with her sketchbook under her pillow. She'd wake at dawn, take her paints down to the beach and sit on the cool damp sand trying to capture the beauty of what she was seeing. It had been her way of channeling all the emotions she couldn't express in other ways and it had been the one thing about her that had attracted the interest of her mother. They'd never baked together or done any of the things mothers and daughters often did, but Kathleen had always showed interest in Liza's art. When Liza had won the art award at school her mother had turned up and clapped loudly. Given how rare it was for her mother to appear at a school event, it had been Liza's proudest moment. That award represented so much more than a recognition of her art, which was why she was so disappointed that her mother had packed it away.

"Yes." She forced her attention back to the present. "I thought of myself that way."

"What medium did you work in?"

"Everything. Early on I painted in oils, but later I tended to paint more with watercolor and then pastels. Acrylic, occasionally. I dabbled in mixed medium and I still love to sketch."

"Do you have any photographs of your work? I'd love to see what you do."

No one had showed interest in her paintings for years. "I don't—oh wait—" She brought up a website on her phone. "Years ago I painted a series of oils that they exhibited in a small gallery near here. They still have the photos on their website. Goodness knows why."

He took the phone from her and was silent long enough for her to wish she hadn't shown him.

"They're probably not to your taste, and it was a long time ago—"

"These are stunning. I can smell the sea. The

depth of color. And the way you've captured the movement of the waves—I bet they all sold?"

"Yes."

He handed her phone back. "Do you accept commissions?"

"I told you—I haven't painted anything for years."

"So maybe it's time. And what better place to start again?" He rubbed at the shell in his hand. "Do you miss painting?"

"Yes, although I hadn't thought about it in a while." But now she was thinking about it. "It would feel selfish to paint when life is so busy."

"I would call it self-care. We need to make time for the things that are important to us. Here—" He handed her the shell. "Inspiration. You can put it in your studio."

She slipped the shell into her pocket, feeling as if he'd given her something special and significant. "I don't have a studio."

"Where do you prefer to paint?"

"When I was younger I'd paint in the summerhouse at the bottom of my mother's garden. Big windows. North light. In London, we don't have the space." She wasn't used to talking about herself. Uncomfortable, she bent and rolled her trousers up further and waded into the sea until the water rushed past her ankles. "Is this where you do your best work?"

"Here and Ireland. I have a place in Galway.

280

It belonged to my grandparents on my mother's side."

"You're Irish?"

"American Irish. I was born in California, but we moved back to Galway for a few years when I was in my teens. That was when I got serious about music." The tide swirled up around his calves. "How about you? Your family aren't here with you?"

"No. Sean is an architect and he's in the middle of a big project. And the last thing my twin girls need is to be dragged down to the middle of nowhere." She didn't confess that she'd all but run away from them. Or that the girls would have taken the first high-speed train down to the West Country if they'd thought there was a chance of meeting Finn Cool in person.

"Is that why you look sad?"

"I look sad?"

He lifted his hand and brushed a strand of hair away from her face. "Yes. Or maybe it would be more accurate to say you're trying hard not to look sad. Also, you're not painting. Or drawing. Or sculpting. Whatever your chosen form of expression is. And an artist not creating art, is never a good thing. If that part of you lies dormant, you become a shadow of yourself."

How could this man, this stranger, see something that Sean hadn't?

When had Sean last asked her what she wanted?

When had he last looked at her the way Finn was looking at her now, with such close attention and interest? Was it simply that familiarity blinded a person? Did people see what they'd always seen, rather than what was there?

"I'm tired, that's all." Tired. Hurt. Confused.

"Then it's a good thing Kathleen encouraged you to take a break."

She sensed that some sort of response was needed, so she kept it neutral. "Family life can be all consuming, especially when you have teenagers. I don't expect you to understand."

"I understand. Why do you think I'm single?" His smile was so compelling she found herself smiling back.

"I thought maybe you stayed single so that you could cause the maximum amount of gossip amongst the locals."

"There is pleasure in that, I admit." He waded a little deeper. "Do you want to swim?"

"Here? Now?"

"Why not?"

"I'm not dressed for it."

"I wasn't suggesting you swim in your clothes. Leave them on the beach. Keep your underwear on if you're shy." He said it so casually that for a brief moment she considered it.

Then she came to her senses.

"You're being ridiculous."

"Swimming is the most natural thing in the

282

world. And swimming in the sea is the best feeling. What's ridiculous about it?" He studied her. "Do you ever do anything spontaneous, Liza?"

"No." Although coming to Oakwood Cottage had been spontaneous. And so had her decision to visit him today to apologize in person. Both actions had required her to dig deep. "Occasionally."

"And how does it turn out when you do?" He was standing disturbingly close to her, and she took a step back, flustered by his teasing.

"I'm not sure. Ask me in another week." Instantly she was embarrassed. That made it sound as if she was expecting to meet up regularly.

"I'll hold you to that. Come and swim on my beach. Bring your bathing suit."

"Are you staying here all summer?"

"Until September. Then back to LA."

She couldn't imagine living such a globetrotting lifestyle. "Why hadn't you written for a year?"

He paused. "I lost someone close to me." He turned and strolled back to the shore, leaving her wishing she'd kept silent.

"I'm sorry."

"Don't be. Death is part of life, isn't it? Doesn't make it easier, though." He crouched down by a rock pool. "Seaweed is algae, not a plant. Did you know that?"

"No." She crouched down next to him, but it didn't feel awkward. It felt companionable.

She was ashamed of herself for all the assumptions and judgments she'd made about him.

The pool was teeming with life. Tiny hermit crabs darted under the shelter of the seaweed. Limpets and mussels clung to the rocks, and anemones wafted in the still of the water. She could have watched it for hours, but the tide was licking at their heels, reminding them that it was about to claim back the beach.

Finn rose. "We should go before the tide turns. Having already had a run-in with the police, I don't want to add the coast guard to the list."

"You get an extra-massive lemon meringue pie if you have to call the coast guard on my account."

He laughed. "I'm tempted to throw myself in the water. Who taught you to cook lemon meringue pie?"

"I taught myself. My father was a practical cook—" She paused. "Actually he was a terrible cook. He cooked on the highest heat, so everything was burned. My mother traveled a lot, so I took over. I enjoyed it, but to alleviate boredom I liked to experiment."

They walked across the sand and back to the tiny path that snaked up to the garden.

"Is everything you make as good as your lemon meringue pie?"

"I hope so." The path was steep, and she was already out of breath. She needed to make time in her life to take more exercise.

"In that case, invite me to dinner." He held out his hand and pulled her up the last section of the path.

She hadn't planned to cook, but for some reason she liked the idea of cooking dinner for Finn. She'd had a more honest conversation with him in the last hour than she'd had with anyone in a long time. His company had lifted her mood. Why not? He'd obviously been a good neighbor to her mother and she would thank him by cooking him something delicious.

"Are you allowed out without security?"

"You can protect me." He smiled. "I'll walk across the fields. No one will see me."

The dogs bounded round the garden, snarling, barking and tumbling over each other as they played.

"In that case come for dinner on Friday." It would be a chance to indulge her love of cooking, and she hadn't done that in a while. Meal preparation was usually another chore at the end of a long list. "What's your favorite food?"

He picked up the cups they'd abandoned on the table and carried them through to the kitchen. "I eat everything. I'll bring wine. We can discuss the painting you're going to do for me."

Liza was already planning dinner. The heat

wave was predicted to continue, so they could eat outdoors. She'd use vegetables from her mother's garden.

"Here—" Finn handed her the bag she'd brought. "I'm glad you came over."

So was she. It had stopped her stewing on what was happening with her family and made her think about life in a way she hadn't before.

Feeling lighter, she'd walked back down his drive, along the lane and across the field that led to Oakwood Cottage.

She stayed in the house long enough to put the bag in the kitchen and pick up her car keys.

What had he said?

You have a corporate look about you. I wouldn't have guessed artist in a million years.

Her clothes didn't reflect who she was, they reflected the life she lived.

Having a neutral wardrobe with pieces that matched meant she had fewer decisions to make in a day that was packed with them. What would she choose to wear if she wasn't driving the girls around, rushing to the supermarket, teaching a class?

Determined to find out, she drove to the village, parked the car and walked along the twisty high street until she reached the small boutique that was nestled between a bookshop and the deli.

With a touch of defiance, she pushed open the

door. When was the last time she'd shopped for herself? Too long ago.

The shop was cool and spacious, with mirrors covering two walls. For a moment Liza saw herself as others probably did. Straight blond hair that settled on her shoulders, a narrow face and blue eyes. If she had to find one word to describe her look it would be *ordinary.* Her clothes didn't say "look at me," they said "don't look at me." And it wasn't even as if she intended to send any message at all with the way she dressed. She had enough to do without thinking about messages.

"May I help you?" A young woman with cropped red hair and immaculate makeup emerged from a room at the back. "We have more stock in the back if you can't find your size."

Liza felt a moment of insecurity, and dismissed it. She was an artist. She knew color. She knew shape. She knew what looked good. She didn't need help with that. All she needed to do was give herself permission to be that person and allow her creative side some freedom. It had been suppressed for far too long.

She headed to the racks of clothes, studied each piece and then selected a few items. And then a few more.

When she finally left the store half an hour later, she was carrying two large bags filled with a selection of pretty sundresses, linen tops in pastel shades, shorts, shoes, flip-flops for the beach and a pair of oversize silver earrings made by a local artist.

Happy Anniversary, Liza.

She'd tried on outfit after outfit. Even trying them on made her feel summery and relaxed, although she couldn't use that excuse for her most extravagant purchase.

"How do you feel about red?" The woman had handed the dress to Liza. "With your coloring, it would look fantastic."

The dress was red, strappy and totally unsuited to her lifestyle.

Liza had bought it, along with a pair of shoes most definitely *not* designed for walking.

Did she feel guilty? No, she felt light-headed and young. Instead of buying a dress to suit her lifestyle, she was going to choose a lifestyle that matched her dress.

Liza walked from the boutique to the delicatessen next door.

One of the advantages of being here on her own was that she didn't have to think about creating meals for a family.

Balancing a basket on her arm, she picked up a stick of crusty French bread still warm from the oven. Then she added Italian ham, a couple of French cheeses, ruby red tomatoes still on the vine and a jar of plump green olives.

"Liza?"

If she could have hidden, she would. She'd

been enjoying her freedom. She didn't want to connect with anyone. She wanted to be able to focus on herself without being considered selfish.

"Oh my, how many years has it been?" The woman looked as if she'd stepped out of a yoga session, her hair in a ponytail and her face shiny and pink. "You *do* recognize me?"

It took Liza a moment. "Angie? Angie!"

"Why so surprised? I live here, remember?"

"You moved to—" She racked her brains. "Boston. Your husband's job?" What was his name? Jeremy? Jonah?

Angie pulled a face. "He's still there. We're divorced."

"I'm sorry." *Life,* Liza thought. It bit chunks out of all of them. "I wish you'd emailed me or called."

"We hadn't been in touch for a while. I didn't want to be the moany friend. It was rough at the time and for a few years after but we've both moved on. John remarried and has a baby."

John.

"A baby?"

Angie rolled her eyes. "You don't have to be tactful. He's fifty-three. My revenge is imagining him dealing with nappies and sleepless nights. Not that he handled those things first time around. Oh Liza—it's so good to see you. Do you have time for a coffee? There's a place around the corner."

Her instinct was to say yes. It was what she did, every time. To every person in her life.

But there were things she wanted to do with her afternoon and evening, and she'd been looking forward to them.

"I would love to catch up, but there are things I have to do this afternoon." Saying it felt hard, but she said it anyway. But she was truly pleased to see Angie. "Why don't you come over to the house tomorrow?"

"To Oakwood? You're staying with your mother?"

"She's driving across America. Route 66."

"Your mother is amazing. Still living the life of *The Summer Seekers*. I can't imagine doing that now, let alone when I'm eighty. So if she's not at home, why are you here?"

I'm escaping. "I'm cat sitting."

"With your girls and Sean?"

"No. They had things they couldn't miss at home."

Once, she and Angie had been as close as sisters. They'd told each other everything. But that was a long time ago. College and life had separated them and then Angie had met John and moved to Boston and gradually their communication had dwindled. They were long past the stage where Liza felt comfortable exposing the details of her life to scrutiny.

She felt a sudden pang. She missed the deep

friendship she and Angie had once had. The sort where you laughed until your sides ached and knew everything there was to know about one another. They'd shared clothes, stories and makeup. When Sean had kissed her, Angie had been the first person she'd told.

Once she'd had children her friendships had changed in nature and tended to be connected with lifestyle. At first, the common factor had been babies, then it had been school. It was friendship of sorts, but not the deep, authentic friendship she'd once enjoyed with Angie. Perhaps she'd treasured it all the more because she didn't have that closeness with her mother.

Still, those days were long gone and she and Angie were different people now, their bonds torn by time, distance and life experience.

"Come tomorrow. We'll take a picnic to the beach. We could swim if we're feeling brave. We have so much to catch up on. Where are you living?"

"In my mother's house." Angie selected a jar of jam from the shelf. "My home, now. She died last year and I came over to sell it, but then decided to keep it. It's small, but there's room for Poppy to come and stay. Did you have more children?"

"No. The twins kept me busy!"

"I can imagine." Angie gave Liza a hug. "It's good to see you. Until tomorrow."

Liza felt Angie's hair brush her cheek, breathed in her floral scent.

She clung for a moment. She missed friendship. She missed intimacy.

Having hauled her many purchases back to the car, she arrived back at Oakwood Cottage feeling a thousand times better than she had when she'd started that morning.

She unpacked the food, put a selection onto a plate and the rest in the fridge.

Feeling decadent, she opened a bottle of wine, poured herself a glass and took it out onto the patio.

Popeye sat there, licking his fur. He paused long enough to throw her a look of disdain, and then carried on his grooming ritual.

"Have you always been this emotionally distant, or have you learned it from my mother?" Liza sat down, feeling summery in her new shorts and T-shirt, her feet finally comfortable in pretty flip-flops.

Her mother was right. She needed to try and capture this light, holiday feeling all year round, not only for a few weeks in August.

The rest of the afternoon and evening stretched ahead.

She should probably use the time cleaning her mother's house, but she had no intention of doing that. The dust could stay where it was. She had better things to do.

She noticed a missed call from her mother on her phone and felt a flicker of concern. Her mother rarely called her. Liza was the one who did the calling.

She sat in a shady spot on the patio and sipped her wine while she waited for her mother to answer. When she did, her voice was faint and a little groggy.

"Mum? Did I wake you?" Had she calculated the time difference incorrectly? "Is everything all right?"

"Everything is better than all right. I'm living the dream."

Something about her voice didn't sound quite right. It was unsettling to realize she didn't know her mother well enough to be able to read her. "Are you sure? You called me." *And that's not like you.*

"I'm sure. Do you know how long I've wanted to do Route 66? Martha is taking wonderful photographs."

"I'm enjoying them. Please thank her. Where are you exactly?"

There was a pause and Liza heard muffled voices in the background before her mother came back on the line.

"Martha tells me we're staying somewhere outside Springfield, and today we're driving through Kansas. How about you? Are you calling me from the car while you take the twins somewhere?"

"I'm not in the car." Liza stretched out her legs, admiring her new sandals. "I'm drinking wine on your patio, having enjoyed an excellent lunch from the deli in the village that you recommended."

"You're in Oakwood?"

"Why so surprised? You asked me to come here, remember?"

"Yes, but I never thought—" Her mother's voice tailed off. "You went to the deli? Try the mini goats' cheese tartlets—they're divine. And Sean would love the chocolate brownie."

"Sean isn't here, but I'll buy some for myself next time I'm there."

There was a pause. "You're on your own?"

"Yes. I came to check on Popeye, as I promised you I would." She glanced at the cat but saw nothing even vaguely approaching gratitude in its feline features. "And yesterday I found a stranger in your kitchen."

"No! Another intruder?"

"Not exactly, but I didn't figure that part out until after I'd called the police. Why didn't you tell me you knew Finn? And that you'd asked him to feed the cat?"

"Ah."

"You also forgot to mention that the two of you meet up for coffee regularly and that you swim in his pool several times a week."

"I'm old, Liza. My memory isn't what it was."

294

Liza raised her eyes to the sky. "Says the woman who is currently crossing America in a sports car."

"It's every bit as wonderful as I thought it would be."

"Good. But why did you ask me to come to keep an eye on Popeye, when someone else was already doing it?"

"It was a spontaneous thing. I thought you needed a rest and sea air. I knew you wouldn't do it for yourself, but I knew you'd do it for me if I asked. Because that's the kind of person you are. And now you're going to tell me off for being a hypocrite and interfering even though I never allow the same interference from you."

Liza grinned. "Actually I was going to thank you."

"Oh?"

"Yes. For encouraging me to do something I wouldn't have done without a nudge." She watched as Popeye basked in the sunshine. She never made time in her life to do nothing. Why was it that a busy life was valued more highly than a quiet one? She'd spent so long sprinting between tasks that she'd forgotten how to stroll. A moment of inaction made her feel stressed and guilty.

"I wasn't sure you'd do it. Or at least I thought you'd take Sean."

Liza finished her wine. "It didn't work out that

way." There was a long pause. "Mum? Are you still there?"

"Yes. Liza—is everything all right?"

It was so unlike her mother to ask that question, Liza almost spilled the wine. "Everything is fine. Why?"

"Nothing. Ignore me."

Why did it feel as if she was missing something? "Are you okay, Mum? Did you call for a reason?"

"I was worried about you, that's all."

Liza had to stop herself checking the number on the phone. Was this really her mother? "You called to check on me? Why? You're not usually a worrier."

"I worry about many things. I worry about leaving this earth before I've done everything I want to do. I worry about Popeye. I worry about whether I should have had that old apple tree pruned."

"Wrong time of year." Liza glanced at its thick gnarly bark and spreading branches. "I'll make a note to remind you in the winter."

"What did you think of Finn?"

"He was—nice." It was an inadequate word, but also a neutral description that wouldn't invite further questioning. If she'd described him as charismatic, charming, or sexy—all of which would have applied—the conversation would have gone down a route she didn't want.

"He's nothing like the rumors."

"I realize that. We had a good chat."

"What about?"

Life. Her painting. Creativity. A hundred things she hadn't talked about in ages.

"Nothing in particular." And as well as being charismatic, he was possibly the world's best listener. "The house is spectacular."

"It's the garden I love. And the pool, of course. And those beautiful dogs."

"I had no idea you knew him. Why didn't you tell me?"

Kathleen laughed. "I thought you'd lecture me on having unsuitable friends."

Liza felt an uncomfortable pressure in her chest. Was she really that bad?

"I'm sorry you feel you have to censor things you tell me. If I nag you, it's because I love you." She knew her mother didn't feel comfortable with demonstrations of affection, but she felt the need to say it.

"I know you do, dear."

Liza held her breath. Waited. Hoped. "Are you still there?"

"Yes, I'm here."

But she wasn't going to say it back.

Liza knew she should have accepted that by now. "How's Martha? Where are you both now? It must be, what—" she checked her phone "—ten o'clock in the morning where you are?"

"Nine. We're about to eat breakfast before we hit the road."

Liza smiled at the description. "I'm pleased you're having fun. By the way, that nice police-woman called. Given that your intruder was drunk, apologetic and apparently had no previous convictions, she thinks it's unlikely that you'll be called in this matter."

"That's it?"

"Seems like it."

"Well, good. Poor man. Now what are you doing this afternoon? Please don't say you'll be cleaning."

"No cleaning. I'm going to the beach with my sketchbook and paints." She hadn't felt the urge to paint in years, but she felt it now. She was excited at the prospect, and that excitement grew as she heard her mother's murmur of approval.

"Promise me something? Whatever that painting looks like, I want you to leave it for me."

"Why?"

"Because I'd like another of my daughter's paintings in the house."

"Another?"

"To go with the others, although they were painted a long time ago of course. Too long. You've neglected that talent."

Her mother had kept her paintings? Liza felt a warm glow and then felt irritated with herself for being so needy.

"I'll leave you a painting."

She didn't mention that Finn had asked if she took commissions, or that he was coming to dinner at the end of the week. "I wanted to ask you—you know those old DVDs of your shows? Where are they? Can I watch them?"

"Why? You were never interested in the show. You always hated that part of my life."

Liza felt a twinge of guilt. She could hardly say that talking to Finn had piqued her desire to look back at the way her mother had been back then. "I was young. I missed my mother, that's all."

There was a silence and she wondered what her mother was thinking.

"Are you still there?"

"Yes! Sorry. I was distracted. The DVDs are in my study. On the shelf, I think, beneath the travel guides. The key to the study is in the drawer by my bed. But Liza—"

"What?"

"Don't tidy. Don't throw anything away."

"I wouldn't do that." She heard clattering in the background. "What's happening?"

"Josh, the hero, has organized breakfast for us. It's just arrived. Goodness, what a feast!"

"Who is Josh?"

"He's someone we picked up yesterday. A delightful man, and adept at procuring breakfast it would seem."

Liza opened her mouth and closed it again. "You—picked up a stranger?"

"Well, he's no longer a stranger. In fact without him I'd—" Her mother stopped talking.

"You'd what?"

"Nothing. I must go. You know I can't bear cold oatmeal. And Liza, about Finn—"

"Yes?"

"Some of the rumors about him *are* true. He is charming, and absurdly handsome of course, but a little on the dangerous side, especially when it comes to women. Be careful."

"I can't believe *you're* telling *me* to be careful. You picked up a hitchhiker!"

"I know. It's only because I don't want you to do something impulsive that you regret."

Why would her mother say that? Liza had been with Sean since she was a teenager. She'd never been at all interested in another man. Had her mother somehow sensed how unsettled she was?

With a final goodbye, Liza put the phone down. Regrets? Right now she had a feeling that she was more likely to regret things she hadn't done than things she had. And she had no reason to feel guilty or uncomfortable. She'd invited Finn to dinner, that was all. It was the neighborly thing to do in the circumstances.

There had been no reason at all to mention it to her mother.

14

MARTHA

SPRINGFIELD~KANSAS~TULSA

Martha put a loaded breakfast tray on the table and pulled it close to the bed while Josh poured coffee. She was grateful for his calm, steady presence. "Why didn't you tell Liza the truth?"

"Because then she would have worried and this is the first time in as long as I can remember that my daughter hasn't seemed anxious. She's staying in the cottage on her own. Taking her paints to the beach. I have no intention of saying anything that will draw a gray cloud over her blue-sky day."

Martha hoped it was the right decision. She still felt shaken up after the night before. The responsibility weighed on her. If she were Liza, she'd want to know. But she wasn't family, so she had to respect Kathleen's wishes. "All right, but you heard what the doctor said. You overdid it yesterday. Too much sun, not enough water. You were dehydrated. I'm blaming myself."

"Why? I'm old enough to decide whether I'm thirsty."

301

"Apparently not. And today I'm going to be nagging you to drink every half hour."

"Does gin count?"

"No." Martha piled fresh berries into a bowl, relieved that Kathleen appeared to be back to her usual outrageous self. "This breakfast looks delicious, Josh. Where did you find all this?"

"I raided the kitchen. Friendly people." He pulled a chair closer to the bed and sat down, nursing a cup of strong coffee. "I agree with Martha. I don't think you should rush to go anywhere this morning, Kathleen. Take it slowly and see how you feel later."

All the antipathy and suspicion Martha had felt had vanished. She had more than one reason to be thankful for the fact that they'd picked up Josh Ryder in Devil's Elbow.

Josh had been the one who caught Kathleen before she could hit the floor, and it had been Josh who had located a doctor in virtually the same time it had taken Martha to settle Kathleen on the bed.

He seemed to have a way of making things happen, and for that Martha was grateful.

She wouldn't have wanted to be on her own with this. When Kathleen had collapsed onto Josh, Martha had felt terrified for her, vulnerable and a long way from home.

What if something happened to Kathleen? It was something she'd considered, of course, but there was a big difference between contemplating the possibility of something and experiencing it.

The doctor had proceeded to give Kathleen a thorough checkup, while Martha hovered in attendance.

Reassured that there was nothing that fluids and rest wouldn't cure, Martha had then insisted that Kathleen follow instructions and rest on her bed for the evening. She'd intended to stay with her and keep her company, but Kathleen had insisted she wanted to be left alone to sleep. Martha had reluctantly agreed to spend the evening in her own room, next door.

She'd assumed Josh would do his own thing, but he'd insisted on keeping Martha company.

At first she'd protested. "I don't need a baby-sitter."

"If Kathleen gets worse, you can sit with her while I call the doctor." He'd refused to discuss it, and she'd been relieved to have him there for moral support so she hadn't argued too hard.

The drama had broken the ice between them, removing the barriers she'd erected.

Truthfully, he'd impressed her. He could have walked away, but he hadn't.

They'd passed the next few hours playing cards, and despite her anxiety he'd managed to distract her and make her laugh.

Eventually he'd vanished to track down food and Martha had checked on Kathleen.

She'd done the same a few times in the night, using the flashlight on her phone to leave and enter the room quietly.

All the same, it had been a relief when sunlight had finally peeped through the curtains. Things seemed less scary and generally more manageable in daylight.

"What did you two do last night when I was having my long rest?" Kathleen accepted the bowl of berries Martha handed her. "Did you dress up and find a lovely restaurant?"

Did she think it was date night?

Martha didn't know whether to be amused or exasperated that a health fright didn't seem to have dented Kathleen's enthusiasm for matchmaking. "We split a pizza and played cards. Yogurt?" She handed one to Kathleen.

"Thank you, dear. It's all very healthy and delicious, although I do miss crispy bacon."

Josh finished his coffee. "I'm sure I can track down bacon." He left the room and Kathleen put her bowl down and reached for Martha's hand.

"I apologize. You didn't sign up to be a nurse. You've been very kind, but if you wish to resign, I understand."

"Resign? No way. Don't you fret about anything. You need to drink." Martha poured her another glass of ice water and watched while Kathleen sipped it.

"I'll be right as rain in a few minutes. Particularly if Josh tracks down bacon. Isn't he a wonder?"

"He's been a big help." Martha was careful not to be too effusive in case Kathleen's next request was that they book a wedding venue. "Are you sure I can't call Liza back? I think she'd want to know that you weren't well."

"What would be the point? You'd give her something else to worry about and she already has more than enough. I can't believe she's actually in Oakwood by herself. You have no idea what a step forward that is, although I'm a little worried about what it means for her and Sean. I do hope the man comes to his senses. Do you think I should call him?"

"I do not." As someone who had been on the receiving end of Kathleen's energetic attempts to meddle with relationships, Martha was swift with her response. "I think you should leave it to them. How are you feeling, really? And don't put on a brave face."

"I'm better. You heard the doctor, it's nothing serious."

"Doctors don't know everything." Martha poured Kathleen some juice. "You know what my diagnosis is? Too much meddling with my love life." She was relieved to see Kathleen smile.

"That part has been relaxing. And look how well I did. Isn't he perfect? I chose him for his shoulders and his nice eyes, but it turns out the rest of him is equally magnificent."

"Kathleen—"

"If Josh hadn't caught me, I probably would have knocked myself unconscious. I now have firsthand experience of his superior muscle tone. Maybe you could try fainting on him, that might accelerate the relationship."

"Or kill it dead."

"I wonder if he will find bacon?"

"I'm sure he will. He seems to be good at getting people to do what he wants them to do." Martha poured herself a small cup of coffee, wondering how deeply to delve. "Did all that talk of the past upset you, Kathleen?"

"You heard the doctor—I didn't drink enough, that's all. I was too busy chatting to our lovely Josh because you were giving him the silent treatment."

"I was focusing on the driving. And if you don't stop matchmaking, I'm going to call Liza."

"That's blackmail."

"It is. I learned it from you." Martha sipped her coffee. "I wonder if we should spend another day here. I could amend our bookings."

"Today is Kansas and Oklahoma. No need to amend anything."

Was it safe for them to travel? What if Kathleen collapsed while she was driving and they were miles from the nearest big town? What if she needed to find another doctor? Where would she start?

Josh returned with bacon and after they'd finished eating they headed back to their rooms to pack up their gear.

Martha caught up with him by his door.

"Are you leaving?" Yesterday she'd been more inclined to drive over his foot than offer him a ride, but that was before the drama of the night before. The calm and kindness he'd shown had changed her opinion of him.

"Martha—" his voice was gentle "—the last thing you wanted was me coming along on your trip."

"That was yesterday. And it wasn't because I didn't like you. It was because—" Oh this was so embarrassing. If she told him about Kathleen's matchmaking she'd never be able to look him in the eye again. "I'm not good with strangers. It takes me a while to warm up."

He studied her for a moment. "Since we arrived here, you have engaged almost every member of staff in conversation. If you were any warmer, you'd be a risk to the planet. I've rarely met anyone as friendly as you. Except with me."

Okay, so that excuse wasn't going to work.

She felt a rush of desperation. "You don't understand—Kathleen has this misguided idea that I need her—help."

"Help?"

"I had a bad breakup."

"How bad?"

"Well, it ended in divorce, so pretty bad—he cheated." She blushed. Why was she telling a stranger all this? "I needed to get away from everything—by which I mean my life—so I took this job. And somehow Kathleen managed to get me talking, because that's the kind of person she is, and I told her the truth, and she came up with this ridiculous plan to—"

"To?"

"Match me up with someone to help me get my confidence back. And I know how ridiculous that sounds. I've been telling her the same thing."

"You mean a rebound relationship?"

Martha ground her teeth. "Believe me, it was *not* my idea."

"I was the chosen one?"

She should have let him leave. "She thought you had potential. Are you laughing? Because there is nothing funny about this."

He pulled off his sunglasses and rubbed the bridge of his nose. "So that's why you didn't say a word to me on the journey yesterday?"

"I was mad with her. And frustrated. And embarrassed in case you worked it out. And also a little nervous because back then I didn't know that you were a really decent guy who could find a doctor, and food, and produce a good bottle of wine—that was lifesaving by the way—and be generally fantastic. I don't know what I would have done if you hadn't—I mean, I wouldn't have caught her the way you did. She would have banged her head. Injured herself."

"That's a lot of feelings for one small person." Smiling, he reached out and squeezed her shoulder. "She's going to be fine. You heard the doctor—heat, travel, dehydration, jet lag—it all adds up, particularly in someone of her age."

"I was scared. And you were wonderful. I didn't have a chance to thank you properly last night, so I'm thanking you now." She was conscious that his hand was still on her shoulder, warm and strong.

"You're welcome. I'm glad she's feeling better, and I hope the rest of your trip goes well."

"But that's just it—if you leave now, she'll blame me. She'll think I got rid of you. And that will stress her. She seems determined to travel today, so can I persuade you to travel with us? For one more day at least?" Or was that the last thing he wanted? "Or maybe you'd rather find a cooler ride than the two of us, especially if you haven't taken a vacation in so many years. This one is probably special, and I know there's nothing special about my driving. I'm not that experienced, as you probably guessed, although if we'd picked you up in Chicago you would have had even more reason to be nervous. I've improved a lot in a few days. By the time we reach Santa Monica I'm hoping to be competent. And now you're probably thinking that you'd rather not risk your life. Which is ironic, really, because there was me worried for our safety picking up a stranger, whereas the person who should have been worried was you—" The words died as he covered her lips with his fingers.

"Yesterday I couldn't get you talking, and today I can't stop you talking."

"It would reassure Kathleen to have you there and we *are* traveling in the same direction." She took a breath. "Say something."

"I was waiting for a gap in the flow of words." The laughter in his eyes made her feel better.

"Will you come with us? For one more day. After that if you're tired of us, I'll let you go."

"May I speak? Because I have a question."

She folded her arms, nervous. "Go for it."

"Why did she think I'd be your perfect rebound relationship?"

"You'd have to ask her that. Because you're male and have good shoulders? Her list of criteria didn't seem long. Also you were the first man of appropriate age she happened to spot after she'd come up with her thrilling plan. But honestly, you don't need to worry. She can plot as much as she likes, and frankly if it distracts her from feeling unwell, that's fine by me. You know the truth now, and in case you're wondering I should reassure you that you're safe. I'm not remotely interested in any sort of relationship right now, even a rebound one. I took this job to get away from all that. You have no idea how much I'm loving having no emotional complications."

He looked thoughtful. "So you don't know her that well?"

"I have known her for less than a week." But funnily enough she felt as if she did know her well. In the time they'd been together, Martha had told Kathleen things she'd never told anyone else.

Why was that?

She stared across the river. It was because Kathleen was interested in her, and never judged. Not once, even about the driving, had she made Martha feel like a failure.

"You have such an easy relationship I assumed you were her granddaughter."

Martha felt a pang of loss. Spending time with Kathleen had made her realize how much she missed her grandmother. And she realized that there was nothing wrong with her life. Her unhappiness stemmed entirely from the people she was spending time with. Her family. Steven. She'd never be who they wanted her to be, and she didn't want to be that person.

"If I could have a second grandmother, I'd choose her." With her own family she was defensive the whole time and braced for conflict.

She didn't talk to them the way she talked to Kathleen.

On this trip she was able to be herself, and she felt happier than she had in a long time.

Josh smiled. "She's lucky to have found you to drive her. And now I understand why you're doing it—but why is she doing it?"

"Route 66?" Martha forced herself to concentrate on the conversation. "She was a big traveler of course—a pioneer. But you already know that. Route 66 happened to be on her wish list I think." Although she was starting to wonder now if Ruth hadn't had something to do with Kathleen's choice. She said she didn't want to get in touch, but she was driving to California and she had to wonder, surely? It had to be on her mind. Maybe Martha would prompt her again. But it wasn't something she could discuss with Josh. "Will you come with us today?"

"It would be my pleasure."

The sense of relief was as welcoming as a cold shower on a hot day. "Thank you, thank you, thank you."

"You're welcome. I'll talk to the staff at reception, and then I'll help you load the car."

She wanted to hug him, but after the conversation they'd just had she was afraid her gesture of gratitude might be misconstrued so she settled for a friendly punch on the arm.

"Oklahoma, here we come."

Kathleen wasn't wrong about his muscles, she thought. But that didn't mean she was interested.

That was one bad decision she was *not* going to make.

15

LIZA

"It's been nineteen years since we saw each other. Can you believe that?" Angie sat on the picnic rug, a large sun hat pulled down over her eyes as they dried off after an invigorating—freezing, Liza had called it—swim in the sea.

Liza lay on her back, staring up at the cloudless blue sky. Why had it taken her so long to do this? And how lucky was she to be having her escape time in the middle of a heat wave?

The day before, after she'd spoken to her mother, she'd strolled to the beach and spent hours sketching and then painting. At first the blank sheet of paper glaring up at her had felt intimidating, almost like an accusation. She'd made a few strokes with her pencil and her hand had felt stiff and uncertain. She was used to guiding and teaching. Less used to creating something herself. But who was going to see it? Fortunately the beach had been virtually empty and no one had seemed interested in looking over her shoulder. Eventually her hand had started to move with more confidence, as if it had finally remembered what to do. She'd stayed on the beach until her skin had started to burn, and then piled all her equipment into her bag and strolled home. She could have used any room in the house to continue her painting, but instead she'd rummaged in one of the kitchen drawers for the old rusty key that opened the summerhouse at the bottom of the garden. These days it was used for storage, but at one time it had been Liza's favorite place.

The lock had been as rusty as the key, but with a little oil and lots of maneuvering she'd managed to open the door. All the memories had come rushing back. The summerhouse had been the focus of so many of her childhood games of make-believe, constructed to fill the long weeks when her mother was away. It had been a bookshop. A hospital. A pirate ship. She'd been a wild child who lived in the woods. A fairy princess. A good witch.

And now, today, she was an artist.

Energized by this project that was all for her, she'd cleared out cobwebs and broken plant pots, brushed a thick layer of dust from the floor and polished the murky windows to let the light flood through the glass unrestricted. After a few hours of hard work she'd turned the place into something that could be described as a studio. She'd rescued her old easel from the back of her mother's garage and set out her paints on the table. Pastels, watercolors, oils—

she'd worked in a variety of mediums in her time and was excited to do so again. She'd experiment with all of it and see what she found most absorbing.

Too excited to take a pause, she headed back to the house for long enough to make herself a simple sandwich with the remains of the fresh crusty loaf she'd bought from the deli and some thick sliced ham, poured herself a glass of chilled white wine, and carried both down to the summerhouse.

With the windows open she could hear the sound of the birds in the garden and the occasional bleat of a sheep from the field behind the house.

She'd painted until she lost the light, absorbed in her own creation. Finally she locked the door, headed back to the house and remembered to check her phone.

She'd missed two calls from Sean, and a text from Caitlin, asking how long a packet of ham would last once it was opened.

Soon, she thought. Soon she'd talk to them about how she was feeling, but for now she wanted to focus on herself.

She'd fallen asleep, exhausted but happy, and now here she was on the beach with her oldest friend, wondering how they'd ever managed to lose touch. Like so many things in her life, it had happened gradually so that she hadn't even noticed the change until it had slipped away. Was this what had happened with her mother and Ruth?

"I can't believe it has been so long." She stretched out her legs. She was wearing shorts and a T-shirt and her legs and feet were bare. For the first time in as long as she could remember she had nothing tugging at her. No little voice telling her there were things she should be doing, which was good because the only thing she wanted to do was lie with the sun on her face and listen to the waves break onto the shore. She hoped this heat wave wouldn't end any time soon. "It was at our wedding."

"I know. And your anniversary was a few days ago. Unbelievable how fast time passes."

How was it that a friend who she hadn't seen for almost two decades could remember her anniversary, but her husband couldn't?

"It was a hot day, do you remember? My hair was limp and my makeup was shiny."

Angie removed her hat and lay back next to her. "I remember every moment of it. You looked beautiful. And I had never been more envious of anyone in my life."

Liza turned her head. "Why would you have been envious of me?"

"Because no man had ever looked at me the way Sean looked at you."

Liza's heart gave a skip. "It was our wedding

day. Every man looks at his bride like that on his wedding day."

"Not true. This wasn't a *Hey, you look great in that dress look,* or anything like that. It was a look that said everything he ever wanted in life was standing right there in front of him. That was the kind of look you read about in romance novels and hardly ever see in real life." Angie sighed. "Sean was an incredibly sexy guy. Brain and brawn—always a killer combination. Women were falling over themselves to catch his attention, and he literally didn't see anyone else there. Just you. It was one of those rare weddings where you knew the couple really would be together forever, however long that happened to be. Who doesn't dream of that?"

Liza was engulfed by a swell of sadness and nostalgia. Angie wasn't wrong. The only thing she really remembered about that day was Sean. He'd been her focus, and he'd stayed her focus for all the years that had followed. In the beginning she'd been dizzy with happiness, unable to believe her luck. Even after that initial feeling of euphoria had faded, she'd still felt utterly content with her life.

They'd celebrated the highs and weathered the lows. They'd laughed, hugged, talked, listened, had plenty of sex and planned for their future. They had so much shared history, but somewhere along the way life had chipped away at the bonds that kept them close. They'd forgotten how to be a couple. How had that happened?

"It's a shame for you that Sean couldn't get away this time, but it's a treat for me." Angie sat up and brushed sand from her legs.

Liza felt guilty for thinking only of herself. "I didn't even know you'd moved back here."

"I've only been here six months and I didn't get out much to begin with. I was feeling too sorry for myself. You know what village life is like. I didn't want people asking questions."

"How did Poppy take it?"

"She was mortified that her father was having an affair—no teenager wants to be forced to think about a parent having sex, particularly with someone closer to her age than mine. She didn't speak to him for months. And that was hard because I was trying to do the good mother thing and not say anything bad about him. I clenched my teeth so hard I almost needed dental work." Angie pulled sun cream out of her bag and rubbed more onto her skin. "We muddled through. Poppy already had a college place on the East Coast, but she came home for Christmas. Then in February John broke the news about the baby."

"Oh Angie—" Liza reached across and hugged her.

"It hurt, which made no sense because I wouldn't have taken him back if he'd begged. Anyway, bring me up-to-date with your news.

Sean is a big shot architect now? You live in an amazing mansion in London with glass everywhere?"

Liza curled her toes into the sand. "Not a mansion, but it's true that Sean has made the most of the space. He extended our kitchen a few years ago and yes, a great deal of glass was involved. It's a lovely big family room that opens onto the garden."

"And you two are still married and happy. You see? I knew it."

Eight signs that your marriage might be in trouble.

How could she talk about it with Angie, when she hadn't even raised it with Sean?

He should be the one she was talking to. And she would. *She would.*

"Liza?" Angie's voice brought her back to earth.

"Sorry. I was miles away."

"Dreaming about Sean." Angie nudged her. "It's good to know that absence makes the heart grow fonder even after two decades together. When is he joining you? I'd love to see him again."

"We haven't made firm plans. He's in the middle of a big project and it's hard for him to get away. And the girls have summer activities—" It was a part truth, and she didn't want to say more.

"You two are an inspiration. Do you know the crazy thing? Despite everything, I still dream of one day meeting someone special again."

"That's good." Although she wasn't sure she should be anyone's inspiration. She felt uncomfortable for letting Angie believe she had a perfect marriage.

Angie slipped her feet back into her sandals. "After everything that has happened, I should be bitter and twisted and hate all men, but honestly I don't feel that way. Life is too short and precious to waste a moment of it being bitter, isn't it? And it's not that I *need* to be with someone—I'm financially independent, I have a house—small, but it's mine. I have friends, a job and hobbies. I can be single. But I'd rather share my life with someone who cares about me, and who I care about. I want someone who is going to be interested in me, and care about what happened in my day."

Liza swallowed. *She wanted that too.*

She thought about Finn, and how it had felt to be listened to. Connecting was so important for intimacy and somewhere along the way she and Sean had ceased to connect on all but the most superficial level.

"I'm sure you'll find that."

"Maybe." Angie glanced at Liza. "Don't look so worried. My disastrous romantic life isn't catching. You and Sean are a forever couple if ever I saw one."

Liza stood up quickly. "It's hot and we're both burning. Let's go back to the house."

Angie stood up too. "Why don't I cook us both dinner on Friday?"

On Friday she was cooking dinner for Finn. Something else she didn't plan to share with Angie, and not only because it would be an invasion of Finn's privacy.

"I can't do Friday. How about tomorrow?"

"Tomorrow works." Angie slung her bag over her shoulder and they walked across the sand and back to the path that led across the fields to Oakwood Cottage. "Did you know that Finn Cool lives around here?"

"Mmm?" She wasn't used to being evasive. How did her mother do it?

"Poppy almost went wild when she found out. I keep hoping I'll bump into him in the supermarket, although I expect he has staff and doesn't relate to normal humans."

Liza thought about how friendly he'd been. And how he'd helped her mother. "It must be difficult trying to lead a normal life when you are high profile."

They arrived back at the house and Angie dug in her bag for her car keys.

"You're probably right. But if you happen to see him make sure you tell him I'm available." Laughing, she unlocked her car and threw her bag on the passenger seat. "Thanks for the picnic. This was fun."

Liza waved her off and then headed straight to

the summerhouse, desperate to get back to her painting.

The afternoon passed without her noticing and it was hunger that eventually drove her back to the house.

Her hair was stiff from her swim in the sea earlier and she intended to take a shower, but first she wanted to watch some episodes of *The Summer Seekers*.

She made a quick snack, found the key in her mother's bedroom and unlocked the study.

Every available space in the room was taken. Bookshelves rose from floor to ceiling against two of the walls. The other walls were covered with maps. Two large windows let in the light and showed every speck of dust. And there was plenty of it. The desk in the corner was piled high with more maps, guidebooks and stacks of papers.

And there, in prime position, was her art award.

Her mother had moved it from Liza's old bedroom into the study where she could see it.

Liza felt a pressure in her chest. She'd had no idea. She never came into this room.

She touched the award, remembering that day she'd seen her mother clapping loudly in the audience.

She'd wanted so badly for her mother to be more demonstrative, but sometimes it wasn't about what you said, it was about what you did.

She wouldn't have kept the award if she wasn't proud, would she?

Liza forced herself to focus on the shelves. She found the guidebooks, but there was no sign of the DVDs.

Searching randomly, she pulled open the large drawer in the desk and there were the DVDs.

"Aha!" She pulled them out and was about to close the drawer when something glinted. She reached into the drawer to investigate and found a ring. The stone was huge. It couldn't be a real diamond. Could it?

She lifted it out carefully. It had to be fake.

Was it fake?

She turned it over in her hand.

Who had given it to her mother? This wasn't her engagement ring. Her mother's engagement ring was an emerald and it was always on her finger.

This ring had been tucked loose under a piece of string holding a bunch of papers.

She checked the drawer and discovered that what she'd thought were papers were letters. The postmark was California, and they'd been mailed at regular intervals dating back to the early sixties. Her mother would have been in her early twenties.

Why hadn't she opened them? Was there a reason the letters and the ring were together, or was that coincidence?

Her phone rang and she almost dropped the letters.

She slid the ring onto her finger for the time being, returned the letters to the drawer and locked the study door. Only when she'd done that did she answer her phone.

It was Sean.

"I've been calling you all day. Where were you?"

"I've been out. I forgot my phone."

"You never forget your phone."

These days she was doing a lot of things she didn't normally do.

"I was busy." She sat down on the edge of her mother's bed. The ring felt heavy on her finger. Did that mean it was real? If it was real, then it must be valuable. Surely not even her mother would leave a valuable ring loose in a drawer.

"Busy doing what?" Sean sounded tired. "Caitlin is going crazy because she washed her white shirt, which is apparently precious, and I'd left a red cleaning cloth in the machine."

Liza watched a woodpecker land on the apple tree. "I did tell her to check the machine is empty before she put anything in it."

"Well, apparently it's my fault, because I should have noticed. Girls are exhausting. Alice's hair straighteners broke, and I'm told this is a tragedy. I tried to point out that this does not come under the heading of a crisis, but before I had the door slammed in my face for that remark I was told that I couldn't possibly understand. The bathroom smells so badly of hairspray and perfume I'm having breathing issues. When are you coming back? How much attention does Popeye need?"

"I'm not staying for Popeye, I'm staying for me. I need a break." It was the closest she'd come to admitting that something was wrong.

"A break? Knowing you, you've probably worked nonstop since you arrived."

Did he know her? Or had he assumed she was the same Liza she always had been? No one stayed the same throughout life, did they? Things happened. Life happened. And each event and experience sculpted you into a slightly different shape. Maybe when you'd been with someone for a long time you saw the old, not the new. It was important to keep communicating. Keep listening.

But she hadn't done that with her mother.

She'd assumed the house was too much for her, and that moving would be the best thing. She hadn't said, *What is it you'd like?* She hadn't listened. Instead she'd motored forward with a plan that seemed sensible to her without consulting the person who mattered most.

She assumed she knew her mother, and the unopened letters in the drawer and the ring had reminded her that there was plenty she didn't know. And she hadn't asked. She was just one part of her mother's rich and varied life.

Liza had thought she had all the answers, but now she realized she hadn't asked the right questions.

Feeling guilty, she stood up and walked to the window.

"I haven't done much around the house." Apart from finding something she was pretty sure she wasn't supposed to have found.

"We'll probably need to get professionals in to have a clear out when she finally decides to sell."

Liza stared across the garden, at the blur of bright color that tumbled from the pots on the patio. The place was idyllic. The thought of never standing in this room again, never running across the fields to the sea, never feeling the air cool on her skin in the evenings, left her bereft. "I don't think she should sell it."

"Really? Why have you changed your mind?"

"I've had the time to think." About many things.

"Good. Your life is a mad rush. Fortunately, we're going to France in a few weeks. You'll be able to relax."

Would she?

"France is a lot of work for me, Sean."

"What are you talking about? It's a brilliant family holiday that we've done for years. You love it. We always have a relaxed time."

It was time to tell at least part of the truth. "You all have a relaxed time, because I do all the organization. For me, it's relaxing for about two hours a day when you're all enjoying watersports. Here I have time to myself and it's not limited. I'm staying a little longer." It was the first time she'd given thought to what was going to happen next. "I have things to sort out."

There was a pause. "Is everything all right, sweetheart?"

A breath caught in her chest. The kindness and warmth in his voice sounded like the old Sean. This was her chance to tell him the truth. To be open about all the things she'd been feeling. But was that really a conversation to have on the phone?

No. It had to be face-to-face. She'd do it, but not yet.

"I'm tired, that's all."

"After spending this week with the twins with no help, I can understand that." There was humor in his tone. "I'm going to need a month to recover. What about you? If you haven't been clearing the house, what have you been doing?"

She thought about Finn. About her shopping trip. About her painting.

For some reason she didn't understand, she wasn't ready to tell Sean about it yet.

She looked at the DVDs. "I've been trying to

find out a little more about my mother. I don't think I've paid enough attention to who she is or what she wants. I'm about to watch her old shows." She didn't say anything about the letters she'd found. Nor did she say anything about her painting. "I bumped into Angie."

"Your old friend Angie? From our wedding? What's she doing there?"

"She and John divorced, so she moved back here. We had a picnic on the beach together today." She didn't mention that Angie was using them as the model for a perfect relationship.

"Sounds fun. I should go—I promised Caitlin I'd try and rescue the white shirt."

They were doing it again. Talking about life and the children. Never about themselves.

But he'd asked her if she was all right. He'd cared enough to ask her.

She thought about what Angie had said about their wedding day and felt a rush of anxiety. They'd been so happy. Tears stung her eyes. "Sean—"

"Have fun. I'll speak to you tomorrow."

Resisting the temptation to call him back, she returned the ring to the drawer in the study, picked up the DVDs and headed downstairs to the living room.

She made herself a tea with fresh peppermint from the garden, slotted in the DVD and curled up on the sofa.

She started right at the beginning, with her mother's first show.

The Summer Seekers had been one of the earliest travel shows, and its immediate popularity had surprised even its creators. It had run for almost two decades, with Kathleen the face of the show.

As she watched, she saw her mother as others probably saw her—a vibrant enthusiast, hungry to explore all that the world offered and share it with a wider audience.

The show was dated, of course, and in different circumstances she might have been amused by the outfits, the use of language and the places they'd chosen to stay, but even now there was an energy to the show that made its record audience ratings easy to understand. It had been aspirational, and yet somehow still accessible. Her mother drew the audience to her, until you felt as if you were there by her side, traveling with her, laughing with her.

In many ways Kathleen hadn't changed much. Yes, she had more wrinkles and her hair was shorter now, but she still had the same fierce expression in her blue eyes, and the same buoyant approach to life.

How could she ever have thought her mother would be content in a residential home?

Liza watched several episodes, and then walked across to the shelves where the photo albums were kept. She carried them back across the room, piled them on the floor next to the sofa and started to go through them one by one.

The photographs charted her mother's life history, from her childhood through to college and the early days of her twenties. Liza was interested in those early days.

When she reached the photo of Ruth, she paused.

Ruth and her mother had obviously been close. Why had they lost touch?

She and Angie hadn't fallen out. It was more that life had pried them apart and they hadn't tried hard enough to bring themselves back together. The most likely explanation was that the same thing had happened between her mother and Ruth.

The letters had been mailed in California. So did that mean they were from Ruth?

She put the album down, thinking about herself and Sean.

Not all relationships ended in an abrupt way. For some it was a slow easing apart. In some way that was more dangerous because it could go unnoticed amidst the pressure of life.

She felt guilty for not asking him to come and join her. And guiltier still when she was forced to admit she didn't want him to join her.

She was a family person. Her family was everything.

And yet here she was, happier than she could remember being for a long time.

Alone.

So what did it all mean?

16

KATHLEEN

OKLAHOMA~AMARILLO, TEXAS

Kathleen sat in the back seat, dark glasses covering her eyes. It was a hot day and Martha had insisted on keeping the roof closed and the air-conditioning on so the car was deliciously cool.

Kathleen stared out the window, taking in the landscape.

What would Route 66 have looked like in its heyday? She wondered what experience those earliest people to travel the road would have had. Nothing like the comfort of this, that was certain.

"Are you all right back there, Kathleen?" Martha glanced in the mirror and Kathleen produced her most reassuring smile.

"Never better."

She'd been a great deal better, but Martha was already anxious enough and to admit how she felt would stimulate a flow of follow-up questions that she wasn't able to answer. She'd never been a person who shared each and every feeling. And how could she share something she didn't understand herself?

Her dizzy spell had shaken her up. What if that had been it? She would have died not knowing what was in those letters. And perhaps that would have been a good thing. What if the contents upset her? The events of that summer had shaped her. She'd made the hardest decision of her life and she'd believed, truly, that she'd done the right thing.

But what if those letters told her otherwise? Without opening them, she had no way of knowing.

She should have destroyed them. If something happened to her on this trip, someone else would open them.

She thought about it. Hands tearing through sealed envelopes. Curiosity. Shock, maybe. Revelations. Those hands would probably belong to Liza, who would never dream of disposing of letters without first reading them in case they contained something important. It wouldn't sit well with her sense of responsibility.

The secrets of Kathleen's past would be exposed in a way she couldn't control. They would reveal a picture she couldn't yet see. And she knew that no matter what they said, those letters would only be part of the story.

Kathleen knew the beginning of the story, but not the end. There could have been any number of outcomes and the only way to find out was to open those letters.

The thought made her physically uncomfortable. She shifted in her seat.

Brian was the only person who knew the truth. He was the only person she'd shared everything with, and even then it had taken time and gentle coaxing.

Her chest ached. How she missed him. His wry sense of humor. His quiet way, and his wise counsel. He'd been gone for five years and yet she still found herself turning to talk to him in the night.

She'd never fully shared herself with anyone except Brian. Not even with Liza. She'd protected herself for so long it had proved an impossible habit to break.

Until now.

She felt a twinge of guilt that she'd shared more of her past with Martha than she had with her own daughter.

In front of her Martha and Josh were engaged in conversation about where they should stop for lunch and what they should eat.

"Catfish and crispy tater tots," Josh said and Martha pulled a face.

"I don't even know what that is."

"It's good old Oklahoma food. Cover the fish in cornmeal, fry it. Delicious."

Martha shook her head. "Not convinced. Not a big fish lover to be honest. And a kitty-fish doesn't tempt me to change my mind."

"How about onion burger? They used onions to bulk out the meat during the Great Depression and their attempts at economizing led to the most delicious burger."

"That sounds better than catfish."

"I'll order catfish and you can try it. You should try everything once."

"That's what I thought about marriage and look how that turned out."

"You're also driving Route 66 for the first time and that's turning out okay, isn't it?"

Kathleen saw Martha smile at him.

After the drama of the night before, they'd developed an easy camaraderie. It seemed that her funny turn had forced them together in a way she'd failed to manage with her heavy-handed attempts at matchmaking.

Oh how well she remembered those days of flirtatious looks, the air heavy with sexual tension and anticipation.

It cheered her to think that although her own life might be a tangled mess, at least Martha's was looking hopeful.

She focused on that, in the hope of calming the emotional turmoil churning inside her.

"How are you feeling, Kathleen?" Martha glanced in the mirror, asking the same question she'd asked at least ten times since leaving the motel.

"I'm alive," Kathleen said. "I took my pulse

to confirm it. You may continue, reassured."

Martha grinned. "You sound like you again. Don't you think so, Josh?"

"Yes." He turned. "If you need to stop—"

"You'll be the first to know."

Dear boy. Although "boy" was hardly the right description. Josh was a man, and a fine specimen at that.

Like Martha, she was relieved he'd opted to travel with them a little longer, and not only because she hoped it might culminate in a little romance for Martha. Josh had proved himself to be steady and capable.

In some ways he reminded her a little of Brian, although Josh appeared to have a drive and ambition that her husband had lacked.

It hadn't bothered her. She'd had drive and ambition enough for both of them.

After Adam, she'd never let herself become too close to anyone, and her job had facilitated that approach. Maybe that was part of the reason she'd chosen that line of work. Even before *The Summer Seekers*, she'd traveled around the country as part of her work.

And here she was, doing it again. Dwelling on the past.

Maybe it was a feature of age, that the past seemed more relevant than the future.

They stopped for lunch at a roadside diner, and Kathleen found she wasn't hungry.

And of course Martha noticed.

"You're not eating. You need to eat."

"I ate a large breakfast."

"You eat a large breakfast every day and it has never interfered with your lunch before. Can we order you something else?" Martha was obviously poised to fuss over her and Kathleen gave her what she hoped was a quelling look.

"If I feel the need for something else, I can order it myself."

"I know." Martha, never easily quelled, beamed at her. "But I thought I'd save you the bother."

To avoid an argument, Kathleen nibbled a few pieces of salad.

Josh excused himself to go to the restroom and Martha leaned forward.

"I've been thinking—"

"Should that admission make me nervous?"

"You could ask Liza to open the letters. That way you'd know what was in them."

It was unsettling to know that Martha's mind had been moving in the same direction as her own. "And she would also then know what was in them."

"What's wrong with that? Why not let her share it with you? You've said you're not close. Sounds as if you'd like to be. She might like the fact you're involving her. It might bring you closer."

Or it might have the opposite effect.

"If I'd wanted to open the letters, I would have opened them."

"You didn't want to open them before—I get that. You must have been so mad with Ruth. Trying to move on. But things change, don't they? I mean, if you asked me now if I wanted to marry Steven I'd say definitely no way, but there was a point where I wanted to, obviously, or I wouldn't have done it. People are allowed to change their minds."

That wasn't it. That wasn't it, at all.

Kathleen felt something flutter inside her.

Martha had no idea.

She didn't understand that the reason she hadn't opened those letters wasn't out of some childish wish for revenge, or even a wish to keep the past in the past. It was because she'd been afraid of what they'd say.

She was still afraid.

Martha thought she should read the letters, but Martha knew only a tiny sliver of the story. That was all Kathleen had shared.

"I appreciate your concern."

"But you want me to stop talking now." Martha gave a good-natured smile. "I don't want you worrying, that's all. And I know you *are* worrying, even though you won't admit it."

"I don't know why you would think that."

"You're quiet. And you've stopped actively trying to fix me up with Josh."

"I consider my work in that area to be complete. If you can't see what a perfect rebound experience he would provide, then I'm at a loss to know what more I can do to convince you."

"I'm not going to have a rebound experience, Kathleen." Martha finished her fries. "But I admit it's good having him with us."

Yesterday Martha had given Josh the silent treatment. Today she'd been chatting away, very much back to her usual self.

Sometimes it took a while to get used to an idea, Kathleen thought. You had to plant a seed, water it and let it grow.

Josh returned to the table and he and Martha promptly started arguing about dessert.

Adorable, Kathleen thought.

She tried to push thoughts of Ruth to the back of her mind, but her old friend hovered like a dark cloud on an otherwise bright day, her presence threatening change.

She could ignore those letters, Kathleen reminded herself. She didn't have to read them.

But then Liza might read them.

Oh if only she knew what they said, she would know whether she needed to read them or not.

The ridiculousness of that thought made her laugh.

"What's funny?" Martha glanced up from the menu with a smile.

"Nothing."

Martha ordered ice cream, and Josh did the same. "What was Brian's favorite food, Kathleen?" Martha handed the menu back. "Are you a good cook?"

"I'm an appalling cook. Brian wasn't overflowing with talent in that area either. Liza was always the one who showed a skill in the kitchen. She still does. She treats food like art. Everything she puts on the plate looks pretty." Had she ever praised her daughter for her cooking skills? That day she'd sped down to the West Country after Kathleen's accident bearing a casserole, had Kathleen even thanked her? She had an uncomfortable feeling that she might have said something impatient.

Liza had probably thought her rude and ungrateful. It was only now with some distance that she could understand the reason for her less than admirable behavior. She'd been terrified. Terrified that they might persuade her to sell her home and move into residential accommodation. Terrified that it might, in fact, be the best decision for her.

The house had been the best gift Brian had ever given her, apart from love.

When she'd finally accepted his proposal, he'd taken her on a car ride to Oakwood and pulled into the curving drive.

I've found a house with nothing between you and the sea.

The fact that he'd understood her deep need for independence and freedom had cemented her decision to marry him.

She hated the idea of staying in one place, but then she'd fallen in love with her cottage by the ocean. It made her feel that she was on the edge of a journey. That she could sail away at a moment's notice.

Why had she not said that? Why had she not said, *Liza, I'm afraid.*

Because she handled life by not letting it get too close.

In their last phone conversation Liza had said *I love you,* and what had she said in return? Not *I love you too,* even though she did love her daughter very much. She'd said *I know you do.*

It was evidence of Liza's great love for her that she hadn't given up on her mother.

Kathleen's heart ached.

She should do better. She *would* do better.

She watched as Martha dipped her spoon into Josh's chocolate ice cream and he tried her strawberry.

Sharing. Sharing was an essential part of fostering a good relationship. It wasn't enough to tell Liza she loved her, she had to show her. Actions meant so much more than mere words, although of course words mattered too.

She needed to show Liza that she trusted her and valued her opinion.

And there was a good way to do that.

She needed to ask her daughter to read Ruth's letters.

She needed to be honest about the past.

17

MARTHA

AMARILLO~SANTA FE, NEW MEXICO

Martha glanced in the mirror. They'd spent the morning touring Amarillo's historic district, and now Kathleen was sleeping in the back of the car as they headed across the top of Texas toward New Mexico.

Since her dizzy spell, Kathleen had been more subdued. The day before they'd driven from Oklahoma City to Amarillo and Kathleen had dozed for much of the journey. Martha had asked if she was feeling quite well, and been told that she was, but she'd insisted on an early night, leaving Martha and Josh to spend another evening together.

Josh had suggested a steakhouse, but Martha hadn't wanted to be too far from Kathleen, so they'd ordered in pizza again, played cards and watched a movie.

"Do you think she's matchmaking?" Josh had asked at one point but Martha had shaken her head.

"I wish she was. She's very unlike herself.

Anyway, I could never be with someone who didn't eat the crust from the pizza." She eyed the crusts on his plate and he shrugged.

"I hate crusts. Give me gooey cheese any day. This is a tiring trip for her. Could be that."

"Maybe." But Martha didn't think so.

She felt uneasy. She had a strong feeling that the reason Kathleen felt out of sorts wasn't physical, but emotional, and it didn't feel right to share that with Josh.

Was she thinking about Ruth? About the letters? They'd talked about it enough for Martha to know what a big deal it was.

She glanced in her mirror again and saw Kathleen's head resting against the back of the seat. Sleeping?

Martha turned her attention back to the road.

To stop herself worrying about Kathleen, she focused on Josh. "What are you going to do at the end of this trip? Are you worried that you don't have a job to go back to?"

"No."

"I admire you. Must feel good to be able to walk out and slam the door in your boss's face, metaphorically speaking. Not many people would do that. I'm guessing he won't give you a reference—" She glanced at him, saw something in his face and suddenly she knew. "Oh—"

"Oh what? Why are you looking at me like that?"

"It's you, isn't it? This awful boss of yours—"

"I never said he was awful."

"Scary and focused then. It's you! You were the boss." She felt foolish and embarrassed. "I see it clearly now. The way you paused a little too long when Kathleen was telling you what she thought of your 'boss,' as if you weren't sure whether to defend him or not. Why didn't you say something?"

"Because this is a vacation." He sounded tired. "I needed a break from it all. Work. Being the boss. All of it. I didn't want to talk about it."

This car was crowded with things no one wanted to talk about, Martha thought. And what good did that do? Kathleen had obviously been carrying the weight of her past around with her for decades. As far as she could see, nothing got fixed by burying it.

"So basically although you're hitchhiking, you're a gazillionaire."

"I never said that."

"But you're super successful, and not exactly having to wonder where your next meal is coming from." And she almost wished she hadn't figured it out because now she felt intimidated.

No *way* would she have a fling with someone like him.

They were totally wrong for each other, and not only because he didn't eat the crust from his pizza. He was a career person. Driven. Probably ruthless. The type of man who chose work over a good time. *The type of man her mother would kill to see one of her daughters with.*

That itself was enough to put Martha off. He probably had a million qualifications. He'd judge her, the way her family judged her. He'd tell her to get a proper job and take life seriously. With him, she'd never feel good enough.

"Life isn't all about money." Josh sounded relaxed and she rolled her eyes because of course he was relaxed. He wasn't the one who had made a fool of himself.

"That's easy to say when you have plenty. Believe me, when you don't, it becomes something of a focus. Not that I'm greedy. I don't need diamonds or anything—not that I'd say no to diamonds—but money, even a small amount, does give you choices. If I had money, I wouldn't have to live with my family, and that would be good for everyone's mental health. You're able to take a break because you don't have to worry about where your next meal is coming from."

Underneath her humiliation was a layer of envy.

Josh gave her a long look. "I hope my next meal is coming from that diner up ahead, because it's recommended in the guidebook."

Martha barely managed to raise a smile. "You can joke, but this changes everything."

"What does it change?" He was calm. "You

347

want me to pay for the burgers? I was going to do that anyway. My contribution."

"This problem goes a lot deeper than who pays for the burgers. I was comfortable with you, but now I'm not."

"Why? What does my job have to do with anything?"

It was probably a lot easier to be casual about success when you'd experienced it. "Tell me about your company."

"Why?"

"Because I want to know."

He sighed. "I design and sell DBMS."

"I don't know what that is."

"Database management software."

"Still no idea what that is. Time to stop the conversation. It's not making me feel good about myself. I don't even understand what it is you do, let alone how you do it."

"Basically I design software that make databases run smoothly."

"So you don't make something I'm likely to have used, or any individual."

"Not directly. Our products are used by big companies."

"And you set up the company."

"Yes."

Martha felt herself shrink. "From nothing."

"Yes."

"And now it's worth—a lot."

"I guess. The diner we talked about is up here on the right so you need to turn."

Martha turned, and parked outside the diner. "I'm not sure I can drive knowing I have a tech tycoon in the seat next to me." She was hit by a wave of depression. She'd been enjoying the trip so much, but it was all an illusion. Or maybe delusion would be a better word. This wasn't a new life. It was a pause in her old life. Yes, she was having fun but it wasn't real. She couldn't spend the rest of her life driving old ladies across America. What lay ahead wasn't a sun-soaked adventure in California, but a return home to the less than welcoming arms of her family. It was all very well realizing that she needed to distance herself from people who made her feel bad about herself, but how?

"What does my job have to do with anything?"

"Let's put it like this—if my body was my ego, right now I'd be skinny."

"I have no idea what you're talking about."

Wasn't it obvious? "Being with you makes me feel small. You're intimidating."

"Intimidating?" He looked astonished. "How?"

The fact that he could laugh made it worse.

"You may find this funny, but I don't." When she'd been with her grandmother she'd never seen the importance of striving for a career, but even she had to admit that what she'd achieved so far in her life couldn't be described as impressive. "Maybe you should be a little more sensitive."

"Maybe you should have a little more self-confidence. You're too easily intimidated, Martha."

"That's easy to say when you're a massive success."

"There are many definitions of success, Martha, and they don't all involve money. You're making assumptions about me based on your own prejudices. I'll go get us a table." He left the car and slammed the door behind him.

Martha flinched. Prejudices? He was accusing her of having prejudices? His success was a fact, not opinion.

What did he have to be angry about?

She watched as he strode across the parking lot and saw him pause outside the diner. He ran his hand over the back of his neck and she saw his shoulders move as he breathed deeply and composed himself.

Behind her, Kathleen stirred. "What's the matter with Josh?"

"When he talked about a boss who wouldn't let him take a vacation, he was talking about himself. He's the boss."

"I know."

"You *know?*" Martha turned to look at her. "And you didn't think it was a fact worth sharing?"

"I knew you'd be intimidated, and I didn't want that to happen. I wanted you to get to know each other a little first. Did you fight about something?"

"Sort of." Why did she feel guilty? Because she'd upset him in some way, and he'd been nothing but kind. It was a strange situation because being closeted together in the car created a false intimacy. They were close, and yet not close. The fact that she'd upset him and had no idea why was a sharp reminder that they didn't know each other at all.

It shouldn't have mattered, but it did.

Kathleen reached forward and patted her on the shoulder. "You like him, don't you?"

"Not anymore."

"You like him."

"Okay, I like him but I'm not getting involved with someone who makes me feel bad about myself."

"No one can make you feel bad about yourself unless you let them."

"That's a great theory. In practice it's not that easy."

"Character is more important than bank balance. Josh has been heroic in his actions."

"Because he found a doctor?"

"He also found bacon, which tells me he's a man who has his priorities straight." Kathleen lowered her sunglasses and looked at Martha.

"Talk to him. I need to use the restroom, and I'm going to be at least fifteen minutes."

"*Fifteen?* Are you planning to redecorate or something?"

"I plan to give you enough time for a proper conversation with Josh."

"I'd rather have a conversation with you," Martha said. "You've been quiet and tired the last couple of days. I should come with you."

"You're my driver, not my nurse although after my fainting episode I do understand why you might think your job description has expanded somewhat." Kathleen gathered up her bag and her wrap and emerged into the bright sunlight. "Go. It's the perfect moment."

Was it? He'd walked away. That could be taken as a clear indication that he was annoyed with her and didn't want to continue the conversation. On the other hand he was reserving a table, which implied that he expected them to join him.

And Martha believed strongly that issues shouldn't be ignored. If there was one thing she couldn't bear, it was an atmosphere.

She slid her arm into Kathleen's as they walked to the door of the restaurant. "Is it the letters? Is that why you're quiet? You've been thinking about them?" She felt a tug on her arm and stopped walking. "I know a parking lot isn't the place for this conversation, but I don't want to say anything in front of Josh and I'm worried about you. I know those letters are important to you. You have to be wondering what they say. I don't really understand why you haven't read them before now."

"Because I was afraid I might not like what they say."

Kathleen was scared.

Why hadn't she realized that before? Fierce, fearless, Kathleen was scared. Even she had her vulnerabilities. She was as human as Martha.

She covered Kathleen's hand with hers. "But if Liza reads them, then you can talk about it together."

"I'm considering it. As I told you, we don't have that kind of relationship. We're not particularly close—my fault, of course."

Because Kathleen protected herself, Martha thought. And no one understood that better than her.

But she knew how hard it must have been for Kathleen to admit that and was quick to reassure her.

"Liza loves you. I saw that when I came to meet you that day. And I see it in the messages she sends, and the way she sounds on the phone when she asks how you are. You don't have to protect yourself from someone who loves you. She's an adult, Kathleen. Whatever is in those letters, she'll handle it. She'd probably like the chance to support you."

"I don't need support."

"We all need support." Martha glanced at the diner, where Josh was sitting alone. Did Josh need support? "I'll do what you suggest and talk to Josh. But if you're more than fifteen minutes, I'm sending in a search party."

Kathleen squeezed Martha's hand. "You are a very special young woman. You have high emotional intelligence."

Martha felt her throat thicken. "You say the nicest things."

Kathleen sighed. "I speak only the truth, and the sooner you stop mixing with dreadful people who make you think less of yourself the better. Did you delete Steven from your contacts?"

"Not yet."

"Well, do it, while you still have the confidence to get out of bed in the morning."

Why hadn't she deleted his number? He didn't add anything to her life except stress. She didn't *want* him in her life.

"Perhaps you're right." Martha paused in the doorway of the diner. She could see the back of Josh's head in a booth by the window.

"Go." Kathleen patted her arm. "You, Martha, are smarter than you think you are." She headed to the restrooms while Martha joined Josh at the booth.

He passed the menu across to her.

"Thanks." She took it and then put it down

again. If she was going to do this, then she had to do it right away before Kathleen joined them. "I know I upset you in some way, and I'm sorry. If you'd like to talk about it, then I'd like to listen." She stopped as the waitress arrived with coffee and iced waters. "You're not crossing Route 66 for the fun of it, are you?" Presumably he could take a private jet if he wanted to. Or hire his own chauffeur. There had to be a reason that someone like him would want to hitchhike.

Josh picked up his glass of water. Condensation misted the side of the glass. "I was supposed to do this trip with my brother."

It was the first personal thing he'd told her. "And he couldn't make it?"

"He's dead."

"Oh Josh—" She reached out and covered his hand with hers. She remembered how she'd felt when her grandmother had died. How empty, and alone. She felt him tense and waited for him to pull away from her, but after a pause his fingers closed over hers.

"It's been—hard. The toughest time of my life."

When her grandmother died many people had said clumsy things. Some hadn't been in contact at all because they hadn't known what to say, and that had been bad too. All of it had added to her sense of isolation.

She knew it was important to say *something*,

but she also knew that the words she chose mattered.

"Grief is a horrible, cruel thing. People talk about going through stages, but honestly it wasn't like that for me. I think of it like being on the ocean. One moment things are calm and you start to relax, and you feel almost confident and think 'I've got this,' and then the next minute you're swamped by a wave and you're gasping for air and drowning."

"You've lost someone close to you?"

"My Nanna. It's different, I know, because she'd lived a full life, but she was the person I loved most in the world. She understood me. When she died it was as if I'd lost a layer of protection. I felt raw. My whole world changed shape. Losing her was the biggest thing I've had to handle—worse than my divorce to be honest—and she wasn't there to help me through it."

"But you coped."

Martha stared down at their hands, still locked together. "Not really. Not in a way that makes me proud. I was lonely, vulnerable, desperate to connect with someone and feel close and understood, the way I had been with Nanna. When Steven suggested marriage, I said yes. I thought it would fix everything. It didn't. It made everything worse. Feeling lonely inside a marriage is a thousand times worse than feeling lonely outside.

The whole thing was a mistake really. I guess he thought so too."

Why had she been so hard on herself? She'd been beating herself up about making bad decisions, but when she laid the facts out like that her decisions made more sense.

He nodded. "Your grandmother sounds like a special person."

"She really was." She paused. "Had you been planning this trip with your brother for a long time?"

He put the glass down. "He'd been threatening me with it for two years, but I was always too busy."

"Threatening?"

He gave a faint smile. "Red and I were very—different."

"Red?"

"His name was Lance, but everyone called him Red because if there was danger to be found, that's where you'd find my brother. I was the serious one. Tech addicted, focused, driven. He was a laid-back cool surfer dude. He loved water. I hate water. When we were teenagers, I built a surfing game that I could play from my bedroom so that we could connect—it was our joke. That I managed to find a way to surf on dry land, while he was out there doing the real thing." He stared into the glass of water. "I used to ask him when he was going to do something

357

serious with his life, and he always told me that serious was overrated and that looking at me made him realize he'd made all the right choices. He thought my life was insane. I felt the same way about his. Despite that, we were close. That probably sounds unlikely to you."

"No. One life does not fit all, a bit like clothes. Just because you're wearing something I wouldn't wear, doesn't mean I don't think you look good."

He smiled. "That's an interesting way of looking at it."

Why hadn't it occurred to her before? Just because her decisions seemed bad to her family, didn't mean they *were* bad. For some reason she didn't understand she was programmed to believe her family were right in all things.

She forced her attention back to Josh. "Is that why you're hitchhiking? You're wearing his clothes? Doing it his way?"

"In a way. He said I'd forgotten how to connect with real life. He wasn't right, but still—" He let go of her hand. "He died in a surfing accident, which is exactly how he would have chosen to go. It's been two years, and I miss him every day."

He'd been traveling the road alone, thinking of his brother. Missing his brother.

She'd been thinking that he had life all figured out, and he didn't have it figured out at all.

"I think it's great that you're doing this trip. It's the perfect way to honor him and remember him." Martha felt her throat thicken. "What was on his list? What would he have talked you into doing?"

Josh sat back in his chair and smiled. "You're right—we would have wanted to do different things. I would have tried to drag him to museums and places that highlight the history of the road. He would have been using my credit card to book an expensive river rafting trip. I would have complained the whole time."

She made a mental note to research it. She was going to make him do something he would have done with his brother.

"Do you have a photo of him?"

He dug his hand into his pocket and pulled out his wallet. "This one was taken when he visited me at my offices. It was one of the few days when I was wearing a suit. He wouldn't let me forget it, even though I'm usually in jeans." He pushed it across the table. "He joked that he wore his only clean shirt."

Martha picked it up and saw a smiling man with shaggy blond hair and a wicked smile. "You're alike."

"We're nothing alike, Martha. Apart from my aversion to water, he's vegan and I'd drive seven hours for a decent steak. He can name every breed of shark, and I can build a computer from scratch. I don't think there's a single area where our tastes aligned. And I'm doing it again—talking about him as if he's still here." He paused, emotion close to the surface and she felt a stab of sympathy. She'd done the same thing herself, many times.

"I'm not talking about what you enjoy, or the way you're dressed. But you have the same smile. And eyes."

"That's what you see when you look at that photo?"

She saw love.

And pride, in both their eyes. But maybe this wasn't the time to say that. "I see brothers." Sadness punched through her. She didn't have a single photo like this one with her sister. Josh and his brother looked comfortable together. She and Pippa had never willingly appeared in a photo together. They'd never been comfortable together. Maybe she should stop trying to fix that and accept that it was the way it was. "Do you have more?"

He flicked through his wallet and pulled out a couple more. "These were taken when he took me surfing. He joked that the ocean was his office. I was never sporty. I can fix your laptop but don't ever ask me to catch a ball or a wave."

And yet he'd gone surfing with his brother. And he lit up when he talked about him.

She handed the photos back. "You had fun."

"Spending time with him was fun, although I would have chosen to spend it on dry land. I wish I'd done it more often. I wish I'd spent less time fixated on work and more time having fun with Red. I'm not big on life advice, but if I were to give some it would be 'do it now, because there may not be a tomorrow.'"

And now she understood why he'd reacted so strongly to their conversation about success. His success was a wound. He was being tortured by every moment he'd spent at work and not with his brother.

She could see the regret in his eyes. "Can I ask you something?"

"Go ahead." He put the photos back in his pocket.

"I don't pretend to understand what you do, but it does seem to me that you love it. It's your passion, yes?"

"Yes. Since I was a kid. I was as crazy about my computer as my brother was about his surfboard. I had as much fun with my virtual surfing game as he did with the real thing."

She sipped her water. "You both followed your passion. It wasn't as if you'd gone down the route you chose because you were chasing money, or corporate success—not that there's anything wrong with that. Money is a necessity, that's a fact. But the point is you loved the job. So did he. You were both doing what you loved. You said you had nothing in common, but you had that. I don't claim to know much about anything, but doing what you love is the very definition of a life well lived, surely? That's the success I see, not the money. And I think that's something to be proud of, not a cause for regret."

He was silent for a long moment. "You're wise, do you know that?"

"No. Usually I'm told I know nothing about real life."

"I think you know a lot more about life than you think, Martha. Maybe you should spend less time listening to other people and listen to yourself."

Kathleen had said the same thing.

She put her glass down. Did she have the confidence to do that? Ignore the people around her, and follow her own instincts?

What would she do if people weren't constantly putting her off and minimizing her ideas?

Something that involved connecting with people. But that wasn't a passion, was it? Not like surfing or tech.

Josh seemed about to say something else when Kathleen finally joined them.

She'd timed her entrance so perfectly that Martha wondered if she'd been listening or lip reading.

"Do they have tacos?" Kathleen sat down next to Martha and pulled the guidebook out of her bag. "Planning time. Josh, I hope you'll join us for the next phase of our trip."

Martha held her breath and focused on her menu. She'd assumed he'd leave, but now she knew his story she badly wanted him to carry on his journey with them. She wanted to do what his brother would have done and encourage him to have fun. She sensed he needed that, and she wanted to be the person to help him do it.

Josh glanced up from the menu. "I appreciate the offer, but there are things I need to do."

And now she knew why he was making this trip, Martha was determined that he wasn't going to do those things alone. "Just because you hitch a ride, doesn't mean you have to stick with us like glue. Kathleen and I will probably be out and about getting up to serious mischief anyway."

"I don't doubt that." There was a smile in his eyes. "But I'll want to stay a little longer in the Grand Canyon than you had planned."

"We don't have plans as such—" Kathleen waved a hand. "Take as long as you wish. Martha will amend our booking. I can't think of a better place to linger."

Josh hesitated. "If we do this, then I'd insist on being in charge of the accommodation."

"We can argue that part later."

"So that's settled?" Martha's mind was already working. She needed to research trips on the Colorado River. She didn't want to leave

Kathleen for long, so it would have to be a day trip. And anyway, if Josh was going to complain and moan about getting wet the whole time, a day would probably be more than enough for both of them.

Their food arrived, plates heaped high with refried beans, spicy enchiladas and tacos for Kathleen.

"I confess I like having you around for reassurance, Josh," Kathleen said. "What if I collapse again? You proved to be most useful when it came to finding a doctor."

Martha reached for the salt. "I could find a doctor if we needed one."

But she too, wanted Josh to continue with them on the trip, even more so now that she understood how much this journey meant to him. He shouldn't be on his own for this, should he? It was clear he was finding it difficult. He might need a friend and he seemed a little like Kathleen—so used to handling life's challenges on his own that he didn't know how to reach out. And if he continued alone, who would step into his brother's shoes and nudge him to do the things he wouldn't normally do?

She was going to stop thinking about his job and that he was so successful in his business. Just like Kathleen, there was a person behind the success. A human being, who felt all the same things every person felt. He was a man grieving for his brother. A confused man, who somehow felt he'd let his brother down.

A person wasn't defined by their job, and she was going to keep reminding herself of that.

They finished their meal and returned to the car.

Filled with a sense of purpose, Martha slid into the driver's seat. "You're lucky to be traveling with us, Josh. You probably haven't heard, but I'm a great driver."

"I heard that." He slid into the passenger seat. "I heard that roundabouts and reversing are your favorite things, so I'll try and find a route that gives us plenty of both."

"Very funny."

He smiled at her and her heart bumped hard against her chest. He'd smiled at her before, of course, but this was different. This smile was slower, intimate, the type of smile shared between two people who knew each other.

Her insides did an elaborate dance that included a spin and possibly a pirouette.

No, Martha. *No, no, no.* Yes, she felt sympathy, yes he was sexy—but none of that changed the fact that Josh Ryder was absolutely not her type.

He was a planner. She was spontaneous. Maybe she should embrace that side of herself instead of constantly trying to shape herself into the person others wanted her to be. She was never going to be the corporate type. She was more like Red Ryder, living life in the moment.

But Josh thought she was wise.

Wise.

Martha focused on the road. She was conscious of Josh in the seat next to her, his knee within touching distance and his hand resting close to hers. It made it hard to concentrate.

She kept thinking of Kathleen, so bruised by her early experience of love that she'd kept herself at a safe distance from emotions until she'd met Brian. She was urging Martha not to make the same mistake.

Martha didn't want to have regrets.

She didn't want to make another bad decision, but which option would be the bad decision? Having a fling with Josh, or not having a fling?

She'd never felt a fraction of this chemistry with anyone else.

She glanced in the mirror to check on Kathleen and the older woman gave her a cheeky wink.

Kathleen didn't say a word, but she didn't need to. Martha already knew what she was thinking.

18

LIZA

Liza stood in the kitchen, humming to herself as she grated ginger and chopped lemongrass for the salmon fillets.

She'd spent the day painting, experimenting with a large canvas, applying bold swipes of aqua and green to reflect the colors of this part of the coastline.

Halfway through the day she'd broken off and jogged to the beach, taken a skin-numbing swim in the freezing ocean, and then jogged back. It was something she'd been doing every day. She felt horribly unfit, her face red and her heart pounding. Sean had a gym membership, and he tried to go at least twice a week. During Liza's three-month membership she'd managed to go on precisely two occasions, and one of those had been cut short by the school calling asking her to pick up Alice who had fallen during a game of hockey. Deciding that there was no point in paying to sponsor other people's fitness, she'd canceled her membership. She'd planned to try a yoga class, or maybe jog in the mornings, but there was always something more pressing demanding her time. And when she did find herself with thirty minutes to herself, she couldn't bring herself to spend it pounding along a path.

As she'd showered off the salt water, taking time to condition her hair, she'd thought more about her dream to live somewhere like this eventually. There had been a time when she and Sean had talked about it, but like many other things that dream had been squashed out by reality. Why?

Spending time with Angie had made her ask herself that question. Her friend's life had changed radically over the past few years, and that change had been forced upon her. But why did you have to wait for a crisis life event to rethink the way you lived?

And now here she was in the kitchen, preparing dinner for a man who wasn't her husband.

Should she feel guilty? *Did* she feel guilty?

No. Finn had been generous to her mother. Also, she enjoyed his company.

And it wasn't as if Sean was going to know anything about it. If it came up in conversation then she'd talk about it, but otherwise why raise it? It was all perfectly innocent.

She put the salmon back in the fridge, whisked egg whites with sugar to make meringues and slid them into the oven.

Feeling thoroughly unlike herself, she selected

a track from Finn's most recent album and danced round the kitchen.

When the track ended she stopped, breathless, thinking how embarrassed the girls would have been if they could have seen her. They thought she was too old to dance.

And she'd thought her mother was too old to do a road trip.

Behavior shouldn't be dictated by age, she thought. If she wanted to dance, she'd dance. If her mother wanted to travel, she should travel.

And if she wanted to stay in her home, she should stay in her home.

The doors and windows were open to the garden and Liza could smell the climbing rose that clustered on the wall next to the window. An idea formed in her head, but she pushed it away. Ridiculous. She was stepping into fantasyland.

When she was satisfied that she had dinner preparation well in hand, she headed upstairs to change.

She surveyed her new wardrobe. The problem with so much choice, she thought, was actually choosing.

In the end she settled on the red dress, because she couldn't imagine another occasion that she might be able to wear it and a dress like this wasn't designed to live its life hanging on a rail.

Her phone rang as she was heading downstairs.

It was her mother.

"How's the adventurer?" Liza fastened her watch. She'd started to look forward to these nightly phone calls with her mother. "How are Martha and Josh? Are your matchmaking attempts working?"

"I am hopeful. But I didn't call to talk about them."

"Oh?" Liza glanced at the time. She had about half an hour before Finn arrived. "Is everything all right?"

There was a pause. "Liza, I need you to do something for me."

Her mother never asked anything of her.

Liza sat down hard on one of the kitchen chairs. "Of course."

"It's—difficult."

Physically or emotionally? "Whatever it is, we'll figure it out."

"Dear Liza. Always so sensible and reliable."

Liza studied her sky-high heels. Fortunately this wasn't a video call, or her mother would see that she'd left sensible and reliable behind in London. "What's troubling you?"

"There are letters—"

Liza sat up straighter. "The ones in your study?"

"You know about them?"

"I found them when I was searching for the DVDs. They weren't where you thought they were, so I checked the desk. The letters were with a ring. Which I assume is a fake diamond?"

There was a pause. "It's not fake."

Liza went hot and cold.

Should she mention that it was a valuable object to keep in the house? No. The ring clearly had an emotional significance that she didn't understand. It was her mother's business. She swallowed down her words of warning. "How can I help?" It took so long for her mother to respond that Liza glanced at her phone screen, wondering if they'd been cut off. "Hello?"

"Yes. I'm here. Before I met your father, I was engaged. His name was Adam."

Liza stared across the kitchen.

Her mother had been engaged. To someone who wasn't her father. Her mother had been in love.

"The man in the photo. With you and Ruth."

"You have a good memory."

"He broke off the engagement?" She couldn't quite believe her mother was telling her this. Talking to her this way. She was afraid she might give the wrong response and cause her mother to retreat again.

"No, I broke it off. When I discovered that he'd had an affair with Ruth."

Ruth. Her mother's best friend.

"Oh no, that's awful—" She'd had no idea. Her mother was so private, Liza hadn't ever given much thought to what lay in her past. "Did Dad know?"

Maybe she shouldn't have asked. She knew how hard her mother found it to talk about anything personal. "Forget it. You don't have to talk about—"

"Your father knew. It was the reason he proposed three times. He understood how difficult I found it to make that commitment. I was never good at being close to people after that." Her usually poised mother was hesitant and uncertain. "I preferred my relationships to be light and easy."

"I'm not surprised." Nor was she surprised that her mother had broken her connection with Ruth. What did surprise her was that her ultraprivate mother was finally telling her this.

"I found it hard to trust. I didn't want to risk my heart again. I protected it carefully, you see. It was my good fortune to meet your father, and he was everything I needed. He is the only person who ever truly knew me."

Your mother needs this.

Liza felt a sudden thud of emotion as she thought of her father, so kind and patient. That was what a perfect partnership was, wasn't it? Knowing another person and accepting them. Allowing them to be who they were. "Are the letters from Adam or Ruth?"

"Ruth. I don't know what they say. I made the decision not to stay in contact."

"It must have been so hard." Surely something

like that would be impossible to forgive? It would break any friendship. "You were never tempted to open the letters?"

"Never."

Liza glanced at the time. The last thing she wanted was for Finn to arrive in the middle of her first proper deep conversation with her mother. "Why have you changed your mind?"

"I had a funny turn. It made me realize that if something happened to me you'd open those letters. Whatever they say, I want you to know the story, Liza. And now you're going to ask me about my dizzy spell."

Finn had mentioned dizzy spells too.

Liza smothered all the anxious questions that bubbled to the surface. "I'm sure you handled it in whatever way you felt was right. If you'd needed me, you would have called."

"I do need you, which is why I'm calling now. I'd like you to read those letters to me, Liza. I know it's a lot to ask. I don't know what's in them. They're deeply personal. Probably upsetting."

But her mother trusted her with them.

Liza sat up a little straighter. "Would you like me to read them myself first and filter them? I could try and judge whether I think you'd be upset before I read them aloud."

"Oh Liza—" There was a pause. "You're the kindest person. Always have been. No, if we're reading them, then we're reading them together."

We're reading them together.

Liza felt a lump in her throat and a weight in her chest. She and her mother had so rarely done anything together. "Okay. Do you think Adam stayed with her?"

"I don't know. I think there's a strong chance he did the same thing to her that he did to me. Anyway, I didn't intend for this to be a maudlin conversation."

"Do you want me to get them now?" She could still cancel Finn.

"No. I'm not ready. I wanted to test the water with you, so to speak. But maybe tomorrow we could open the first couple and take it from there."

"Of course." It was such a lot for her mother to have told her, she was probably drained.

"Tell me about you." Her mother's brisk change of subject confirmed that. "Are you enjoying Cornwall?"

Liza looked at the sunlight on the garden. The small table outside was laid ready for dinner. "I'm loving it."

"Good. That house is meant to be enjoyed. Go and enjoy it, and I'll call you tomorrow afternoon your time if that works for you."

Liza ended the call and sat for a moment without moving.

Her mother wanted her help. Her mother *needed* her help.

She felt closer to her after that one conversation than she had in her entire life.

"Hey—" Finn's voice came from the doorway. "Is everything okay?"

Liza shot to her feet. "Hi there! My mother called and I lost track of time."

"Bad news?"

"No." Although she didn't know what was in the letters so it was possible that there might be bad news. But whatever it was, she and her mother would handle it together.

Together.

"Good." Finn pulled the baseball hat off his head, but kept on the dark glasses. "You look— incredible."

Her conversation with her mother had made her forget that she was wearing her new dress.

She saw appreciation and warmth in Finn's gaze and felt embarrassed. What if he thought that the way she'd dressed had been an elaborate attempt on her part at seduction? The idea was horrifying. She never should have bought the dress. It was too much for a casual dinner in the garden, even if the guest was someone like Finn Cool. But it was too late to rush upstairs and change.

"Come in. As you're not driving, I've made cocktails. I thought we could take them outside."

He stepped forward and scooped up the drinks, the movement bringing him closer to her. He smelled of sun and salt and summer and she felt an unfamiliar heat spread through her and then he started telling her a story about the dogs jumping into the sea and she managed to laugh and behave as if she hadn't just been engulfed by the flame of sexual attraction.

It had been only a few days, but she'd forgotten how easy it was to talk to him. They laughed, chatted and ate the food she'd prepared, and she was glad she'd worn the dress.

Finn helped himself to more asparagus. "What's on your mind?"

Her mother had been in love.

"Nothing at all. I'm relaxed, that's all."

"You've caught the sun."

"I forgot to use sunscreen when I went swimming today." She pressed her fingers to her cheek. "My face probably matches the dress perfectly."

"You look good. Happier than you did when I saw you at the beginning of the week."

"That's what happens when you indulge in a countryside escape."

"What were you escaping from?"

She put her fork down. "I—meant it as a phrase."

His gaze lifted to hers. "Did you?"

She sighed. "No. This was an escape. Of sorts."

"If you want to talk about it, go ahead." He helped himself to more bread. "And if you're worried about confiding in a relative stranger, let me remind you that I live with the knowledge that every single thing I do could end up as tomorrow's news. Because of that, I'm probably the most trustworthy person you could ever meet."

"How do you manage to lead even a semblance of a normal life when you don't know who you can trust and who you can't?"

"I rely on my instincts—" he raised his glass "—which are sharply honed after multiple betrayals and disappointments."

She thought about her mother. "Bad experiences don't put you off? You're not tempted to play it safe?"

"I was eight when I lost my father. There's a lot I don't remember about him, but the one thing I remember clearly was his ability to have fun and enjoy the moment, no matter what the circumstances." He put his glass down. "He was a lot like your mother that way. I try to do the same. It's not an easy thing to do. People think it's frivolous and shallow—"

"But it takes a lot of courage."

He smiled. "That's right. Letting yourself love—live—takes courage."

He didn't understand her mother at all, although he thought he did. Liza could see now

377

that all the traveling, the emotional distance, the way Kathleen lived her life, wasn't selfishness but self-protection. Even though Liza still didn't know the details, for the first time in her life she felt as if she understood and understanding changed everything.

"Yes, it takes courage."

"Trying something knowing you might fail, takes courage. Loving, when you know there's a good chance you'll get your heart broken."

"Yes." How much courage must it have taken for her mother to allow herself to love Liza's father after everything that had happened?

"It's always easier to protect yourself but when you build walls around yourself you don't only keep the bad out, you keep the good out too. I guess that's why I find your mother so inspiring," Finn said. "She knows what she wants and goes for it. She doesn't let fear get in the way. I want to be like her when I grow up."

Liza had thought the same thing about her mother, but she knew better now.

Kathleen *had* let fear get in the way.

She stood up and cleared the plates. "Don't grow up. I think you're fine the way you are."

"Says the woman who tried to kill me with a look when I almost rammed her into a ditch."

"You recognized me?"

"Of course. You're pretty unforgettable, Liza." He'd tilted his chair back. Sunglasses concealed his eyes but she didn't need to see the way he was looking at her. She could feel it.

Her skin heated as if someone had singed her skin with a blow torch. It had been so long since anyone had flirted with her she wasn't sure she recognized it. She certainly didn't know what to do about it.

No man had told her she was unforgettable. It was like pouring water on a thirsty plant.

Flustered, she carried the plates into the kitchen and focused on dessert and coffee.

The light was fading and the tiny lights that her mother had wound around the trees glowed like stars. Liza had always considered the fairy lights to be a surprisingly romantic touch from someone she'd never considered romantic. Her parents had never been tactile or demonstrative. She'd never seen them hug. And yet her father had been devoted to her mother, and Liza understood now that the deep love had been returned.

"So how are you enjoying your new life?" The way he was looking at her played havoc with her senses. She knew she was on the edge of something deliciously dangerous. She wasn't sure if she wanted to step forward or back.

"Not exactly a new life. A break from the old one." She felt breathless. Could he hear that in her voice?

"Are you saying you're going to give up painting when you get home?"

She thought about how much she'd enjoyed the past week. She'd woken each morning eager to return to the canvas she'd left with reluctance the night before.

In London it would be different. She wouldn't have the summerhouse, or the sound of the sea, or the space and time to indulge herself. But still . . .

"I'm not going to give it up." Even the thought of going back was enough to dampen her mood, and not only because of the painting. She'd miss wearing flip-flops to the beach, eating simple food that didn't require her to spend time in the kitchen, summer dresses and a good book. Most of all she'd miss the simplicity. She had things to think about—she knew that. Things to address. She'd been putting it off, but she was running out of time.

She paused as she heard the sound of a car pulling up.

Finn put his glass down, alert. "Are you expecting someone?"

"No." Liza stood up. "Stay there. I'll see who it is."

"I can—"

"No, it's fine." She put out her hand to stop him. "Better not show yourself."

Who could it be? If it was Angie then she was going to have some explaining to do.

Telling herself that she had no reason to feel

guilty, Liza walked through the garden to the front of the house.

Two young women stood there.

"We're looking for Finn Cool."

Liza adopted a vacant expression. "Excuse me?"

"Finn Cool." One of the girls grinned. "You're probably too old to have heard of him."

Cheek! "Is he famous?"

"Seriously? He's only, like, the best musician ever." The girl pushed her blond hair away from her face, her armful of bangles jangling.

"Oh. Well, I think I'd know if I was living next to a musical legend."

"He was spotted in a pub up the road from here a few weeks ago."

"Which one?"

"The Smuggler's Arms."

"He'd probably heard about their famous fish and chips. You should try it as you're in the area. People travel a long way to eat there. And try the chocolate pudding for dessert."

One of the girls turned to the other. "Are you sure you got the right pub? If he lived around here, she'd know."

"Try farther up the coast." Liza waved her arm vaguely. "And be careful driving up the lane. The roads are narrow."

"I know. We got lost twice. Thanks anyway. You should check out some of his music."

"I'll do that." It was a good job they hadn't arrived a few hours earlier and caught her dancing around the kitchen.

Liza waited until the sound of the car engine had faded in the distance and returned to the back of the garden.

The table was empty and at first she thought Finn might be hiding, and then she saw the door of the summerhouse open.

She picked up her glass of wine and walked down the garden.

The air was thick and heavy with the heat but she could see ominous clouds gathering on the horizon. They were forecasting a storm.

"I'm not surprised you were hiding. They were scary." She stepped through the door of the summerhouse to find Finn studying her painting. She felt a flash of insecurity. "Is that what you have to deal with all the time?"

He didn't turn. "No, most of the time it's much worse."

"How awful. What's the going rate for a bodyguard?"

"Mostly it's a voluntary position but it does come with buckets of gratitude. Here, hold this—" He turned and handed her his glass of wine so that he had his hands free. "This is incredible."

"I know. I used to almost live down here when I was a child, but my mother barely uses it. I cleaned it up after I saw you that day and I've been using it as a studio ever since."

"I'm not talking about the summerhouse. I'm talking about this painting. Is this going to be mine?"

"I wasn't sure you were serious."

"Oh I'm serious. I don't believe you've done all these since the weekend." Without apology he started looking through the canvases she had stacked against the wall.

"Some are old. I'd forgotten they were here." And she was a little embarrassed that he was looking at them.

"How can you forget work like this? Thanks for dealing with those women, by the way."

"You're welcome. It was more excitement than I usually have in a day. Do you think I have a future in espionage?"

"No, but I think you have a future as an artist." Finn bent down and took a closer look at one of the canvases. "They're stunning. You have a real gift, Liza."

"Thank you. That's kind."

"I'm never kind. Ask anyone who knows me." He pulled one of the larger canvases out and rested it on the table. "Will you sell me this?"

"Instead of the other one?"

"No. I want both." He studied her work in progress. "This would look perfect in my hallway."

"It isn't finished."

"Then finish it and name your price."

She swallowed. "Are you being polite?"

A smile played around his mouth. "I'm neither polite, nor kind. I'm buying it because I want it, and when I want something—" He left the pause hanging there and it grew and grew, fed by the tense atmosphere.

She wouldn't have thought so much could be said without either of them uttering a word.

His face hovered close to hers and she had a crazy instinct that he was about to kiss her, right here in the leafy shadows of the garden.

She could barely focus, her mind hazy from need and wine. "I'm married."

"I know." His smile widened, seductive and knowing.

She shook her head, acknowledging the differences between them. And those differences, and the lure of the forbidden, were what made him so attractive, of course. It was hard not to feel flattered. Harder still not to be tempted. "Maybe you're as bad as the rumors suggest."

"Maybe I am." His gaze lowered to her mouth and the heat in his eyes almost singed her skin. "How about you, Liza?"

How about her?

She'd always thought she was the type of woman who would never look at another man, but she was looking at Finn.

She was being pulled by an invisible thread to the edge of a cliff, and there would be no recovering from the fall.

His mouth was dangerously close to hers. "Think about it."

She swayed, disorientated. "You mean about selling the paintings?"

"That too." He stroked a finger lazily over her cheek. "Thank you for a great evening. Come over to my place tomorrow."

Come over to his place? For dinner? For sex?

"What exactly are you offering?"

"That's up to you." He was so close that a fraction of movement on her part would have meant they were kissing.

"Finn—"

"Come at 7:00. That way we'll have time for a swim before."

Before what?

She opened her mouth to ask, but he was already strolling up the path away from her.

She stood, torn between calling him back and letting him go.

What was she *doing?*

Of course she couldn't go to his place tomorrow. She wasn't naive. It was obvious that he wasn't inviting her to sample his cooking.

He hadn't even touched her, but she felt as if he had. She rubbed her palms up her arms. Her skin felt warm, her whole body engulfed in a delicious melty feeling.

Shaking her head, she closed the door of the summerhouse and walked on unsteady legs back to the house, but Finn had gone.

She felt different, and it wasn't the dress or the heels. It was the way Finn had looked at her. He'd made her feel attractive. Aware of herself as a woman.

But she wasn't going to go tomorrow.

Or was she? She was going to be opening Ruth's letters with her mother tomorrow afternoon. It could be upsetting. An evening with Finn would give her something to look forward to.

The doorbell rang and her pulse rate doubled.

Finn.

He'd changed his mind about waiting until tomorrow.

Smoothing her hair, she took a deep breath and walked to the door, feeling tall and elegant in her new heels.

She tugged open the door, a smile on her face, and almost fell over.

Sean stood there, hair ruffled, unshaven, eyes tired. In his hand was the article from the magazine, crumpled and torn in places. *Eight signs that your marriage might be in trouble.*

"Hi, Liza."

19

LIZA

Liza slept badly, which tended to happen when your husband arrived unannounced and you were all dressed up and contemplating sex with another man.

She would *not* have slept with Finn, or so she told herself as she lay staring at the ceiling, thinking about Sean who she'd sent to the bedroom across the corridor.

It was the first time in their marriage that they'd been in the same house and slept apart. She'd used the excuse that he must be tired after the journey and in need of a good sleep, but really it was because she wasn't sure there was room in the bed for the two of them and her guilt. She needed to think everything through and she wouldn't be able to do that with Sean lying next to her.

Why should she feel guilty? She hadn't done anything. Thinking about something didn't count, did it? Or maybe it did.

She'd felt like the one in the right, but now she felt like the one in the wrong which was what happened when you put off doing something that needed to be done.

She should have spoken to Sean right away, the moment those first doubts had crept into her head. Like spotting a weed in the garden, she should have said, *Look at that! Let's pull it up right now in case it spreads,* but she hadn't, and she'd let it spread until there were so many weeds she could barely see him through the tangled mess.

She saw now that she was as responsible for their problems as he was, because she hadn't said anything. She'd expected him to *know,* as if he should have been able to read her mind after so many years. As if he had magical powers.

But life wasn't magical, it was messy and real and never more real than when Sean turned up at the door, frantic because he'd found the article and didn't want their marriage to be in trouble. She didn't want it to be in trouble either, but her response to that had been to dig her head into the sand and then run away and press Pause on her life, whereas he'd immediately sped to her side.

She'd always thought she was nothing like her mother, but now she realized that wasn't true. Being honest about emotions was easy when those emotions were positive and clear, but not so easy when there were difficult conversations to be had.

She'd lain awake for most of the night, her head full of Finn, that almost kiss, Sean, their wedding, their hopes, the girls, real life. It had all churned around like an ugly soup until she felt nauseated.

She was grateful when light slowly seeped into the room because the darkness seemed to make her thoughts dark too.

At five, she gave up and headed downstairs.

The weather had broken in the night, and a dramatic storm had turned to heavy rain. It had pounded the roof and the windows and bounced off the garden, leaving plants drooping and cowed under the sheer force of it. The weather reflected the change in her situation. Her days of solitary summer sunshine were behind her.

She walked into the kitchen and found Sean already seated at the kitchen table. One look at his face told her that he hadn't slept either.

Their exchange the night before had been awkward to say the least. She'd broken into a sweat when she'd opened the door and found him there, not because of the heat although that had been overpowering, but at the thought of what would have happened had he arrived half an hour earlier. He would have found her laughing and flirting with Finn in the summer-house.

She'd ushered Sean inside, appalled that he was clutching that stupid article. It hadn't occurred to her that he might find it.

"Are you on your own? Where are the girls?"

"They're at home. I thought this was something

we needed to talk about without an audience." He'd eyed her dress and the stack of plates she hadn't yet loaded into the dishwasher. "You had company?"

"I had a friend over." She'd said no more than that but she'd turned scarlet and knew he'd noticed. Funny how when she wanted him to notice things he didn't, and when she'd rather he missed things he didn't. "That article isn't—"

"Isn't what, Liza?"

"It doesn't mean anything."

"If it doesn't mean anything, why was it in your bag? When you said you were coming to Oakwood I thought you were going to feed the cat. I hadn't realized you were leaving me. It would have been helpful to know."

She was consumed by panic. This wasn't what she wanted, and now the situation felt out of control.

"I didn't leave you! Not in that sense. I needed space, Sean, that's all. I needed to think."

She'd envisioned herself having time to plan what she was going to say, so that her words were thought out and meaningful. And now she felt trapped and defensive. Also tired, and that wasn't good.

"If you'd needed to think about our marriage, don't you think I should have been involved? Even an accused person should have a trial."

"I'm not accusing you of anything, Sean."

He'd picked up the remains of the bottle of wine. "Mind if I finish this?"

"Go ahead." She fetched him a glass and he poured the last of the wine.

He'd always been steady. It had been one of the things that had first attracted her to him, and that had never changed. He'd been steady when the twins had been born prematurely, and steady when her dad had died. At that moment he hadn't seemed steady at all.

"All the way here I was planning this great speech, but now I'm here and I can't think of a single damn thing to say." He looked at her and his eyes were tired. "It's never been more important to say the right thing, after so many wrong things. I was so busy living life I never paused to examine how I was living it."

She understood that, because in her own way she'd been doing the same. "You look exhausted."

"It's been a long week and the traffic was bad." He drained his glass. "Friday night."

"Yes." Friday night. And she'd been having dinner with Finn. And she knew that this wasn't the time to talk about everything. She needed to think, and he needed to rest.

"It's late, and you've had a long drive. Why don't you go to bed while I clear up here, and we can talk properly tomorrow."

"Seriously? This is possibly the most important conversation of our marriage, and you want to delay it?"

"I want to delay it simply because it *is* quite possibly the most important conversation of our marriage. Probably not one to have when we're tired and stressed."

"You don't look tired or stressed. You look energized." His gaze traveled from the skinny straps of her red dress to the heels of her shoes. "You look—incredible. Different."

"I treated myself to a new dress."

"It's not the dress. *You* look different."

It was probably guilt. She felt as if it had been painted onto her skin. Not that she'd done anything to be guilty about. Unless thoughts counted. Did they? "I've had a week in the sun relaxing. And I forgot to use sunscreen, so my nose is peeling."

He'd almost smiled. "I imagined you clearing your mother's house and doing endless jobs. How have you spent your time?"

"I saw Angie. I spent time on the beach. I swam every day. I painted." *And flirted.*

"You painted? Good. You don't do enough of that, and I'm guessing I'm partly to blame."

She shook her head. "I should have made the time."

"How? There are so many demands on you it's a wonder you have time to brush your teeth." He sighed and ran his hand over the back of his neck. "It's humid and close."

"We're going to have a storm." *In more ways than one.*

She fought the urge to have the conversation now and get it over with. She needed time to think about what she wanted to say. She didn't want to have it while wearing a sexy red dress she'd worn to cook dinner for another man. Even though technically she'd done nothing, it felt wrong.

"Go to bed, Sean."

In the end he'd agreed and had taken his hastily packed bag to the bedroom they used when they stayed while she'd slept in the room she'd been using all week, surrounded by memories of her childhood.

And now they were facing each other across the kitchen table while rain dripped onto the patio outside.

"You're awake early." Sean poured her a mug of coffee and handed it to her. "Did you sleep at all?"

"Not much. You?"

"No. Why did you choose to sleep in your old room?"

"I don't know." She took a sip of coffee. Her eyes felt gritty. "I was tired when I arrived and picked that room. I think I needed a complete change."

"From me?"

"No." She put her mug down. The article lay on the table between them, along with so many things that needed to be said. "I didn't plan any of this, Sean. So many things happened that last day, and in the months leading up to it. Something inside me snapped. I felt overwhelmed all the time. And isolated, as if all I was to my family was a fixer—someone to bring them things they'd forgotten, book tables they couldn't be bothered to book, or cook meals so that they didn't have to. I'd ceased to be a person. And that was my fault, because I allowed it to happen and I didn't say anything." And it was a relief to finally say it. A relief to have it out there in the open.

He looked gaunt. "I should have noticed. I've been so damn selfish."

"*I* didn't really notice. Every moment of my day was swallowed up by things that needed to be done. There was no time for reflection. Painting used to be a bit like meditation for me—a time to be focused, and calm. When I stopped doing it, I lost that. I never had the time—or took the time—to stop and wonder if I was living life the way I wanted to. That day I left, all I wanted was space to think."

"I've gone over that day in my head. You suggested dinner and I asked you to book somewhere, after first having assumed you wanted

the kids along—and it was our anniversary—"
He shot her a mortified look. "I don't even know
where to begin apologizing."

"It wasn't your finest moment, but a marriage
is made up of many parts thankfully, and you've
had many fine moments."

"You should have hit me over the head with
a skillet, like your mother did that intruder. If I
hadn't found that article, would you have said
something?"

"Yes. I needed time to figure it out, that's all."

"You didn't want to come home. That says
a lot." His eyes were tired, his jaw dark with
stubble and he'd never looked sexier in his life.

Or maybe she was so shaken up by the thought
of losing him she was noticing things she'd
stopped noticing. Time did that, didn't it? It made
your gaze skim over things that should have
captured your attention.

"I was going to come home, Sean. I was going
to speak to you about the way I felt. I just hadn't
planned how or when. I didn't know you'd find
the article."

"I didn't find it. The girls did."

"Oh." Guilt mingled with anxiety. "How?"

"I sent them to find the spare car keys. They
searched your bag and found it."

It hadn't occurred to her for a moment that
anyone but her would ever read it. "What did
they say?"

"Nothing at first. They didn't know what to do, so they kept it to themselves for a few days and asked lots of questions they considered to be subtle. Then yesterday they confronted me. They had a lot of questions, none of which I could answer, which didn't make me look great. If there are problems in your marriage, generally you're supposed to know about it."

"Are you angry?"

"No. At least, not with you. Maybe with myself, for not seeing how you were feeling, or better still being more thoughtful so that you didn't feel that way in the first place. Mostly I'm—" He shook his head. "I don't know. Shaken. Helpless. Scared, because I love you and I didn't see what was going on. I thought we were happy. It's terrifying to know you were thinking all these things you didn't even share. I don't claim to be an expert on relationships, but even I know you can't fix something you don't know about."

Oh Sean.

She felt a lump in her throat.

"I love you too."

"Then why this?" He touched the offending article with his fingers. "Why didn't you talk to me?"

"When? When do we ever talk about ourselves or our relationship, Sean? We talk about life, about the girls, about practical things."

He fiddled with the paper. "Eight signs. How

many apply to us? I read them, and I wasn't sure. Which again doesn't say much, does it? I mean number two—" he gestured at the paper "—*You never spend time alone together.* That's definitely true, I see that now."

"Sean—"

"We used to have date night. Whatever happened to date night?"

"I think it vanished somewhere between your business taking off and Caitlin getting that drama scholarship." She slid her hands round her mug. "Life is about priorities, isn't it, and we didn't make it a priority. We didn't make *us* a priority."

"There's nothing in life more important to me than you, so if that's the case it was carelessness not design." He reached across the table and took her hand. "I'd forgive you for not believing it, but you *are* my priority. The work, everything I do, is for us."

"I know." She felt tired and emotional, and so, so pleased to see him and to finally be talking. "It was my fault as much as yours. I was too focused on the whole family, and I neglected *us*. I think it all goes back to my childhood and wanting to be present. I went too far the other way—I see that now."

Outside the rain had stopped and a patch of blue sky had appeared. It gave her hope, as did the feel of his hand tight on hers.

"You're the best mother and the twins are lucky."

"That's not true." It was difficult to admit it, but she knew she needed to. "I do things for them, instead of encouraging them to take responsibility. The conflict with Caitlin makes me feel like a bad mother, so I do everything I can to keep the peace. I want her to be happy, and I let her manipulate me. That's my mistake and I need to address it."

"I don't think you're going to need to. The girls have done some pretty deep soul searching since they found that article." On cue, his phone pinged with a message and he checked the screen. "It's Caitlin, wanting to know if we're getting a divorce."

"A *divorce?* That's what they think?"

"That's what the end of that article said. Can you fix things or should you end it?"

"I never read the end of it." The article had made her panic. It had been like reading medical symptoms on the internet and becoming convinced you were dying of something hideous. She hadn't wanted to believe her marriage was terminal.

"On the drive here, I kept going over that last day. I was distracted, thinking about clients, work, anything but the two of us. And you were trying to nudge me into going out for dinner, doing everything you could to remind me it was our anniversary."

"I should have reminded you."

"You shouldn't have to remind me. It was my job to remember. I should have booked a table for dinner and taken you on a romantic night away without making you book it yourself. I'm sorry things had to get to the point where you snapped. You should have felt able to reach out to me and tell me. It's my fault that you didn't. I was rushing, trying to get to work—as you say, prioritizing everything else."

"Maybe I needed this time on my own. It's been good for me." Talking to Finn had been good for her too. It had helped her clarify what was important to her.

"You're sure you were planning to come home?"

"Of course!" She was appalled that he felt the need to ask. A shaft of sunlight shot across the kitchen and she stood up. "Let's go to the beach."

"Now?"

"Why not? We used to love going there after a storm."

"We were teenagers."

"And? Fun isn't only for the young." She thought about her mother. "There are no rules that say you can't still enjoy the things you used to enjoy. The waves will be rough, it will be blowy and there will be no people."

He drained his coffee. "Are you planning to get dressed? And do you want breakfast first?"

"We'll take breakfast with us. The light will be wonderful after that storm. I'm going to take some photographs I can use later for painting."

They dressed quickly and Liza grabbed some fruit and a couple of muffins she'd bought the day before and pushed them into a bag.

Sean emerged, hair damp from a hasty shower and a sweatshirt looped around his shoulders. "I haven't seen you in shorts for years. You seem to have bought an entire new wardrobe."

"I didn't have the right clothing." She slid her feet into flip-flops and together they walked across the field and down onto the beach.

Apart from a lone dog walker in the distance, they had the place to themselves.

Liza kicked off her flip-flops and walked barefoot to the water's edge. The sea was choppy, but the storm clouds had cleared, and it promised to be another sunny day.

"We met on this beach." Sean put his arm round her. "I was intimidated by you."

She leaned into him. "That's ridiculous. You were the cool guy. The one all the girls wanted."

"And you didn't look twice at me."

"I looked. But I was shy." The water surged over her feet and ankles, freezing cold, numbing skin.

"You were thoughtful. I liked that. You seemed to live so much of your life in your head."

"I'd learned to be self-contained."

He glanced at her, understanding. "Have you spoken to your mother?"

"Every day." She saw his surprise. "We've talked more during the past week than we have for months. Years, maybe."

"About what?"

"Everything. Her life. Martha is posting details of their trip on social media. Images, videos—they've called their account *The Summer Seekers*. I'll show you later. They're obviously having great fun." Should she tell him about the letters? Maybe later. "I'm starting to understand her, and that helps." She slid her arm round his waist and they walked along the water's edge together. "I love it here."

"Me too. Remember when we used to talk about buying a place? We had so many dreams. Whatever happened?"

He remembered. She'd thought he'd forgotten those conversations, but he hadn't.

Her mood lifted further. "We grew up. We became sensible."

"Maybe it's time to do something about that." He scooped her up without warning and she shrieked as he waded into the water with her in his arms.

"Sean! If you drop me, I'll—"

"*If* I drop you? I'm going to drop you, sweetheart. It's a question of *when,* not *if.*"

"You'll ruin my new shorts." She gasped as a

wave crashed into them and the water splashed onto her face. "It's too rough."

"I'm here for you." He kissed her. "I'm always here for you."

Her heart turned over. When had they last said things like that to each other? She couldn't remember.

Their clothes were wet and clung to them.

"You're ridiculously irresponsible."

"I know. And about time. If you ask me, we've been far too adult lately. As you say, fun isn't only for the young." He lowered her into the water and pulled her close. "We're going to do more of this, Liza Lewis."

"Spend time wet and freezing? Drowning?"

"Being spontaneous." He stroked her soaked hair away from her face. "You're shivering. Let's get you home and into a hot shower."

They raced back up the beach hand in hand and trailed sand through the kitchen on their way upstairs.

"We should have rinsed our feet—" Liza was giggling as they stumbled on the stairs.

"We'll clean up later." Sean kissed her and together they squeezed into the shower in the main guest bedroom. "This isn't built for two."

She closed her eyes as the shower rained down on her, washing away the sand and the salt, and the stress of the past few weeks. Sean's mouth was on hers, delivering kisses and hope.

Constrained by the tight space, Sean switched off the flow of water, wrapped her in a towel and carried her through to the bedroom.

His hands were bold and sure, his body hard and familiar. He touched her with expert knowledge, smoothing away all the knots and doubts, removing the last of the distance between them. And for once she wasn't worrying about the past or the future. There was nothing but the present and Sean and the ultimate intimacy of being known and truly loved.

How could she have forgotten how this felt? How could she have questioned his feelings for her when they were so obvious? This wasn't sex, it was love, and he showed it with every touch, every kiss, every slow, skilled thrust until the pleasure built and spun out of control, leaving her weak and sated.

It was love, she thought, lying breathless in his arms.

Love.

He pulled her closer. "I missed this."

"Sex? It's not that long since we had sex."

"It's a long time since we had sex like this. Sex that felt close."

She knew what he meant. Intimacy was about so much more than physical contact. "I want to keep this feeling and I don't know how."

"I think if we're both trying to keep it, then we'll keep it. I love you, Liza."

"I love you too." She shifted so that she could see his face. "What happens now?"

"I make you one of my famous bacon sandwiches." He kissed her. "And then we're going to spend the rest of the day sharing our dreams and planning, the way we used to. I want to know every single thing you're thinking. Maybe we should go back down to the beach."

He pulled on his jeans and left the room while she lay there, feeling too lethargic to move.

She could hear birdsong through the open window and when she moved to the window she could see that the hot sun had dried off the last of the rain from the garden.

She could hear Sean clattering around in the kitchen and smelled the tantalizing scent of sizzling bacon.

She took another quick shower, dried her hair and pulled on one of the summer dresses she'd bought in the village. Then she sat on the edge of the bed and sent a text to Finn, explaining that she wouldn't be able to make dinner.

She no longer felt guilt, or regret. She knew that the time she'd spent with Finn had been nothing more than a brief distraction for him, but for her it had helped her refocus. She was grateful for that.

By the time she walked into the kitchen Sean had a stack of thick-cut bacon sandwiches and a fresh pot of coffee.

"We ought to call the girls." She ate one of the sandwiches. "How have they been this week?"

"Their usual selves until they found that article. Then they suddenly started being very caring. It was a little unsettling to be honest." He grinned at her. "Caitlin made me breakfast in bed yesterday. The smoke alarm went off four times because she burned the toast. And the two of them have been spending an hour a day working in the neighbors' garden, although Alice and worms are not a happy match."

"This transformation occurred without so much as a conversation?" She finished the sandwich. "That was good. I haven't cooked much this week. I've raided the deli in the village most days."

"But you cooked for Angie last night? It looked like an elaborate meal."

She could lie, but she didn't want their fresh start to begin with a lie. "I cooked for Finn Cool." She saw a question appear in his eyes. "It's a long story."

"I'm not in a hurry." He listened quietly as she told him all of it, from Finn's appearance in her kitchen, through to dinner.

"It's typical of my mother not to have told me that she knew him so well."

"She's always been secretive."

"I think she's private rather than secretive."

Sean put down his sandwich, half-eaten. "So how worried should I be?"

"About what?"

"About the fact that you'd dressed up to cook dinner for another man. You enjoyed his company—I can see that."

She felt her cheeks go hot. "We talked. He made me feel—interesting. I felt like an individual, instead of someone's wife, mother or teacher. I often think of myself in relation to other people, and that's something I have to change. We talked a lot about creativity and following your passion."

Sean's gaze held hers. "Passion?"

"For art and music." She'd come close to kissing Finn, but she hadn't done it. She'd made a choice. There was no need to share that. This whole week had been about making her own decisions. Decisions that weren't dictated by the needs of others. "Talking to him made me think about things more deeply. This week I've woken up every morning excited about the day. I've walked on the beach. I've read books without feeling there is something else I should be doing. I've sat and enjoyed the garden without thinking about all the tasks building up. I've eaten food I haven't had to cook. And I've painted, and I can't tell you how good that felt."

Sean nodded. "What have you been painting? Oils? Pastels?"

"A bit of everything." How much should she

tell him? "Finn wants to buy two of my paintings for his beach house."

Sean was silent for a moment and then gave a brief smile. "He's clearly a man with good taste. How does he know about your painting?"

"I talked to him about it. And I showed him some pictures of my old work."

Sean breathed deeply. "I haven't seen you this fired up and enthusiastic for a long time."

"Our conversations helped me make sense of what I wanted."

Sean pushed his plate away. "I'm sorry I made it difficult for you to have those conversations with me. That was number four on that article, wasn't it? *Do you still share your dreams with your partner?* That one hit me hard. I realized I don't know your dreams, and there was a time when I did. I remember the first time you told me you wanted to be an artist. You'd never told anyone that, and I felt like the king of the world because you'd shared that secret with me."

"That was an impractical dream. It's hard to make money that way, and I never wanted to be a starving artist."

"But as life got busy, I didn't nourish your creative side. I feel terrible about that."

"It was my responsibility."

He stood up and held out his hand. "Show me what you've been painting."

She slid her hand into his and led him to the

summerhouse. "I had a big clearout before I turned it back into my studio." She opened the door and Sean stepped past her and looked at the canvases stacked against the wall.

"These are all new?"

"Some I've painted this week. Some are old works that I dusted off."

She didn't mention the one she'd painted in a fever of inspiration that was now upstairs in her mother's bedroom ready to surprise her on her return.

Sean stood in front of the canvas that Finn had admired. "This is it?"

"Yes. He likes the ocean."

"It's stunning."

"So is his house. An architect's dream. You'd love it."

"We have to find a way to build you a studio in London."

She tidied away a few paints, more for something to do than because it needed doing. The shell that Finn had given her rested on the narrow windowsill, a reminder of that morning on the beach. Was it wrong to keep it? No. It didn't make her think of Finn, it made her think of the moment she'd decided to take up painting again.

"We don't have the space for a studio."

"Then we'll make the space." He stepped closer to the canvas, studying the brush strokes. "You have so much talent."

Pleasure rushed through her. "Thank you."

He turned and pulled her close. "So what's the dream, Liza? If you could design your perfect life, right now, how would it look?"

"Fantasy or reality?"

"Start with the big dream. And we'll see how we can make it reality." It had been years since they'd played this game. *Big Dreams, Little Dreams*.

The big dream. She rested her head against his chest. "I'd like to move out of the city. I'd like to live in a house like this one, full of character, close to the ocean. I'd like to live an outdoor life, filled with good friends, good food and good books. I'd like to paint. I'd like to not worry about the twins all the time. I'd like to know you're fulfilled and happy too. I don't want my dream life to come at the expense of someone else's happiness."

He stroked her hair. "We always dreamed about living near the beach. It's my fault we're in London."

"It's no one's fault." She glanced up at him. "It was a joint decision. You've worked hard to build your client base, and I'm grateful for the security it has given us."

"But—" He eased away from her. "This life we're living is not looking the way either of us wanted it to twenty years ago."

"I doubt anyone's does. And what you want at

twenty isn't the same as what you want at forty."

"I'm not sure. I could live here without too much of a struggle." He stared out across the garden. "Maybe when the twins leave for college."

Her heart bumped against her ribs because his mind was going in the same direction as hers. "Do you mean that?" She felt a spark of excitement and tried to temper it. "It isn't practical though, is it? There's my teaching. And your practice. I can't see how we could make it work."

"Maybe we need to try harder. Let's think about it." He kissed her. "In the meantime, let's keep sharing those dreams so at least we both know what we're aiming for."

She kept her arms round him and for a moment it felt as if they were alone in the world, as it had all those years before.

She didn't want fantasy, she realized. She wanted her reality, but an improved version.

"I'm glad you drove here."

"Are you? When you opened the door last night, I thought I might have made a mistake." His arms tightened. "Don't give up on us, Liza. I won't let you give up on us. We can do so much better."

She'd missed him. Not the limited part of Sean she'd had access to recently, but the whole Sean. The man she'd fallen in love with.

"I'll never give up on us." She rested her head

on his chest. "We ought to call the girls. Also, there's something I need to do before I speak to my mother later."

"That sounds mysterious."

"It is, a little." She took his hand and they walked back through the garden. "I never asked my mother much about her life before she met my father. She has these letters she wants me to read—actually I probably ought to check with her before I tell you everything."

"I understand. I'm pleased you feel closer to her. I know how much you wanted that. You focus on your mother and I'll call the girls and put them out of their misery. I was thinking—shall we stay here for a few more days? Call it our anniversary gift to each other."

She'd been assuming they'd head back to London.

"What would we do?"

"I have a few ideas." He flashed her a wicked smile. "Go to bed early, get up late, walk on the beach, eat dinner together outside. You can paint and I can watch you. We can read or do nothing. Talk. What do you say?"

She didn't need to think about it. "I say yes." She stood on tiptoe and kissed him. "I should probably speak to the girls too."

"Time for that later. Go and get those letters and call your mother."

Feeling stronger and steadier than she had in

411

a long time, Liza took the letters through to her mother's bedroom and untied the ribbon holding them together. She separated the first one and the second one, and put the others carefully on the table next to her mother's bed.

One at a time.

It was tempting to open them in advance, so that she could find a way to prepare her mother for what was inside, but she knew her mother didn't want that.

Popeye walked into the bedroom, eyed her with slightly less disdain than usual and then sprang onto her lap.

Liza was so shocked she didn't move. The cat nudged her hand and she tentatively stroked him. It was the first time Popeye had ever sought attention or affection from her.

"What's going on with you?" She stroked his fur and heard him purr. Maybe the cat was finally warming up to her. A bit like her mother.

The thought made her laugh.

Popeye was still on her lap when Kathleen called, at exactly the time they'd arranged.

"Do you have the letters?"

"Yes. I've made sure they're in date order and I have the first two right here." Liza slid off her shoes and lay on the bed, careful not to disturb the cat. "You haven't changed your mind? I'm worried if it might be difficult or upsetting." It couldn't be easy handling the fact that the man you'd loved and planned to marry had conducted an affair with your best friend. No wonder her mother had walked away. No wonder her mother hadn't been in touch with Ruth, or opened those letters.

"I'm sure. Martha and Josh have gone out for breakfast and to explore some of the local sights recommended in the guidebook, so I have this time undisturbed."

Liza opened the first letter. It was dated September 1960.

"Dearest Kate,

I'm not sure if you'll read this. I won't blame you if you don't, but I'm writing it anyway. There are things I need to say even if you're not going to hear them. It's ironic, isn't it, that the one person I was always able to say anything to (you!) is now no longer here to listen. It is a great loss, and the blame for that loss lies entirely with me. You've been the very best friend to me since that very first day at college, and you stayed that way until the end.

This should never have happened of course, and if I had been as good a friend to you as you have always been to me, then I would not find myself in the position of having to write these words. But I am not you, no matter how many times in the past I have wished to be blessed with even a few of your qualities.

I should be wishing this had never happened,

and yet how can I? I cannot begin to explain the emotional turmoil and confusion that comes from knowing that my greatest joy came at the expense of your happiness, and our friendship. The knowledge that I hurt you deeply is something I live with every day.

I know that my feelings for Adam vastly eclipse his for me. Perhaps I should care more about that than I do, but unlike you I never had expectations of grand passion or romance. I know he is marrying me because he feels driven by obligation. His feelings for me are a fraction of his feelings for you, and we would not have found ourselves in this position were it not for the baby . . ."

Liza stopped. Baby? *Baby?*

"Liza?" Her mother's voice came down the phone. "Why have you stopped?"

"Ruth was pregnant?"

"Yes. Please keep reading. I want to hear all of it."

Pregnant.

No wonder her mother had walked away and not tried to fix it.

Liza forced herself to carry on reading.

"You know that all I ever wanted was a child, and a family of my own. You used to tease me about it. What was the point of a college education if I had no intention of putting it to good use? Where was my ambition? But I was never

like you. I know that Adam came to see you after he found out—" Liza heard her mother's indrawn breath. That part obviously came as a shock. Should she pause? No. Not unless she was asked to. *"He told me that he went to you and begged you to take him back. To forgive. And he told me that you refused to listen and that you told him to live up to his responsibilities. He tried to see you again, but you'd left. You walked away to give us a chance. You removed yourself as an option. Even in our parting you were a better friend to me than I was to you."*

Liza broke off, her throat thick with tears. "Mum—"

"Don't stop, Liza. It's hard to hear and I'd like to get through it as fast as I can. You have no idea how relieved I am you're the one reading them."

Liza swallowed. Her job wasn't to judge or ask for more detail. Her mother needed her to read the letters.

She wiped tears from her cheeks and focused on the words.

"And now he resents me, and for that I don't blame him even though he is at least half responsible for this child we made. I have no expectations that he will be faithful, and next time I write to you—and I will write, even if you don't read these letters—I may well be a single mother."

Liza cleared her throat. "He wanted you back. You loved him, and you could have had him back."

"I loved him more than anything, and I was heartbroken, but I knew I would survive without him. I wasn't so sure about Ruth. She was always vulnerable. From that first day we met in college, I protected her."

Did her mother want to say more? This type of conversation was new to both of them.

"It must have been a special friendship." Liza trod carefully, wanting to be sensitive. "What was she like?"

"She'd had a difficult childhood. Lonely. Very strict parents. They were older, I believe, although I never met them. They didn't visit her."

Liza put the letters down. "How did you meet Adam?"

"At drama club. I dragged Ruth along with me. Adam was there. He was a medical student and rather full of himself I suppose, but I found him entertaining." She paused. "I've never told this story to anyone before."

Liza heard the uncertainty in her mother's voice. "I'm glad you're sharing it with me."

There was a pressure in her chest, a swell of emotion that threatened to overwhelm.

"So am I. Where were we? Oh yes, Adam. He was one of those annoying people who was good at everything. He seemed to achieve what he wanted with remarkably little effort. I remember we did *Much Ado About Nothing* the following summer. I was Beatrice and he was Benedict. You know how I love that play. The banter. The energy. It mimicked our real-life relationship. Ruth was forever intervening and begging us to stop arguing. She was a gentle soul."

Liza lay back on the bed, picturing it. "I didn't know you loved drama." She was learning so much about her mother.

"Only at college. After that I never stayed in one place long enough to commit to rehearsals."

Because of Adam and Ruth. Because her mother had walked away from that part of her life. This had to be a tough conversation for Kathleen. "I bet you were an incredible Beatrice."

"I believe *feisty* was a word that came up in more than one of the reviews."

She could easily picture her mother in the role. "That must be where Caitlin gets her love of drama." She diffused some of the emotion by steering the conversation away from the personal for a few minutes. Her mother wasn't the only one who needed a breather. Liza did too. She was struggling to hold it together, but she knew it was important that she didn't overreact or make her mother uncomfortable by revealing her own feelings. And hers were complicated, of course. For her it wasn't only about what she was hearing, it was about how it finally felt to have her mother's trust. "We can blame DNA for all those stage-worthy moments."

"Perhaps. Although she seems to give her best performances away from the stage."

They both laughed, and Liza pulled the phone a little closer. She was laughing with her mother. *Laughing!* And it felt good. "She does indeed. Tell me more about you and Adam."

"We were a cliché, really. Our romance onstage spilled offstage. But Ruth and I were inseparable. I wasn't going to be one of those people who ditched their friends when they fell in love, so invariably we ended up doing things together, the three of us. Ruth had gone to buy a picnic the day Adam proposed to me on the riverbank. Our exams had ended that day. I'd had a glass or two of champagne and was feeling excessively cheerful and optimistic about life. He produced a ring."

Liza heard the wistful note in her voice. "The one in the drawer."

"Yes. I believe it's valuable, although I don't know for sure. You're probably wondering why I still have it." Kathleen paused, as if she wasn't sure of the answer herself. "He refused to take it back, and I couldn't bring myself to sell it. I don't quite know why. Maybe I thought it might act as a caution."

At some point Liza would urge her to store it in a safer place, but that wasn't the priority. Right now her thoughts were only for her mother. "You accepted his proposal. So where did Ruth come into the story? How did that happen?"

Her mother didn't immediately answer. "I was naive. I believed Ruth to be impervious to his charms. She was the one person he didn't seem able to impress. And Adam, being Adam, would have felt compelled to convert her into an admirer. I'm sure he would have done the hard work, because Ruth would never have proactively gone after him. Not that I'm absolving her of blame. But I see how it might have happened. Adam was godlike, and she would have been flattered. But it turned out her feelings ran far deeper for him than I'd thought."

Liza's chest ached as she thought about how her mother must have felt. Her fiancé and her best friend. The betrayal had upended her life in every possible way.

"Had it been going on for a long time?"

"No. It was after the Summer Ball. I was due to go with Adam. Ruth hadn't planned to go at all. She didn't enjoy that kind of thing, but then I ate something that disagreed with me—it won't surprise you to know that I lacked caution in my eating even back then—and went down with a vicious bout of food poisoning. So Adam took Ruth instead." There was a pause, and the sound of her mother taking a breath. "And that was it. They didn't tell me right away, although I suspected something because they both behaved differently around me. And then a few weeks later Ruth discovered she was pregnant. And in those days being a single mother was greeted with horror and judgment of course."

"Oh you poor thing." Liza found it hard to imagine. "How did you cope?"

"It was hard. I'd lost my lover and my best friend. Ruth was distraught. She was worried about telling her parents. Worried about how she would survive. Guilty at having hurt me. Adam came to see me and begged forgiveness. Until you read the letter, I didn't know he'd told Ruth. He said it was a silly mistake." There was a hint of irritation in Kathleen's voice. "But that 'silly mistake,' even if that's what it was, couldn't be easily undone. Ruth was pregnant. She needed support. Her parents wouldn't give it. I could hardly give it. That left Adam. I told him he had to do the responsible thing. Then I packed up all my things and left. I didn't believe their relationship would sustain, or even that Adam would be there for her, but I knew there was more chance of that happening if I wasn't in the picture."

Liza closed her eyes. As a child she'd seen her mother as being apart—almost detached—as she pursued her own life, with her family an adjunct to that life. To her great shame she'd often considered Kathleen to be bordering selfish in her decision making, and yet here was an example of the most selfless behavior Liza could have imagined. Would she have been as strong willed in the same circumstances? She didn't know. All she knew was that she now had a very different view of her mother. "Did Dad know all this?"

"Yes. I avoided close relationships after that, as you might imagine. Both male and female. I was fortunate to fall into a job that I found exciting, and then came *The Summer Seekers*. I had a life that didn't allow me time for more than the most superficial of friendships, and that also absolved me of all need to reflect on my life. Had your father not been the steady, persistent man he was, I doubt I would have married at all."

"I'm glad you told me. I'm glad we're reading these letters together."

"I should have done it before, but I preferred to keep the past in the past. I've given you the impression that it was easy, and it wasn't. It really was the most terrible mess. Of course in those days we didn't have mobile phones or email, so communication wasn't as instant and continuous as it is now. That made it easier. Martha has Steven's name popping up on her phone all the time. I didn't have to handle that. No wonder the poor girl needed to escape."

Martha had been escaping from a bad relationship?

Liza had suspected there was something. She

also knew that her mother probably shouldn't have told her something so personal, so she didn't pursue it. Everyone had their own story, didn't they? Things were rarely as they appeared on the surface.

Her mother was obviously enjoying Martha's company, and Martha had made this trip possible. For that, Liza was grateful.

"I'm sure you're right that it was easier to make a clean break."

"I worried about Ruth terribly. I was angry of course—I'm not a saint, but I did worry. I was afraid Adam would leave her alone with that baby. Maybe she lost the baby. I don't know. I didn't want to know. But now—I suppose I'm about to find out—"

Liza heard her mother's voice wobble and tightened her grip on the phone. "*We're* about to find out." She was part of this story now. She wanted to know how it ended.

"I'm afraid reading them might be something I regret. What if I did the wrong thing, Liza?"

Her mother, who never asked or even seemed to value her opinion on anything, was asking her opinion and looking for reassurance.

Liza considered her answer carefully. "Whatever is in these letters doesn't change the decision you made. Regret achieves nothing, and it isn't even valid because looking back with distance, isn't the same as looking forward when you're close up." It was advice she intended to take herself. There was no point looking back and wishing she'd been a different type of mother. There was no point in wishing she'd spoken to Sean sooner. She'd done what felt right at the time. "You did what was right for you and we're going to remember that as we finish reading these letters."

"Yes. You're right of course. Thank you. You've always been sensible. You're like your father, and that's a good thing."

Liza had never heard her mother like this. After her father had died, she'd been sad but practical. After the intruder she'd been feisty. But now, facing her past, she was showing a side of herself that Liza had never seen before. A vulnerable side.

"Maybe we should take this slowly." She looked at the little stack, and wondered what other shocks and revelations lurked in those folded pieces of paper. "We could do a few a day. Or I could read them all and summarize them for you."

"Oh Liza—" Her mother's voice wobbled. "I don't know what I did to deserve a daughter like you."

The words unlocked the emotion Liza had been trying to keep under control. "You should have had an adventurous daughter, someone who wanted to travel the world. I wanted you to stay home and read to me."

"You deserve a mother who doesn't give you constant anxiety attacks."

Liza managed a smile. "I'm working on that. Given time I might even become what Caitlin would describe as 'chilled.' "

"Don't change too much. I admire the way you are. I know I was absent a great deal when you were young. The reasons for that are complicated. Yes, I loved my career, but it was so much more than that. Part of me has never stopped being afraid of loving deeply. Of course that doesn't mean I don't love deeply—I do. But I was always afraid to give that love too big a place in my life. Like being afraid of heights, and not looking down when you're standing on a cliff edge."

She'd always thought she was to blame for the fact that she wasn't close to her mother, but she could see now it wasn't anything to do with her.

Now, finally, she understood.

Her mother's character had been formed long before Liza had arrived on the scene. Beliefs and behavior arose from unseen events. Something that had happened to her mother sixty years before had continued to send aftershocks through her life. Her mother had been hurt, so she'd distanced, and that feeling of distance had made Liza determined to be closer to her own children, except that she'd got it wrong and now she needed to unravel that.

If Adam had married her mother then Kathleen might have been a different type of mother, which was a ridiculous thought because if Kathleen had married Adam then Liza wouldn't have existed. But it was a reminder that everything was shaped by events and her own children would be shaped by events too. Perhaps they'd forever be cautious in relationships because they'd remember finding an article entitled "Eight Signs That Your Marriage Might Be in Trouble." Perhaps they'd decide not to get married or perhaps they'd get married and watch for every one of those eight signs and be happier in their relationships because of it.

"You lived the life you needed to live," she said. "I respect that. It's inspiring, and I'm planning on doing more of that myself from now on."

"You are? Tell me more."

"Later." There was time enough for that. "Let's focus on these letters. What do you want to do?"

"Read them. All of them. Now we've started I don't think I can bear the suspense of not knowing. Do you have the time?"

Liza glanced up as Sean walked into the room bearing a large glass of wine and a cheese platter.

He put it down quietly on the table next to the bed, raised his eyebrows when he saw Popeye curled into her lap and handed her a piece of paper that said "I love you."

She smiled at him and then turned her attention back to her mother.

"I have all the time in the world. Let's do this."

20

KATHLEEN

ALBUQUERQUE~WINSLOW, ARIZONA

Our baby was born today. A little girl. We named her Hannah Elizabeth Kathleen. Perhaps you'll think that foolish, or even thoughtless, but it's important to me. Adam resisted. I suppose he didn't want to be reminded, but I will always think of you as my true and best friend, even though I no longer have the right to call you that.

Kathleen stared out the window as they headed through the deserts of northern Arizona and took a scenic detour through the Petrified Forest National Park.

They'd set out early so that Martha and Josh could do a short hike, which their research had told them was best done early in the day. The hour was irrelevant to Kathleen, who hadn't slept at all.

Somehow the rhythm of the car and the blur of the landscape was more relaxing than a still, silent hotel room filled with nothing but her thoughts.

They drove to the trailhead for the Blue Mesa Trail that wound its way to the valley floor.

"It's not far, so we shouldn't be long, Kathleen. Is that okay?" Even though it was early, Martha pulled on her sun hat and smothered her arms in sunscreen.

"Take your time. Enjoy." She was looking forward to being alone so that she could spend time with her thoughts and memories.

She waved Martha and Josh off, delighted to see that Josh took Martha's hand, and stepped closer as he pointed out something on the horizon.

The view was spectacular, but Kathleen stared at it for only a few seconds before closing her eyes.

Hannah Elizabeth.

Ruth had become a mother at twenty-one years of age, and Adam a father.

What a challenge that must have been for him, and yet it seemed he'd risen to that challenge.

She'd lain awake all night thinking about the letters Liza had carefully read aloud. Her memory was unreliable and frustrating much of the time, but for some reason she'd been able to recall every word and she'd reexamined the contents line by line.

She'd been able to picture Ruth clearly. She'd heard her friend's voice in the words on the page, measured and thoughtful. There was an assurance by the end that had been missing in those early letters.

Kathleen had absorbed every one of the facts, delivered in chronological order. Each letter had been an update on Ruth's life, another piece of the picture revealed.

She knew now that Hannah had been born with a heart defect that had required surgery when she was a few months old. That had fed Ruth's maternal anxiety, even though the child had been strong and healthy since. It had been Hannah's condition that had driven Adam's choice to be a heart surgeon. *Cardiothoracic,* Kathleen thought, imagining him masked and gowned, with another person's life in his hands.

In those early days, Ruth had doubted Adam's love for her, but had never doubted his love for their daughter. She credited Hannah with being the reason he hadn't left. Adam adored his daughter.

Hannah had been smart and creative, a talented violinist, with a love of sport that had brought her close to her father. In the winter they'd skied at Lake Tahoe, and in the summer they'd hired a boat and sailed down the Pacific Coast.

There had been photographs with that letter, which Liza had described and offered to send to Martha's phone.

Kathleen had refused. Hearing it was one thing.

Seeing was another. She could absorb only so much of the past at one time.

Adam's career had taken them to Australia for a year, and then to Boston, before they returned to California and settled there.

The letters were filled with updates on Hannah and Adam, Ruth's pride in her family as obvious as her love. She described a contented life, cemented in place by family.

Kathleen felt a sense of relief. She'd done the right thing. By stepping away, she'd given them a chance to make it work and they had done that.

She was pleased. Also sad that she'd missed so many of those years.

If she'd stayed in touch maybe she could have been a support to Ruth when she'd had that brush with cancer, or when Adam died suddenly ten years before.

But Ruth had other sources of support now, of course.

She had Hannah, who lived close by and worked as a pediatrician. She'd followed her father into medicine.

Kathleen imagined a woman who was part Ruth, part Adam, and wished now that she'd asked Liza to send the photos.

Ruth was proud of Hannah, just as Kathleen was proud of Liza.

Had she told her daughter she was proud?

She felt a moment of panic. Did she know?

The car door opened suddenly and Kathleen jumped and opened her eyes.

"Sorry. Were you dozing?" Martha was smiling down at her, her face pink from the sun. "That was amazing! Although I'm glad we came so early—no way would I want to slog back up that hill in the heat of the day."

It took Kathleen a moment to compose herself.

"The word *amazing* conveys nothing. I can't picture your experience from that sparse description." She felt unsettled and raw. She wished for a moment that Liza was here. Liza would understand.

Reading those letters couldn't have been easy, but her daughter had been compassionate and sensitive. She'd checked how her mother was feeling, without in any way smothering her or forcing her to reveal the emotions that were swirling inside her. Liza had asked few questions, even though she must have had hundreds.

Kathleen's eyes stung. Her biggest regret wasn't the years she hadn't been close to Ruth, but the years she'd wasted when she could have been closer to Liza. That bothered her more than the lost relationship with Ruth. She'd held herself back from the people who were most important to her.

She tried to focus as Martha slid into the car next to her. "You enjoyed yourselves?"

"It's magnificent. There are multiple layers of

rock, all different colors. Blues, and purples—wait—" Martha pulled out her phone and showed Kathleen the photographs. "This will give you a better idea than my totally inadequate words. Do you see the petrified wood?"

Kathleen was touched by Martha's insistence on including her in the parts of the trip that were beyond her capabilities.

"It's the result of extensive erosion." Josh leaned forward from the passenger seat, every bit as enthusiastic as Martha. "You're looking at layers of exposed sandstone and bentonite clay. The mineral deposits are a few hundred million years old. It was formed in the late Triassic period."

"Your brother would accuse you of being a nerd at this point," Martha said and Josh gave her a smile.

"He would. And I'd point out that it wasn't politically correct to call someone a nerd."

"At which point he would roll his eyes and open another beer."

From Josh's laughter Kathleen thought it safe to assume that Martha's guess had been correct. They'd obviously been talking about his brother on their walk.

The dead never left, she knew that. They walked alongside you.

What would Brian have said, if he could be with her now?

You read the letters? Good. It will make your mind feel tidier to have that chapter complete.

Kathleen smiled. She'd never been the tidiest of people.

"A few hundred million years." She studied the rocks in the photographs Martha was showing her, because that seemed safer than studying her feelings. "I feel young by comparison. The colors are striking. Like an artist's palette." She thought how much Liza would love it and felt herself wobble. "You must send those to Liza. She's been painting again. She uses a lot of blue. She likes blue. She's always loved to paint the ocean." She was engulfed by a smothering cloud of homesickness. Oh how she wished she was back in Oakwood Cottage, feeling the afternoon sun on her face and smelling the sea in the air. Everything here was arid, baked dry by the scorching sun. At home the garden would be lush and green, and her favorite rose would be flowering in scented profusion. Popeye would be lying on the patio, basking in a pool of sunshine. "You will send them to Liza?"

"I'll do it as soon as I have a strong signal." Martha was no longer smiling. "Is everything all right, Kathleen? Are you drinking plenty?"

"If only she said that when I had a gin in my hand." But Kathleen took the water Martha handed her and took a sip as she glanced at the

432

view. "Are you going to upload the photos to our social media?"

"Listen to you—upload—" Martha nudged her "—we'll make a technology lover of you, yet."

Kathleen shuddered, but more because it was expected of her than because she felt a particular aversion. It was technology that was allowing her to talk to Liza.

"I thought maybe I'd call Liza when we stop for lunch."

"You can call her anytime. Josh and I can go for a walk to give you some privacy if that would help."

Kathleen pulled herself together. "Lunchtime will be fine. She'll probably be at the beach with Sean at the moment and the signal isn't good there."

"Sean is at the cottage? I thought Liza was there on her own?"

"He joined her, so they're spending a few days together."

"That's good."

It was good. Was Liza happy? All Kathleen wanted was for her daughter to be happy. She'd always wanted that, of course, but now that the barriers between them had been removed it was as if their happiness was somehow connected.

"Shall we record a piece to camera?"

It would be an excuse to send something to Liza without appearing needy.

With Martha's assistance, Kathleen maneuvered her aching, uncooperative limbs out of the car and shaded her eyes.

"It's already hot."

"We'll do this quickly." Martha found the right angle, gave Kathleen a cue to start talking, and recorded a piece. "Such a pro. You never fumble or stumble."

"Where next?"

"We're heading to Winslow, Arizona." Martha started to sing and Kathleen lifted a hand.

"We had an agreement—I suffer your excruciating playlist, providing you don't sing along with it."

"It's not excruciating—I've chosen each song specifically for its relevance to where we're going. And after Winslow, we're headed to the Grand Canyon, via the Meteor Crater which is fifty thousand years old which is *definitely* older than you, Kathleen. We've booked an extra day at the Grand Canyon. Woohoo! And Josh has got us rooms with a view so you can sit on your balcony and watch the sunrise and sunset."

She'd talk to Liza, Kathleen thought. She'd find a way to share the view with her daughter.

"Sounds like a perfect day," Josh said and Martha shook her head.

"You won't be sitting anywhere. You'll be river rafting."

"I will not be river rafting."

434

"It's all booked. I've blown the last of my savings, so it would be churlish of you to back out now."

"Martha!" Josh looked exasperated. "I hate water. You know I hate water."

"Red would have wanted you to do this."

"I would have refused."

"And he would have found a way to persuade you." Martha stood on tiptoe and kissed his cheek. "It's amazing what you can enjoy when you push yourself out of your comfort zone."

That was true, Kathleen thought, delighted to see that they'd reached the kissing stage. Although technically Josh hadn't kissed Martha. It had been the other way round. And Martha was a naturally tactile and demonstrative person of course, but still . . .

Would she have asked Liza to read those letters if it hadn't been for Martha?

Probably not. She was eternally grateful to her, and wished her nothing but good things.

Photographs and filming finished, they climbed back into the car and headed onward on their journey through Arizona.

Kathleen suggested sampling the playlist, much to the delight of her much younger companions.

Martha's head bobbed in time with the music and occasionally she started singing and then remembered that she wasn't supposed to be singing and clamped her mouth shut.

Kathleen smiled. Even in a short time they'd found a comfortable routine and there was something soothing in that.

The crushing homesickness had passed, fortunately, and she felt excited about the day ahead. She'd see Arizona and California, as she'd always wanted to. Oakwood Cottage would be waiting for her when she'd finished her trip, and she'd appreciate it all the more for her absence.

In the meantime it was a comfort to know that Liza was there, walking on the beach that she thought of as her own, pottering round her garden, tending her plants.

In Winslow, Martha found their hotel easily and they parked and checked in.

It was built in the style of a hacienda, with both a Spanish and Mexican feel.

Revived after lunch, Kathleen joined them to explore the town of Winslow.

Martha waved her phone in front of Kathleen's face, bubbling with excitement. "Look at this! You're trending!"

"Trending?" Kathleen, struggling with the heat, removed an old-fashioned fan from her bag and opened it.

"On social media! Our last post was seen by a TV presenter—must have been the hashtag—and she shared it, and reached out to see if she could cover the story and interview you and now it's all blowing up—" Martha checked her phone again, "well, FOX! You're famous, Kathleen. You're going to need an agent."

"I hereby appoint you to the role." Kathleen fanned herself as Martha scrolled through her messages.

"You can't possibly give interviews to all these people or you'll never get to enjoy your road trip. Why don't we offer an exclusive to one, for now—to the channel you worked for? And then you can see how you feel about doing more once you get home. I can handle that for you. Hey, maybe they'll offer you a book deal."

"I'd rather do something than write about it."

"I'll ghost write it for you." Martha was still scrolling, and Josh shook his head, amused.

"Have you thought about applying for a job in public relations, or media relations?"

"Nah, I already have a job, thanks. I'm Kathleen's personal assistant. I am going to handle her media inquiries." Martha typed a reply to someone, her fingers flying so fast that it seemed like magic to Kathleen. "I am her first line of defense."

"Defense against what?"

"Anyone who tries to give her tea that isn't Earl Grey. Also the paparazzi." Martha sent one message, and then another. "We can't have them knowing about Kathleen's giddy lifestyle."

"Talking of giddy lifestyles, this heat does make me feel a little strange." Kathleen slipped her arm into Martha's and she immediately put her phone away.

"Is it too hot for you? Do you want to go back to the hotel?"

"No. Let's walk for a little."

Whatever would she have done on this trip without Martha?

Josh strolled ahead, but Martha stayed with Kathleen.

"You asked Liza to read the letters, didn't you?" She kept her voice low. "You don't have to tell me about it. But if you need a big hug or anything, I'm here."

A big hug.

Martha was still willing to give emotionally, despite what had happened. It gave Kathleen hope for her.

"It was the right thing to do. Thank you for encouraging me."

Adam hadn't left Ruth.

She knew for sure now that she'd done the right thing.

Ruth had enjoyed a happy life. Adam had stayed with her, although something in the phrases Ruth used so carefully had made Kathleen wonder if there had been an affair in there at some point. It wouldn't have surprised her, just as the fact that Adam had enjoyed a distinguished career didn't surprise her.

Kathleen pictured him, sure and confident

438

standing at a lectern. A little thicker around the middle, perhaps, hair with a few silvery streaks. But he would have had presence. Adam always had presence.

Martha reached across and gave her hand a squeeze. "Did it upset you, Kathleen?"

Upset? No.

"It unsettled me, but it was the right thing to do."

"And are you going to get in touch with Ruth?"

"That, I haven't decided." And it had been weighing on her since Liza had read the last letter.

Martha nodded. "I suppose that depends on whether you want this to be the end, or a beginning. It could be either."

Kathleen stopped walking. The heat pressed down on her.

An end or a beginning. Martha was right.

Which was it to be? Should she view the letters as closure, or should she make contact with Ruth?

She hadn't replied to a single one of Ruth's letters. Her old friend knew nothing about her life, or even that she was still alive.

She thought about it for the whole afternoon, and while she was dressing for dinner. Her room was delightful, with antique furnishings, a hand-woven Zapotec rug and a cast-iron tub.

Ready early, she sat on the chair next to the bed and called Liza, who answered almost immediately even though it was past midnight.

"Did I wake you?"

"No. I was finishing off a painting in the summerhouse so Sean and I ate late. We only just finished clearing up. We stole a bottle of wine from your cellar."

Kathleen smiled. "Steal away. You know how much I approve of indulgence."

"I've been thinking about you all day. Are you all right, Mum?"

"Yes, although I've been thinking about those letters of course."

"I've been thinking about them too." There was a clatter in the background. "She had a happy life. You were partly responsible for that."

"I don't see it that way, but I'm pleased she was happy."

"How is Arizona?"

"Hot." Kathleen gazed out the window. "Tomorrow is the Grand Canyon, and I'm hopeful that Martha and Josh might get together."

"Are you still matchmaking?"

"Shamelessly."

Liza laughed. "Keep me posted on that. Sounds as if Martha could do with some fun in her life. And how about you? Have you decided whether you're going to contact Ruth?"

"I'm still thinking about it."

"Well, if you want to talk about it, or think it through aloud, you know I'm here."

"Thank you." That wave of homesickness was back, unbalancing her. "I don't know what I would have done without you."

"You would have managed fine, the way you always have."

"No." She heard the clink of a glass and thought about Liza sitting in the kitchen of Oakwood Cottage, sipping chilled white wine from one of the pretty glasses she'd picked up on a trip to Venice. "I miss you, Liza. I wish you were here."

"I miss you too—" Liza's voice sounded strange. She cleared her throat. "You're much better off with Martha. You know I'd be nagging you about your alcohol intake, too many burgers and late nights."

"I'm lucky to have a daughter who cares so much."

There was a pause. "Are you sure you're all right? You don't sound like yourself."

Was she all right? Kathleen wasn't sure.

"I'm fine, but—I love you, Liza. I love you very much. I don't tell you that enough." And now she'd finally said it, she wondered why it had taken her so long. It wasn't as if her feelings had changed or deepened. The only thing that had changed was her ability to share those feelings.

It took Liza so long to respond Kathleen wondered if she'd hung up.

"Liza?"

"Yes, I'm here. I love you too. You know that." There was another pause. "Are you sure you're all right? If you'd like me to come, I can fly out tomorrow. I'll get on the first flight."

Kathleen felt emotion squeeze her chest. Oh how she wished her daughter was here, but she couldn't ask that of her. "You have France soon. There must be so much to do."

"Would you like me to come?"

Yes, yes. Please come. She thought how reassuring it would be to have Liza by her side if she decided to see Ruth again after all these years. But Liza had France and her family to think of. Sean. It would be selfish to ask her to come, and Kathleen had put her own needs first more than enough in life. "No." She said it firmly. "There's no need, but thank you. I should go. We have a table booked and it's a popular restaurant."

"Enjoy your evening. Love you, Mum."

"I love you too." Feeling better for the conversation, Kathleen headed to the restaurant. It was crowded with people, the air fragrant with chili, garlic and roasted meat.

She ate red corn posole and it reminded her of the time she'd traveled to Mexico to film *The Summer Seekers*. When would that have been? 1975? No, later.

Martha and Josh were deep in conversation

about their Grand Canyon trip, which left Kathleen time to enjoy the food and the view of the pretty garden.

Ruth had mentioned her garden in California, and her terrace with the view of the Pacific Ocean.

I love to cook, and I still drink Earl Grey tea, as we did all those years ago.

I often think about you and wonder where you are.

I wonder whether you ever think of me, the way I so often think of you. Writing these letters has been my way of staying close to you. When I write them, I feel as if you're listening.

Kathleen put her fork down. "I want to see her."

Martha and Josh stopped talking.

"Ruth?"

"Yes, Ruth." Her heart beat a little faster and she took a sip of water. "I'm here now. I may never make it as far as California again."

Martha smiled at her. "I think she'll be beyond thrilled to hear from you."

"There you go again. Hyperbole."

"Well, let's assess her reaction before you correct my grammar." Martha reached across the table. "Trust me, she'll be thrilled."

"Or she might think it strange that I'd make contact after all this time." Kathleen felt a little shaky. "Maybe she won't remember me."

"Kathleen—" Martha was gentle "—she never

stopped writing to you. If she didn't want to hear from you, she would have stopped writing. If you asked me to guess, I'd say she's been hoping to hear from you for a long time."

"She might be dead."

"Or she might be alive and thinking of her old friend." Martha put down her napkin and stood up. "We're finished here, so why don't we go back to the room and do it right now?"

Josh grabbed his beer and Kathleen's drink. "Good plan."

And that was how Kathleen found herself sitting on the edge of her bed, between these two people who she'd grown so fond of. Martha on one side, Josh on the other, supporting her like bookends.

"This might be foolish. You can never go back."

"This isn't going back, Kathleen. It's going forward." Martha opened the message Liza had sent her, with Ruth's address and phone number.

"That's easy for you to say. I might regret it."

This time it was Josh who spoke. "I think in life we tend to regret the things we don't do more than the things we do, at least that's how it has always been for me."

Kathleen knew he was thinking of his brother. She gave his hand a squeeze but didn't say anything. Her command of the English language and her diction might be superior to Martha's, but her ability to say the right thing in emotional situations was vastly inferior. The last thing she wanted to do was hurt Josh with her clumsy attempts at platitudes.

"And it's because I don't want you to feel regrets that we're rafting on the Colorado River." Martha earned herself a look from Josh before he turned back to Kathleen.

"If you call, I'll treat us to the best bottle of wine you've tasted."

"French?"

Josh winced. "Californian."

Kathleen gave an exaggerated shudder. "What a life you must have led. But you're right, of course. Let's do this." She sat up a little straighter. "Martha. Make that call."

She held tightly to Josh's hand as Martha dialed, and held her breath as Martha spoke to someone on the other end of the phone.

There was a long pause during which Kathleen's chest ached and she concluded that her ability to handle intense emotion hadn't improved with age.

Finally, Martha handed her the phone. Her eyes glistened.

"It's Ruth. She can't wait to talk to you."

Kathleen took the phone, wishing she'd asked Josh and Martha to leave her alone to talk to her old friend, but they must have known instinctively that was what she wanted because

Josh stood up and gave her shoulder a squeeze and Martha gave her a kiss on the cheek and whispered that they'd be "right outside."

As the door clicked quietly shut behind them, Kathleen was left alone.

Her hand was shaking so much she could hardly hold the phone to her ear.

"Hello? Is that you, Ruth?"

21

MARTHA

GRAND CANYON

"I don't like leaving her." Martha and Josh had driven the two and a half hours to Peach Springs, leaving Kathleen asleep in the gorgeous rustic lodge with its views across the Grand Canyon.

She'd assured Martha that she could happily spend a month admiring the view from her suite, and that spending a day alone would be a pleasure not a hardship, but still Martha felt unsettled.

How was it possible that she'd grown fond of Kathleen so quickly? It was partly the circumstances—being closeted together in a car—partly because she reminded Martha a little of her grandmother, but mostly because Kathleen had given her back her confidence.

She no longer doubted her ability behind the wheel of the car. Instead, she looked forward to the driving. She'd stopped punishing herself for past decisions. Thanks to Kathleen, she'd stopped thinking of them as bad decisions. They were *her*

447

decisions, and if her family didn't approve that was their problem.

But this morning she'd felt torn between her fondness for Kathleen, and her desire to do something to help Josh.

"I know she's worried about meeting Ruth. I had a feeling she would have liked Liza to be there." They'd put the top down and Josh tugged his hat down to shade his eyes from the hot Arizona sun.

"Ask her to fly out?"

"Not an option. She has family of her own. They're going to France."

"Then we'll go with Kathleen to Ruth's. If she looks as if she wishes she'd made a different decision, we'll drag her out of there and take her for a walk on the beach instead. Or we can take her home."

"Home?"

"My place. I live up the coast from Santa Monica. I have a great view of the ocean from my deck."

She had an unsettling vision of him sprawled on the deck wearing nothing but board shorts. Her imagination had always been her downfall and now it was presenting her with vivid images of Josh naked. She tried to switch it off and replace it with less provocative images of Josh hunched over a computer screen, looking serious. But that didn't work because he didn't hunch and although he often looked serious, when he smiled it was as if someone had switched on all the lights full beam.

"You live near the sea?" Her voice sounded strange and she cleared her throat. "I thought you hated water?" She wasn't going to think about him emerging from the ocean, with droplets of water clinging to those broad shoulders.

"I like looking at it. Not experiencing it."

"So if I was drowning, you wouldn't save me?"

"I'd save you by alerting the lifeguard."

"That doesn't count."

"You're alive at the end of it, so it counts. The secret of success is the ability to delegate a task to the most qualified person. If I tried to save you, we'd both drown. Talking of which, you might be right about today. We shouldn't have left her," Josh said. "Let's go back. Who wants to go rafting on the Colorado River, anyway?"

Why did he have to make her laugh? She was doomed. "We do."

"*You* do. It always seemed like a bad idea to me. Still does. Particularly now I know I'm expected to save you. Turn the car around."

Was he serious?

The sudden stab of sympathy pierced those unsettling images. "Is this very hard for you? Doing this without your brother?"

"Being without him is hard—it doesn't matter much what I'm doing."

She wanted to stop the car and give him a big hug, but instead she kept the conversation light. "In that case, we might as well go rafting. You can't back out now. Not when I've spent my life savings on this experience for you. *You're welcome, Martha.*"

"You're persistent, Martha. You're a pain in the neck, Martha."

She patted his thigh and then wished she hadn't because the moment her fingers made contact with hard muscle those images came rushing back, along with a scorching rush of attraction. *You're a fool, Martha!* "No need to be scared. And no need to worry about saving me. I'll save you." Although she had a feeling she was the one who might need saving, and not from the water. But she didn't regret doing this, no matter the cost to her. She hated the thought of him taking this long trip alone, hitching a ride from place to place, making small talk with whoever picked him up, thinking about his brother the whole time. He would have carried that sadness with no one to help bear the load.

Although it had to be said that right now he didn't seem particularly pleased that she was by his side. She could feel him glowering at her from under the brim of his baseball cap.

"You're trained in white water rescue?"

"Not specifically, but the people I'm paying to escort us are, and I'm generally resourceful.

If you promise to stop complaining, I'll promise to rescue you if you fall headfirst into the water. You're going to love this. And I honestly think it will be good for you." And unless the searing burn of sexual attraction didn't fade soon, she'd be glad of the excuse.

"Oatmeal is good for me. Doesn't mean I love it."

"Would you have been like this if Red had been sitting in this car with you?"

Josh gave a reluctant laugh. "I would have been worse. Red never would have let me get away with a day trip. He would have booked a week on the toughest part of the river. Probably unguided."

"Terror can bond people, I hear."

"Is that why you're doing this? So I'll cling to you?"

"I don't need an excuse for that. When I'm ready to grab you, I'll grab you." And at this rate, it was going to be sooner rather than later.

"A little warning might be helpful. For example, are you going to do it while driving? Given that you're a relatively inexperienced driver, you might want to pull over first."

"I was inexperienced in Chicago—I have tons of experience now. And I'm not sure when I'm going to grab you." She shot him a look. "I'll do it when the time is right. When it comes to decision making, I'm still feeling my way."

451

"Any time you want to feel your way with me, go right ahead."

Oh Martha, Martha. "Are you flirting with me?"

"Possibly. It's possible I'm trying to take my mind off the nightmare you've so generously planned for me."

"And I need to make sure that getting physical with you is what I want, and that I'm not only doing it to please Kathleen."

He turned his head. "I understand you letting me join you on this trip to please Kathleen, but you'd have sex with me to please Kathleen too?"

"I'm a generally accommodating person. It's something I need to be mindful of when I'm making decisions." She managed to keep her expression serious. "She's vulnerable right now, and it would make her happy to know that her little plan to bring us together has worked. She thinks I need to get my confidence back."

"Do I get any say in any of this?"

It was a good thing he couldn't read her mind or he'd probably decide it was safer to walk the rest of Route 66 than be trapped in the car with her. "Neither of us had any say in it. We're all innocent pawns in Kathleen's game." Thinking about Kathleen triggered another niggle of anxiety. "Maybe you're right, and we should turn round. She put on a brave face yesterday, but she didn't sleep last night. Did you see those shadows under her eyes?"

"She's eighty. And we had a busy day yester-day."

Somehow he always managed to reassure her. And it was true that they'd had a busy day. They'd driven from Winslow to Flagstaff, stopping at the Meteor Crater.

"And you did fill her head with scientific facts, which probably exhausted her." But Martha knew the real cause of Kathleen's fatigue went deeper than that. She was anxious about meeting Ruth. "I have a feeling that now she has made the decision, she wants to get it done. Be serious for a moment—do you think we should have stayed and distracted her?"

"No. She wanted us to do this." Josh rubbed his hand over his jaw. "I've been given strict instructions to show you a good time, which will be a challenge given my lack of affection for water sports."

Martha adjusted her grip on the wheel. "You're supposed to show me a good time? What exactly does that mean?"

"You'll know it when you see it."

She was pretty sure that any time spent with Josh would be a good time. "What if I don't? What if your idea of a good time isn't my idea of a good time?"

"Then you'll have to lie. To keep her happy."

Martha studied the road ahead. "I won't lie. So you'd better make sure I have a good time, Josh

Ryder. No moaning about water. No sarcasm. No blinding me with facts about how old the rocks are or when the Grand Canyon was formed."

"Would you like to know how many hapless tourists drown rafting on the Colorado River every year?"

"No."

"The temperature of the water?"

"Definitely not."

"This is like being with Red."

She glanced at him and was relieved to see a smile on his face. "He had curly, badly behaved hair, an oversize rear end and skin with a tendency to burn in the sun?"

"Mmm." He gestured to the side of the road. "Pull over."

"Now? Why?"

"I can state with confidence that your curly hair is as cute as your freckles, but I might need to take a closer look at your rear end before I can give a definitive answer on relative sizes."

"Josh Ryder! I am not pulling over so that you can stare at my butt."

"My loss." But he was grinning and so was she.

And maybe that should have surprised her as they'd been talking about his brother, but she'd learned after her grandmother had died that sadness and laughter could coexist.

"So how is this like being with Red?"

"You mean apart from the laughter? Like you, he was never interested in any of this stuff and I tried to make him interested. I often tried to persuade him to change his life, and do something more serious and adult, but all he wanted to do was chase waves and have a good time. Interestingly, he never tried to change me, even though my life choices seemed as crazy to him as his did to me."

"But despite all that you were close." She could hear it in the way he talked about his brother.

"Yes. Whenever we were both in we'd get together and share a few beers—more than a few."

"I'm surprised your evil boss gave you the time off. You should have taken yourself to an employment tribunal or something. Cruelty to workers."

"I like to think I was fair with everyone else." He glanced at the roadside. "Make a right. If you're determined to do this, this is our turning."

She turned and found the parking lot. "From here we go on a bus to the bottom of the canyon. I'm excited, are you?"

"Not remotely." But he was good-natured as the bus bumped its way down the road and was still almost smiling as they settled themselves into the boat.

Martha pressed her thigh a little closer to his as their guide introduced himself.

"Prepare yourselves for a wet, wild roller-coaster ride down eight white water rapids."

Josh rolled his eyes. "Thanks, Martha."

"Why the sarcasm? According to the promotional blurb we are going to be thrilled. If it wasn't true, they wouldn't say it."

"I can think of other, safer ways of being thrilled."

"Stop moaning. You, Mr. Tycoon, are about to get up close and personal with the mighty Colorado River." And she was going to get up close and personal with him, if he wanted that too. She'd made her decision, and she was sure about it. Josh was the most exciting man she'd met in a long time, maybe ever. She loved the way he was with Kathleen, and the way he talked about his brother. She loved his sense of humor. Most of all she loved the way she felt when she was around him. With Josh, she never felt less. She never felt as if she should be more or different. He never chipped at her edges, tried to change who she was or make her smaller. Life had shaved pieces from her confidence, but being with him healed all those raw places.

She was happy, and that was enough.

It didn't matter that she didn't know what the future held. No one did, really. They *thought* they did, but so much was out of your control. If her grandmother hadn't died, Martha might have finished her degree but then she would have been on a different track and who was to say that would have been happy? For a start she wouldn't have met Kathleen. If she hadn't needed to get away from her family and Steven so badly there was no way she would have taken a driving job, and no way she'd be sitting here now on the mighty Colorado River with the walls of the Grand Canyon rising up all around her, alongside a man who made her heart race. Basically, there wasn't a single thing about the past she'd change, except perhaps finding a way to make people you loved live forever. But all anyone really had was right now, and she was determined to make the most of right now. And no doubt her family would disapprove of her current choices, but if there was one thing she'd learned on this trip it was that the only opinion that mattered was your own.

She lifted her face to the sun and smiled, feeling good about life for the first time in ages. *About herself.*

"I hope you're still smiling when you're submerged by icy river water." Josh tugged her closer. "The average temperature of the Colorado River at this time of year is—"

"Don't tell me! I'll find out for myself, no doubt."

But she loved his sense of humor, and the way he could recite facts from memory.

"I'm starting to appreciate the task your brother faced. This, my friend—" she grabbed the front of his life jacket and tugged him against her "—is going to be the adventure of your life. Don't panic. Our guide is skilled in river rescue and swift water rescue. This is going to do you good. You're going to love it."

"You sound exactly like Red."

She didn't know what to say, so she sneaked her hand into his and felt his fingers tighten around hers.

"It's been two years and I still hear his voice all the time," Josh said. "I hear him telling me to get outdoors, to stop reading facts, to eat my pizza crusts and stop leaving broccoli at the side of my plate."

"You leave broccoli at the side of your plate? You don't eat your veggies? Shocking. I'm with Red on that one."

"It seems you're pretty much with Red on everything." But judging from his tone of voice, he didn't mind about that. She wondered whether he even quite liked it.

"I still hear my grandmother too, although only when I'm on my own, weirdly enough." And she realized that the voice of the only person whose life advice she should have taken was drowned out when she was with other people. Her mother. Her sister. Steven. She'd been listening to the wrong voices.

"What would your grandmother have thought of this?"

"The trip, or you?" She saw his eyes crease as he smiled. "She would have said a big yes to both." She gasped as the water drenched her, leaving her soaked and laughing. "That's cold!"

She clung to Josh and he muttered something she couldn't make out but assumed it wasn't complimentary, but even he cracked a smile as their guide expertly navigated the rapids.

Later they ate lunch on the banks of the river, devouring delicious sandwiches and homemade cookies.

Martha slipped one into her pocket for Kathleen.

Her hair had dried curly, her face was burning under the hot Arizona sun and she'd never felt happier.

By the time they finally returned to the hotel the sun was setting.

Kathleen left a message that she'd ordered room service and was having an early night, so they ordered pizza and Josh left the crust while Martha ate hers.

Then they found a place where they had a view of the Grand Canyon and watched the sun go down.

"This is the kind of view that makes you think about life. About how small you are, compared to the world. And how all those little things that seem so huge, aren't really huge at all." Martha stood close to him and he slipped his arm round her shoulders.

"Thank you for today. And that's not sarcasm." His voice was soft. "Seriously, thank you. I'm pleased we did it. He would have been pleased."

Martha leaned her head on his shoulder. "You would have had fun doing this together."

He pulled her closer. "He would have liked you."

Warmth rushed through her. "I wish I'd met him."

"He would have flirted with you and pointed out that he was way more interesting than me."

She looked up at him and her heart beat faster because she was absolutely sure she wouldn't have found his brother more interesting than him. "I'm sure I would. We would have laughed together, and he wouldn't have bored me with facts or left his pizza crusts. We would have bonded over broccoli."

He stroked her shoulder. "My brother used to tease me for always planning ahead. He always missed flights because he could never get himself to the airport on time. One year he was a day late to Thanksgiving because he'd left the travel to chance. 'Just catch the wave,' he used to say."

The setting sun turned the rocks burnt orange and the sky fiery red.

She turned and slid her arms round his neck.

"Is that what we're doing? Catching the wave?"

"Maybe." He slid his fingers under her chin and lifted her face to his. "What do you think? Are you going to catch this wave, Martha?"

"Yes." It came out as a whisper. "To get my confidence back, you understand."

"Sure. What other reason would there be?" His mouth was so close to hers they were almost kissing, but not quite.

The suspense of that almost kiss, the burning anticipation, was more erotic than any actual kiss she'd experienced.

He lifted his hand and brushed his fingers over her cheek. "My room or yours?"

"Which is closest?"

"Yours. But that's next door to Kathleen."

"Good point. My room. In case she comes looking for me in the night."

He raised an eyebrow. "That would make for an interesting conversation."

He kissed her briefly, a heated hint of things to come and then he grabbed her hand and they virtually sprinted back to her room. She could taste the urgency in the air and feel it in the tightness of his grip. She wanted him with a desperation that crossed the borders of decency.

Desperation made her clumsy, and when they finally reached the door she fumbled with the lock and dropped the key. "I hate keys. I can't—"

"I've got it." He retrieved the key and thrust it

into the lock, but before they could step inside he grabbed her shoulder. "Wait. Are you sure, Martha? Answer quickly." His tense jaw was a sign of the self-restraint he was exercising, and it made her feel better about her own out-of-control response.

"Yes. I'm a great decision maker, didn't you know that? I never doubt myself." She tugged him into the room, kicked the door shut behind her and pulled him against her. "Come on you meat-eating, broccoli-avoiding, water-hating but seriously hot guy—"

His hands were in her hair, his mouth on her neck, her cheek, her forehead. "You think I'm seriously hot?"

She reached for the buttons of his shirt, fumbled again and decided there had to be something wrong with her fingers. "No, I'm doing this to please Kathleen." She moaned as he cupped her face in his hands and delivered a long, slow deliberate kiss to her mouth, and she thought to herself that the word *kiss* was too generic because she'd been kissed before and it had never felt like this. She was breathing hard, unraveled by the intimacy of his kiss and his sure, knowing touch. Her heart was doing an intensive work-out of its own and she thought he could probably feel it because his hand was on her breast, teasing and then his mouth and she closed her eyes, awash with sensation as he ripped impatiently at his clothes and then did the same with hers.

They hadn't bothered turning on the lights, but the moonlight through the window allowed them to stumble their way to the bed without bruising shins or banging elbows and she tumbled onto the mattress and grabbed his shoulders as he came down on top of her. His face was shadowed in the semidarkness, the details blurred by dim light.

She felt the weight of him, the solid power of his shoulders as he levered himself up, and then the skilled pressure of his mouth as he kissed her. She dug her fingers into his shoulders, desperate, urging him not to hold back, but he wouldn't be rushed.

His mouth moved from her lips to her jaw, and from there to the skin of her throat and then her shoulder. He lingered there, breathing her in, tasting every segment of her skin as if she was a meal he was only going to get to savor once in a lifetime. She'd never felt so much all at once and she shifted under him as excitement escalated. Her body shivered with the contrasts—the chill of the air-conditioning and the warmth of his hands, the slow drag of his tongue over her breast and the rapid pounding of her heart. And she explored him back, touching and tasting, hearing the change in his breathing and the soft murmur of words.

His touch unraveled her but he kept up the

intimate exploration until there was no part of her left unexplored, until she was quivering and writhing and focused on nothing but feelings. *Muscle and strength. Heat and kisses. Arousal and need.*

And then he eased inside her, infinitely gentle and for a moment she stopped breathing because underneath the electrifying excitement was the knowledge that nothing in her life had ever felt so completely right before. She'd never experienced anything like this thrilling, intricate tangle of the physical and the emotional. Never felt so connected to anyone. She was caught in a dizzying whirl of need and he responded with his own urgency until there was nothing but heat and sensation as they tumbled over that peak together.

And afterward, even after the wildness of the storm had eased, they stayed locked together, bodies entangled as they talked in hushed voices, each exchange flavored by the new intimacy.

Often in the past she questioned her decisions, but she wasn't questioning this one. And even if this one night was all they had, she knew she wouldn't regret it.

He curved her against him and she felt safe, and needed, and wanted and so many good things all at once.

Josh said nothing, and after a moment she lifted her head.

"Are you all right?"

"Mmm." His eyes were closed and she wondered if, maybe, she'd read this all wrong that he was having regrets.

"What are you thinking?"

He stirred and finally opened his eyes. "That Steven was a fool to let you go, but his loss is my gain so I can't be too angry with the guy."

She glowed. "Marrying him wasn't a good decision, but I do make some good decisions."

"I count at least five in the past hour."

She grinned. "Josh Ryder. Are you being a scoundrel?"

"I don't know." He shifted her underneath him in a smooth movement. "Tell me what scoundrels do, and I'll tell you if I fit the description." He lowered his head and kissed her. "You're incredible, Martha."

No one had ever called her incredible before. "Just for the record, which bit of me is incredible?"

"All of you, from your cute curly hair to your amazing butt. Mostly your nature. You're the kindest, most generous person I've ever met."

She ran her fingers through his hair feeling it fall, silky soft, between her fingers. "Are you saying I'm a doormat?"

"Doormat?"

"A pushover. Weak."

"Kindness isn't weakness. Kindness is a quality

that is often underrated—" he rolled onto his back, taking her with him "—except by me. I've always been good at spotting value. It's one of my talents."

"You have other talents." She trailed her fingers over his chest and down his abdomen. "Want me to list them?"

She'd been beating herself up about making bad decisions, but every decision she'd made had led her to this moment. If she'd made a different choice at any stage of her life, she wouldn't have been here now. And she wouldn't have missed this moment for the world.

He ran his hand down her bare back. "So now you've got your confidence back, I suppose you're going to go back to your room."

"This is my room."

"Ah. Right. Good."

"And I always think confidence is a funny thing—" She slid her hand lower and heard his sharp intake of breath. "It's fragile. I probably still have a way to go. I might want to use you for a bit longer. Your teeth are clenched. Are you okay?"

He grunted and then rolled her on her back and covered her with his body. "I have a proposal."

"No proposal. One divorce is enough."

"Not that kind of proposal. The kind that involves you gaining your confidence in various places along the Pacific Coast."

She kissed her way down his chest. "What exactly are you suggesting?"

"If you want me to give you a coherent answer, you're going to have to stop what you're doing for a few moments."

She lifted her head but left her hand where it was. "I'm distracting you?"

"Maybe a little." He spoke through his teeth and she smiled.

"This is fun."

"For you. For me it's an exercise in self-control and sexual frustration. When we've delivered Kathleen and found out what she wants to do, I thought we could take a drive down Highway One. I'll show you California. The Big Sur. Monterey. Cliffs. Redwood forest."

Her heart flew. She felt as if she'd won the lottery. "Don't you have to get back to work?"

"I should. And if you say no, it's true that I'll probably revert to my old workaholic ways."

"That's blackmail."

"It's negotiation."

"And what excuse will you give to your boss for not going back?"

"I'll tell him I met a girl . . ." He scooped her up so that she was lying on top of him, and smoothed his hands down her back. "So what do you say? Do you have to get back?"

To what? She needed to make a plan, but that could wait. It could all wait.

"Well, I feel a certain responsibility for making sure you don't slip back into your old, serious ways—so yes."

"You're sure?"

"Totally."

She'd never been more certain of a decision in her life.

22

LIZA

Sean sprinted across the sand to Liza, dripping with water from a final early morning swim. "Invigorating." Shivering, he reached for a towel. "Despite all the exciting things that lie ahead, I confess I don't want to leave. I'd forgotten how much I love it here. When we come we don't use the time for relaxation. It's always about doing jobs."

Liza felt a twinge of guilt. "That's my fault. I always prioritize other things over having fun. That's going to change, I promise. Fun is going to be at the top from now on."

"For both of us." He sprawled down next to her on the picnic blanket, droplets of water clinging to his leg. "It's so easy to get into a routine, and never question an alternative. I'm picturing what life could be like if we lived here. I'd finish work and instead of sitting in commuter traffic and getting home late and tired, we'd go for an evening swim. In the winter we'd take wild, blowy walks on an empty beach and grab something to eat at the Tide Shack."

They'd talked about it, but was he really considering it?

"You have a thriving business. In London."

"Mmm. The way I see it, there are two options. One is for me to keep that business as it is and commute from here a few days a week. Delegate more."

"You'd be on the road the whole time and pulled between two places."

"I could make it work. I'd go up to London Monday night and be there Tuesday through to Thursday night or something."

She reached out and swept droplets of water from his cheek with her thumb. "Then we'd have to keep the London house and we can't afford both."

He grabbed her wrist and pulled her in for a kiss. "You're putting up obstacles."

"I'm being practical. That's what I do."

"Well, don't do what you do." He sat up. "Alternatively, I talk to my partners and explore the idea of opening an office down here, focusing on coastal properties. Plenty of people want to reimagine the space they're living in and I'm good at that side of things."

She thought about how he'd transformed their small terraced house in London into a light-filled space. "Yes, you are."

"I'd still have to do the occasional trip to London, but the bulk of my work would be here."

She thought about what her life could be like living here. She'd have the beach. She'd be able to focus more on her art. She'd be able to see more of her mother, and also Angie.

Liza had visited her the day before, not wanting to leave without saying goodbye.

In the end she'd been honest with her old friend, as Angie had been with her, and that one conversation had reminded her why the connection between them had always been so strong. There were few people in life with whom you could trust your innermost secrets, but Angie was one of those.

She shifted her attention back to Sean. "Do you think you'd get enough work to justify setting up an office?"

"I don't know, but I'm excited to try."

It was fun to plan, but she still couldn't see it as reality. "There is no way the twins will want to leave London. And do we really want to move them at this stage, when they're heading into important exams?"

"Life isn't all about the twins, Liza. Our lives are important too. But whichever option we choose, it's going to take a while to make it happen. So why don't we agree to spend the next year thinking about how we are going to make this work, with the aim of moving down here when Caitlin and Alice head to college."

The future that had so recently seemed

pressured and full of dark clouds, now glowed brighter. "I love that idea."

"It will give me time to look for exactly the right property." He pushed the damp towel into the bag. "Ideally there will be some unloved coast guard cottage with beach views that I can turn into a project for the next couple of years."

"And I can take my time furnishing it." She imagined herself picking up pieces from the many local shops selling Cornish crafts along the Atlantic coast. And she'd improvise too, because that was something she loved. She'd collect shells and driftwood, sand and stain the floors of their cottage to a bleached white. "It's fun to plan." And most of all it was fun planning together. They'd stopped doing things together and somehow started to live parallel lives. But not anymore.

"Let's come back soon." Sean put his arm round her shoulders and stared out to sea. His skin was turning a deep bronze. She'd forgotten how easily he tanned.

"Yes." Liza stood up and started to gather their things together. "You haven't changed your mind about what we agreed last night? In the cold light of day it seems impulsive and extravagant."

"Impulsive is good. We need to do more of it." Sean took the bag from her and they walked back to the house, took a shower and loaded their things into his car.

They'd decided to leave hers parked at the cottage for the time being and collect it later in the summer.

Liza checked the front door for a final time. She'd fed Popeye and the evening before she and Sean had driven over to Finn's to deliver his paintings.

For Liza it had been an awkward moment, but both men had been surprisingly relaxed. Finn had given her a good natured wink, and he and Sean had discussed the architectural design of the house while they had drinks on the lawn.

The other painting she'd done during her visit, the more personal one, was leaning against the wall in her mother's bedroom. There had been no end of possible subjects for the canvas, but she'd known right from the beginning what she wanted to do and when she'd finally shown it to Sean she'd been reassured by his response.

"Oakwood," he'd breathed, gazing at the painting of the sun setting over the cottage. "It's perfect."

Liza hoped her mother would think so too.

And now they were heading back to London.

Sean took her hand. "Are you sad to be leaving?"

Liza glanced back at Oakwood Cottage. It had provided her with a sanctuary when she'd needed it the most. "We'll be back very soon. I've missed the girls."

They'd had a long chat the day before, and Liza had been honest about the way she felt. It hadn't been an easy conversation for her, but the girls were obviously so shaken by that article they'd found, and by the thought that their parents' marriage might be in trouble, that they were reflective and apologetic.

"You do so much," Caitlin had said in a subdued tone, "and I'm sorry I didn't notice or say thank you more. I'm going to do better."

"A thank-you would be appreciated," Liza had replied, "but mostly I need you to start taking more responsibility."

"I will. We will."

Alice had agreed, and Liza had to admit that on the whole the conversation had gone better than she'd hoped. Whether or not it would last remained to be seen.

"If we're home late afternoon, I'll be able to call my mother before they set off for the day." Liza fastened her seat belt. "It's weird, isn't it? You don't expect your relationship with a parent to change this late in life. I assumed that we'd never be close." But she and her mother had talked about everything and anything. All the barriers that had kept them separate had vanished.

"I'm pleased for you. Funny to think Kathleen had so much going on in her past. What a life she has led."

Liza waved a mental goodbye to Oakwood as

Sean pulled out of the drive. "I've been wondering what her life would have looked like if she'd married Adam."

"We can all play that game. If I hadn't met you on the beach that summer, where would I be now? If you hadn't left and woken us all up, what would have happened to our family?"

"I didn't *leave,* Sean."

"Sorry—you came to 'feed the cat.'" He glanced at her and smiled. "You do know that from now on all you have to do is threaten to go and 'feed the cat' and I'll be booking dinner tables and buying you elaborate gifts."

"I'll remember that."

"I should probably warn you that the kitchen wall is now home to a giant spreadsheet. Alice allocates tasks for people."

Liza winced. "That doesn't sound like a particularly tasteful design feature."

"It isn't, but if it reminds them to do their share then it's worth the visual pain." He pulled over suddenly and parked in the gateway to a field. In the distance the sea was a streak of blue against the cloudy sky.

"Why are you stopping?"

"Because these last few days have been special and leaving here makes me nervous." He turned in his seat. "I'm terrible at remembering anniversaries. There's no excuse for that, and I'm going to do better. It's one of my flaws, I know that. I can focus on work, but not have a clue where my blue shirt is. I try and approach everything calmly which I know drives you crazy because you work at a pace that would shame a racing driver, but here's the thing, Liza—I love you." He took her face in his hands. "I love you, and I have loved you for every one of the years we've spent together, even if I sometimes forget to mark the moment. And part of the reason I forget to mark the moment is because I feel lucky every day I'm with you and picking one day a year to celebrate is almost like saying the rest of it isn't special. It's all special." There was no doubting the sincerity in his voice.

"Sean—"

"Let me finish—" He smoothed her hair away from her face. "Yes we're swamped by things to do. My job is busy, having twins has always given us more than enough to do and you bear the brunt of it, and we both have constant demands on our time and we have to prioritize, but since when has our relationship come bottom of the list? It should be top priority, not bottom. It should be the first thing we pay attention to, not the last."

"I know. And we're going to do that."

How had she ever prioritized washing Caitlin's strap top over a conversation with Sean? How had they stopped prioritizing themselves? She made lists of all the things she had to do, but spending time with Sean where they did nothing but focus on each other wasn't on that list.

Sean kissed her gently and then steered the car back onto the road and headed for home.

As they pulled into their road, Liza felt a flicker of nerves. It felt strange, being home, as if she'd been away for a lifetime even though it was only a matter of weeks.

But then the front door opened and Caitlin and Alice raced out to greet them, as they'd done when they were very young.

"Mum!" Caitlin grabbed Liza so tightly she couldn't breathe, and Alice did the same.

"We missed you."

"And not because we can't find anything when you're not here." Caitlin finally released her. "You look *amazing*. That dress is cute on you. Is it new? Come inside, we've made a surprise for you both." She and Alice glanced at each other and then ushered their parents through to the kitchen.

The house was sparkling, and the kitchen table was loaded with plates of food. Tiny finger sandwiches, scones, cupcakes, chocolate chip cookies—

Liza put her bag down. "You did all this?"

"We thought you'd be hungry after your journey. Alice did most of the cooking. I did the cleaning." Caitlin looked nervous. "I did the mirrors and even cleaned behind the bed in your room. And we're going to help get ready for France. Alice and I are going to do everything, so you can relax."

"Ah—" Liza looked at Sean. "We need to talk to you about that."

Caitlin's face fell. "We're not going to France?"

"I'm afraid not."

"Because it's too much work for you?" Alice looked anxious. "Is it our fault?"

"It has nothing to do with you. And this is all wonderful, as is the tidy house. I'm touched. Goodness, it looks delicious." Liza reached out and picked up a cupcake. Were her girls really capable of this? She'd underestimated them. Or maybe it was simply that she'd never given them the chance. "But we do have some bad news about France. They called yesterday—they had a burst pipe and the downstairs is flooded."

"Oh no!" Alice slumped onto the nearest chair. "But it's our special time away as a family. We wanted to spoil you, and—can we find somewhere else? Caitlin and I can do a search."

"That was our first instinct, but then we had a different idea." Liza took Sean's hand. "We have another plan, which I hope you'll be excited about. It's not France."

"Not France?" Caitlin caught her sister's eye. "But whatever you think would be fun, works for us, Mum. We want family time, that's all."

Family.

Liza smiled. "We can guarantee you family time of the very best type."

23

KATHLEEN

BARSTOW~SANTA MONICA

Kathleen stood on the pier at Santa Monica and stared across the waves.

She'd crossed prairie and desert, seen the Grand Canyon and the bright lights of Las Vegas, and now she was here, at her final destination.

She felt Martha's hand close over hers.

"We made it, Kathleen, and I didn't drive into a lamppost."

Kathleen said nothing, but clung to her hand. She couldn't find the words to describe everything she was feeling.

Josh took her other hand and they led her closer to the beach. "That's the Pacific Ocean, Kathleen."

"Yes, I can see that. My eyes are the one part of me that still work." The Pacific Ocean. Kathleen felt the sun on her face and the warmth of the breeze, but she couldn't relax. All she could think about was Ruth. "She lives near here?"

"Not far."

Kathleen turned back to the car. "Then let's go.

Let's do this. I don't want to wait any longer." She saw Martha glance at Josh, as if they were calculating something. "What are you two plotting?"

"Nothing."

She knew they weren't telling her the truth, but she was too anxious about her meeting with Ruth to probe further.

What if it felt awkward? It had been almost sixty years since they last saw each other. They would have nothing in common except the past, and that wasn't exactly a comfortable place to linger.

She slid back into the car that had been their home since they'd left Chicago. Kathleen had grown ridiculously fond of it, and also fond of Martha and Josh.

There was a new intimacy between them. Kathleen saw it in shared smiles, the brush of fingers, the promise in a look. She was thrilled for them, but their new closeness made her feel alone.

She'd always been an independent person. So why did she feel the need to lean on someone for this trip?

She made a supreme effort to pull herself together. If seeing Ruth ended up being an upsetting experience then Kathleen would simply make an excuse. She'd drink a cup of Earl Grey, say how nice it had been to see Ruth, and then she'd check into a hotel with a view of the ocean and pretend she was at home.

Having decided that, she wanted to get it over with. "Are you sure we're going the right way?" She clutched the back of Martha's seat, the other hand securing the hat she was wearing to protect herself from the California sunshine.

She'd agreed they should ride with the top down for this last section of the trip together.

It should have been relaxing, but how could she relax knowing that she was about to see Ruth after so many years?

"Yes." Josh checked the navigation. "You need to make a left up ahead, Martha. And then pull over and wait."

Wait for what?

"Turns no longer scare me, although I will never love a roundabout." Martha glanced in the mirror. "Are you all right, Kathleen?"

"No." Panic got the better of her. "I think this is a dreadful mistake. One should never revisit the past. Don't make a left. Head straight down the coast." She saw Martha glance at Josh.

"Kathleen—"

"If you're about to reason with me then don't waste your breath. I know what I want."

Martha pulled over, swerving into a parking space in a manner so decisive that Kathleen was forced to shoot out a hand to steady herself.

"I thought your driving was vastly improved, but it seems I was premature in my assessment. I have no idea why you're stopping. We should keep going, moving forward."

Martha unclipped her seat belt and turned. "We're visiting Ruth. She's expecting us. But we're going to wait here for a few minutes."

"For what? You work for me, Martha. I decide on the itinerary."

Martha reached between the seats and touched Kathleen's knee. "This must be very scary—"

"Don't soothe me, Martha. It's patronizing."

"I'm being a friend. Just as you've been a friend to me on this journey."

Kathleen felt her eyes sting. Sand, of course. They'd spent too long near the beach. "Nonsense."

"If it hadn't been for you I wouldn't have met Josh. I was so busy protecting myself I would have missed out on all the fun we've had." Martha's eyes twinkled. "Not to mention the best sex of my life."

Josh cleared his throat and slid down in his seat. "Is this really—"

"Yes, it is." Martha ignored his discomfort. "We've all done things that felt tough on this journey. I picked up a hitchhiker and deleted Steven's number from my phone—"

"And about time," Kathleen muttered.

"Josh went rafting—"

Josh pulled a face. "Not sure I want to relive that."

Kathleen sighed. "Since when did this become a competition?"

"It's not about competition. It's about the support of friends. And you won't be on your own today. We've got your back, Kathleen."

She felt a strange pressure build in her chest. "You are nowhere near my back. You young people are so careless with language."

"I know you're scared of seeing Ruth," Martha said. "You're scared of feeling things you think you can't handle, but you *can* handle them, Kathleen. You've handled so much already. And if you don't do this, you might regret it."

"I will not. I make a point of never looking back."

"But this isn't looking back. It's looking forward. You and Ruth will be building something new."

"I'm eighty. It's a little late to be building something new."

Martha raised her eyebrows. "This from someone who drove two thousand four hundred miles across America? If it's not too late for that type of adventure, how can it be too late to call on a friend?"

"She's a stranger, Martha. I haven't seen her for almost sixty years so don't romanticize the relationship."

"You had a deep and special friendship. That kind of bond doesn't go away."

"Your generation are so emotional." Kathleen fiddled with the strap of her bag, kneading it, twisting it. "Fine, let's do it. It will be a disaster, and then I will take great pleasure in firing you."

Martha smiled. "If it goes badly, you'll need me as the getaway driver."

"If I'm relying on your driving skills to escape then we're all doomed." What should she do? Martha was right, of course. She was terrified. Seeing Ruth could rip open everything. "In case we have a major falling out, I should probably give you this now." She leaned down and retrieved the parcel she'd tucked into the car a few days earlier. "It's a thank-you."

"A thank-you for what?"

"For not singing even when you were bursting to do so. For humoring a cantankerous old lady on the trip of a lifetime. For being the best company. And for smiling even when you were terrified." She saw Martha's eyes fill and waved a hand. "No! No crying."

Martha brushed her hand over her eyes and opened the box Kathleen had handed her.

"Oh Kathleen—" She lifted the teapot out of the box and stared at it in wonder. "It's perfect. Where did you find this?"

"I am fortunate in having well-connected

friends who can make things happen." She sent silent thanks to Liza who had sourced it, and Finn who had navigated the astonishing complexities of transportation.

"Red cherries." Martha sounded choked. "It's exactly like the one Nanna had."

"Your grandmother would be proud of you, Martha."

"I'll treasure it. I'm never going to use it."

"That would be a pity. A teapot is designed to hold tea, just as a human being is designed to live life no matter how hard it seems at times." She felt her voice waver, and knew that Martha heard it too. Kathleen saw her glance at Josh.

"Could you go for a walk? We're five minutes early, anyway."

"Early for what? We're having tea, not watching the opera." Kathleen's fingers were white on the bag. The moment had come, and she couldn't delay it any longer. "And why does Josh need to walk anywhere? Given that I'm already in possession of far too much detail regarding the extraordinary regeneration of your sex life, I can't imagine any conversation that would require his absence."

Martha turned back to her. "I know you're anxious, but there really are only two outcomes here. One is that you no longer have any bond with Ruth, you find her boring and we leave after a very painful cup of tea."

"Tea can't be painful unless you spill it shortly after pouring."

Martha ignored her. "Two, you bond as you did the first time you met and can't stop talking. Then you have the best afternoon you've had in a while. That's the one I vote for."

"A third outcome is that the meeting rips open a part of my life I left in the past for good reason."

"How can it?" Martha's tone was gentle. "You're not going to regret your decision, Kathleen. You wouldn't want to turn the clock back, even if you could. You *know* that. Because of what happened, you had an amazing career."

"You know how much I dislike the word *amazing*. It conveys nothing."

"It conveys amazingness," Martha continued unrepentant, "and your career was amazing."

"It's true," Josh said. "It was."

Martha nodded. "If you'd married Adam he would have driven you crazy."

Kathleen wrinkled her nose. "*Crazy* is another word I dislike. Could we aim for more descriptive language? Have I taught you nothing over the past few weeks?"

"You've taught me persistence." Martha leaned forward. "If you'd stayed together, you would have wanted to kill Adam. Think about those articles we read. I'm sure he was very eminent, but he probably had an overinflated ego. Maybe he wouldn't have liked you being a big star.

Maybe you wouldn't have been able to travel the world. Maybe *The Summer Seekers* never would have happened."

"I'm not sure there is evidence to support that." Kathleen brushed nonexistent fluff from her skirt. "You could be right. I wouldn't have described him as supportive when I expressed certain ambitions."

"But Brian was. Wait a minute—" Martha grabbed her phone and fiddled for a moment before thrusting it in Kathleen's face. "There's Brian when you received that big award in London. Presenter of the Year or whatever it was called."

Kathleen felt her eyes mist. *Oh Brian.* "I have no idea why you are showing me this."

"Look at his face! What do you see? Pride. Joy. And so much love. I'd give anything for a man to look at me that way just once."

"Perhaps if you wore something other than jeans—"

"We're talking about you, Kathleen. And Brian, who you loved as much as he loved you. He was *not* second best. He wasn't your consolation prize. Wasn't that what you said to me when we pulled up at Devil's Elbow? A good relationship doesn't need a miracle. All it needs is the right person at the right time. Which is a whole lot harder than it sounds, actually, but that's not relevant right now."

"I used the word *require,* not *need.*"

"Same thing."

"Actually it's—"

"Kathleen!"

"Give me a moment." Kathleen closed her eyes, and thought of Brian. His patience. His ability to always make her laugh. The way they'd argued about the best way to mark a place in the book. Their love of the sea. Their home. Their daughter.

He had, without doubt, been the best thing that had happened to her in her life. Better even than *The Summer Seekers*.

He'd been her biggest and best adventure.

Martha was right. She wouldn't change a thing. She wouldn't trade a day of her life, either when she was single or with her dear Brian, for more time with Adam.

Her throat ached. How she missed Brian. She missed his steadiness and the way he'd known her. There was no better gift in life than being known, and yet still loved.

And Brian had known and loved her.

She opened her eyes. "Tea then, but only tea. And we should have some kind of signal. In case I need moral support or a rapid exit, although I'm not sure I'm capable of making a rapid exit with my hips the way they are. You may need to throw me over your shoulder, Josh." She saw Martha and Josh exchange glances again and gave a sigh of exasperation. "Now what?"

"You'll have all the moral support you need, Kathleen." Martha turned her head to look at the road.

A large car approached and glided to a halt in front of them.

"She's here." Josh stepped out of the car and so did Martha.

"Who is here?" But Kathleen was talking to herself. Before she could call after them and tell them that all this drama and subterfuge was frustrating, the door of the car was opening and a woman stepped out into the sunshine.

She looked exactly like Liza.

Kathleen felt something flutter in her chest. No. It couldn't be. Liza was in France, with Sean and the girls.

But it *was* Liza. A different-looking Liza, whose shoulders were back and whose smile was sure and confident. *Happy*. Right here in California, wearing a dress that flipped around her legs. She was hugging Martha, and shaking hands with Josh, and then she walked quickly to the car and smiled down at Kathleen.

"Hello there, Summer Seeker! I have to admit I had my doubts about the car, but it suits you."

Kathleen couldn't find any words. She wanted to get out of the car, but in the end she didn't need to because Liza slid into the passenger seat next to her, wincing as she tried to squeeze her legs into the limited space.

"You drove all the way across eight states with your legs cramped like this? It's a wonder you can move." She leaned forward and hugged Kathleen. "I hope you don't mind me coming. I wanted to be with you for this part. I thought we could see Ruth together."

Together. She wasn't on her own. She had Liza.

She'd been so afraid of losing her independence, but she saw now that you could lean on someone and accept support without giving up any part of yourself. Accepting help didn't make you weak, it made you human. Perhaps it was even a strength because it meant you could face things you might be unable to face alone.

Kathleen clung back, only vaguely aware of Josh and Martha getting back into the car. "Why aren't you in France?"

"It's a long story. Why don't I tell you after we've had tea?"

"But what about Sean and the girls?"

"They're here too." Liza fastened her seat belt. "Last-minute change of plan. It probably won't surprise you to learn that the news that we were coming to California, instead of France, was greeted with joy by the girls. They're currently in our beachfront apartment—arranged at short notice thanks to Josh—planning a future that allows them to move here permanently. It might even be the boost Caitlin needed to focus on her studies. They can't wait to see you, by the way. They're cooking dinner for us all tonight."

Kathleen was finding it hard to keep up. "Did you say that the twins are cooking dinner?"

"Don't be scared." Liza patted her leg. "Turns out that they're better at it than past experience would suggest. I have a lot to tell you. But let's get to Ruth's now. No point in delaying a moment longer. How far is it?"

"Not far." Josh glanced at the directions and told Martha to make a left. "It's halfway down this road. Close to the beach. Adam can't have done too badly if they bought a property here."

Kathleen's mind was spinning. She had so much to say, and she needed to say it now. "I can't sell Oakwood, Liza."

"You're right. You can't."

"I know you think I'll have an accident there, but—" She paused. "What did you say?"

"I said you can't sell it. I don't think you should and I'm sorry I ever suggested it. Stay, and if the time comes when you need help there, we'll figure it out together."

Kathleen eyed her daughter. "I won't wear an alarm."

"I know." Liza smiled. "Or lift the rug, or stop using the stepladder. It's your decision. Your life. Your adventure."

She'd never seen Liza so relaxed. "I might stop using the stepladder."

As Martha pulled up outside a set of large iron

491

gates Kathleen felt nerves flutter again, but it was too late for second thoughts because Martha had already spoken into an intercom and the gates swung slowly open and there, standing at the head of the drive, supported by a woman who was presumably her daughter, was Ruth.

She hadn't changed at all, Kathleen thought. Not one bit.

Martha parked and Josh was out of the car in a flash but it was Liza who helped Kathleen. Liza who took her arm and didn't let go. Liza who was by her side as they walked the short distance to greet her old friend.

And it turned out that Kathleen needn't have wasted time planning what to say, or being anxious about it, because Ruth hurried forward and wrapped her in a tight hug, and she realized that sometimes words weren't needed and that touch could convey everything.

It was only when she heard Ruth sniff that she realized her cheeks were wet too.

She'd displayed more emotion during this one morning than she had in the lifetime that preceded it.

"I'm Martha—" Martha held out her hand to the woman with Ruth who greeted her warmly.

"I'm Hannah. Ruth's daughter. We spoke on the phone. And you must be Liza. Welcome. We're so pleased you could join us." She shook Liza's hand. "Why don't you all come in? We've made tea. We can sit on the deck in the shade." She led them inside and finally Kathleen and Ruth released each other.

"Look at you!" Ruth brushed her damp cheeks with her fingers. "So glamorous. You haven't changed one bit. It's like having a movie star in my home. I want to hear all the details of your life. You must have so many stories. I watched every episode of *The Summer Seekers*."

The possibility that Ruth knew about her career hadn't crossed Kathleen's mind. "How is that possible?"

"Adam tracked down the videos for me. They were in the wrong format but he managed to get them converted."

It felt strange and a little uncomfortable imagining Adam and Ruth sitting together watching *The Summer Seekers*.

Ruth tucked her arm into Kathleen's and led her into the house. "Come on in. I have Earl Grey and Hannah made homemade shortbread."

Hannah.

Ruth's daughter. Adam's daughter.

And there was Liza, her own daughter, watching her closely, giving her reassuring smiles, and Kathleen realized that this trip hadn't only brought her back to Ruth, it had brought her closer to her own daughter. They had so much to talk about, and time to do it.

Her epic road trip had delivered her so many

new experiences, but none so satisfying as sitting here with her old friend and her daughter, sipping tea while they gazed across the Pacific Ocean. The past had finally found a comfortable place in the present and she felt utterly content with her life.

Maybe that had been the destination all along.

ACKNOWLEDGMENTS

The story of *The Summer Seekers* popped into my head a few years ago as I was driving the car on a weekend away. My first and biggest "thank-you" must therefore be to my family who patiently stopped all conversation when I yelled, "Nobody speak for a minute because I just had an idea and I need to think" and patiently complied when I said, "Please can someone write this down so I don't forget it." I was busy writing a different book at the time, so I filed the idea away in my brain where it grew and grew until finally I knew the time was right to tell the story. The fact that I've been waiting to write this book for a few years may be part of the reason I enjoyed the writing process so much.

Every idea I have is made better by my talented editor Flo Nicoll who brings insight, calm and her special brand of positivity to each project we work on together.

I am immensely grateful to the publishing teams around the globe who handle my books with such enthusiasm and dedication. Putting a book into the hands of readers is a team effort and involves huge complexity with many people and departments involved. Listing everyone would probably mean this book would have to be published in two volumes, but particular thanks go to Lisa Milton, Manpreet Grewal and the whole UK team, and also to Margaret Marbury, Susan Swinwood and the team at HQN books.

I doubt I'd finish a book without the support of friends, and I'm sending an extra big hug to RaeAnne Thayne, Jill Shalvis and Nicola Cornick.

My final thanks go to my readers who are so endlessly supportive and continue to buy my books. I feel fortunate that with so many books on the shelves, you choose mine. I hope you love *The Summer Seekers*.

Sarah
xx

Center Point Large Print
600 Brooks Road / PO Box 1
Thorndike, ME 04986-0001 USA

(207) 568-3717

US & Canada:
1 800 929-9108
www.centerpointlargeprint.com